FOOTSTEPS OF THE TEIGN

In 1690 the French Fleet had won and had England in its grasp. Instead of visiting unprotected London, their Admiral visited Teignmouth, a small estuary on the River Teign. They ate cream scones and played boules on the Back Beach. A few days later they left with their tails between their legs, defeated not by military force but by lack of booze. The good people of Teignmouth had smuggled their whole store of brandy and claret off their ships and hidden it. Centuries later their descendants were still masters of the old West Country art of smuggling without menaces. But a very small privileged few of them also were masters at keeping hidden a world-shattering secret which their forefathers had also smuggled off the French flag ship. This had lain hidden by them for three centuries; an ancient secret of such importance that the French Admiral burnt the town down in an angry attempt to find it. Why did the French admiral turn away from defeating England and reinstating King James Stuart on the royal throne to visit a small unimportant provincial English West Country town? What was lost from his ship that caused him to nearly destroy the town?

Well, what it was will change the world forever.

Now a descendant of the French admiral is about to discover and reveal that secret…and she must be stopped at all costs.

Also by Davey J Ashfield

A Turkey and One More Easter Egg
Contracting With The Devil

FOOTSTEPS ON THE TEIGN

DAVEY J ASHFIELD

And did those feet in ancient times walk upon England's
mountains green?
'Jerusalem' William Blake

APS BOOKS
Stourbridge/Teignmouth

Cover art by Clare Jenkinson

ISBN 978-1-78996-037-2

Print edition authorised for charity by permission of APS Books

APS Books/APS Publications,
4 Oakleigh Road,
Stourbridge,
West Midlands,
DY8 2JX

www.andrewsparke.com

Frogs On The Teign

Bardy Cask

Steve Collings

♩ = 120

Al - bert of Teign-mouth was a smu - gg-ler bold. Now dy-ing Kee - per of the Sec -

- ret so old, Was to pass on to his pro-gen - y that they should hold, Were not

there at the end so to his his nur - se he told. When Frogs on the Teign were so mean, so

mean. When Frogs on the Teign were so mean. The clues to a trea-sure that's nev-er been seen, can be

found in pubs near the Teign.

2. In sixteen ninety when the French came ashore,
   After beating the English off Beachy once more,
   Were quickly sent packing, with their tails between their legs,
   Having lost bottles of claret and fine brandy kegs.
   Chorus

3. The skill of the Devon Smuggler's never seen,
   Nor by the Frogs on the Teign, all mean,
   Without their strong booze to give stout courage and heart,
   Were forced to weigh anchor, set sails and depart.
   Chorus

4. What is this secret that's been kept for so long
   Not heard in a myth, fable, story or song.
   History tells of the buildings burnt down to the ground
   But no mention of treasure has ever been found.
   Chorus:
       When Frogs on the Teign were so mean, so mean,
       When Frogs on The Teign were so mean
       The clues to a treasure that's never been seen,
       Can be found in pubs near the Teign.

To all the 'buoys' who have allowed me to tell their story so that the world may know what life was like before: *'you cannay say that these days'*. May your Footsteps on the Teign never die out.

Thanks to those great people who care for and support all those who need a little bit of help; especially to the families, children, and supporters of AIMS.   www.aimsfamilies.org

'Not everyone can do great things but everyone can do small things with great love'
Mother Theresa

To all the good people who are acting in this story. Crazy or not, and by God there are a lot of crazies in this epic, you make the world a better place to live in.

Thanks to everyone in the shops, restaurants and particularly the ale and cider houses who contributed both financially and in good spirit to the book and the charity treasure hunt.

And always, beaucoup de bisous to Françoise our own Frog on the Teign xx

Big thanks to **Steve** *of* **CASK SHANTY DUO** *for his cracking song* **FROGS ON THE TEIGN**

To Clare for the beautiful cover www.clarejenkinson.co.uk

To Charlie, the umpteenth Earl of Devon for being such a good sport and for offering his home to help our children in need.

Come to beautiful Devon any day to meet the crazy cast, sing 'Frogs on the Teign' with Steve and his Cask Shanty Duo at the various festivals and carnivals and in the treasure hunt pubs.

www.teignseashantyfestival.co.uk
www.teignmouthfolk.co.uk
www.teignmouthcarnival.co.uk

CHAPTER ONE

The old man knew he was dying. So did the lady sitting holding his hand by his bed. She had seen the death mask come and go many times. The old man looked up through tired darkening eyes and smiled. Françoise wondered if he was remembering his youth. Many of her patients had clearly reverted back to their childhood as they were dying as they brought back memories in their ramblings of long-lost parents, brothers, sisters and friends and always in childhood. The old man smiled again, coughed violently and fell back exhausted again into his bed. Françoise wiped his mouth with a tissue and spoke gently. 'Would you like a glass of water Albert?'

The old man looked kindly at her and grabbed her hand. He whispered with a voice hoarse from months of coughing from the illness which had been slowly killing him. 'No thank you my dearie. Us could murder a pint of zider though.'

Françoise laughed and said, 'I bet you would, you old devil you.' And she grabbed his hand more firmly. She had grown to like this man so much. He made her laugh with his tales of his and his friends' past exploits as they had rampaged across the West Country and this quaint estuary town in particular, smuggling, drinking, fighting and mainly laughing. She had moved here among them all some years before when she'd travelled with her English husband from her home in Brittany, France to take up a nursing career. It had taken time for the particularly close knit and sometimes xenophobic reprobates in the town to come to the conclusion that she wasn't a French spy, tax inspector or customs officer. But now she had 'grockle clearance' by the MI5 officers in Devon's GCHQ, which masqueraded as The Teign Brewery public house, she was accepted as one of their own. Well, not completely, no one who was an incomer could ever be completely 'cleared'. And she was French of course. But now she was comforting one last time one of famous characters of the area and he was about to reveal something to her which would change her life and maybe those around her forever.

'Come closer maid. I wan tell ee summat.' The old man struggled to talk now and his voice was getting softer and distant. Françoise moved closer still tightly holding his grizzled and wrinkled hand. She moved her head closer to the man. He sighed deeply and took a breath, waiting to speak, as if he was hoping he would have enough breath in his failing lungs to say what he wished. He finally spoke in his broad Devon accent. 'You are a good maid my dearie. I thanks you for all you've done for this owld pirate. I don't deserve it you know that don't you?' And he smiled again. Françoise just nodded and stroked his hand. He took another breath and continued. 'Us be dying now. I've lived long enough. It's time to let some other work and keep family going. Lazy wassels these days.'

Françoise smiled at him. She knew he was the patriarch of a broad family. He hadn't worked the mines, docks or the fishing boats for some years and he'd been housebound for many months. His body was worn out by the physical hardships of shovelling day and night on the docks and hauling nets and pots in the stormy English Channel winters and summers. But he was still the boss to his family and to many in the town.

The old man coughed, not as violently as before, and lay back exhausted again. With another minute's rest he turned back to Françoise. 'You are a good friend to us here maid. You deserve to be one of us. It's bloody strange that I tells this to a French maid, after what you French devils brought here all those years ago. But in some ways its right that you know and that you decide what to do with it. The world has changed from when I was a lad and maybe he can cope with knowing what we've kept from he for so long. Us be tired maid, tired in my bones and tired of keeping the secret. I wants you to be...' and he began coughing violently, with blood coming out of his mouth. Françoise held his thin, shrunken body close to her and wiped the blood. Worryingly it didn't stop until he laid back again exhausted, eyes glazed. The dying man tried to speak but Françoise hushed him and wiped his brow. 'Shush, mon ami, Shush.' She knew it would not be long now. He lay back silent except for the wheeze from chest. She sat down and waited. She had phoned his son up one hour before but he had been up country and was driving down fast. His daughter was tied up at a care home and her call hadn't been able to get through. She hoped that someone would come before it ended.

Suddenly the man's eyes opened and he took a deep breath. He exclaimed in a hushed voice. 'Are you there, maid?'

Françoise whispered, 'I'm here cheri. Just lay still, your family will be here soon.'

With great effort the man turned his body. She could see in his eyes that the pain of it was almost too much. He laid the side of his head on the pillow and looked at Françoise, his eyes fading fast. He gently spoke through pursed and cracked lips. 'Maid, find the treasure...,' and he fell back again. With some effort he began again, 'the Cornish..., but failed to finish in his weakness. She just could hear his through his gasps. He tightened his grip and pulled with what strength he had left, trying to get her nearer, he whispered, 'Charlie will tell…Chalice.' His head fell backwards and he lay flat. He breathed intermittently in bursts and then exhaled slowly and his chest lay still. A dark shadow of a cross came across his brow. And he passed from this world.

CHAPTER TWO

'The old man has finally died.'

'Was anyone with him at the end?' asked the man on the end of the mobile phone.

'Yes. A nurse: She was alone with him. There was no one else we could see boss.' The man on the other end of the line answered. He looked around to check if there was anyone listening. All he could see were yachts bobbing in the Teign estuary and an empty beach. It was just dawn on a beautiful summer's day in Devon the morning after Albert's death.

'Do we know if he told her anything about the secret?' the boss asked.

'The recording from the bug in Albert's room is a bit hazy boss. Not sure if the signal works that well down here. But I fear from what we analysed he seems to have been telling her something about it. His last word mentioned the Cornish, we could pick that out and also Charlie, but the rest is unclear. Its gobble de gook to us boss.'

'Merde,' the boss exclaimed and went silent. *This is bad news*, he thought, *another possible leak and someone to monitor and if necessary, get rid of.* He held the phone and sighed again, 'Merde.'

'Are you there boss?'

The boss put the phone to his mouth and whispered, 'Yes I'm here. I want you to watch her and follow her. We need to know if she talks to anyone. We may have to bug her place too. Phone me each day. Change phones regularly as usual and be careful no one notices you following her. A bientôt.' And he finished the call abruptly.

The man in Teignmouth put his mobile into his pocket and looked over the estuary towards Shaldon village. *What a rude man. Bloody French, typical*, he thought. *What the hell was this secret he was so bothered about?* He shrugged his shoulders and knew it wasn't his position to know that only to take action if asked. It's what he did, watch, monitor and take orders. To kill if necessary; it's what he was trained for and he was very good at it. He walked back to his camper van parked on The Point car park.

The Frenchman sat on his apartment balcony. He took a drink of his Espresso and thought deeply about this latest setback and the heavy responsibility he had carried for too many years now. As he was thinking he looked across at the magnificent Château de Saint-Germain-en–Laye and the ancient parish church next to it. There lay his problem. If the Catholic English King James and the French had won the attempt to regain the throne and replace the Protestant King

10

Billy after the Glorious Revolution then that French fleet would never have sailed into that English town. And he now might not have to eliminate a perfectly innocent fellow lady citizen. 'Merde,' he whispered again and he reflected on the historical web of revolution, secrecy, religion and power that had been spun around him and entrapped him.

The château was indeed magnificent but had not been good enough for The Sun King, Louis IV, and he left it to go to more glorious and expansive Versailles. He left the Saint-Germain château to the deposed English King James II in 1688. His bowels remain in the parish church, a constant reminder to the man on the balcony of the lost secret. He cursed those Scottish Jacobites who lived there for years until The Revolution and caused so many problems trying to put their Divine King on the English throne. All the latest stories about the Stuarts having a direct blood line to Jesus Christ did was alert the non-cognoscenti to seek the secret that he had been holding for two centuries.

He knew all about the current revelations and investigations in the theory that Jesus Christ did not die on the cross and that Mary Magdalene carried his child across the Mediterranean and eventually to England. He had read the *'Holy Blood and The Holy Grail'* and watched *'The Da Vinci Code'* movie and their conclusions that a secret society The Prieuré de Sion (Priory of Sion) formed many, many years ago in 1099 in Jerusalem, by Godfrey of Bouillon and the Knights Templar protected the secrets of the Sang Graal. The Sang Graal, the Holy Grail, and the Priory's purpose was to act as guardian to Jesus and Mary Magdalene's sacred bloodline.

He also knew that the secret Priory was formed to return the French Merovingian royal dynasty to power; this dynasty was directly descended from the offspring of Jesus and the Magdalene and some had shown that the Royal Scottish line of the Stuarts was the current direct descendent; hence their 'Divine' Right of Kings.

Its leaders or Grand Masters included the likes of Isaac Newton, Victor Hugo and Leonardo da Vinci; the dynasty was protected by the Knights Templar, the Masons, the Cathars, the Rosicrucians; you name it, some secret society protected it. The Catholic Church had tried for centuries to prevent the secret blood line coming to light mainly in order to retain the absolute belief of a line of spiritual dynastical Bishops of Rome, Popes. They had maintained this Papal dynasty for nearly two thousand years, instead of the legitimate hereditary succession through the Stuart line in Britain that began with Mary Magdalene.

He knew all about the discovery of a world changing secret by a Catholic priest, so important that the French royalty and the Vatican supposedly paid him millions of dollars in today's money, never to reveal what he had discovered. What he had discovered in the church in Rennes le Château, Languedoc, France and deep inside the Cathars' protective territory, was thought to be absolute proof of the facts of the Holy Bloodline; hence the Church and State trying to prevent it coming to light.

In 1891 Father François Bérenger Saunière when he was renovating the church discovered something that would change the world. He became a millionaire overnight and famous about town in Parisian society. The secret was so destructive to society that he was refused absolution on his death bed by an ordained priest; a secret which was now thought to be buried in the catacombs of the Vatican.

The man sitting drinking Espresso coffee in Saint-Germain-en-Laye knew exactly what that secret was and he knew that a copy of the secret parchment had been made centuries before Saunière found it in Rennes le Château. The original had been taken by the Knights Templars to a secret location over the water from France somewhere and lost in history. Why did he know this? Well it was simple. He was Saunière's illegitimate great grandson - and he had the copy of the original.

And he also knew where the original parchment was lost...

It was stolen in 1690 from the flagship of the French fleet that was the last foreign enemy to invade England. Someone in the small estuary town in Devon knew where it was now and they were sworn to protect it. Now it seemed a French woman may well find and, dangerously for his shadowy organisation and certainly for her, she may reveal it. And that could never happen...

At the same time, three thousand kilometres away, a man was also worried that someone may find this secret. He knew that for two centuries the Russians had tried to prevent the unification of Europe, either as a Holy Roman Empire or an enlarged European Community. His successors had used all their powers to prevent this through espionage, intelligence, war, nuclear threats, oil and gas disruption and now cyber warfare and political disruption. They had been particularly successful with preventing Britain joining the EEC in the fifties and sixties, De Gaulle an unlikely ally, and those actions stopped the secret plans to unify France and Britain under one crown – the ultimate threat as it would inevitably lead to the rise of the new European Empire and a military and economic alliance to rival the USSR. And lately they had been extremely successful in their infiltration and manipulation of the

British right of centre political parties and the media with their Brexit misinformation and cyber implantations. He knew that this Brexit process must not be stopped and that Europe must break up. The only thing that could stop it was this damned secret that might now be found. *If this long-hidden secret is found, who knows, what might happen to his carefully thought-out strategy?* A knock came on his door. He told the person to enter. The man in uniform opened the door and spoke. 'Mr President, I have the President of the United Sates on the secure line. It seems he is concerned over events in Devon, England.'

CHAPTER THREE

'Ee be dead now of course.'

Françoise was standing in *The Teign Brewery* with a pint of beer talking to Charlie and a few other old friends of Albert. She had just said goodbye to Albert at a nice send off at Torquay crematorium and they had retired to the iconic Teignmouth pub for a final drink after the family goodbye wake at Teignmouth Rugby club. She had remained silent about his death bed confession and was still quite in shock at what he had tried to reveal to her. *What secret that would change their whole world? How and why had they kept it so quiet for three centuries? What on earth had he meant about Cornwall and who was Charlie?* She talked to her husband who worked as a marine engineer for a local contracting company, but he had just said the old man was delirious, let it drop. The thing was she couldn't. She was intrigued that her own Gallic past was catching up with her.

Three years ago she had heard briefly from her great Aunt in France that she was now living in the town where her long lost great, great, great and probably even greater grandpapa had actually set foot. He was the Compte Anne Hilarion de Tourville and he had commanded the fleet of ships that were victorious against William of Orange's joint Dutch and English fleet at the battle of Beachy Head. The French instead of pursuing the enemy decided they'd enjoy the sun and beaches of Devon and Cornwall and sailed to the West Country instead. It must have been summer as the French have always taken the whole of August off, nothing much had changed in 1690.

After a nice few days in Cornwall, sampling the pasties and the warm hospitality of their fellow French, the Cornish Bretons, they decided to go to Torbay and then after another day they sailed up Labrador Bay and began to rape and pillage Teignmouth, just as they'd done before in 1340. Teignmouth was becoming like Juan les Pins to the French, a great holiday destination, but sadly without Brigitte Bardot on the Back Beach.

Françoise had spoken with her grandmother who lived in Rennes in Brittany about her family's involvement in the last English invasion. She had been very circumspect and said that it had been passed down the years through the family that the invasion had not achieved what it was planned to do. Their old relative had lost something in Teignmouth which could have changed the course of French and English history and maybe the world. She told Françoise that only her old Auntie knew more. She was now living near the worst place on earth for Bretons – Paris, so, no one talked to her now.

Françoise was no wiser but very intrigued that it was quite possible that Albert's death bed revelation may not have been the hallucinogenic result of years of drinking scrumpy zider' (cider to normal people) but be true. Maybe, there was a mystery and a lost secret. She decided to keep quiet to her husband and all others in the town and see if she could find out more. Then she would take a trip to Paris and talk with her great Aunt, whom she knew liked her a lot. She would put up with the rude Parisian waiters and the hell of the Boulevard Périphérique, the worst road in the world, and she would hopefully learn more about the French mystery.

Now she was talking with Charlie as he was one of Albert's old colleagues on the old Quay and the docks. Maybe he was the Charlie he had mentioned. She decided to find out. Charlie was talking about a funeral that had taken place some years ago of a real well-loved character in the town, Schutz the German. The fact that he was 'dead now' wasn't the point he was making. What he was alluding to was that the free and smuggled booze they all drank habitually when they worked the Quay was sometimes not of the correct quality. And the fact that Schultzie could drink more than most and actually liked the 100% proof illegal distilled spirit that some captains brought in, may have helped the mercurial man on his way to the Reichstag in the sky.

Indeed, Charlie was reminiscing about a certain bottle of spirit that no one, even the most hardened drinkers on the Quay could drink. It had been given to them by some Rumanian captain who drank half another bottle himself. Everyone took one smell and taste and nearly collapsed. It was a zillion percent proof and smelt of turpentine. This morning as usual Schultz had arrived in time for their breakfast livener at 6.00 am after his early morning visit to Brixham harbour. 'Is there anything in your locker Charlie?' Schultz enquired, as he did most mornings. The dockers' lockers those days, long before the new company took over, and when health and safety regulations were shall we say a little less invasive, contained not clothes or things pertaining to work. They just contained booze that had been given to them by the ships captain's or the shipping agents; a vital stimulant to get them through a day man hauling and shovelling large cargoes on and off the ships, but it was of course duty free and eagerly sought in periodic raids by Her Majesty's Customs and Excise.

'I've none today buoy,' answered Charlie, much to the disappointment of our Teutonic early riser. Shultz looked dolefully at

Charlie and Charlie took pity. A kind and thoughtful man that he was, he offered Schultz a way out of his thirst and a decent liquid breakfast. 'There is the bottle under the sink Schultzie. You could try a drop out of that.' And indeed, the lovely man did, and drank the whole bottle, with seemingly little effect. Hence Charlie's laconic end to the tale. 'Of course, he be dead now though.'

The captain had given them, as was the custom then, several bottles as a favour (bribe) and then a thank you for moving the cargo quick. The Quay boys could make or break a captain and the sailors knew it. The reward for getting their ship either unloaded or loaded was always booze or cigarettes. Some which was just for drinking with the captain or for sharing with the team. Other was smuggled through the Quay and into the town. Another ancient Devon tradition the 'buoys' were keeping strong.

'Was there much stuff you couldn't drink Charlie?' Françoise asked, still smiling at the last story about iron stomached Prussian.

'Not a lot. We did get some queer brews though. Captain Jim loved bringing in his stuff. One day he gives us a huge bottle of wine shaped like a brandy bottle but it was about two-foot-wide at the bottom and three foot high. He be wrapped in that raffia type stuff, just like the Chianti bottles that came out in the seventies. Me and Kev drinks he on the day of the Teignmouth carnival. He be horrible but he got supped.' Charlie smiled and then drank another slurp of his lager.

'You must have been pissed you old bugger,' asked Françoise rhetorically.

'Aye we were maid. When we leaves the quay, we were staggering and bumped straight into the Temperance Society float. The float was pulled by a large horse. Those days all the floats had booze on them and everyone was pissed. I jumps on the float and asks the maid in the hat if she had a spare bottle. *It's the Devil's brew my son,'* says she to me and I realises, and thinks *oops wrong wassel,* and I jumps off.'

Françoise chuckled, 'Bet they were shocked?'

Charlie replied, 'No me booty, they prays for me as I jumped. The horse neighed and stamped a bit as I think I'd frightened he and the religious maids looked scared. So, I grabs the horse's bridle and pulls its head down and I blows up its nose, making Indian sounds. The ladies looked even more scared and leader shouted down, *'What are you doing? You silly man!'* I shouts back, *'it's an old Apache Indian trick, seen it in a John Wayne movie. Don't be feared maid',* and the horse stopped. God knows why, I'd never held a horse before. The float moved on with the ladies crossing themselves. I fell over pissed.'

16

He laughed and then, when he'd recovered, he concluded the horse whispering tale. 'When I'd calmed the savage beast, Kev's wife and family arrives to go to the carnival and he just says hello through his laughter. He was laughing so much and was so pissed that he staggered backward and over a wall into a six-foot ditch they were digging for a new pipe. His wife just looks at him unconscious in the ditch. She shakes her head, gathered the kids around her skirt and they looks at daddy lying comatose in the muddy ditch and she says to them, '*Say goodnight to your dad, he won't be home before you are in bed.*'

Charlie took another drink and Françoise laughed and said, 'Yes, I heard the carnival was a riot in those days. It's a lot more civilised now that Sarah and the folks organise it.'

'He sounds some character that Captain Jim. What nationality was he Charlie?'

'No idea. Maybe Portuguese I think, we got them all in, French, German, Dutch, and Portuguese. The Russians came in numbers after Gorbachev and his perestroika and glasnost. We had boats from Asian and African crews too; loads of stories and many, many characters. They were happy days then. Mind you Captain Jim's parrot took some beating.'

'His parrot? Sounds like it was a pirate ship Charlie?' Françoise asked.

'No maid, it wasn't Long John Silver's parrot Captain Flint, but that bloody bird caused mayhem. When us were in the holds of any ship, the captain would shout down sometimes encouragement and sometimes instructions and us'd shout up to ask for lifting strops or something to be lowered. First time on Captain Jim's I be hearing him shouting down, '*you buoys ok there?*' We shouts back, '*Aye Captain*' I shouts up, '*do you want us to move the bags to port side?*' and there be no answer. We thinks ignorant bugger. Then a few minutes later, '*All Hands on Deck!*' So, we climbs out and stands there to see no sign of Captain Jim. Again, we just thinks typical foreigner, no bloody manners and back down the ladders we'd go. Sometime later we hears his voice again, '*You buoys ok?*' Us shouts back, '*Aye aye sir*' and again no answer. This went on for our entire shift until we finished and Captain Jim was waiting with a bottle for us all to share with him. His parrot was sat on his shoulder. He opened the bottle and the bird said, mimicking his voice exactly, '*bottoms up!*' The bloody bird had been talking all the time.'

He chuckled away and Françoise giggled. He continued. 'We let other gangs work his boat sometimes just to laugh like hell in *The Quay Pub* at elevenses listening to them saying what a rude and ignorant captain he was! Mind you maybe the parrot compensated him in conversation

17

because he always brought his deaf and dumb son with him: Poor lad. He probably talked a lot to his parrot because of his dumb son. It talked back to him I guesses. That bloody bird picked his accent and words up magically. We should have shot the bugger!'

'To Shultzie!' a shout went up in the bar and they all raised their glasses in toast of the iconic German who was taken before his time. Without doubt he'd been a well loved and influential character in the town. And his funeral had seen him driven on a horse drawn carriage through the town. Not a thing for anyone who wasn't respected and loved.

'How did he get here Charlie? I thought I was the only foreigner here?' said Cockney Jim, who was drinking next to Charlie and Françoise.

'Hell, no buoy,' said Dawn from behind the bar, 'you are just from up country, just a grockle. Schultzie was German, a real foreigner.'

'Well, his name was actually Polish but he came from Flensburg. He always said he was a Danish white Viking. He just arrived one day off a ship, walked down the gangplank and never went back. The ship left and he stayed,' explained Charlie. He continued, 'He was some man that buoy. If the Germans ever won a football match or Schumacher an F1 race he'd smash open the pub door and scream at us all joyously, *you bloody English. We beat you again*'. He'd get annoyed when the whole pub would chant *'two world wars and one world cup!'* If anyone wanted to challenge him, he'd tell them all *'to shut up or they'd get a 'smack in the mouse'*.

'One of the hardest men and best workers we had down the quay Françoise,' interjected Marty, the now retired leader of the old Quay dockers. 'One day he had his whole thumb squashed flat by a crane grabber in the cargo hold. He worked through his shift and we got the ship turned around. We took him to hospital and he took his thumb with him. He be so squashed they couldn't fix it on. The maid on reception fainted when he showed her. He used to keep the thumb in his pocket and show everyone. He be turned green and mouldy eventually and the thumb shocked many a maid in the bars when he pulled he out. That's some man. The captain that day was so pleased even if we had chopped Schultzie's thumb off that he gave me a case of vodka too.'

'Aye you old bugger, we saw none of it!' said Appsy standing at the bar.

'He went into the kitty buoy; all for one and one for all,' Marty said, with a mischievous glint in his eye swallowing another gulp from his beer. Marty had controlled all the jobs and the rewards on the Quay. He had managed hide the spoils mostly from the constant vigilance and raids of the customs and excise men on the Quay and on the workers houses in the town; the grand master at the noble art of attaining and concealing contraband which his antecedents had been perfecting since the French invasion.

'Remember that bloody Captain Sex and his donkey and monkey caused us some environmental grief. The Colorado beetles were the next buggers to cause mayhem,' interjected Marty.

Françoise was listening and enjoying the nostalgia. But she was no farther forward in finding out if Charlie was one of the secret society or even who the Charlie she should be trying to talk with. She looked around and smiled at her fellow customers in the bar. The bar in *The Teign* was like the Follies Bergere without the tarts. A wheeling mass of unforgettable Harlequinesque characters dancing with the Devil in haze of cider, beer and cigarette smoke from the back garden, smelling not unlike the Gauloise she had once loved to smoke at the Follies herself - a madhouse of course. But then again it always was.

She had been in town for some years now and been accepted and surprisingly, given her *incomer* background; it had not been too much of struggle. Being French of course didn't help, but mainly what helped her immensely was that her husband was known; he was a 'local buoy' who had come home after seeing the light. So, her vetting by the MI5 members, masquerading as the patrons of *The Teign*, was pretty straightforward. In fact it only took a few visits for her to be accepted. This was simple really, she soon understood. It was purely because Rollo, the pub's huge Staffordshire bull terrier had taken a fancy to her. The crafty canine was a master at vetting strangers who come into the bar.   He had a nose for policemen, taxmen or welfare benefit inspectors. Tony the now retired welfare inspector still had the scars to this day of his leg being gnawed on his first visit.

Many, many years ago in the old days before the new companies took over and the buoys were working and when the docks, or the quay was affectionately called *The Quay*, it was not like now a professional, modern efficient enterprise of the highest management and HSE standards. Now the old customs and behaviours of the past, and the buoys are long gone. Those days Rollo's granddad was the crème de la crème of customs and revenue men sniffers. The present-day Rollo, nearly blind, slept most of the time on the quaint old-world wooden benches that are the bar seats only leaving his slumbers to sniff at new visitors and then bark loudly and aggressively at any that might be suspicious. He was remarkably accurate in his vetting!

Françoise looked around at the clientele. At the far end of the bar was someone like a wizard. The only difference was this ancient mystic loved to drink Diesel/Natch, not the stuff that powered the cranes on the nearby docks, but real, potent scrumpy cider. This should not be surprising because any genuine wizard or druid would surely sup cider? You could not imagine Merlin drinking a chilled glass of Chablis or a Two Drifters Black sails rum and ginger.

As Françoise looked over at the great man, she wondered given his mystical status in the bar, maybe he was the holder of the esoteric secret. *Of course*, she thought as she remembered the dying man's last words, 'chalice'; *maybe it was an alchemist's cup?* Could this be the special man to talk to? It made sense; Gandalf could hide it forever in the paradise of Rivendell, guarded maybe by Rollo's offspring. The fruit of Rollo's overactive loins would, like Cerberus the multi headed hound that guarded the gates of Hell, guard the French ship's secret forever.

She was just thinking of ordering a beer when Dave the Painter got quite agitated and in his loud voice he was remonstrating with someone about their lack of appreciation of his love everything artistic, especially post-modernist work.

'Heh man! You have no idea about art. You are philistine man. Carl Andre's a genius man!'

His protagonist, and latter-day Goliath to King David the painter, just looked up from his stool at the tall, flowing locks Essex man and throw back to the swinging eighties. Goliath quietly appraised the cultural significance of great artistic talent and then through pursed lips he made his judgement to the whole bar - 'Art is shite.'

Dave went into apoplexy and hurled expletives and words of artistic historical significance at his Philistine opponent. Françoise chuckled as she listened; well she couldn't help hear, as even the good customers of *The Blue Anchor* public house up the road could hear Dave when he was in full flow. He fired a few more sling shots at Goliath and then shaking his locks, still shouting out loud, he looked around for support from the good patrons of *The Teign*. Disgusted and distraught at the lack of anyone in bar's interest in the world of art and into the post-modernist movement, he retired from the debating society. He dragged Bournville his lovely chocolate Labrador hound with him to the beer garden at the back of the pub. He joined the other members of the Teignmouth Botanical Society in smoking his roll your own Rizla and Golden Virginia and discussing the cultivation of exotic plants.

As Françoise watched the hound following his master to the meeting room for The Society for the Advancement of Botanical Science, or TABS, for short, she wondered if she should join this esteemed society. She knew it held its meetings daily in the tropical gardens of the back of The Teign. After all, maybe one of the professors of Pharmacognosy in the learned society may be able to shed some light on the mystery she sought to solve. Then she heard Painter Dave shouting again about the wonder of art, particularly sheep pickled in formaldehyde, and thought maybe she'd give the tropical garden and its fragrant aromas a miss.

She turned to Charlie and asked him if he'd ever been interested in exotic plants and the study of therapeutic substances that came from them.

'Not really Maid, I just liked beer and making money. Isn't that so Marty?'

Marty looked over and asked what he'd said and would he repeat himself. In his older age Marty suffered the deafness induced by the loud noises of his past work.

'Us were greedy bastards weren't we buoy!' Charlie shouted over the mayhem.

'Oh arh, us certainly were Charlie. We'd worked our way up from waiting in line for work and scrabbling for the odd few hours day work to finally we were the top gang on all ships. It was the way of quay those days always the survival of the fittest, maid. The new starters and young' uns had to wait for work we'd give them. Us took the cream of the boats and cargoes first. Aye, we were greedy bastards. Mind you we worked like hell, shovelling day and night to get the boats out. No one could beat us. Charlie was the best: a beast. He could shovel more shit than any of us.'

Charlie looked up took a drink and said, 'I was like the kids in the movie *'Patton'*, with George C Scott, when he faced a bunch of recruits back home in America before they were sent to France to fight and he said, *'Would you be like to be remembered as the kid who stayed at home and shovelled shit in Louisiana or a hero who fought and died for his country'*. I was that man shovelling shit!'

Marty laughed. 'You shovelled some shit that Christmas Eve when Schultzie helped you.' All in the know chuckled away again, knowing the Charlie would have to reply and tell yet another old Quay tale.

'Yes matey, I did. Its early Christmas Eve morning and we has to get this boat out so we can go on the piss. I needs Kev with me but he has been drinking since six along with Marty with the boat's Captain. Marty is on the hatch directing Colin with the crane, who was also pissed. Marty gets a fit of the giggles and then keels over unconscious on the deck. Kev's head is so messed with drink he says he's off home. I'm left on me own. No one to shovel with so I gets stuck in. We has to get the ship out afore I can get home. Matey heads to the Quay Pub and asks for help. Schultzie is in pub already from the night shift on the trawler but when he hears about our plight he volunteers to come down and help. Me and Schultzie worked all bloody day to get the ship out whilst the buoys are in the pub or unconscious. We never gets to the pub till ten at night. Everyone is mortal! My first Christmas Eve lost, for God's sake. But I'll never forget Schultzie for that. Hard, hard man but what a shoveller!'

All who were listening laughed. Françoise curious to know how the whole thing worked asked, 'If both of you and Marty were so good then the management must have thought a lot of you?'

'Dear God, maid, the management just sat up in their central heated offices in their short sleeved white shirts looking down at us grafting away in the sleet and howling gales coming up The Teign valley. They never moved out. And when they did, Dangerous Dick the Destroyer came down and watched us shovelling and just said, *'I love to hear the swish of shovels in the morning.'*

Everyone laughed again at Charlie stark description of leadership in the old days *'Patton'* and *'Apocalypse Now'* style. 'So, maid, we were too busy earning money and shovelling to bother about plants. Mind you we did manage to make a bob one day out of plants but it wasn't what we expected.'

Marty chuckled, and shouted across, 'Aye, but not what we wanted eh Charlie?' and he strolled over, his short very wide powerful body moving a few bodies at the bar aside. Françoise noticed his solid gold neck chains and gold Krugerrand rings glittering in the bright bar lights. She mused that Marty had indeed been 'the man', and made some money from hard work on the quay and maybe possibly also from extracurricular activities. She chuckled to no one but herself when she remembered travelling through the Tyne Tunnel most days when she had taken a nursing training course in Newcastle. She had noticed every time she went through the tunnel twice a day certain hands would come out of the toll booth with everyone of them containing huge gold rings and bracelets on to take her cash toll money. She spoke to a fellow nurse on the course who was a local Geordie lady. 'These toll guys must make have a huge salary Mary? I wouldn't mind their job.'

'Everyone wants their job pet, 'she said, 'it's a bloody goldmine; salary's shite mind, only about five grand a year. But somehow they can afford the whole of De Beer's output in Kruggerands.'

'That's a puzzle then Mary?' said a very naive Françoise.

'Uhm pet, you are French, I guess. You must think outside the box sometimes. I guess you never pay by card or cheques do you when you use the tunnel?'

'No Mary I don't. Always cash...oh!' and suddenly she was educated to the inventive ways of the British working man to earn a 'bob or two.'

Marty sidled up to Charlie and said, 'That was the summer when Teignmouth won the Britain in Bloom competition. We Quay buoys did all that. Proud of that weren't we.'

'Proud! We should have been keel hauled for the cock-up man,' Charlie answered, looking distressed. 'That secure store that KP had hired out to outsiders should have been a goldmine. Us were told it was full of food or booze. It was below my carpenter's shed, The Carpenters Arms, where there was a hidden small trapdoor between the joists. The only one who could fit through was Peter, Jackie's dad. We lowers him down through the roof on a rope tied to his legs. He keeps handing us back up sacks of what us thought were full of spring onions or oranges and some were cardboard boxes which us hoped might have cigarettes in. After a few hours of bloody hard work, us had emptied enough of the store and managed to get the boxes stacked ready to take off the Quay. I fits the hatch cover back and us takes the haul back up to the house in Kingsway. We shared a bottle from Marty's cases of vodka he'd been given off the Captain of a clay boat and opened the boxes. For Christ's sake all they contains is hundreds of bloody daffodil bulbs and other flowers and then the bloody boxes were full of *Radon'* the soap powder.'

Charlie just stared at Françoise and Marty who were chuckling away and he finished. 'It wasn't bloody funny at the time. Anyway, that's the summer Teignmouth looked bootiful in bloom and the nappies were cleanest ever seen on the washing lines in Kingsway.'

Marty grabbed Françoise's arm with his strong gnarled hand. 'The next lot that KP rented out, Peter tried to get some of that as well. When he opened the containers, they were full of bird's nesting boxes!' He laughed out loud, 'Every council house in Kingsway had a full bloody aviary of birds nesting that spring.'

Françoise smiled again, took a drink and asked another naive question. 'Did you manage to get anything as a thank you but booze for all your hard work?'

'Bloody hell maid, most of Teignmouth is built out of what came off the Quay,' said Charlie. 'Whole houses were built out of timber from the timber dunnage used hold the cargoes in place. Twelve by six joists mind. The chipboard came from the chipboard boats and plaster board, it was a godsend. The Eastern bloc boat's plasterboard cargoes were a bonus but they were mainly shite, but they were free so everyone took them. Cement came from the cement boats and the sand from the sand quay when we had three quays to work from. So, my hansom, yes, the Captain's were good to us those days.'

'Mind you we had to do some things to get a drink on some boats. Do you remember the boat *'Ebenezer'*, Charlie?' Appsy asked, 'that Mormon boat?'

'Aye I does. None of them drank! But they weren't daft woz them buggers. They had lots of booze for us. But matey made us kneel down and pray while he preached about the evils of drink before he gives us our bottles. First time I prays for my booze!'

Charlie and Marty raised their glasses in toast to the old days. 'But it's a lot different now. Thank God we got out of the docks in time,' said Marty, and everyone nodded in sympathy.

Françoise sat down on a stool, feeling very happy. She loved to hear the stories of days on the Quay before the new company took over many years ago and modern management brought secure, long term and safe, well paid employment to the good folks in the area. But looking at the age of most of the old stalwarts she began to realise that she had better hurry up and find some answers to the secret that Albert wanted her to share. It could be gone forever if the ancient cognoscenti had not passed it on to their offspring.

She was broken out of her thoughts by a growl, a huge bark and then another growl as Rollo flew off his chosen perch and promptly bit Denis the Taxi driver who had come to pick up Charlie and take him back to Kingsway. It seemed he disliked taxi drivers as much as customs inspectors. She decided it was time to leave. She would begin her search another day. This was indeed a mad house.

CHAPTER FOUR

Françoise woke up with a start. Her husband was getting up out of bed to head off to work; a small project in Falmouth docks upgrading the quayside. She watched as he dressed and he kissed her, and said, 'See you Friday' and left. The light was just coming through their bedroom window and she realised it was going to be another warm and sunny day. She had woken suddenly as she had been dreaming of wizards, rabid dogs and curiously Peter Pan. She couldn't quite work out where Peter Pan had come from and this had caused her to wake up confused. As she lay watching the sunlight stream through the slightly open curtains, she remembered why. It was Captain Hooke, the bill -hooked pirate nemesis of Peter Pan and Wendy and her dream had ended with him been eaten whole, not by the tick tock crocodile, but by a gigantic Rollo dog. She shook her head, rolled her legs out the bed into her slippers and thought, *no more scrumpy for me.*

After a nice steaming cup of coffee, she gave her small French bulldog, Piaf, a few biscuits for her breakfast and returned to the bedroom to get dressed. She dressed casually in shorts and tee-shirt as she had a two-day rest period from her nursing duties. She opened the curtains and the window and took a deep breath of the warm sea air. *This has been a lovely summer so far,* she thought. As she sat on the bed and put on her walking trainers, she remembered suddenly why she might have dreamed about the canine spy hunter devouring Captain Hooke. Maybe it was another sign or omen. She really needed to talk with the Hook family as they had been around for centuries and maybe one of them was in the secret circle. There was a hell of a lot of them around the area she knew that. It was an ancient name around these parts; *it has to lead somewhere* she murmured to no one but her pet hound who was sitting panting at her feet waiting for her early morning walk on the Back Beach.

She put the hound on her leash and walked out of her terraced house into the small back lane that lead down Northumberland Square and then walked past *The Devon Arms* and then *The Jolly Sailor*, the oldest pub in Teignmouth. As she passed, she was sure the pub may well have been around when her countrymen invaded. *Maybe it contained a hidden treasure or map in there?* She'd definitely have to talk to someone about that.

She looked into *The Quayside* bookshop and noticed an old book on Donald Crowhurst, the local man who attempted to sail around the world to win the Golden Globe race. She and her husband had watched the movie of the story, *The Mercy*, with many locals at the new

Teignmouth theatre and performing arts centre, *The Pavilions*, some weeks ago. Only thing she really liked about it was Colin Firth, he was a bit of an homme sauvage. She got mildly jealous when her husband grunted a few times at Rachael Weisz but like a lot of the locals she was disappointed that Teignmouth and Shaldon, its sister village over the estuary, weren't shown more in the movie. Plus, the yachtsman was a cheat; not a great local advertisement they thought.

She checked if there was anything in the window of the book store that might be useful in her quest, but saw nothing that interested her. As she walked on, she thought that maybe one day she'd write her own book about the whole quest and call it *'Frog on the Teign'*. They would make a better movie than *The Mercy* out of that she was sure.

The small hound pulled harder at her lead as she could smell the sea air and smells coming from the estuary coastline and Back Beach. Françoise looked briefly into the tattoo shop and saw one photo of a pirate and considered that if she was successful, she'd have one tattooed on her buttock as a thank you to Captain Albert. Then she gave up that thought as she realised her husband might well think she had lost her marbles. Maybe she'd put Peter Pan on instead. She shook her head and tried to think of something else; this was getting obsessive. She turned down the street past *The New Quay* pub and onto the fish quay. A couple of boats were unloading crabs and carrying them into the small Simmonds's fisherman's warehouse where they would be boiled and sold to the general public in their small delicatessen opposite to *The Newquay*. She smiled as she remembered seeing the two boys Joe and Matt helping their father with the crab pots when they were young. Now both had graduated from Teignmouth Rugby Club through the successful Exeter Chiefs to play for England. The French always know that sea food is good for you she mused, *why don't our Rugby team we eat more? We might win a few games then!*

The hound pulled harder and she pulled the leash and checked her. She bent down and unleashed her. Piaf, named after Edith, the Little Sparrow, ran excitedly past *The Ship Inn* and onto the Back Beach, rolling around in the sand in pure ecstasy. Françoise sat on the small wall outside *The Ship*, lit up a cigarette and looked out over the Estuary towards Shaldon Village, about half a kilometre over the River Teign. It was beautiful morning and she looked up the river following up the valley and she could see clearly Dartmoor and its majestic granite Tors. As it was low tide, the leisure craft, fishing boats and yachts were lying scattered over the mud and sand with those in the deeper moorings bobbing gently on aquamarine water in the early morning westerly breeze. She loved this place and she said this to herself every morning it was sunny like this; hard to beat it, even in her native Brittany.

Her hound was playing happily with small miniature Schnauzer. She finished her cigarette and walked onto the beach and say good morning to her owner. 'Bonjour Jack, C'est beau n'est–ce pas? Ca va?'

'Oui, Françoise, ca va. C'est beau encore. Et-tu en forme?' the dog owner replied.

'Yes, Jack I'm fit. But only just mon ami. Had a night in *The Teign* last night after Schultzie's funeral. Bit delicate this morning.'

Jack nodded and chuckled, 'Aye, it's not unusual that though Françoise is it? And he threw a small stick into the river for his small German hound to swim the short distance and fetch it back. The tide was on the turn and the stick was accelerating with the pull towards the estuary mouth and the small gap where the sea and river exited and entered between the beach point and The Ness Rock on the Shaldon side. His hound just managed to get the stick before it floated out of her tiny legs reach.

'Guess not, but yesterday was a big one,' Françoise replied smiling. 'Plus, I spent most of the night drinking with Charlie and Marty. You can't get your hand in your purse before they have another round on the bar.'

'That's for sure. You never get away from that lot from the old docks without a gallon at least,' Jack answered.

'What a morning Jack it is today and thank Christ I don't have to work today. You, you lucky bugger don't have to worry about that though. One day I'm going to retire and spend my whole first day in bed. The dog can just have to wait till the bar opens for her walk.'

Jack smiled, certainly he was indeed lucky. He had retired from the purgatory of working in the UK and then the paradise of a life working in Asia, and after a brief visit to hell that is a life in Paris, he had moved here, Initially he felt he had holed up in a remote land, forgotten by anyone North of Stonehenge and regularly cut off from normal society and civilisation; it's called Devon.

During his first year he often asked himself; why? Well it is a wonderful and beautiful spot and the local natives are smashing friendly people but mainly it was because they don't eat you, and it was a good spot to be hiding from such people as people may read about in *'A Turkey and One More Easter Egg'*. Especially the real contractors in that book who would never find him because they would never come here, simply because of one fact alone, there is no Four Floors of Whores. Whilst there are pretty young

27

girls like Rosie hidden in the cider orchards, most of the women he was now acquainted with were mainly like your wife or more likely in this geriatric haven, your grandmother. Mind you a lot of grandmother's here were very good looking. He had to say that as the Tina from *The Kings Arms* and Norma from *The Castle* and all the other lovely barmaids would bar him if he didn't.

As he attempted to settle and bond with the locals, he felt forgotten by all but a few fellow outcasts from the real world, retired, bored, stuck in a time warp and surrounded by people who drink cider from porcelain jugs and mugs, as it rots normal glass and dissolves the lead from pewter tankards. You can guess what it does to the cerebral cortex.

But now, despite the beauty, the wonderful people and no work, some days he believed he was in Jack's Inferno again. But now the Nine Circles of Hell were the nine pubs he visited and inhabited day by day across this beautiful part of the world, constantly moving from bar to bar, tortured daily by the local demons......and always there is Gus. He believed he may well be all the Circles of Purgatory in one.

Here in Jack's Inferno he had made acquaintances in all the bars. As the years went by, he realised that he could never be a real Teignmouth lad as he was an in comer, but he was beginning to think maybe they did accept him as they had named him Singapore Jack; a breakthrough in human and international relations. He knew Charlie and Marty and most of the lads well now, so he understood Françoise's hangover and her angst at never been allowed to pay. He also after a life of *Contracting with the Devil* had great sympathy for her having to work. It just isn't fair.

'Anyone else there last night Françoise?' he asked as they walked towards the point and the end of the Back Beach. The water was racing back out of the estuary now and past the Point out to a virtually flat blue sea. The small sand dredger that dredged the entrance and surrounding sea was just off the Point. It dredged perpetually 365 days a year to ensure the channel between the Ness and the Point was clear and ready to take the commercial vessels which came into the modern docks for loading and unloading. It was a wonderful sight to see the harbour master guide the ships past the Point and through the deep-water channel into the estuary harbour and guide them through the host of yachts and small boats to the waiting dockers on the Quay. Some days it was almost possible to touch the hull of the ship as it passed through the narrow channel - wonderful feat of sailing skills from harbour tug and ships captains.

Françoise answered his question about the funeral. 'Yes, there were loads there Jack. Most were at the *Rugby Club*, only a few went back to *The Teign.*'

By now they had walked around the end of the Point and were facing the sea. Françoise looked back to look for Piaf and she noticed that a man stopped as she turned and began to light a cigarette. She was sure he'd been sat opposite *The Devon Arms* on the public seats when she'd past. Was he following her? She shook her head and thought *'don't be silly madam; you are getting paranoid.'* But it prompted her to think again about Albert's confession and where on earth could she begin to find out what he had meant. She decided maybe she could use a bit of help so she decided to let Jack into some of the story. He knew a lot of people across the area, mainly because he was pissed in most of the bars most of the days, so maybe he could spread some light on the thing. 'Jack, you know an author here don't you?'

'Yes, I drink sometimes with a lad, Davey. He moved here some time ago to write.'

'Does he know anything about the history of the town and the characters?'

'He seems to know a lot about the old days and he researches a lot of obscure stories. He's a bit of a conspiracy theory freak. Thinks everyone is linked to a secret society or spying for the NSA. Drinks with that wizard in the Teign. But he knows his stuff on some things. Why do you ask?'

Françoise threw a small stick for Piaf and her and the German hound ran off, competing with each other to get there first. She looked at Jack and thought should I really tell but she bottled it. 'It's just I'm really interested in the French invasion. I think one of my distant relatives was on one of the ships. My aunty told me years ago that maybe they left some buried treasure or something. Be good to know if anyone knows anything about it; might be a book in it for Davey.'

Jack laughed. 'Buried treasure, how many times have I heard that in this place. Have you heard the tale of The Black Pig?'

'No. Thought The Black Pig was Captain Pugwash's ship? Françoise asked.

'It was, but it was also Frankie and Gordon's. Mind you they didn't have a Master Bates or Rodger the Cabin Boy onboard like Captain Pugwash. They were master smugglers. They even have their exploits and ship in the smuggler's hall of fame in Polperro. Sadly, they were caught red handed just off the shore about to come into the estuary with a hall of cigarettes and booze by the customs and the Royal Navy. It was a massive thing at the time. In the News of the World and a TV crew came to make a documentary about it. Pity they caught a local policeman outside of *The Dawlish Inn*, which is *Dicey Reilly's* now of course, sitting down drinking a nice cup of tea, instead of directing the traffic; Teignmouth yet again shown up on national TV.'

'I didn't know we were that famous Jack,' said Françoise, thinking maybe this might lead somewhere to help her quest.

'From what the lads tell me Françoise, Teignmouth and Shaldon particularly, seem to have a chequered past in the scheme of all things politically correct. Esther Rantzen did an exposure on her Saturday Night popular show in the seventies which didn't go down well at all with the town. A restaurant owner had asked a local care worker not to bring his mentally disabled people into his restaurant at peak holiday times on evenings. It seems he was losing customers as they were embarrassed and disturbed by the seriously mentally handicapped people in his care. Sad but, I guess he didn't stop them coming but asked them to avoid his peak weekend and school holiday evenings. Anyway, Esther's show portrayed Teignmouth to the world as a cruel and heartless bunch in line with Nazi Germany. She isn't too well liked here.'

'That's terrible. Everyone I know is amazingly tolerant. We have an amazing reputation for accommodating and integrating with the visually impaired and have great disabled facilities at the beaches and town.'

'Aye Françoise, for sure; they let us in and haven't eaten us yet,' and Jack laughed. 'Did you know about the people who lived in Shaldon? Dear me, it's a worry.'

Françoise, still smiling about the 'eaten' comment said, 'No, not really. It's a beautiful spot and a lot of wealthy people move there.'

'Famous ones as well in the past; Great names like Gary Glitter and Jimmy Saville. Jimmy Saville even had a dedication and his signature on the wall in the fish and chip shop. It's been painted over now.'

Françoise looked shocked and Jack continued, 'Mind you they've had some less controversial people come and stay there, The Beatles I'm told played once in *The London Hotel* and of course Norman Wisdom came to make the movie *'Press for Time'*. It was filmed a lot in *The Jolly Sailor*. It seems he was a sensation here, great man and so friendly. Guess with *'The Mercy'* as well we may well become the next Hollywood. Mind you Shaldon has had some characters you could make a good movie about. Roy, the Teignmouth Yank, tells me when he was a young apprentice plumber in the sixties he had to work over there. Old man Hook who was the man who knew all the ways of the tides and how to move ships to ensure they were never grounded on the old Quay told him as he puffed away at his wooden pipe, *'You don't want to know what happens there buoy.'* Roy would walk over the bridge crack of dawn every day and work in the houses. He says he is still scarred now, years after. *'Us young buoys shouldn't have been exposed to the goings on over in that place. Sodom and Gomorrah buoy. Mind us enjoyed some of it.'* Yes, Roy saw some things a boy shouldn't have had to see.'

Françoise looked shocked again: 'Surely not that bad Jack? Who was there then?'

'Well Mandy Rice Davies for one; Stephen Ward and Profumo as others. I think Roy may well have been the man in the picture that was published in all the press and in the episode in the Netflix, *The Crown*, on the scandal that brought down a Minister of the Crown and maybe well have destroyed the monarchy. It showed the back of the head of a man at a party thrown by Stephen Ward and Keeler. Everyone alleged it was the Duke of Edinburgh. Your Royal Highness you have nothing to worry about, it wasn't Phil the Greek. It was taken in Shaldon of course - and I now know it was Roy.'

Françoise laughed out loud and then looked around for Piaf. They had crossed the beach and walked through the gap between the beach huts and were back on the Back Beach. She couldn't see Piaf, and then the little pug looking hound came running through the beach huts. Behind her was the man with the cigarette. As she looked behind, the man looked down and picked up a shell and looked as if he was examining it. Françoise turned to Jack. 'Don't look now but that man behind us. Do you think he's following us?'

Of course Jack turned around immediately, as most do when told not to. The man had thrown the shell away and still stood still just behind them and when Jack looked he turned around and picked up another shell, turning it around in his hand. Jack turned back. 'Come on you daft Frog. You are getting like that Davey; thinking there is a plot under ever stone. Let's head and get a cup of coffee. It's a pity it's a bit early for Adam and Jane's cracking bacon sarnies in *Relish* cafe and Naema won't be out of her kip yet for sure. Let's try *The Whistle Stop* at the train station.'

Françoise shrugged her shoulders and brushed off her fears yet again and walked with Jack. She brought him back to his original story about the treasure and smugglers. 'What happened after the lads were arrested by the customs and navy men?'

'Well I was told they were banged up in Exeter Jail and then moved to Haldon open prison, where they managed to get home for marital activities. Think they must have still been smuggling. But this time cigarettes and booze in for the guards who to let them escape as a favour.' Jack chuckled again at the thought. He continued. 'I was told the customs didn't get anything like the real goods they had on board as they'd dumped that to another mate with another boat. There are rumours in town that there may have been a treasure hoard on board and more than just cigarettes. It is thought by those in the know that it's buried under the sand on The Salty, the island in the Teign Estuary. Long John Silver and Captain Flint's buried treasure and all that Françoise; Devon has a chequered history of pirates and smugglers. We have the impressive rock hewn Smugglers tunnel in Shaldon, Smugglers Lane in Holcombe and *The Smugglers* pub there too. There could be anything buried around here.'

Françoise's heart skipped a beat. *Maybe the Salty held the key. But who would know?'* Jack, does anyone really know anything about this treasure?'

'Well Charlie told me about it but I think he just knows it from the old lads on the docks. One name is mentioned who knew the Black Pig and the boys. Hook, not the Captain Hooke but one of the Hook's; mind you I'm told there are loads of them. Why are you so interested Françoise?'

Françoise stopped walking. She turned around again and sure enough the man with the shells was still behind. She shivered in the summer morning's warm air. Had she now also brought Jack into danger? *Surely not, get real woman,* she thought. But she decided maybe she tell Jack a bit more, if he was now implicated, he should at least know some more. 'Jack lets walk and get that coffee. I'll tell you there about what happened to me a few weeks ago. A man called Albert, maybe he was Captain Hook, I'm beginning to think this is a fairy story we are in, told me something about a treasure and to keep it secret to myself. But I think you should know what he said and by the way I think the man behind **is** following us.'

Jack bent down and leashed his dog and as he did, he looked behind. Sure enough the man was there. He looked at Jack and immediately sat down wooden benches outside *The Ship* pub and turned his back and looked out across the yachts and fishing boats and up the Teign Estuary, which was now shimmering silver and gold reflecting the rays of the rising sun over the sea and the Ness rock. He stood up and thought, *Yes, maybe Françoise wasn't paranoid like his mate Davey, let's go and talk more.* 'Come on the Françoise. Get Piaf on her lead and let's have that coffee.' They both walked much more quickly.

They passed Laura Wall's studio the renowned local artist. Francoise couldn't help think that the boy and girl holding hands, sitting together cuddling that she added to many of her paintings, could easy have been Jack and her that sunny morning as they walked and sat among the same landscapes and features Laura painted so affectionately and distinctly.

They passed *Relish* cafe where Naema held daily counselling sessions for the patrons and next to it Françoise stopped to look at a painting in the window of the *Teignmouth Arts and Community Centre.* It was a spectacular, colourful and moving expression of colour by an artist called Clare Jenkinson. She couldn't help notice a beautiful moody painting of Dartmoor by a local lady called Kate. She made a note in her head to come back and buy one of them.

The man watched them go and stood up. He tapped his mobile phone and made an international call. The man on the other end of the call put down his café au lait, pushed his croissant almond across the table and answered the call. He listened to the man on the River Teign. After listening he whispered down his phone in very good English, 'Merci Paul, follow them and find out who the man is. It's time to step it up. Fix her phone; a bientôt.'

He switched his phone off and looked out over the Château and broke off another piece of his croissant. 'After all these years I am close now to securing grandfather's legacy.' He turned on the radio and he could hear the tones of an aria sung by a female opera singer. He smiled as he thought of his great grandfather Father Saunière mixing in those exclusive Parisian esoteric circles all those years ago in the 'naughty nineties'. How he had carried out an affair with the most famous singer in the world, Emma Calvés, and that he was the result of that illicit liaison. How the errant pastor had mixed with artists, sages, and high society. He had known Claude Debussy. But all the time he was being groomed by the controller of the Seminary of Saint Sulpice. They cared nothing for him as a lowly country Catholic priest only for the secret he had discovered. And they were prepared to pay millions to his Catholic great grandfather to secure it and keep it safe from the rest of the world. Now he had the only copy. The original was lost in Teignmouth and soon he would have that. When it has in his hands, he could demand the world and gain retribution from those that manipulated his grandfather to his grave and the ultimate shame and disgrace of excommunication.

He opened his small briefcase and laid out a ragged, faded, brown stained piece of parchment. He turned it over and took out his half-moon glasses and put them on his aquiline nose and peered at the parchment. The map clearly showed an ancient faded drawing of a river entering La Manche, with two large villages on either side. He traced the river back to what he assumed were large hills or mountains with small village hamlets marked all around the river in a couple in the mountains. He peered closer at the writings on the parts of parchment that were obviously indicating positions of interest. The writing was in 17th century French, of which he was an expert. He read one of the notes, near a drawing of a large rock on the part where the hills were. This led him to a Castle, East of the smaller river but on a larger river estuary. He read carefully the note beside a large cross which indicated a church or cathedral. He took off his glasses, rolled up his parchment and placed it carefully in his briefcase, closed the case and picked up his cup of cafe au lait. As he drank, he smiled for the first time that morning.

Across the channel at the same time, The Cornishman was sitting at a table outside *The Whistle Stop* café. The Whistle Stop was host to all the bikers and scooter riders from the West Country as well as being the one café that offers free food to the local homeless.

He was drinking a cup of tea and reading *The Western Times*. He was also listening to everything that Jack and Françoise said. He had observed as the man who had been following the couple made his phone call and left to his camper van on The Point. The Cornishman then followed the two to the café and made sure he took up a place nearby them. From their conversation he knew the parchment could be his very soon, if only this Teignmouth French lady could persuade the guardians to reveal where it was.

He was the last of the Cornish searchers of the secret, for three centuries they had tried to identify the guardians and force them to reveal the location of the document. Now, Albert had broken, and this lady knew more than any of them had known. He knew that their long search to reveal to an innocent world what was long lost was almost over. He would protect this secret with his life. No one could be allowed to hide it again once it was found. He would kill to ensure that didn't happen.

CHAPTER FIVE

Françoise was worried again. She had been at work and had lost her mobile phone. She wasn't sure if she had lain it down in the *Rowcroft Hospice* staff room or it had left it on the reception counter when she gave the new young lady there her number. For two hours she searched and enquired with her colleagues in between her care duties and no one had seen it. Then when she finally searched her handbag in her locker for the third time in that period, it was there. At first she cursed herself that she was so untidy in her bag. Her husband never stopped giving her stick about it. The she thanked her lucky stars that it was there.

Now as she drove home, she was worried. She knew *it had been there. She was certain. But maybe not...But I'm sure...*dear me she was losing her marbles she thought. Stop the paranoia, accidents happen. Just then an all-black car moved up behind her riding her bumper. Its windows were blacked out and she couldn't see any faces. The car was so close she thought she could feel her small Fiat 500 being pushed forward. She was on a small side road driving from Newton Abbot up towards a meeting she was having with a girlfriend in the castle coffee shop at *Powderham Castle*. She had taken the country route to avoid the rush hour traffic and the lanes like many in Devon were single traffic and the hedges high, so no visibility of anything, even potential oncoming traffic. She started to panic. She accelerated as fast as she could given that she had no idea if she would meet a vehicle head on as she rounded the tight blind bends. The dark car matched her speed and stayed on her bumper. Her heart was racing so fast she could hear it and in the summer sun, she was sweating profusely.

She slowed as she came around a very tight bend and the black car just pushed her bumper as it kept up its speed. She felt her car accelerate around the bend much too fast, she closed her eyes monetarily in fear of a head on crash. As she blinked and hurtled around, she breathed a sigh as she saw clear road again, still narrow but no cars to face. Up ahead she could see a passing place, a farm gate with a small gap in the hedge. She accelerated in an attempt to shake off the lunatics in the black car and hoped she could drive quickly into the gap and brake and the pursuing car would just drive past unable to stop and hit her car again. As she neared the gap and passing point, the black car had caught up and was riding her bumper and pushing her little Fiat ahead.

Fifteen metres from the gap she turned her steering wheel left and braked hard in an attempt to slide into the gap and let the car past. She slid into the gap and the black car overtook, the car scraping on the hedge on the right-hand side, and as it drew level the car suddenly threw left hand down and pushed the Fiat's front end to the left. Françoise hurtled out of control, the Fiat hit a small ditch near the farm gate and it rolled over and through the gate, smashing the wooden gate into pieces. It rolled one more time in field of yellow rape seed and ended upside down.

The black car braked and reversed and stopped alongside the broken gate. The two men observed the Fiat and one wound down the passenger window and listened to the engine humming and no sound of any human coming from inside. He took a photograph on his mobile and then closed the window, the driver accelerated away. The passenger took his mobile and dialled a number in Paris.

'Did you hear what happened to Françoise?'

'Yeah: Terrible wasn't it. Bloody kids these days; and you try and get a policeman. It's impossible.'

Jack was talking with MI5 Mick and Jimmy the Hat in *The Blue Anchor* pub. MI5 Mick was so called because of his propensity in his friendliness and attempt to socially interact with the locals he never stopped asking them questions. Jimmy the Hat's moniker was simple. He wore a trilby type hat. Unlike his drinking buddy MI5 Mick, The Hat was a man of few words. The long winters' nights would indeed fly by with Jimmy the Hat and that other man of few words from *The Kings Arms*, Silent John, locked in an igloo together.

Jack explained to his fellow customers of Adele and Luke's garden centre and zoo masquerading as an excellent real and music ale house. 'She's ok mind. I went to see her at home. Just a few bruises and shocked still. She was lucky really. She couldn't tell the police anything as she never really saw the driver or the number plate,'

Two new tourist looking customers came in and MI5 Mick lost interest in Jack's conversation and he entered into his interrogation. As usual he was desperate to find out why they were here and what job they did, which football team they supported and what they had for dinner last night and had they ever been a member of the Communist party or pray to Mecca...Jimmy the Hat stared at the wall. Jack decided he'd talk to wall too.

As he stared at the wall and MI5 Mick enrolled the two innocent non-Marxist tourists into membership of Exeter City football club, Jack thought about his chat with Françoise. *God, she had been lucky. Was it just a bunch of thugs?*

She didn't think so. 'Jack, I know I had my phone with me. I think someone stole it and has taken my information off it. I had texted Viv Wilson, the lady historian who knows everything about this place and asked to meet her to discuss the French ships just two hours before. As you know, I also texted you to get an update on things. You sent me a full update. What if someone doesn't want us to find out? That man on the beach for Christ's sake.'

'I can't believe someone would try deliberately to harm you. It isn't that important surely? Have you told your husband?'

'No definitely not. I don't want him hurt or distressed. That's why I told you.'

Jack thought, *well thanks a lot for that.* But didn't say it; the lass was still in shock. 'What did the police say?'

Françoise took a drink of her Lucozade that Jack had brought her. Sarcastically, she chuckled to herself; *he knew how to charm a sick woman.* 'I didn't tell them of my fears. They just think it was kids, probably a stolen car. Thank God a couple of walkers came along. It was those two you know Jack, the mad Professor who likes to look at Ur-anus and thinks time doesn't exist. Dear me I listened to his summary of his new book on what is real and what isn't with you the other day in here. He is normal? His lovely wife phoned the ambulance and he managed to get me out of the wrecked car. They were on their way back to *The Castle Pub* in Holcombe Village. I will have to buy them a drink one day. But if you are with me don't get him on about time, quantum physics and reality, I haven't the time to talk about real things?'

Jack was excited now. 'But that's the point: does time exist and is anything real? and...'

'Oh, just shut up! My bloody head hurts.'

'Sorry. I told him to make the book more interesting to normal people. Like Hawkins's *Brief History of Time...*'

Francois interjected again and howled, 'Interesting! It's unintelligible to normal people.'

'Well I guess it's not easy, but he sold millions. The Proff might do the same if he can explain it for readers without them having a PhD in String Theory. Davey the author told him he'd write his advertising blurb for him. He's already written the back-page quote. What do you think? *'This book makes Einstein's General Theory of Relativity read like a Harry Potter Novel'* or *'The Lady Bird book of String Theory'.'*

'I think you are all touched and I don't give a merde. Jack, get real man, someone nearly killed me and you are also involved if this wasn't an accident. I am worried. I think I am going to go and see my aunty in Paris. I'll call her tomorrow and fly out in a week's time. I have a week off work sick leave. Maybe she can give some closure on all this. I think you should talk to the crazy docker mates of yours in the bars and see which one of them might confess something. Try the historian, the Museum- the Teignmouth and Shaldon Heritage Centre, the bookshops, maybe that nice man you know, the author who is a brilliant historian and some think a spy. Anyone but that crazy professor for God's sake. If we can get some information maybe we can find something positive for me to talk to my Aunty about.'

And now in *The Blue Anchor*, Jack was hoping to do just that while Françoise was in France.

MI5 Mick was bored again. The tourists had little more information to give now the Scopolamine had worn off. Jimmy the Hat was also bored he'd counted the mega number of bottles of Adele and Luke's speciality Gin and Rums, many times now. But luckily for Jack, in walked Charlie, Kev and Kev's brother Steve on their Wednesday afternoon walk around the sights of Teignmouth. He could talk with them about the old days and maybe the secret of the French boats before they got too mortal drunk – as per the norm.

'I was chatting to Françoise the other day. She was still laughing at the story you told her about Captain Jim and the parrot. You must have had some crazy Captains those days Charlie,' Jack asked, knowing this would prompt tales of old.

'Yes buoy. And this pub was the pub all the Captains and crew came to. All we Quay buoys went to *The Old Quay Pub* which was right on the docks and the ship's crew came here,' Charlie explained.

'Why *The Blue Anchor*?' Jack asked.

Kev interjected: 'Because he be where all the ladies of the night came. And sailors were the same the world over, the first place they all asked for was *The Blue Anchor'*. He continued as he does,

39

'One of the craziest captains who used to come here was Captain Sex.'

'Aye, what a character he was. He nearly got us all sacked that bugger,' said Charlie.

'Why was that Charlie?' Jack asked again.

'Because he was mad that's why,' Kev jumped in again. 'He arrived one day in a small freighter. Think he was Dutch but can't be sure. He had a baseball cap on with Captain Sex on it. He also kept a parrot like Captain Jim. This parrot sat on his shoulder like Long John Silver. He looked like a bloody pirate to be fair. But the real problem was he also had his pet donkey on board. It was tethered on the well deck and he wanted us to lift it out with the crane. He gave us a few bottles of booze and we put strops around the thing and Pete lifted him out with the crane.'

Charlie drank a large part of his Carling lager and interjected too. 'I think Pete had only drunk one bottle of Brandy that day, so the animal was saved from the torture what the bastard used to do to us when he was drunk with his crane and bashing the grabs and chains off us and the deck heads. One day he was so pissed he hooked the crane hook onto my belt and lifted me up. The only thing that saved me was Marty grabbed me and matey kept hauling up, so pissed he had no idea as usual. Marty was pulled off his feet and he managed to holler enough for the bugger to hear both of us, just before we were going to be swung out of the hold and into the dock. He should have done the same with that bloody donkey the trouble it caused.'

Kev continued his tale of the story of the errant crane driver. 'He picked up Carne with his grabs. He missed the load he was aiming for. Carne was sawing away some timber on the deck. He howled in pain and fear as he was lifted high. Our crane driver decided best drop him – straight into the grain cargo. Marty had to sort the captain out for that one. I sorted another captain out too when he asked Pete to move something across deck. Pete told him through one closed eye, *'I can't see that, I'm on my second bottle of brandy.'*

Charlie chuckled and finished off the hapless crane driver stories. 'I once took his real egg out of his sandwich and put a plastic fried egg into it before he climbed up the crane in the morning. He never climbed down for his elevenses, just took a bottle and his egg sandwich, which he loved. We watched him killing ourselves with laughing as he chewed and chewed and kept looking at his sandwich and trying again. He looked down and saw us pointing and laughing and the next thing we saw was the fried egg flying down at us. We ducked as it was lethal. He be the first Frisbee we had ever seen.'

Jack chuckling at the last story and remembering that Charlie had also told him that they used to tell the Captains who questioned the safety of having a pissed-up crane driver, 'It's ok he's only had one bottle today and one eye is still open!'

'Yeah, us hauled the donkey out and us all shared the booze with Captain Sex. That crazy bugger got drunk and put his parrot on his shoulder, his hat on his head and climbed on board his donkey, Jesus of Nazareth style. He rode it along the Quay out of the dock gates and right into here, *The Blue Anchor*. He rang the brass ships bell you can see hanging here for all his crazy drunken crew to have yet another round of drinks. They all rode back down to the Quay, mortal drunk, girls in tow.'

Charlie finished his beer and ordered yet another round. Jack took a nice pint of Dartmoor *Jail Ale* and puzzled over why this would get the dockers sacked so he asked the question.

'Well Jack. The Quay was changing by now. The new management weren't like the old days. Dangerous Dick had come and was intent in changing everything. So, lifting live animals that were not cleared for rabies nor permitted to carry live stock by pissed up crane drivers out of ships didn't go down well. Even worse was allowing drunken foreign crewmen to ride said animals around town and transporting whores into the dock on the back of a donkey also didn't go down so well,' Charlie laughed as he finished.

Kev explained the company's angst at all this. 'Yes Jack. Someone reported the whole thing to the customs and quarantine people and all hell broke loose. We were all put on warning and the Quay then introduced much more stringent controls on rabies prevention and posters and everything. We were lucky to survive another one of Dangerous Dick's purges. That bloody Captain Sex and his donkey and monkey caused us some environmental grief. The Colorado beetles were the next buggers to cause mayhem. If the buoys found one in the cargo Marty had to halt the job and the bosses would come and then the environmental men in black suits and white coats. We were all then sent off the Quay. No bloody pay and the job stopped. Also, the captains wouldn't pay up the booze as Marty couldn't finish the job on time; Bloody beetles.'

'I finds a bugger one day.' Charlie confessed. 'Marty was driving us so hard to get the ship out I thinks, bugger this I'm not handing him in to matey, they'll stop the job. So, I thinks I'll put him in a matchbox in my pocket; so, I does. Then bugger me a half hour later I finds another bugger. I pops him in the same box. We get the job done, Marty gets the piece work signed off and he gets the booze and the lads are in the pub by twelve thirty. But I has a conscience so I goes upstairs to the bosses before I meets the buoys in the Quay pub and I gives the matchbox to the bosses. We woz supposed to get a reward for helping with the beetles and I goes for a drink with buoys thinking I'd be flush. Us sees the cars arrive and out gets mateys with black suits and glasses just like the movie *Men In Black*. The buoys got their money and booze and the Ministry got their beetles. I never did get a reward - the bastards.'

'It's just as well he wasn't here when Bill had *The Quay Pub* on the dock and when Ringo was there,' Steve, Kev's boxer brother said.

'Yeah, 'said Kev, laughing. 'Ringo was a monkey, Jack. He belonged to Stan, Marty's stepdad. Stan used to bring him on the Quay and he used to run riot in the *Quay Pub*. Stan used to keep him in the rafters of one of the warehouses, along with his greyhound. Jackie's dad, Peter, used to also keep his pet Jack Russell called Fred in his fork lift cab with him all day. The ships cooks would throw him bones. The only problem was he'd bury them in the animal food stock cargoes! Yes, health and safety wasn't like it is now. Dangerous Dick put an end to our animals on the Quay.'

'Seems Dangerous caused some grief lads?' Jack asked.

'Aye: He didn't like me,' Charlie said with a sigh and then continued. 'He arrived after they had sacked a smashing boss. He was so clever and good that he modified the whole Quay structure. For his efforts he was promoted. Marty and me loved him because he came to talk to us first and admitted he knew nothing about working the Quay and wanted us to educate and help him. He was the one who built my carpenters shed, The Carpenter's Arms, as before he built it, I used to store wood and work in rain leaking buildings. He'd come to The Carpenter's Arms drink a few with Marty and me and we would educate him. But they sacked him and brought in Dangerous Dick. The first thing he said to us was now *that out last boss had sorted the Quay physical structure out he was here to sort us buoys out'!*

Charlie shook his head. Kev interjected again to follow up why the new boss disliked Charlie. 'The new boss gave us a pep talk and said he was here to change things, to bring the place into the twentieth century and the next. Charlie shouted out, *'And how long will you last then!'* He was a marked man from there; Mind you same with Marty. Dick carried on explaining how they were doing away with the piece work system and stopping only paying men to work when there was a ship in. No more would lads have to stand in line waiting for work each morning while the top of the pecking order old crews like Marty and Charlie took the best ships. Dangerous was putting everyone on a salary. No more paid for the amount and type of cargo you shifted. Marty shouted out to him, *'You've just cost me eight grand a year buoy!'* And Dick did just that; the bastard.'

'Yes, things were never the same after that,' Charlie explained. 'Why would we work our arses off to get a cargo out and a ship turned around when now we all got paid the same whether we moved ten tons or one. Captains used to pull Marty aside and give him hell for not turning the ships as fast we always had. The worse thing was the booze dried up because of it!'

'Dear me lads no free booze, that must have been like hell; surprised Dangerous wasn't shot,' Jack said sympathetically.

Charlie continued the tale of woe. 'Yes, it was a bloody nightmare. Us always left the Quay for our elevenses. Us usually has a bottle with the Captain early doors about 6 or 7 when we had moved a lot but us all liked a beer at eleven. When the *Quay pub* was there it was easy. We walks off a ship into the pub. Then we walks out of the gates into *The Blue* or go around to *The Ship* or *The New Quay*. After Dangerous Dick put security cameras into the yard, Appsy and me would have to slide along with our bodies to the wall where they couldn't scan. We were like the buoys from *Mission Impossible* shuffling along the wall, squeezing and shuffling our bodies up against the dock walls. One manager saw us one day and asked *'What the hell we were doing?'* We said we were doing a fitness regime. Once we'd escaped it was hardly worth going back and dodging the cameras as we always used to come out anyway for a lunch time pint after returning from elevenses; so, we'd just stay and get pissed in *The Ship*.'

Charlie continued after getting a round of drinks in. 'To be fair Dangerous was only doing his job to modernise the Quay. He was good at that. He told us one day that even he didn't realise it would but so tough and he had been sold on the job by the company telling him it was tropical paradise down here on the English Riviera. He was standing on a ship with us the rain and sleet hurtling up the Teign Valley into our faces, the biting wind chilling him to the bone. Unable to stop shivering he stammered through chattering teeth, almost in tears *'they told me there were palm trees down here.'*

'They tells everybody that buoy,' Marty said, and took a bottle of brandy out of his coat pocket with glass and said, 'Here take a few glasses my lover it'll warm you up nicely. Dangerous Dick just looked shocked and then bewildered, he moaned through the biting gale, looked at the drink and sighed, *'Dear me, it never stops'*. And he turned to walk down the gangplank. He looked back and shook his head despairingly. *'Palm trees, they are no bloody palm trees,'* muttering to no one who really cared anyway.'

'Nightmare he was. He was far too bloody sharp and good at sorting us buoys out,' Steve said, shaking his head, 'much better when KP was boss. Aye KP was the best. He knew how to keep the buoys working and earning but also how to let them make a bob or two with the booze and cigs plus other stuff. *'It oil's the wheels of Industry,'* he used to say. The agents and Captains were happy and Marty kept everyone, including the Revenue, off our backs. Wee Shoey would allocate lists and Marty controlled it all. The best boats were the clay and grain boats if they had no bulkheads and nooks and crannies, so we could get in and out quick, earn the money and get on the drink quicker than the others. Marty and Charlie always got the best ones. Mind you we were all weekend millionaires those days when the cargoes were good. You knew if there had been a good cargo and ship in because all the dockers were in their best suits and smoking cigars in all the bars. Great days then...'

Charlie took up the story. 'KP was legend. Those days we would always have a drink 'across the rail' and 'one for the other leg' with the captains' at 8 a.m. That was if Wee Shoey MacBride hadn't pinched 'ee. At 6 am the foreman was supposed to see the captain and get the lists of cargo and work. The captain then gave out the booze. Wee Shoey stole his foreman's tally board and used 'ee to con the captains and get the lists and the booze and he'd sup most of the bugger before we got there!'

Charlie took a drink. 'KP's office used to be above the buoys' rest area and when the captain gave out the early morning booze

44

we bangs on the roof. KP comes down for his share and he always carries his own glass in his pocket when he comes or when he visited the captains on their ships. Once we'd had a few over the rail it was time for elevenses in *The Old Quay Pub*. KP dropped dead in *The Kings Arms* with a gin and tonic in his hand. He was one of us.' And they raised their glasses to a managerial legend.

Jack reflected on the three of them drinking the health of yet another character. Surely one of these must know something. It has to be Charlie he knew that. Albert had said, 'ask Charlie.' So, he decided to do just that.

They drank up and as usual started to move on to another one of their Wednesday afternoon pub crawl haunts, *The Devon Arms*. MI5 Mick shouted over, 'Hi Charlie, where are you buoys off too now?' and was a bit miffed when all three shouted back:

'He got bugger all to do with 'ee.'

Jimmy the Hat began counting the bottles of whisky, but as he did, he surreptitiously adjusted a small listening device receiver in his hat. Once done, he sat staring at the wall.

Charlie, suffering from the old back and leg injuries caused by falling sixteen feet into the hold of a ship was slower than the other two. Jack decided to front him as he walked alongside.

'Charlie, you might think I'm nosy but I'd really like you to help with something.'

'What's that matey?'

'Well, I am not sure if you know that Albert told Françoise something very important on his death bed?'

'Word travels Jack. Us is a small town and wassel like that spreads among the ones who know,' Charlie whispered, looking at Jack with a glint in his, despite his age, still young blue eyes.

'So, you know what he told her?' Jack asked surprised at his friend's knowledge.

'No not what he said, but I think I have a feeling I know what he might have said. He was awful miserable in his last months. He told me he wanted to confess. I told him that could be dangerous. But he said he be time everyone knew.'

'Knew what?' Jack teased.

'I don't bloody know. Do you?' Charlie said, again looking quite sheepish.

We are getting nowhere here, Jack thought. He decided to be straight. 'He told Françoise that a few of you here are keepers of a secret and that it was time you all revealed it. He asked her to talk to you. She has asked me to help her. She really wants to fulfil his last wishes.'

'Albert was a very wise man and was very much a leader and one of us. I guesses if he wants something to be done; maybe he be time to do it.'

Jack was excited; maybe he was on the edge of a breakthrough. 'So, do you know what and where it is Charlie?'

Charlie looked at his new found friend, and he knew in his aching bones and strong heart that maybe the burden he carried should be lifted. After all Albert had never ever revealed anything, even to his own family and he was indeed the lead guardian. He sighed and confessed. 'I was only told some facts and they are a code, I think. I only know Albert as the one who held all clues. I don't know anyone else who has any. I was never told by my Uncle. Anyway, we are nearly at *The Devon,* and it's Kev's round, so here we go, this is all I know.' And he told Jack.

CHAPTER SIX

Five days later Jack and Françoise booked into a two-bedroom apartment in *The Rugglestone Inn* in Widdecombe on the Moor. They were lucky as the rooms were normally booked solidly in the tourist walking season a week at a time. But this time it was a change over and the owners had let them have just one night. They had both thought they may need more than the afternoon Françoise had off work to find what they were looking for. Françoise was feeling much better and had gone back to work, but only for a day. Her husband was away working for the week again so she never mentioned her trip. They travelled in Jack's car through Newton Abbott and up through Bovey Tracey and up into Dartmoor National Park. It was a beautiful day again and as they drove, they enjoyed looking out to the right over the moor towards High Tor, the ancient mound of granite stones that defined the moor. Both Exmoor and Dartmoor were littered with these geographical features.

The famous Ten Tors foot race had eluded Jack. His days of running across beautiful moor and hills and dales to touch ten mounds of granite had been replaced by a gentle stroll to the pub. But he loved Dartmoor, winter or summer, especially winter when he would walk in the snow and frost and photograph the beautiful and iconic wild Dartmoor ponies. Exmoor similarly fascinated him.

Françoise was thinking about the first time she had come up to see the famous Dartmoor prison. It had been a horrible damp, foggy and cold day. The prison still looked foreboding and she could well understand how no prisoner escaping into that wild and dangerous moor could survive for long in winter. It was 2009 when she came and she was tracing the roots of her ancestors, The French prisoners of the Napoleonic war who had been imprisoned and died there. Between 1809 and 1816 around 1200 French prisoners of war died there. Also 271 American prisoners died there captured in the Anglo-American War of 1812. The graves of these prisoners are still there. On the 24th of May 2009 a bicentennial ceremony was held at the French cemetery in Princetown attended by descendants of the prisoners of war and French dignitaries. Françoise was one of those.

Today the weather was so different and as the sun shone through the windscreen, she thought of the French prisoners who had also been held in the old jail opposite *The Blue Anchor* and on the dockside. Many of these had drowned in there when the River Teign flooded. She assumed few lived to tell the tale. Drake's Island prison in Plymouth harbour also held American prisoners. Jack also had visited Princetown, but he had little interest in French prisoners, only the excellent *Jail Ale*, brewed by Dartmoor brewery there. He liked breweries, especially Dartmoor.

They drove past the turning to Hound Tor, famous scene of the Hound of the Baskervilles movie, she wondered if the hound still roamed the moor as the legend still said. She shivered, as she remembered what had happened to her just a few days ago. She had her real and alive nightmare hunting her.

When they had driven through the beautiful moorland village, famous for its Widdecombe Fair, Jack pointed out Saint Pancras Church and its churchyard they were going to visit, once they had checked into one of his favourite pubs, the Rugglestone Inn with its lovely landlord and landlady Richard and Vicki. After checking in, they sampled a pint of the landlord's excellent real *Jail Ale* and Jack quickly ordered another pint. Both ate the wonderful fish and chips sat in the small bar by the now unlit fire. In winter the last time Françoise had been there she had sat shivering warming up in front of the roaring fire after a long walk through the moors.

'So now we try to find the clue to it all?' Françoise said as they relaxed in the bar.

'Well not it all. Charlie said he only had part of the code.'

Françoise opened up an A 4 sheet of paper and read the words again. 'Are you sure this is what he told you?'

Jack checked the words he'd typed out and confirmed it was all he'd said.

They both sat reading the words.

Look for the stone in Widdecombe that marks the hook. The answer lies behind.

'Well do we start in the church or outside in the grave yard. And how do we know they mean the church at all? It could be any old stone,' Françoise asked, perplexedly.

'As we discussed Françoise, we can only assume that it must be in some closed space or how could anyone check the whole of the area for bloody stones?'

'Well let's get started then. We'll take a stroll back into the village to walk off the fish and chips and beer.'

They strolled along a delightful country lane into the village. They entered the church yard through a small wooden gate and archway. Immediately they were taken by the age of some of the grave stones and the view over towards the moor was breath-taking. There were two crosses that stood out on a hill at the end of the grave yard, framing the whole moor.' Why don't we start with that one?' Françoise said. 'Maybe they are the clue as they stand out from the rest.'

They both looked at the inscriptions and markings. The graves were relatively new, nowhere near 1700 or the 18th century; and nothing to be seen with a hook. 'You try that end and I'll try this one. If all this fails, we'll try the church next,' Françoise said to Jack.

So, they roamed the graveyard in the afternoon heat. It was frustrating and boring work and they just could not find anything that related to a stone or a hook. They were about to give up and go into the church when Françoise shouted out to Jack. 'Come here Jack I think I've found something. Here: near the iron gate at the back and facing the large tree.'

Jack quickly walked around the church. He was thinking it's time to give up and go back for a nice beer. *Sod this; the whole bloody quest is a one big fraud. But what about Françoise's accident? Well maybe that's what it was - an accident.*

He reached Françoise. She was kneeling down and looking a small grave stone about 300 cm by 300 cm which was placed in a line of adjacent sized grave stones. The stones had clearly been taken from their original graves and lined up on the side of a small grass bank. They looked very old. 'Look Jack this one has a single capital H marked in the stone and I think the date says 1698, but it's so faded.'

Jack kneeled down and looked carefully. 'I can't say its 1698 but it's definitely a letter H. Bloody hell well done girl.'

'The H could stand for hook, or more likely Hook! It is certain from what you told me there are lots of Hook's and the family were part of the smugglers who stole the drink and the chest or parchment or whatever. Maybe it is the grave of the man who stole it; the original guardian?'

'If it is, we are buggered my dear. This stone has been taken from its original spot and placed alongside all these other seventeenth century stones. If we have to look for the grave we are indeed well and truly.'

'Maybe not: The clue said 'look behind the stone'. If it was on a grave it would have said look under or below. I think whatever is hidden was placed there much later than when our original Captain Hook died and when the stone was moved. We have to dig behind the stone Jack.'

'For heaven's sake girl, we can't just rive the stone off the hill and dig up everything. For one we don't have any tools and two we'll end up with our bowels roasting in Hell. Besides, it's a busy summer's day anyone could come through that side gate.'

'Ok makes sense. Let's come back tonight. Have you got anything in the boot to dig with?'

Jack looked at Françoise and realised that she was truly committed to getting this clue and the answer. He had better go along with this, if only to keep her out of HM Prison Dartmoor. 'Yes, actually I have. I left a trowel in I used to dig up some worms for fishing the other day.'

'Good. Let's go back and have a nice walk. I'll take a shower before dinner while you no doubt drink and we can have dinner and a few beers and come back when it's dark.'

After a lovely dinner and many beers, they were waiting in the bar for the light to fade. When dusk arrived, they staggered along the country lane towards the church. They noticed the sky had turned really dark and clouds were swirling ominously. It looked like a thunderstorm was brewing. 'That's bloody magic that is,' Jack said as he saw the clouds and felt the heaviness in the air. 'We've no coats or anything.'

'Oh, stop whining you gloomy man. It's lovely tonight, listen to silence. I love the silence of nothing, don't you?' She was tipsy after too many beers and a bottle of wine.

They reached the church and entered through the main gate again. There was no one around. Everyone was either in bed or had left visiting to go back to their homes. Both of them did not see the man who stood against the church wall and behind an alcove in the darkness.

They walked towards the area where the small stone marked H was positioned. Françoise began to laugh and grabbed at Jack's arm. 'Whoo whoo, it's an owl, hoot, hoot. Are you frightened mon protecteur?

'You're pissed. Let's get this sorted before the rain comes.'

A lightening flash could be seen in the darkening clouds and overhead the thunder clapped loudly. The first drops of rain fell. Jack knelt down facing the stone. He carefully started digging directly behind it into the bank. It was hard going as the bank and soil was firm due to the long drought. The beer didn't help and he soon wished he was back in bar. After getting about 100 centimetres down he felt the trowel hit a harder object. 'This might be it Françoise,' he said his voice full of emotion now. Françoise was sitting down on another grave stone, singing La Marseillaise. Jack shook his head and began to dig around the object.

He soon had isolated a small brass cylinder. He pulled it from its hiding place and held it up. *'Eureka!'* he shouted, as the clouds burst and the heavens opened and the rain poured down; And just as the man came out of the shadows.

CHAPTER SEVEN

The man had been following them all day. He followed them to *The Rugglestone* after they had searched the churchyard that afternoon. They had not noticed him even when he took up a dinner table in the dining room. He heard them talk of their plans and had left the pub after his dinner to find a place to hide and wait. He was skilled at concealment and stalking so they had not heard a thing as he had crept up upon them. Françoise was too occupied with singing and the ambience of the night and Jack was concentrating on the digging. Once Jack found the object, their stalker knew what he had to do.

'Hand it over mate or you'll get hurt,' the man quietly but forcefully said.

'Tell him to piss off!' Françoise shouted, still feeling the effects and brave with the alcohol.

Jack was shocked. His heart was beating fast. *Who the hell was this?* Even with the booze he realised that this was probably the man who had tried to harm Françoise in her car. He didn't look like a vicar. Mind you it was hard to see through the pouring rain. All three were standing now and were looked like drowned rats in the downpour. Overhead the thunder roared. *What should he do?* Jack had to make a quick decision, to fight or surrender the cylinder.

The man seemed to be aware of his thinking. 'If I were you Jack, I'd just hand it over. You see hurting and killing people is what I do for a living. I know you don't. I'm good at it, you aren't. But if you want to have a go, maybe this will persuade you.' And from the back of his trousers he pulled a gun and pointed it at Jack.

'He'll not use that. He's just a coward. Go on Jack hit him!' Françoise clearly still not sobering up to the danger made a move towards the man. Before she could get near him, he'd stepped towards her and rammed his fist into her stomach, doubling her up. He immediately turned to face Jack, gun pointing ahead. 'Don't try anything mate or you'll end up worse than her.'

Jack was now stone cold sober. This was it. The rain was dripping down every gap in his clothes, Françoise was writhing in the floor in the developing mud and he was scared. He looked down at the cylinder and his last thought was *what the hell this is? Is it worth dying for?* He decided it wasn't and he began to hand the object over. Just then the man crumpled in front of him into the mud as another man, dressed in black hit him across the back of his head with the branch of a tree. The gunman collapsed and fell head first at Jack's feet. Jack just stood hand outstretched, stared at the body and then at the shadowy figure with the branch through the pouring rain. *This was a dream surely? These things didn't happen in Devon.*

The figure knelt down and picked up the gun. He looked down at the body and at the cylinder in Jack's hand. 'That was good timing. If I were you, I'd pick your lovely lady friend up and head back to your rooms and lock the doors. But I think that's the last you'll see of this one tonight. That thing you dug up, I assume it's part of the code you were given by that Devon yokel?'

Jack was just shell shocked and couldn't speak. 'Well is it?' the man shouted.

'Yes,' Jack uttered, stammering.

'Well you two are doing a lot better than we have done in centuries. Go on then take it back and open it. We will be watching your every progress. You will find this secret and then you will give it to me and I will use it for our good. You will tell no one else. I will contact you and I will expect an update on your search. We will be watching you all the time so do not go to the police, tell the Guardians or try to hide it from us. If you do, well, look around you. We have buried better men than you. Go and let me get rid of this.'

Jack picked up Françoise who had been sat holding her stomach after vomiting. 'Come on. Let's get out of here. I just don't understand any of this.'

He dragged his friend past the man in black through the rain and through the church gate. They arrived at their lodge just after midnight, bedraggled and muddy but mainly scared and confused. Françoise needed to wash her mouth out with her mouth wash and another shower. Jack got out of clothes and showered too. He knocked on Françoise's door and she let him in.

'I think you should sleep in my room tonight Françoise, we need to stick together. I'll drag the mattress in and I'll kip on that. I'm going to put the sofa up against the door. Do you think we should phone the police?'

Françoise was sat on her bed. She looked dazed still but now sobering. 'No Jack: what the hell do we tell them? Secret scrolls, Guardians of the Secret, violent hit men; do you think they'd believe us? And if we do, we can say goodbye to anyone helping us find it. Maybe that nice man in black has sorted the bad men out and that will be it?

Jack thought a bit. 'I have a feeling that that nice man in black isn't so nice. He wants the secret and threatened to kill us if he doesn't get it. Surely that's enough to get the police?'

'What are you Jack a man or un souriceau?'

'What the hell is a sue ee sow? Jack said laughing for the first time since the incidents.

'A baby mouse! Come let's keep the adventure going. Let's open the box!'

They put the cylinder on the table and Françoise began to screw the brass top off. It would not budge, so Jack placed it in the door jam and jammed the door on it and began to twist. Slowly it opened. Inside was a small rolled up parchment. They opened it up and spread it out on the table. There were just a few words on the paper written in black ink.

Look for the rabbits in the church who point to the nuns and he who wears the crown will show the Grace of God.

'What the hell does that mean?' Jack grunted. He was tired weary and a bit hung over.

The fear had gone but left him drained not excited. 'And why on earth did that man in the black bash that other one. He seems to want us to find the clues and then the secret and hand it over to him. The other one wants to stop us finding it and keep the clue which would allow us to find it. I'm confused and sick of it all to be honest. I think we should just go home and give it all up.'

'Mon souriceau, cheer up. One of them looks as if he's not going to harm us anymore and the other won't do anything till we find the clues and the mystery is solved. We can buy time and decided what to do if and when we get there. I think I know where to look tomorrow?'

'And where's that?' said an unimpressed Jack

'We go back to the church and this time inside. Let's hit the sack Jack. It may be an eventful day tomorrow again.'

The Cornishman had changed out of his soaking wet black clothes. He'd left the body by the side of the road. If he recovered so be it, if he didn't, well they might think it was a hit and run in the poor visibility of the storm. He was happy now. The two searchers seemed to making great progress. He'd let them proceed as they were his best chance. He had managed to sneak into their apartment while they were dining and had placed a small tracking device and bug into their phones. He noticed the first bug in Françoise's and smiled, so many people wanting to find this. *I wonder who these are? And why do they want it kept hidden?* For him and his masters it was best the whole world knew the truth. It had been lost for too long.

CHAPTER EIGHT

Jack awoke first. He dressed and went out for a short walk. He loved the ducks that swam in the little stream next to the pub and goats and chickens and turkeys they kept. The whole place was soaked after the storm but it would soon dry off as the weather was forecast to be scorching again. As he walked, he reflected on what had happened. He hadn't slept too well. He had never had a gun pointed at him or seen a possible murder so it was no wonder he was still distraught. *Should he go with this?* He puzzled over who were the two groups chasing them and why? It was undoubtedly dangerous but something inside said why not? Life had become boring in retirement and since his wife had been so tragically killed all those years ago. He was beginning to like Françoise a lot. He couldn't let her down.

He returned to apartment, Françoise too had woken early; she had dressed and was sat drinking a cup of coffee. 'Let's get down to the church when it opens and look for the rabbits and nuns and the one with the crown. I'm sure the nun reference must relate to there.'

Three hours later they were searching around the lovely ancient St Pancras church. They looked around for two hours and could see nothing to decipher the coded text. Jack sat down on one of the pews. Françoise kept searching the walls and stones on the floor. Jack then had a thought, he always jumped in when he got a new gadget and just started to make it work. He only read the manual after hours of trying to make it work and then breaking it. Surely there is a manual here that tells all about the church, there must be some mention of the code words. And sure enough there was - on nice very visible presentation boards. And there in black and white was the answer to one clue.

'Françoise come here; I think I've found one.' Françoise came over. 'Read that,' Jack said. 'And now I know why the Rugglestone were selling *Dartmoor Three Hares Honey Beer*. I should have tried a pint.'

And she read the story of the three rabbits:

The church was built in the 14th century and built out of Dartmoor granite. It was developed many times using wealth given from the Devon tin mines. The famous roof boss in the chancel was painted to resemble a circle of three hares sharing three ears between them. The Three Hares symbol was often called the Tinners' Rabbits. But more commonly it represented The Holy Trinity.

'So, let's look at the bloody rabbits then. How didn't we see them?' Françoise lamented.

'What's a boss?' Jack asked.

'It seems it's something they put over joints in the roof and they carve and paint them to depict local and religious symbols. Look up there!' And she pointed. 'There they are.'

Sure enough they were there above the altar.

'Well that's great, but where are the nuns and the crown?' Jack asked wearily.

'I haven't a clue. I've been up and down this place and there are no nuns that I see or anyone wearing crowns that could mean anything. Let's go and have a coffee at that little place over the road where the car's parked and take some time out and think.'

They sat thinking. The coffee grew cold. And then Françoise jumped up, 'That's it! It must be. Come on Jack we are heading back to Teignmouth. The answer lies there.'

As they drove back along the moor road and past High Tor again, Jack asked Françoise to explain. She did lucidly and with a big grin. 'It's simple really Jack. The man buried there must have been a Hook and he would have come from Teignmouth. I have no idea why they hid the clue up here and why he's buried here. Maybe because it was in his memory, or it may have been hidden forever so far away from Teignmouth. Whatever, the answer must lie back there. Think about it, the rabbits' ears form the Holy Trinity. And who are linked to the Holy Trinity?'

'Dunno, who?' said Jack.

'Nuns of course: And where do you find nuns?'

'In a convent?'

'Correct Jack, but also in a school. And what is the school called where the nuns once lived and taught?'

'Bloody hell Françoise! You've cracked it - Trinity School; in Teignmouth.'

Françoise looked pleased with herself yet again. 'Yes, and I think we might find the one with crown there. This has turned out a smashing day; bien sûr mon ami, tres jolie.'

They travelled back down the beautiful road to Bovey Tracey. Jack thought they should treat themselves for such a good job and suggested they would stop off maybe on the River Teign at Kingsteignton and have a carvery lunch in *The Passage House* pub. He loved walking his dog along the river there and in the Hackney Marshes nature reserve with the ancient reed beds, but Françoise said she'd fancy the other side of the river for a change. As they drove, they debated where to go. So much choice; *The Wild Goose*, the charming 17th Century Inn in the heart of Combeinteignhead or *The Old School House* an eight-hundred-year-old coaching house pub in the lovely Stokeinteignhead. Both just minutes away from the river but beautiful villages and thatched roofs.

'You know what I'm hungry. I could eat one of those gorgeous steak and kidney puddings in *The Linny Inn* in Coffinswell. It's a tossup between there and *The Smugglers Inn* for the best Steak and Kidney puddings in the world,' said Jack, smacking his lips.

'Yes. They are both smashing. But after spending the day and night we had around coffins I don't fancy another coffin location,' answered Françoise laughing. 'You know what I've never know so many places that vie for the best of something in the world here.' And she laughed again, 'We have the two fish and chip shops in Babbacombe, *Hanbury's* won third best in Britain and *Drakes*, '*Top three fish and chip shop Devon and Cornwall*', and now we have the *Jolly Good Fish Shop* in Teignmouth which is the best fish and chip shop in Britain, according to TripAdvisor - spoiled for choice mon ami.'

Jack smiled and looked across at his passenger. 'Aye, don't get me on about the best Pasties in the world and the best Cream teas. Or eating the Cornish or Devon way - Jam first or cream first. I saw a car the other day with the Cornish flag bumper sticker on and across the white cross was written *jam first*. For Christ's sake they fight wars for that! There are many that compete for best food around these parts. You could eat yourself to death here. And that's what I fancy - as well as a pint.'

'It's another beautiful day the river will be wonderful today. Why don't we drive along through Combeinteignhead and go to *The Coombe Cellars*, you won't get a better view and location anywhere on a day like today. The tides out and the birds will be wading right outside our table. We can look back up the river to Dartmoor where we came from and reflect on last night's adventure. We can then look up to Teignmouth and think about next steps. The foods my type, a bit posher and fine dining than you like, but you can get your pie or your fish and chips and maybe *Jail Ale* or *Devon Mist* and I'll have a nice fillet steak salad with a Black Sails spiced rum and ginger beer.'

'Done deal,' Jack said, 'but you pay!'

As they sat outside *The Coombe Cellars* with the graceful white swans swimming along the river's edge and the wading birds feeding around them in the estuary sand and silt and watched the crews of the gig rowing boats practicing on the river up towards Newton and back down to Teignmouth and the open sea, Jack wondered if things couldn't be better.

A man sitting at table quietly sipping his white wine, purportedly watching the boats and the birds on the river, was listening to all they said. He was about to make a call to Paris that would make things, not better, but a whole lot worse.

CHAPTER NINE

Françoise had flown off to Paris to see her great aunt in Saint-Germain-en-Laye. Jack had taken her to Exeter Airport and she had taken a Flybe early morning flight. Jack had seen her off and as usual had found himself having a *Jail Ale* beer in *The Kings Arms*. Gareth the landlord had opened up with his enigmatic Welsh wife Tina and was serving before Jackie one of his four lovely barmaids came in. His only barman Barry the Scouser had just retired; a smart ex-military man who was still extremely fit after a life time in military service training recruits in PT and sport. He had been a very good sportsman still was in many sports. Jack had played golf with him a few times and he always turned up looking immaculate. His shoes were polished to perfection and his trousers pressed with knife edge creases. Jack looked down at his muddy old borrowed golf shoes and baggy creased shorts and sometimes thought; maybe he should have had a stint in the army. Barry always beat him too.

Barry was famous because he was perpetually tortured by both Gareth and Tina. Sadly, Barry loved sport so much, especially his beloved Liverpool FC, that he loved to watch anything on the pub telly that pertained to sport or read about it in the newspaper on the bar. And also, he talked with Cliff, the perennial bar attending large man who sat at the end of the bar every day and also, much to Gareth's annoyance; he'd talk sociably to any other customer who liked sport. Sadly, in the eyes of his employers, this caused them eternal angst when they came downstairs or back from their afternoon break. Especially if some of their potentially new customers were standing waiting to spend their hard-earned cash in the tills of the entrepreneurial bar owner.

Gareth had in his past life been a successful banker and financial broker for the aerospace industry and knew all about pounds being prisoners and Tina; as you know, she was Welsh which on its own should be enough but also her Gallic temper was pretty well known. She had once bashed a rude aggressive drunken local customer over his head with a darts trophy and knocked him out. Both would be almost apoplectic at their biased opinion of Barry's nonchalance and laissez faire approach to customer service. And sadly, the wonderful man would have his sport's telly viewing switched off (and co-incidentally all the other customer's viewing who loved it too) and he'd receive a managerial melt down from his loyal employers. Gareth switched |The Sun paper to The Financial Times so he could avoid the sports pages being worn out by Barry and Cliff, and again all of the other normal people in the bar were denied their pleasures of reading anything but stocks and shares and banking liquidities.

But Barry was loved by all the regulars and staff simply because he was human and very pleasant and helpful in his role. If he was lost in another world of the golf scores on telly all the regulars knew was to shout affectionately, 'Heh you Scouse bastard, pour us a pint!'

Big Kev, another Liverpool fan, was particularly good at gaining his attention. New customers just needed a short while to warm to the culture of the place and anyway the beer was always better after a short wait; did they never go to Paris?

Many stayed forever and loved the Scouse man's politeness and immaculate manners in face of attrition from all sides both from his devoted regulars and his employers' Welsh Inquisition. It was a sad day when he retired.

Gareth and Tina, despite their perpetual angst, really did love the man. In lasting memory of his loyal and dedicated service, Gareth immortalised the man with his own 'blue plaque' eulogy which has pride of place on the bar.

Jack talked with Gareth about his trip up to Dartmoor, avoiding mention

of the real about his trip up to Dartmoor, avoiding mention of the real reasons and violent incidents. He just explained that he was following a lead from a bar conversation that a famous man had been buried there and that maybe he had been buried with some secret about Teignmouth. Gareth was mildly disinterested, which was his normal manner, so this was no worry to Jack, it was normal conversation. Not known to suffer fools gladly Gareth could be classed as well, blunt. He had been a banker.

Jack was about to try to get a response from the great man when into the pub came two old ladies. Gareth just carried on cleaning the brass on his beer pumps. One dear lady came up to the bar and asked, 'Do you have coffee?' Jack chuckled to himself; he loved it when this happened.

'Read the sign!' Gareth growled, not looking up from polishing the beer pumps.

'Oh, where is it?' asked the little old lady.

'It's just over here,' Jack kindly answered, hoping to avoid any small misunderstanding and he picked up a small chalk blackboard just the same size as Barry's testimonial which sat next to the coffee notice board on the bar. He showed it to the ladies. Gareth grunted.

On reading it, the smaller of the two ladies asked, 'Oh! So you don't do Cappuccino?' Before Jack could calm the waters, Gareth put down his cloth and explained loudly; 'No madam. For Christ's sake can you not read? This is a pub not a coffee shop. Teignmouth has at least thirty places you can get your foreign coffee. My instant coffee is, as I have said, tolerable and cheap. Do you want some?'

Jack spoke quietly to the blue rinsed haired one, again trying to play Henry Kissinger 'You could try my *Jail Ale* if you'd like a taste and the coffee really is ok. Lots of people like it. Tina's Scotch Eggs are divine too.'

'Oh ok, we'll have two cups. Maybe, we take an egg later,' they both said in unison, smiling happily.

Gareth dropped his head and shook it. 'For God's sake,' he said out loud as he walked out to put the kettle on in the kitchen.

Jack chuckled to himself yet again. He loved Gareth; his perverse manners amused him. He reminded him a bit of The Iron Chancellor from whom he had suffered the hounds of hell working for him when in Asia. He took no prisoners either. But then again, he wasn't serving little old ladies in his pub, just torturing real contractors at work.

Gareth was precious; a hardnosed successful business man trying to be nice to people whom not so long ago he would have closed their bank accounts and repossessed their homes and thrown them onto the streets. But he tried very hard. Jack wondered if he too should go back to his old profession of coaching leaders of men and he should coach Gareth and help him adjust to normal people and not just bankers. Maybe he'd tell him when he returned from doing the small task of making the coffee that Mother Theresa once said: 'Not everyone can do great things. But everyone can do small things with great love.' Somewhere in Gareth Jack could see a Mother Theresa.

Marty and Appsy came into the bar. 'Hello buoy: You in here again?' shouted Marty.

'Aye Marty, same as you mate,' Jack replied. 'Been up *The Smugglers* in Holcombe with Colin?'

'Yup: He's just coming in. We met Dave an old Quay buoy up there. Dear, did we have a laugh at the old days?'

'You always do Marty. Was this Dave as crackers as all of you?' Jack asked, really prompting yet another tale of the Quay which he loved to listen too.

'I guess he was Jack, but we were a lot more careful than Dave with our wages. The day his wife found out his fiddling was hilarious buoy. You should have been there.'

Appsy, was stood next to Marty, not as stocky as Marty, and certainly not as many Krugerrands, but a man who had been one of the hardest around. No one picked a fight with him in the old days. Jack had observed he was quite laconic in his ways with a dry wit. The hat he perpetually wore Jack believed must cover a bald head but just two weeks previously Appsy's mum had died and Jack had bumped into a man at the bar of the Social Club wearing a black suit and black tie and a full head of black hair. Jack said sorry and the man said, 'Ok Jack.' Jack said, 'Sorry do I know you?' And the man said,' It's me Appsy'. Yes, hats can be deceiving.

Appsy spoke. 'It was bloody hilarious. Dave had swallowed a couple of bottles of brandy we think over the rail with Captain Sex. He be so drunk the bosses told him to go and sober up and come back and get his wages when he be sober. Dave goes for more drink in the rugby club. As he be returning for his wages he collapses with the drink. The club phones for an ambulance and also for his wife. She arrived and took one look at him, and says, 'He's pissed. Take him home.' They does and she goes to the Quay and wages office to pick up his wages. They asked her did she want both of them. *'Both of them!'* she howled and took both packets. When she opened them she went ballistic.'

'Why was that Col?'

Marty interrupted before Col could explain. 'Simple buoy: For years Dave had played the two-wage packet trick. He kept the one with one hundred pounds in and handed over the false one less hundred pounds to his wife, unopened, as many men did those days. So, for years she gives him his pocket money out of the false wage packet to go on the drink without knowing he already has one hundred nicker to spend anyway. She had brought up the family and fed and watered Dave in booze on a pittance! Yes, that was a bad day for Dave!'

They all chucked at poor Dave's plight, little concern for his wife's struggle of course.

'Us thinks it was Dave that was sick every time he put those new teeth of his in.'

'Why was that Col?' Jack asked.

'Well he had his new teeth and was wearing them in. He got up in the morning to empty the chamber pot under the bed. He didn't know his wife had had a huge turd in it, so as he carried he downstairs the smell caused him to vomit and his teeth fell into the po. Every time he put them back in his mouth, he was sick again. We laughed like hell at work when he tried to put them in at elevenses in the Quay to eat his bait and he had to run to the toilet to be sick.'

Everyone laughed at this poor man's dental problem. Marty concluded it. 'He looked like Champion the Wonder Horse with those huge bloody teeth.'

Jack added his own story. 'Mushroom Les told me the other day about a mate of yours who went Bass fishing. He was sea sick and when he vomited over the side of the boat, he lost his false teeth. His mate took out his own teeth unknowingly to the bloke who lost his teeth and put them on his own hook. He dropped the line over the side and waited. After a while he reeled in and shouts out in surprise that he's hooked his mate's teeth. He takes them off the hook much to the lads in the boat's surprise and especially the lad with the lost teeth and hands them to him. The lad is over the moon, puts them in his mouth and tries to chomp with them. They look like the ones you talked about, Champion the Wonder horse. Disgusted the poor toothless chap takes them out and says, *'they are too big, not mine.'* and promptly throws them over the side.

His mate looks at his disappearing teeth, chomping his toothless gums in absolute horror.'

Everyone howled at this poor toothless man's misadventure - the best intentions and all that.

'Us had some laughs with *The Quay Pub* buoy,' Col continued, in nostalgia mode again. 'The bosses asked Kev and me to dig a huge hole one day. He be was next to the mess and the *Quay Pub*. So, I ties a cable to the handle of the windy pick and Kev and me goes into the mess to play Brag. I keeps pulling the handle to keep the pick sounding as if it's drilling in the hole. Bill keeps us supplied with booze from a tray he brings in from the pub. We get pissed and Kev loses his wages. When we goes out to see the hole the bloody pick has drilled its way six feet under and is stuck under a pile of rock. We does a runner before the boss could catch us.'

They laughed again. Happy days indeed; Well, not for The Quay Company

'Is Jackie on today?' Appsy asked.

'Yeah, she'll be here soon Colin, 'Gareth replied. Gareth also loved to hear the stories of his old customers long gone by.

'I gets talking with Dave about her dad. What a buoy he was,' Appsy said. 'Now Peter was a character. Dave was there when the new supervisor caught Peter with the dog sitting with him and a pint of Guinness on the dashboard of his fork lift. Matey says, 'The new boss won't like that?' Jackie's dad be saying, 'No problem, tell him I've got a bottle of lager in my locker.'

They laughed at the memory of Jackie's dad. Marty continued in the same vein. 'Mind you Jack, in them days us was having lots of bottles in our lockers. We has so much booze coming in we couldn't get it all out sometimes. Charlie's carpenters shed was the best place. He be called The Carpenter's Arms there was so much booze in he. Many times, they comes into Charlie and asks him what he had in his locker and they sits there drinking themselves silly, till time to go to *The Quay* pub. The problem was those bloody customs men.'

Appsy agreed with some passion. 'Chiefly was the best among them, he'd warn us if the black gang for Plymouth were coming. They were the bad bastards and were the Revenue's SAS. They had more power than the police. The first time they came, Charlie gave Chiefly a couple of drinks of vodka and he said they may as well drink the lot before the black gang arrived. They gets mortal drunk. But when the gang arrived, they begins smashing up the buoy's locker even Charlie's special one in The Carpenters' Arms. Chiefly just wanted an easy time and the buoys did too so us would tell him if there was any hint of drugs or anything like that trying to be smuggled and he would let us have our share of the booze. It worked; it was trust. We never dealt in them drugs and we helped him. One day a man from London came down asking for our help with smuggling drugs. We told Chiefly about him because we only ever wanted the freedom to have the booze and cigs that the captains gave us. The good customs men turned a blind eye to booze not drugs. This next time these were the bad boys from Plymouth. Kev showed them some booze in his top locker so they foolishly let him off the quay (this wasn't normally done as the wise customs ones knew what would happen). Kev phones his wife to put his home booze over the fence. They want get into Charlie's safe but he was at home so they escort Wizzel to his house but again they let Wizzel go in on his own first, so the booze was quickly thrown over fence to neighbours.

Marty took up the story. 'I used to take all the good customs men to my place and feed them smuggled booze every night after work when they were on a raid. They loved it, but these back gang were bad buoys. Luckily Col managed to phone home and tell his wife so she was passing loads over the fence and had shifted a hell of a lot before they arrived at his.'

Colin interjected. 'Yes, that was lucky. I even managed to get Charlie's place warned and they managed to get some booze over into the neighbours but he was more worried about them finding his collection of antique guns. Luckily, they came to mine first. It was just getting dusk and they spent a couple of hours getting all the booze and cigs out in bags. Marty heard them say, '*Let's get out here back home to Plymouth. If we search every bloody house in this place, we won't have enough vans to store the bloody stuff and we'll be here all night!*''

Marty laughed out loud. 'Col saved us all that night. He got locked up but they never found the rest.'

Into the pub came a lady with a small water bottle. She came up to Gareth who was standing listening to the tales of Colin's fate with the police. 'Can I have some water for the dog?'

Gareth looked down at her and his face twisted haughtily. 'There is a large dog bowl outside madam.'

'Yes, I know. But I'd like some fresh from the tap,' the lady said pleadingly.

'I have just filled the dog bowl up this morning; it's fresh,' Gareth explained, not too kindly.

'My dog doesn't like to drink water from a bowl. He will only drink fresh from a tap or a bottle.' *Oh dear*, Jack thought when he heard the dog lover's answer, *I think this won't go down well*. And true to his Basil Fawlty roots our esteemed landlord exploded

'Look outside woman: This is Teignmouth. Where the bloody hell does the bloody dog think it is? The spring waters of Evian? The melting glaciers of Greenland? The end of the Ice Age. The water is fresh, let the bloody dog drink it.'

Marty attempted prevent a further melt down (sorry about the pun). 'Maid, if I was you us would go to the back beach, its high tide and there's plenty of water coming down The Teign from Dartmoor. Fair fresh and good Devon water my lover.'

'I'm leaving. I'll buy him a bottle of water in the Co-op.' And she left. No one cried for her, or the dog.

Jack liked the pub and the owners. Gareth was a dedicated landlord who kept his place spotless and safe and more importantly for Jack, his beer and cider in excellent health. Tina was proud of her decoration and her clean pub and hotel bedrooms upstairs and worked hard to maintain it. She would help anyone and was a great supporter of charity and the disadvantaged; After all, she had married Gareth.

The old wood carvings on the heavy wood tables and the bar which depicted the Kings of England were iconic and amazing in their artwork and carpentry skill. Jack could not help wondering if in here, this old building and surrounds, which stood on French Street after all, scene of the worst sacking by the French, here may lay a clue or even the secret itself. He decided to talk some more with Gareth and let him into part of his quest.

They sat at the table next to the bar section with King Henry's head on and chatted. Jack asked if Gareth or his family had heard of anything related to a secret parchment or chalice that may have been left by the French or a society that may be keeping that secret.

'Well my father was very high up in the Freemason's and I guess they retain many secrets but the only thing he ever spoke about to me was the two ladies who lived at Cliffden. That place and Rowdens were owned by Doctor Rodger Mules given to him by his Aunties, Annie and Bertha who kept it as a retreat for women with psychiatric problems. Rodger Mules kept it on as psychiatric care home and gardens and sold the Rowdens to Teignmouth Urban District Council when Annie finally died. His family moved into a new wing of Cliffden. My father had come down from Essex as a successful engineer and he had a contract from The Guide Dogs for The Blind to find and develop a hotel to provide recreation for visually impaired people. Cliffden was the ideal place, with extensive secure grounds for the dogs, easy access to Teignmouth Sea front and town and with bedrooms and care facilities already. Doctor Mules wished to sell but would not do so until two sisters who were the only residents by then died. So, Dad and the Guide Dogs for The Blind had to wait.'

'All sounds great Gareth, but where's the mystery in that?'

'Well Jack, in the end Doctor Mules moved into Trafalgar House, over the way, and all that were left in the huge mansion were the two sisters and those who cared for them. No one could develop the house or grounds as anything but institutional use and nothing could be done, even when it was sold, until the two ladies died.'

'Seems some guy that Doctor Mules,' Jack said, drinking his pint of *Jail Ale*.

'Yes, he was. Dad liked him a lot. In the end he donated the whole of the East Cliff grounds to the people of Teignmouth in memory of his family. That is why it is called Mules Park.'

'Nice bloke then,' Jack confirmed. 'What was so special about the old ladies?'

'Well, they lacked for nothing. They had their own staff, were served every night silver service five course fine dining with just the two of them in the huge dining room building. They had an ex two Michelin star private cook and they drank the finest wines and travelled first class in the finest car and rail travel escorted by personal maids and grooms. No one had a clue about who was paying for it. Doctor Mules and the accounts did not reveal. It came from a blind trust controlled by a merchant bank in London. My father heard from his Masonic friends in high places that the ladies had some knowledge which was extremely valuable and secret and that was why they were kept virtually locked up and in luxury. They were sometimes visited by a shadowy French person and one day a Minister of Margaret Thatcher's government. He thought Doctor Mules also may have known something more than he ever said.'

Jack perked up. Whilst he liked to hear about old Teignmouth and the area - little old ladies and beautiful oriental and tropical gardens in East Cliff Park didn't excite him as much as ladies of the night, mad drunken Dutch captains and smuggling. However, a mysterious secret and immense wealth did. 'What happened in the end?'

'Well father agreed a sale and a development plan, but had to wait till the ladies died which they eventually did after two years. He built the Cliff Den hotel for the Guide Dog association in 1990. But he did tell me that he was told something which he kept to himself as it was probably arcane and maybe linked to his Freemason roots. He never talked again about it before he died but I have lot of his personal memorabilia and his Masonic regalia and things. I can look through them in more detail Jack and get back to you. Or we could talk to Mum. She knew everything he knew I think and maybe more.'

'Sounds great Gareth; let's meet up next week.'

Gareth nodded and then looked around as he heard a tap on the bar. 'Oh shit! There are customers in. What the hell do they want? I hope it's not a bloody coffee,' he said, looking gloomily at a men and woman standing at the bar. And he walked behind the bar.

'Can I have a pint of that Thatcher's scrumpy cider please? We have just arrived on holiday and I'm told Devon is the place for cider. Smashing town this and can my wife have a gin and tonic please?'

Gareth grunted and pulled a pint of natural Thatcher's and then a gin and tonic. He handed them to his customers. 'Oh, can I have ice please?' the lady asked looking at her gin lying alone at the bottom of her glass.

'For heaven's sake!' Gareth exclaimed, shook his head and went back over the few yards to his ice bucket and dropped one ice cube with a plonk, splashing a few drops of gin up and over the glass. He put in front of the lady. She looked at the lonely cube:

'Have you not got crushed ice?'

Just as Gareth was about to hurl a *'for God's sake this is Teignmouth not the Costa ********* Del Sol,'* Jackie, stepped across between him and his victim and said nicely and calmly, 'Isn't it time to get to the bank Gareth? I'll take over now. Now then my lovelies, I'll see if I can get some ice crushed for you.' And she took the glass back. As she brought it back to the customer the lady said:

'Can you slice me a lemon and small piece of cucumber thin please as well?' Jackie smiled at the lady walked back again, gripped the trembling hand and took the knife off Gareth and said, 'Maybe you should take your walk now Gareth.'

Jack chuckled to himself, thinking, *how lucky the innocent aficionados of fine drink were to have Jackie start work at that moment. Mind you if they carry on like that much more with her, she'd have them barred in an instant. No prisoners taken with our Jackie – a human Gareth in some ways, but with a pretty face and an actual heart.*

He went back to talk to the throng who had now assembled at the bar. Big Kev, so called because he was, well big, said rhetorically about the new fussy customers, 'They'll not last long then?'

Yorkshire Tom, glowered at the new customers, 'Fussy bugger, she wouldn't deah that in't Yorkshire. Bloody slices of cucumber, whets wrong wit woman!' Silent John said, well, nothing. Little Pat was sitting on her personal carved wooden bar stool talking to her great mate, the ample bosomed lovely friendly Chris. Jack moved closer to the crowd. 'Not working today Kev?' Jack asked the big man with a smile, knowing the answer.

'Nah; weather's not good Jack.'

It was rare now for Big Kev to be seen in his personal taxi. Sadly, his new chosen business and profession was not what it had seemed for the mercurial private man. Not being particularly customer originated and like most gorillas, rather aggressive when disturbed, Jack had been surprised this service career as a self-employed taxi driver had been his new career move. If Jack had still been a management consultant, he may well have advised Kev that a career as a nightclub doorman, in the French Foreign Legion or a lone Antarctic explorer may have been preferable than meeting and servicing the needs of little old ladies with their shopping from Waitrose, or drunken idiots puking up in his car. Maybe he'd take his advice next time.

Bed and Breakfast Pete came over, ordered a pint of rough cider. 'Got many in this week Peter?' Jack asked the sometimes very grumpy owner of an establishment for the bed and breakfast of visitors to this lovely area.

'Full house,' was the answer.

'That's good then,' Jack said comfortingly.

70

'Would be if those bloody Welsh weren't wasting my electricity,' Pete replied, twisting his thin face up in a grimace that showed he was in pain with the thought.

'Oh, they are back then?' Jack asked.

'Yes, the buggers are. Do you know how much electricity a mini- fridge in a bedroom uses per hour?'

'Sorry Pete, no idea,' Jack replied, knowing fine well that Pete would know. He was extremely cautious with his money was our Pete. Jack knew he had been full of angst about his guests, particularly a Welsh couple who came every year for one week to donate their hard-earned money in his fine establishment. Every year they had brought several cases of cheap supermarket Eight Ace type lager beer and drunk it in their room. Last year they had requested a mini fridge to chill it off. Pete had provided it but had gone apoplectic when he realised, they left it on 24 hours to keep their holiday libations cool.

'I've worked it out; it costs me seventy-five pence a day for that bloody fridge. Last year I kept switching it off when they went out but they put it back on the greedy buggers. They left the windows open too as it was boiling hot. That meant the fridge was burning even more electricity so each morning I shut the windows. The buggers complained their rooms were always boiling when they came in from the beach. Complain, complain and cost me money that's all the buggers do. I've installed a trip switch for the fridge this year. That'll stop the buggers.'

He took a large slurp of his 7% cider. 'This year I am going to add the five pound twenty-five to their final bill. I can't go on subsidising them on my income.'

'Aye; these customers are a nightmare Pete. That's why I sit here,' interjected Big Kev.

'That's why I come out for a pint,' said Pete, and swallowing another large slurp.

Jack chuckled; Pete came out a lot for a pint - well pints. 'Are those Arabs still with you Pete?'

'No, thank Allah. Pain in the arse they were. Six of them in two rooms, all dressed in black camouflage. They were good for saving cash though. They only ever ate were two fried eggs between them on a morning. It was Ramadan think. I was chuffed to bits, no bacon, pork sausage; saved a fortune.'

'Bit like that kid a few weeks ago then?' Jack prompted, hoping for another meltdown on cost.

Pete supped the pint off and ordered another. 'Don't get me on about that lot. From Birmingham, I think. I take their breakfast orders and of course the greedy buggers all want full English. But a ray of hope, the kid asks for just a bacon sandwich. I serve the breakfasts and the kid his sandwich. When I clean up, the kid has only eaten the bacon and the two slices of the Co-op's finest sliced white are left. The next day the bastards all order full English again. Bloody hell I thought, these buggers will bankrupt me. They order the kid his bacon sandwich again and sure enough when I clean up the little horror has left his bread again. Bugger this I thought, I'm not wasting money on bread if the little sod won't eat it.'

Gareth, who had come back from his trip to bank and was avoiding the gin and tonic lady who seemed to be having a great time talking to Maynard Martin the rough cider loving, retired government economist, agreed. 'I'd have slapped the little bastard.'

'So would I if his parents hadn't been there,' Pete said, 'but you can't seem to get away with that these days.'

Everyone in the bar nodded in sad agreement. Yorkshire Bob looked down at Pete sitting on the bar stool and grimaced; his furrowed brow and bald head seemed to ripple with angst. 'In't army if fussy buggers didn't eat their bread, the buggers would be made to clean the shit house with their toothbrush and rogered silly afterwards by the sergeant major in the sangers. Never did 'em any harm.' Silent John looked thoughtful and nodded in tacit agreement of the joys of military life, then Jack thought he was about to comment as his lips moved, but when he burped, he realised, of course, it was only wind. Barry, who was watching the golf on the telly, shouted over, 'Calm down, calm down lads; Tiger just got a birdie.'

Pete continued with his tale of woe. 'Anyway, the next day the bastards had the full breakfast again. I even left a couple of pamphlets I'd pinched from the doctors on obesity, diabetes and cholesterol on their pillows the night before. Greedy sods. But I just brought the boy two slices of bacon. The father says, *'Heh what's this? The boy ordered a bacon sandwich.'* He never eats the bread; I told the daft bastard. *'He won't eat the bacon if it's not in a sandwich,'* the dad told me. Is he thick? I asked. And that caused a melt-down; sensitive sods.'

72

Pete took a drink and continued, *'I've paid for the bread and I want the bloody bread,'* the dad shouted at me. I'll knock it off your bloody bill then. I told him.' The poor tortured bed and breakfast man looked up at Jack morosely. 'In the end I just brought the bacon and two slices of bread on a plate. I refused to put them in a sandwich and spoil them with fat from the bacon because afterwards when the horrible little sod didn't eat them, I served the two slices back to them as toast; miserable sods.'

The way of the hotelier is hard, Jack mused, especially when as tight as Pete.

'Oh God not another bloody old folks' trip!'

Like the movie *Jaws* just as he thought it was safe to enter the water and go out for his stroll around the bars in town, Gareth, cried out his woes from behind the bar. Jack had always thought *The Kings Arms* could easily be like the pub in the end of the TV series of Alan Bleasdale's work, *The Boys from the Black Stuff.* This was a series of black humour comedy about Liverpool during the Thatcher era when the work and the jobs were collapsing around the characters neighbourhood. It introduced the manic depressive Yossa Hughes and followed his breakdown as he was made redundant from normal family man to suicidal homicidal maniac. His laconic plea to anyone and everyone being, *'Giz a job,'* before he head-butted them. The last episode was particularly epic as it brought all the tragic characters and tales together in one Liverpool pub. The pub was surrounded by desolation, as factory after factory around had been knocked down and laid in ruins. It was the last building standing. The landlord just stood behind the bar, ignoring the mayhem around. *Shake Hands* a huge man who went around bars asking people to shake hands and then crushing their hands as they writhed around in agony on the floor met his match in this series ending episode. In this final *Gotterdammerung* episode he meets his match as he asks Yossa to shake hands. Yossa just takes his hand as the big man crushes and stares into his eyes. Shake Hands eyes bulge and the pain spreads across his brow because he can make no impact on the one black eyed, staring Yossa. Eventually Shake Hands is about to give up when Yossa head buts him. The big man breaks into tears and is comforted by his mates. The landlord shakes his head yet again at the pathos of it all.

The next scene jumps to an old drunken man in the window seat who is a whistler and he has his two hands in his mouth whistling and singing, '*If I had the wings of a blackbird*'. He is told a couple of times '*to shut the **** up*' by all in the pub. He ignores and keeps on whistling and singing. Two men, not unlike Big Kev and Yorkshire Bob, Jack mused as he reflected on the show, go over, pick the whistler's chair up and throw him through the window. They go back and drink their beer as if nothing had happened. The Landlord shakes his head again and cleans a glass with his bar towel.

Then the door opens and into the bar piles another load of drunken lunatics. The barman puts his towel down and says to the two stood with him chatting.

'That's it! Not another bloody redundancy party. I'm off.' And he walks out of his bar leaving it free to all the out of work crazies.

Jack chuckled to himself as he heard Gareth's painful cry, '*Oh no! Not another bus trip!*' and he saw the lovely old ladies and men walk into the bar from their long-anticipated holiday bus journey to the English Riviera. He chuckled and believed passionately that *Gareth could easily have made it as tortured landlord in the remake of Boys from the Black Stuff.* He would write to his friend in the London agency and recommend him. Sarah, the lovely and friendly Teignmouth carnival organiser, who had come in to take over from Jackie, patted the trembling Gareth gently. 'You goes and has a walk now Gareth. I'll look after the old dears.' And she did.

Jack noticed that Bill Hook had arrived and he decided to see if he would have chat. Bill was a marine man and long serving member of the community. A proud and professional captain whose company *Riviera Tours* offered wonderful tours of the estuary and sea and also excellent fishing trips for mackerel and deep-sea fish. He was also a member of one branch of the ancient Hook family and may well be one of the guardians.

Jack decided to broach the subject of the French invasion with Bill and that Françoise may be writing a book about it, if there had been anything smuggled off the boats. 'No, never heard anything about that. There are a few branches of the Hook's buoy. I know ours in Teignmouth have nothing to do with smuggling. They might have many years ago, but he be much more likely he be the Shaldon or the Bishop buoys. You're best having a talk with one of them or the Job's, they were definitely at the invasion as the bloody French burnt their ships and they lost their living. I wouldn't be surprised if they got their own back. There is a man who drinks in The Ship, Old Jim Smith. Best you goes and sees him my handsome. How's that French maid, Françoise these days? I didn't know she was interested in history. I haven't seen her for a while. I had heard that she'd been in a serious incident.'

'Oh, she is ok. Had a few things hit her lately; hopefully nothing can go wrong again.'

But he was too late; over on the banks of the River Seine something was about to go terribly wrong – and to Françoise again.

CHAPTER TEN

Françoise had flown into Charles de Gaulle airport and taken the RER B to Chatelet Les Halles and changed onto the RER A line towards Saint Germain-en-Laye. Her destination and the home of her aunt was Le Vésinet, a small market town on the River Seine. Her Aunt, Edith, had worked for her whole adult life as a French teacher at the junior school of the British School of Paris, located in the banks of the River Seine at Croissy –sur-Seine. She had been one of the founder teachers having joined as a new teacher after leaving Nanterre University College in 1954. Now she enjoyed her last year's partially wheelchair bound living in a beautiful old house of the Route du Grand Lac a stroll away from the beautiful Lac du Vésinet.

Edith was delighted to meet Françoise, her favourite grandniece; her two French bulldogs were also delighted to see her niece again. Françoise had named her own small hound after her auntie and had chosen a French bulldog over the English springer spaniel her husband had wanted because of her aunt's dogs. Edith had a live- in Moroccan helper and she helped Françoise with her bag and took it upstairs to her bedroom. Her aunt was mobile in the house, her legs just not up for long walks or standing, and she showed Françoise into her lounge overlooking through wooden French patio doors a beautiful manicured garden. She shouted to the helper as she descended the wooden carved grand staircase that bent in a semi-circle from top to bottom, 'Safaa, please bring Françoise a cup of coffee please when you get down.'

'Yes, Madame, would I bring one for you Madame?

'No thank you, just one cup please.'

'How was your journey my dear?' Edith asked.

'Very pleasant thank you, apart from the usual RER from Charles de Gaulle. When will they tidy that up?'

'I have no idea; I never leave here these days. I hope you can take me around the Lac before dinner. I have booked a table at *Le Pavilion des Ibis* on the island. I think it's time I treated you, Françoise. I see you so rarely these days.'

'I know Aunty, I will come again soon I promise.'

Safaa brought in the coffee with a couple of petit fours, placed on the small wooden antique table at Françoise's side of the high-backed sofa they were both sitting on. 'Thank you Safaa; I don't think I shall need you now. Françoise will look after me until bedtime. Please go and see that lovely boyfriend of yours. The weather is so fine for a walk on the Seine.' As Safaa said thank you and hurried out, taking off her apron as she rushed, Edith turned to Françoise, 'Now then Françoise, your mother tells me you are worried about something and that you have been in an accident. Tell me more about what has happened since I last saw you.'

Françoise told Edith everything she knew up to now. She brushed over the car incident and did not mention the two men at the graveyard, only that a man was following them all the time and he looked dangerous. Edith listened, her old body was wearing out and her hearing not so good but she understood every word and she thought deeply about what she should tell her niece. What she knew was so dangerous and deeply hidden for so many centuries by her family and the society that she was not sure Françoise should take on its burden. She decided not to tell all but to try to get her to give up her quest for the secret knowledge. She would feed her enough to maybe put her mind at rest and put off those who she knew must be hunting her down to stop her finding out.

'I think you should freshen up Françoise. I'd like you to help me dress for dinner and as it's such a beautiful evening then you can wheel me around the lake and we can talk over a nice bottle of Montrachet. I will take a nap now and see you here at seven; à tout à l'heure ma cheri.'

Françoise kissed her aunt and helped her climb the stairs to her room. She sorted her suitcase out and put her clothes away. The room was furnished in old antique French furniture. Françoise pondered that her aunt had a lot of valuable items in this wonderful old château of a house. She knew this area on The Seine, commuter distance and only 30 minutes from Paris, was extremely expensive and sought after. Only the inherited wealth of many years or the nouveau rich or the Russians could afford to live here. Her aunty had been a teacher. To her knowledge Edith's deceased husband was not wealthy; he had been a librarian in the Bibliothèque de France. To her knowledge her mother or her aunt's relatives did not have wealth. They came from marine backgrounds in Brittany, and some had been high up in the French Navy long ago but most were fishermen or pirates. It was a puzzle as to how they could have afforded a house this

77

expensive and the antiques that filled it. Maybe it was her husband's line. They came from Monségur Languedoc region, near Carcassonne; nothing rich about that place as far as she knew. She took a shower and forgot about the history and the money; she had more to worry about.

At 7 p.m. her aunt had walked a short distance out of her grounds and through the huge wooden automatically opening gates which barred the way into her mansion. Françoise loved to see the old French house with their chateau type styles, wooden shutters and house gates. Nowhere is the world could you see such grandiose and architecture; a time past she always thought but up to now the modernisation seen in many towns across Europe had not touched the typical French villages and small towns. As they approached the lake Edith tired and asked to sit in her wheelchair. Françoise pushed her around the path that followed the contour of the lake. In the middle of the lake, accessed by a road and footbridge bridge were the Isle de Ibis and a five-star restaurant, gardens, tennis courts and home. She was getting hungry now and was looking forward to dinner on the island with Edith. She continued to push her aunt around the idyllic lake, swans, ducks; small song birds were all around as well as fishermen trying with not much success to catch trout and carp from its sparkling blue waters. It was a perfect summer's evening and they retired for dinner in the restaurant on the Isle du Ibis.

Over a delightful meal and in charming ambience Françoise talked with her aunty. What the old octogenarian told her was astonishing and mind boggling. She had lived in complete ignorance of her family's past and significance on the world stage. And now with this knowledge she had an awesome responsibility laid upon her petit shoulders.

'Françoise ma cherie, I have great fear for what has happened to you and the misfortune of what was told to you. I fear you are in danger and should be aware of the reasons why. If only that you can make what mind up to tell all and got to the security forces of your adopted country. However, I caution you on who you can trust. The society and the people who want the secret are of the highest positions in both our countries. Only 'the one who holds the secret of the vine' is thought to know all and that person is unknown to many of us. Let me start at the beginning and tell you as much as I have been told or I know.'

And Edith asked for two more glasses of Montrachet to be poured by a waiter from the bottle in the ice bucket by their side. She looked around again to be sure that their table in the alcove that overlooked the sparkling lake was free from close and listening ears and she recited what she knew.

For many centuries a secret order had protected a secret that if revealed could cause a world- wide schism of the Christian faith. *How did she know this?* Well, it was because their family was descended from the Knights Hospitallers or the Knights of St John. Originally a monastic order in Jerusalem founded around the same time as The Knights of Christ, The Knights Templar in 1113. Along with The Templars they were the joint military Holy orders in the Holy land. However, by 1312, the Catholic Church had fallen out with the Templars and they were persecuted, tried and hanged for heresy. This was mainly as they became a huge influence and most wealthy and threat to the Holy Roman Church and there was verbal circumstantial evidence that they did not believe in the resurrection of Jesus Christ and that Christ had not died on the cross. Under the Inquisition members of the order confessed that their ritual was to spit and stamp on the Cross and they worshiped a severed head called Bathomet. Some linked this to the cult that worshiped John the Baptist and more expansively the Knights Hospitaller who were founded as protectors of the primacy of John the Baptist. In the end they effectively died out suddenly as the bankers of Europe and the most powerful religious order when their leader Jacques de Molay, the Grand Master of the Order by King Phillip IV in 1314.

Françoise listened intently to this history lesson of the religious and esoteric orders of ancient times, not having a clue how this could involve a small town in Devon or her own family. Françoise continued to explain.

The Templars were ordered under a Papal Bull from Pope Clement V to be dissolved and their property and wealth to be handed over to the Knights Hospitallers. Many Templars joined the Hospitallers who had by now spread and formed 'langues' ruled by a priory and a Grand Prior, across the Mediterranean, Spain, France, Holy Roman Empire, and Italy. The main citadels were founded in Rhodes and in Malta. And the Knights of Rhodes and the Knights of Malta founded as protectors of the Order or St John.

Over the centuries the order protected the Christian world against Muslim tide in defensive and offensive actions of crusades and jihads. It fell from power and resorted mainly to piracy and mercenary work for its power and influence. Where the supposed wealth and treasure brought to it by the Templars went is lost in history and speculation. The Templars themselves were thought to have sailed from France with most of their treasure in a fleet of 18 ships from La Rochelle just before papal bull dissolved the order. No one knows where this ended up, though many speculate.

Françoise was beginning to get bored with all the history, and she asked her aunt what was the relevance of all this to Teignmouth and her. Her aunty explained and revealed something quite amazing.

'Françoise, the man who burnt and sacked Teignmouth on the 26th June sixteen ninety was your relative and a Grand Knight of Malta and he was bringing back to France the secret knowledge that the Knights of Saint John and The Templars had discovered in Solomon's Temple. He was carrying The Holy Grail.'

Françoise was shocked; Thoughts whizzed around her confused brain. *This couldn't be true. Our family had the Holy Grail? Has the old lady lost her marbles?'* 'You look worried ma petite? Let me explain a bit more; please bear with the history lessons. In the eleventh century a group of people who believed in a thing called Catharism or Dualism, an idea that there were two Gods, one good and one evil appeared in the Languedoc region of France. They were known as the Cathars or the Albigensians after the city of Albi in Southern France where the revival started. The Catholic Church and the Pope decided that this was heresy and a crusade was hurled against the Cathars, The Albigensian Crusade. They fought valiantly and but finally ended up besieged in the town of Montségur for nearly one year until in March 1244 they were massacred. However, it was popular knowledge in the region around Montségur that a party of priests escaped the fortress with the Cathar Treasure. It is also speculated that The Knights Templar fought with them and that the secret scrolls may well have been those Templars and Hospitallers excavated from the Temple Mount in Jerusalem.'

Edith took a small drop of her wine. 'Would you like me to carry on Françoise? You look tired?'

'It's ok Aunty, I'm just taking all this in. It's a bit weird this entire secret scroll, Holy Grail stuff. Isn't it just a fantasy?'

Edith put her glass down and smiled: 'Yes, many, many things have been written about these things. The Knights Templar, The Freemasons, The Holy Grail, your King Arthur and of course the books on the secret society's that control the secret that Jesus did not die on the cross and that Mary Magdalene carried his child to France. The Holy Grail, or Sang Graal is supposed to be the Sang Réal, The Holy Blood, Christ's bloodline.'

'I never knew any of that Aunty Edith. It's all knew to me. Christ had a child?'

'Read *The Holy Blood and The Holy Grail* and then *The Da Vinci Code*. They will bring you up to modern day speed. But the fact is they are not exactly correct. What the Templars found was a library of scared scrolls placed in the Temple by a society of Gnostic, believers in the first century after Christ's death. It was that arcane knowledge which is the true Templar treasure of the Order of the Temple of Solomon. And it was hidden with the Cathars in Montségur and taken by the Templars, first to Malta and then to Britain. It contained a revelation that was so amazing that they have kept it hidden for centuries. And then it was lost in Teignmouth by your great, great, great, grandfather.'

Françoise sat looking over the table at her aunty in a dream. *Surely this wasn't true or real?* The waiter brought over two cafe gourmands as their desert and placed them on the table. 'Can I bring you anything else Madam?' he asked the old lady.

'No thank you Paul, just bring the bill,' she replied kindly and leaned across at her niece. 'Françoise, I think maybe we should finish off and head home after this. I detect you are feeling a bit confused and tired. Let's talk again in the morning. I am looking forward to a promenade au bord La Seine. You can ask any questions tomorrow.'

Françoise took a drink of her cafe and took a small fork to one of the four tiny samples of the dessert menu. She really wanted to know more but she also needed to take in what her aunt had told her. But she couldn't just leave it at that, that her long lost relative had lost the greatest secret in the whole world, maybe the Holy Grail. 'That's fine aunty, but can you just explain who was this relative and how did he find and lose what people have been searching for centuries?'

The old lady took a taste of the meringue with Chantilly taster. 'Well, your long lost great, great, great grandfather was Admiral Anne-Hilarion de Contentin, le Compte de Tourville. He was the commander of the French fleet that defeated the Anglo/Dutch fleet in The Battle of Beachy Head on the 10th of July 1690. The fleet had been sent by King Louis the fourteenth to defeat the English and also prevent the English fleet from supporting King William of Orange's army from defeating the French/Scottish and Irish armies of the deposed King James the second who had landed in Ireland in an attempt to regain his throne from King William after the Glorious Revolution.

Sadly for the French, King William defeated King James at the Battle of The Boyne on the first of July. But the whole of England was still in panic and mobilised as they believed the French who now controlled the channel would attack King William as he returned from Ireland and also then invade England.'

Edith took and the other dessert and examined it with her fork before halving and eating one piece. 'Are you getting all of this Françoise?'

Françoise leaned back in her seat.' I never was any good at history Aunt Edith but it's getting there. What's this got to do with Teignmouth?'

'Well your ancient grandfather, instead of attacking London and winning the war, he left the battle to drop off his wounded and then for some reason he sailed the fleet to Torbay in Devon and seemingly did nothing for 10 days. Then for some reason he sailed up the few miles of Labrador Bay to Teignmouth, where again for some mad reason he sacked the town. It was the last ever invasion of England.'

'Why did he do that?' Françoise asked, 'he had the English at French mercy.'

'Well that's what a lot of very high-powered French thought and he was relieved of his command on his return,' Edith answered.

'So, we have a family history as traitors to France!' Françoise stated.

'Indeed; it certainly seemed so. But miraculously 'the Compte' was resurrected and he ended up being given the highest honours a Frenchman could gain; a Marshall of France'

'Why would they do that? All he did was beat up some poor fishermen and cider makers in a remote part of England and let William return to his new kingdom and King James I assume never became King again?' Françoise asked, getting more interested in the fall and rise to fame of her disgraced relative.

'Yes, King William returned and effectively James would never get on the throne again. He actually stayed a couple of kilometres up the road in the Château de Saint-Germain-en-Laye. He died there and never returned. Of course, the Jacobites still kept the dream of the 'King over the Water' returning to take over that mysterious 'Divine Right of Kings. Our relative could have helped that happen but he didn't and he was rewarded by our Establishment for not doing so. This has been a perpetual question as we the French supported and fought against the Catholic Pope and the Holy Roman Empire for King James to regain the English and Scottish thrones.'

'Dear me aunty, it all seems very suspicious and conspiratorial. But it doesn't explain what you said before. What did he lose at Teignmouth and why was it so important?'

'Well that is the mystery we do not know and the cause of the problems you are now facing. You see all our family knows is that the Compte de Tourville was also a Knight of Malta, and a high-ranking Freemason. He never revealed to anyone in the family what actually he lost; only how. What was lost he had collected from English conspirators at Tintagel Castle in Cornwall, and then he actually met King William the leader of the Grand Alliance of The Holy Roman Empire, The Pope and The English in Torbay, three days before he sacked Teignmouth.'

'What! Aunty this gets sillier by the minute. Why would two enemies meet?'

'Well that is indeed a mystery ma cherie. The Compte told his son that he had been on a mission from the Grand Master of the Knights of Saint John to return 'that was lost' to its rightful owners and ensure it was kept safe as things were changing rapidly now in Protestant England and Catholic Europe. It had been agreed between people in both the French court, and William and his English backers, who were all members of the Order of Saint John and the Templars that William had agreed to return the secret which had lain hidden in Tintagel since the Templars took it there from Malta because France and England had signed a secret agreement at Torbay '

Françoise just struggled now to take all of this in. She rationalised and summarised her thoughts. *It seemed that an ancient scroll or scrolls had been found by the Knights Templars digging under*

Solomon's Temple. These had been handed down since the death of Jesus Christ in the first century and kept secret by one or several secret societies. The Templars and the Cathars, descendants of the Essenes who wrote them, kept these in Montségur castle, Languedoc. When the Templars were disbanded and persecuted the scrolls were given to the Knights' Hospitaller, the Knights of Saint John, hidden in their priory in Malta and now it seems they had been taken by the dispersed Templars to Tintagel Castle in Cornwall where now, for some reason, the new Protestant King of England, had handed them over to a representative of his enemy and also a Catholic secret order, The Knights of Malta. These had been lost when her relative for some unknown reason he sacked and burnt a small Devon town for no military or plundering reason at all. Now it seemed she had been given clues by a dying man from the town and from his associates of where this secret was hidden and two groups of people one Cornish and one unknown group were trying to gain that secret, and would harm her to get it. No wonder she broke into a sweat on that humid summer evening.

'Here take my handkerchief Françoise; you look very warm, wipe your brow'

Françoise took the petite lace hanky and wiped her brow and asked, 'Aunty, how do you know all this stuff? You were just a French teacher. It is mindboggling for me and for anyone.'

'Well it was for me when I first was told of these things?' Edith admitted.

'Was it handed down through the Tourville family?' Françoise asked.

'Yes, in some way. Through the generations someone from the family has always been involved at high level in the Holy Order but only they knew what the Compte had done and not why or what he had lost. Only I know more than they do?'

'Wow! How on earth would you know more than a secret Holy Order?' Françoise exclaimed, clearly shocked. And Edith told her something that shocked her even more.

'Because I married a Cathar. He was a descendent of one of the priests who escaped the Montségur massacre.'

Wow, Françoise thought, and just sat and started at her old wrinkle faced aunt. She still had such bright sparkling blue eyes and Françoise had never thought that such secrets had lain behind them for so much of her long life. *Her husband had such a past?* He was a librarian for heaven's sake, not a holder of some arcane secret that could change the world. Even though her Aunt clearly looked ready to leave Françoise couldn't just leave it at that.

Holy Order, The Knights of Malta, after his triumphant victory over King William's navy to meet him at Tintagel. He must have taken a route overland from where he was moored at Torbay across Devon into Northern Cornwall and to the legendary Arthurian castle. King William was returning after his victory at the Battle of the Boyne and at a meeting in Torbay or Tintagel they agreed to hand over the Grail documents and sign a secret agreement. On his return to his fleet in Torbay for some unknown reason he sailed the few miles up to Teignmouth, where his ship was plundered while they were exploring the town and beaches and he lost his Grail. She could only assume that it was his wrath and anger and in a search for the Grail that he sacked and burnt the town. It's the only thing that made sense.

Obviously, it appeared to Françoise that meeting William and regaining the grail for his Order and a possible secret society who were seeking it, was more important than pursuing the English fleet for his French King Louis. For this, and what to his appeared to his superiors a futile and senseless use of the best fleet Europe to burn a small Devon town, he was demoted. In any other country he would have been shot. And after a brief period of rest, he regained all his honours and more, all she could think was whatever he had done must have pleased someone in the highest positions in France and the rest of Europe.

None of this really helped her in what she had set out to do. All it did was worry her that now she had powers against her that could change the direction of wars, alter continental power, form alliances with royalty and maybe kill to protect what it knew and sought. She laid all night sweating in the night's summer humidity and worrying that maybe she should just go back to being a nurse and forget it all. *But she couldn't could she now?* The man at Widdecombe had told her she must find the secret location and give whatever was there to him. And now her aunt told her there was another group and a Frenchman who was sworn to keep the secret safe at all costs. So, she tossed and turned until she was stirred by Safaa who knocked on her door.

'Madame, are you awake? Madame Edith would like to see for breakfast on the veranda in twenty minutes if you can make it?'

'That's fine Safaa, I'll be there.'

After breakfast she agreed to push her aunt along the Bords de la Seine, the banks of the river which had cycle and running paths all along them for miles right into Paris and gave the local people a wonderful view of the mighty river and his many huge working barges and cruise boats that ploughed up and down the waterway to the Channel.

They walked slowly along as the cyclists, dog walkers and joggers passed them, most if not all the people who passed each other were in good spirits as the weather was beautiful again and 'bonjour' was passed between the passers-by many, many times. They walked for about a kilometre towards Croissy sur Seine and Edith was feeling so chirpy and fit so she asked if they could carry on until they reached the British School of Paris. 'I haven't seen the old place in a while now. It would be nice to see it one last time. I rarely feel up to coming this far these days.'

As they reached the school, Edith pointed out the small town over the river, just along there is Bourgival and it's where I taught for a while until the merged the schools here in Croissy. It's so pretty there. Push me nearer the Seine and we can see a bit better.'

Françoise adjusted the wheelchair and pushed it towards a large gap in the trees on the bank of the river, next to a ramp which led to a small loading bay on the edge of the Seine. A huge double working barge was ploughing its way up river only about 15 metres from the bank. They could see the captain's car perched on top of the main barge and he waved to them from his vantage point on the bridge of the barge. They were waving back when suddenly, two joggers came up behind them, one grabbed Françoise and pinned her arms behind her back and the other took the handles of the wheelchair and turned it to face down the ramp. Françoise was terrified and screamed, 'Don't harm her. She's an old lady!'

The man holding her said, 'She is going for a swim. It's a long way to Le Havre.'

Edith was trying to push herself out of the chair but her assailant held her tightly in and pushed the chair to the top of ramp.

'We would like you find what you are searching for and when you do you will hand it to us. Do not worry about trying to contact or find us. We will find you. We are watching every day. If you try to run away, go to the police or talk to anyone about what we have told you, you will die. Now do you want us to send your aunt for trip to Le Havre or will you help us?'

Françoise saw the terror in Edith's face and her futile struggle to break out of the chair. She struggled herself but the man was

90

just too strong. She could see no one to help her. The tears started to fall. *Be strong, stop this, think!* Was all she could think? Fear and frustration took over again. 'OK, yes, please let the old lady go. I will help you.'

The man with the chair suddenly tipped it to one side. Edith tumbled out. He then straightened it and gave a slight push and let go of it. It fell down the ramp and off the jetty straight into the huge bow wave that the barge was making as it passed by. It was swallowed up in the grey murky waters as the successive waves lashed over the jetty.

'We will contact you. No police remember or this old lady will be in the chair next time,' the man holding Françoise said, as he released her. He bid his accomplice to come back and as they saw a man cycling along, they both jogged quickly off and turned up the Quai de l'Écluse and into the shadows again.

Françoise ran to her aunt who was lying beating her fist on the hard ground. 'I knew this would happen. The Grail should have been left buried forever. Françoise pick me up please I think I have scrapped my knees.'

The cyclist arrived and climbed off his bike to help.' What happened? Is the old lady ok?' he asked anxiously and helped Françoise get Edith up on her feet.

'I'm alright. Please don't fuss too much. I tried to manoeuvre my wheelchair to see the barge and wave and stupidly it started to slip down the ramp. I had to throw myself out. My dear niece here was looking the other way at the children playing in the school field. I am a very stupid old lady.'

'Let me go to the school and get some help. We can get you to the infirmary and nurse there and then maybe an ambulance.'

'I don't need an ambulance. Just ask someone to help Françoise get me to the school. They'll get me home. Thank you, Monsieur, thank you very much for your help.'

The cyclist climbed onto his bike to cycle to the school but he said to Françoise. 'I am sure those two men should have helped you. Why did they run away?'

'I really don't know. These days there are so many people who don't want to get involved. But thank you for your help monsieur. You have been very kind. When we can get her to school, I'll make sure she is safe and sound in her home soon.'

Three hours later over lunch they both sat in silence for long periods. Both had agreed that maybe they should just go to the police and then after a few more minutes Françoise had come trembling all over, *she couldn't leave her aunt to a watery grave,* she knew that. No, she would struggle on with Jack's help to find what was lost and then hand it over. To which group was her nightmare now? *Why are there two of them? Who the hell is the man in the graveyard who brained the other man? And what the hell does he want it for?* She kept throwing questions and speculation around her head but in the end, she agreed to keep quiet and get on with the search. Edith would not countenance having anyone look after her. Françoise offered to bring her to England, her husband and his friends would take care of any of these who came after her. But the old lady was insistent. 'I have lived a long time Françoise. I would like to know what my husband had been keeping secret for all our lives together and I think you should find that out. Do not worry about me. Your uncle gave me a number to call in the event of anything terrible happening regarding the Grail or Saunière's family approaching me or my family. I have called that number. I do not know who they are or what they will do but all I know is that they will be there. So, go, enjoy yourself, take a trip up to Saint Germain see that English pub you told me about where your friend Jacques asked you to say hello. It's La Fêtes des Logis summer fair there this month in Le Foret du St Germain. Go and enjoy yourself ma petite. This old woman can look after herself.'

CHAPTER TWELVE

Françoise decided to take her aunt's advice and the next day she took and RER to Saint- Germain-en-Laye. When Jack had heard she was going to Le Vésinet he had asked her to pop in and see his old landlord and landlady in *The Bitter End Pub*. He hadn't been back since The Iron Chancellor had sent him from Singapore to live in Paris to sort some suppliers out and told Françoise that she might enjoy a British beer and cider and some real food in that famous hostelry. And Giles and Gina were always worth a laugh with.

She exited the RER and looked across to the imposing Château. Very impressive she thought as she walked through the pretty square with the cafe's buzzing with people outside on the road side tables. She was unaware that above her Saunières' grandson was sitting on his balcony drinking a coffee, he too unaware of her presence, but wondering if she would take notice of his warning of yesterday. He hoped so, because violence was too extreme as it could draw unwarranted attention to him. Attention he did not want. He was happy to remain in the shadows with his wealth and hidden power he had over those who 'kept the secret of the vine'. After all they had been paying him five million euro's a year since he had opened the chest that his grandfather gave him all those years ago. He was the great grandchild of the fruit of an affair that Farther Saunière and the opera singer had enacted in the good priest's happy days of wealth and power, when he was lauded by royalty and gentry alike as well as the Vatican. If only they knew that what he had found and sold to them he had also copied and now his offspring had it kept in a bank in London. His great grandson knew that must continue and no one was going to stop that. He looked down at the thronging masses around the square and the Château. His mind drifted. *How little people know about what controls their lives and who controls the secret organisation that could change their lives forever. Its best they didn't* was his final thought as he stood up, picked up his mobile and called a banker in London.

The banker was worried after putting down the phone and he rang a Minister of Her Majesty's Government in London. Both of them called 'the keeper of the vine'. All were concerned and set in motion a scheme to change Europe and to change Françoise and Jack's lives.

Across Europe and in the old walls of the Tsar of all the Russia's Kremlin, someone else put the phone down. He had spoken to an Italian man in the English cathedral town of Salisbury. The Italian had just left the secret nerve agent facility at Porton Down twelve miles away from Salisbury. He had been instructed to delay his investigation into the poisoning of the ex Russian spy, Skripal and his daughter and to begin plans to go to Devon for a much more important mission. The Italian took his orders without complaint or question as he always did. Like his boss, he too was a member of the Russian secret service but his speciality was in 'wet affairs'. He enjoyed the spilling of blood.

Françoise walked through the old paved streets and quaint old French houses and shops of this pretty and imposing Château town, unaware that one of her nemeses was a short distance away. She eventually found Rue Saint–Pierre and walked down its narrow street into the small place and spotted *The Bitter End* on the right. Already the tables outside on the piazza were filling up with the lunch time dining crowd and she walked into the small bar area. Giles greeting her with smile and asked what she'd like. She chose a pint of *Aspel's* cider as she felt a bit home sick for Devon and even though it was from Suffolk, well it was cider, if not Devon's best. Over a time, she spoke with Giles and his lovely wife Gina and told them of her friendship with Jack.

'Does he still know that author lad, Davey? He wrote a book about Jack and his adventures here. There's a few of his mates still here. Youssef has returned and may be in soon. He'd like to hear how Jack is getting on. And Bernie is still upstairs cooking. No cannibal pots mind these days. Jack used to love chatting with Bernie about his old life in New Guinea. Did he tell you when Bernie went to The British School and he fished all the carp out of the school pond and ate them?' It took him a while to adjust to civilisation.'

'Yeah, he knows Davey, and he tells fondly of Bernie and Youssef. Is Simon the Sorcerer in? Jack loves him. Says he was from Devon; a one off.'

'Can't you recognise him?' Gina said, smiling and knowingly.

Françoise looked around at the clientele. At the far end of the bar was someone who looked like Gandalf from *'Lord of the Rings'*. He was drinking cider. She chuckled when she remembered what Jack had told her about how he had befriended the lovely man and called him after that popular computer game Simon the Sorcerer.

'Françoise, he is one of the most intelligent and well-bred men I have spoken too. Many who never speak to him have no idea and they think he has just fought Sauron on Mount Doom in Mordor or sacrificed a goat on High Tor on Dartmoor, and indeed my wife also did one day when she came to visit me in Paris. We were driving along Le Peq bridge and Simon was walking through town for his daily libation in *The Bitter End.* He was dressed in his usual Sorcerer's long coat, long hair and beard flowing in the breeze off the Seine and carrying his large carrier bag in which he carried we knew not what. My son sat in the back said, *'Look Dad, its Simon the Sorcerer.'* My wife looked horrified and said, *'Who the hell is that?'* I replied, *'It's Simon, my friend from the pub,'* I happily explained. *'He lives in a cottage in Le Peq I think.'* Anyway, my wife was not amused with my new found artistic and mystical friend and she cried out, *'In a house, he looks like he lives in a bus shelter. He's a bloody druid or one of them travellers for God's sake. The Iron Chancellor sends you here, to get away from the bloody waifs and lunatics you knew up North and in that Singapore madhouse The Outback and the first thing you do is end up in that bloody pub and you make friends with weirdoes and crazy people again!'* Yes, women sometimes can't see past their Gucci handbags.

Françoise also chuckled when she remembered what Jack had told her about his son's attempt to help him with his attempt to find a long lost relative. Despite having a wealth of experience in the world of art, antiques, music and business, Simon the Sorcerer was like most of the more mature generation and was clueless with hand held technology. He had been trying to set up Facebook on his medieval phone in an attempt to link into some distant relative who may know where his relative was. His son had kindly offered to help him and set him up through his own laptop and they had arranged to meet in town, not the pub of course. They duly met in a St Germain coffee shop. Simon entered and the young lad said he looked like he had entered a magical world. He was astonished and beaming at what he saw. As he sat down, he told the boy that he had never been in one for years. The son asked him if he'd like a drink, coffee or tea? The wizard looked shocked. He looked around at all the others enjoying their early morning caffeine shot in amazement and turned back to his IT expert and confessed *'I've not drunk tea or coffee for years I only drink cider!'*

As Françoise looked over at the great man, she wondered given his mystical status in the bar, maybe he was the holder of an esoteric secret. He looked a lot like the wizard in *The Teign Brewery. Of course,* she thought as she remembered the dying man's last words about the chalice; *maybe it was an alchemist's or sorcerer's cup?* Could this be the special man to talk to? She realised she was fantasising again.

Giles and Gina were busy with the crowded lunchtime customers, spending their luncheon vouchers on the varied menu. Françoise chose one of Bernie's less carnivorous or cannibalistic dishes, a fried Camembert with salad and enjoyed it. She got talking with an Englishman Graham, who had been in town for a few years and asked him how he liked it.

'Its fine once you get used to the French ways. God, I had some difficult times at first, especially our first Christmas. I was a nervous wreck we'd get it right as we always have the same traditions. I'd never seen any Turkey's in the shop up to now. I fretted that there wouldn't be any. A mate in here told me to go to the butchers in Le Vésinet who would order me one. I spoke little French but he told me it was called 'une dinde'. I also wanted pork, which he said was 'le porc'. But even he didn't know the words for lots of pork crackling. So, two weeks before Christmas, and a nervous wreck I wouldn't get my Turkey, I went to shop. I spoke in my Franglais and was so chuffed when the man put down in his little note book my orders. He looked so confident that I was getting my five kilo le digne and a piece of le porc. I had kept pulling at my skin in an attempt to say lots of cracking. He laughed and said, *'Oui. Oui'*...and pulled my skin... *'trop, trop, bein sûr Monsieur.'* I was told to return on the twenty fourth, Christmas Eve. I was a nervous wreck that if he got it wrong, we would have no Turkey or Pork, and much more upsetting for me, no Turkey dripping or Pork Crackling. But when I arrived there was a large queue of all French women mainly buying Paté Foie Gras, a few however seemed to be buying a 'Dinde'. This disturbed me because when the butcher showed the birds to the ladies, they looked tiny and covered in black feathers and when they were told the bill it was two hundred Euros or one hundred and fifty Euros. Bloody hell I thought that paté fois gras is pricey pleased we don't do that. *And turkeys with black feathers, surely they were crows?* Anyway, it came to my turn. The large butcher and his mate looked into the book, he ran his finger down and grunted a grunt of recognition. He went into the chillier and brought a bag out with a Turkey's head out, covered in black feathers and another bag with a piece of pork. He opened both wide and I looked in. It looked tiny and not what I would call a turkey. I asked sheepishly. *'Une Dinde? Cinq kilo?'*

'Oui Monsieur; cinq kilo and une dinde; aussi, votre porc'...and he pulled his fat arm laughing saying something in French I didn't understand. I bottled it and just smiled and took my wallet out. He said something

like one hundred and fifty euro's, but I just stood there. It couldn't be one hundred and twenty pounds for a bloody sparrow and a piece of porc. But sure enough it was. And I took it home crying.'

Françoise laughed. 'Have to say I had similar issues when I first went to England.'

Graham looked sad and said, 'But I bet you didn't wake up Christmas morning and cry again?' He took a drink and concluded his tale of cross-cultural communication. 'My first thing on a Christmas morning is to go to the fridge and get the turkey dripping out that my wife has collected from the meat tray of the turkey she cooks every Christmas Eve. I love it on bread and have two slices with salt and pepper; I have never failed in forty years. But today there is no dish in the fridge. I come running back into the bedroom distraught with worry. *Where's the dripping?* I shout at my wife. She looks very sheepish and says, *'Sorry dear but there just wasn't any. The bird had no fat on it all. I didn't tell you last night as I know you would have been too upset'.'*

Graham looked gloomily as he recalled his first Christmas morning in France. 'I knew the bloody thing wasn't a turkey. Well if it was it was a bloody queer one with no fat at all. It couldn't get worse I thought but then I found out that the bars were shut in France on Christmas day. Dear God, no dripping and no beer. What next? Later on my wife was cooking dinner and my kids and I were playing games waiting for dinner. How I was looking forward to my pork crackling. I liked dripping and bread and pork cracking better than the meat. Sad, I know but it was my Christmas treat. I could smell the dinner cooking and getting ravenous. My wife came in from the kitchen and quietly beckoned me to come in. *What's up?* I said as I entered. She looked sheepish again and bent down and took out of the oven the roasting pan with the cooked sizzling pork out. She placed it on the worktop and took the pork off onto a carving plate. I looked intensively at it. It was as bald as a coot, and the only fat on it was thin layer of white soggy fat. *What's that?'* I shouted. She took a carving knife and carved a piece off. It was pink, not the pink blood of uncooked meat but the colour of bacon. And indeed, that was what it was – bloody ham. No cracking and no real meat, no bread and dripping and a turkey that wouldn't feed the cat. And one hundred and twenty nicker spent.'

Françoise laughed. 'It happens to us all. Did you learn the word for 'crackling?'

'Yup eventually for the next year and I realised that if I waited long enough Carrefour was selling hundreds of 'Dindes' frozen and natural and legs of pork for thirty quid! I guess the bloody butcher thought when I was pulling my fatty arm, I was telling him I was a fat bastard and liked ham!'

Giles was leaning on the bar, having cleared up several of the last customers tables. He laughed too and he added, 'Indeed, but sometimes the culture faux pas is the other way. The Holy Trinity Church at Maisons–Laffitte always put on a bonfire night and I always used to go and sell tickets at the gate of the church yard where the bonfire and fireworks were lit. A very chic older French couple were strolling down the beautiful tree lined avenue towards me and they saw the large bonfire over the wall and the people and activities and they asked me what was going on and could they come in. I told them in fluent French with a hint of mischief. *'Oh, this is the night where we celebrate in Britain the burning of Catholics.'* They scuttled down the road as fast as they could; France is secular but the Catholic is the majority religion. There's loads of history here of the Jacobites and the Catholic succession; Divine Right of Kings and all that.'

They chuckled at this historical lesson. Françoise thought she'd ask if any of them knew of anything about King James the second and if they knew anything left in the Château or the parish church that might explain anything about his links to secret societies and all the Da Vinci code stuff. As her aunty lived here Jack's mate, Davey, had asked if she's check things out while she was there as he was thinking of writing a book about Saint- Germain and King James' links to a royal and sacred blood line.

'Yeah: there are lots of references and clues to all that in and around the town and the Château. In fact, there may be something in the cellar here,' said Giles.

'What here in your cellar?' Françoise asked incredulously.

'Well when I bought the bar. The sellers handed over some ancient codicil to the deeds. They told me that when they had bought the property the notary had told them that the property was built on the site of the house of the mistress to a King. We always thought that must have been king Louis, but recently I have found an inscription on the cellar walls that might be more relevant to King James and what you are interested in. Do you want to see it?'

'Oh yes please Giles,' Françoise replied, feeling quite excited. Surely this is too much of a co-incidence she mused. But well, things have been a bit a roller coaster lately so why not suck it and see.

Giles opened up the cellar hatch which was in the middle of the room. All of the lunchtime customers had left now. They descended into the cellar, full of beer kegs and food stocks for his thriving restaurant. Giles chuckled and turned to Françoise. 'Did Jack ever tell you about Youssef and his cellar?'

'No, he never did,' answered Françoise.

'Well Youssef and Jack became great friends. Youssef was his surrogate Imam as he spent hours drinking with Jack and teaching him about Islam. Jack was convinced he was about to launch a Jihad on the West. He and Youssef got on together so much that Youssef always promised him that if anyone harmed him or his family - he and his nephews '*would lock them in cellar*'. Every time I come down here, I think of Youssef and his unique protection of Jack from infidels.'

Françoise smiled, 'Yes, Jack said he met some strange people here Giles. Is Whispering John still around?'

'No sadly he has disappeared. Who knows where? But he was another one. Whispering was linked to the East End of London. Jack was convinced he was on the run but again they got on like a house on fire. Whispering promised that anyone harmed Jack's family and they would lose the use of limbs. Both Yousef and Whispering so different, but Arab or Cockney, they had a similar bond, they only ever spoke in whispers and both dealt in extreme violence. And they never spoke if anyone was in proximity. It was as if they were always being watched. Jack left here paranoid, poor lad.'

'He still is. Now I know why,' giggled Françoise.

'Look here is the inscription chiselled into the stone,' Giles said. He realised he too was speaking in whispers. '*Stop it for God's sake. You'll get like Jack*', he whispered again to himself.

'Sorry what did you whisper Giles?' Françoise asked.

'Nothing important, here shine that torch on this.' And he handed a torch to Françoise.

The torch lit up a finely chiselled set of words. They were in seventeenth century French so she struggled to make the whole sentence out. Giles could see her straining to translate and he helped her. 'I have asked a lady from the Lycée International College here in Saint G. It translates as:

Rex quondam rexque futurus. He holds the cup. Avalon is the Vine and the Cornerstone.

'Does it mean anything to you? Loads of people have come up with hundreds of solutions and explanations over the years,' Giles asked his lady cellar mate.

'To be honest Giles, it means nothing to me. I'll take a photograph and write the translation down and take it back to Davey. He might know. My aunty is quite clever with these things she might know something.'

'Come on then. I have to close up. I'll buy you one last drink and have my lunch with you.'

Giles and Gina sat at the bar and had their lunch which Bernie had sent down the dumb waiter for them. Bernie had come down from the upstairs kitchen and warmly greeted Françoise. *What a lovely friendly man* she thought as he left to get on his motor bike for a few hours break with his family before starting cooking again. Graham was still there and they were chatting again about the writing in the cellar and how the translation may be incorrect. Ancient French to Modern French to English could possibly go wrong.

'Nothing went as badly lost in translation as I managed when I first came here.' Graham said morosely again.

'Yes. That was a bit of a cock-up mate,' Giles confirmed. Gina chuckled.

Graham continued. 'I used to go to the bars on Rue de Paris to learn French and get in with the locals. I went to Jackie's bar a lot as I like Jackie and the crowd in there. Jack used to get in there Françoise,' he said. Françoise nodded and he continued again. 'Yes, he was in every afternoon after this place shut and he would be with Yousef. Yousef preached to him most days so I sat at the end of the bar with the, lovely ex actor, the French voice of the character Ross Geller in Friends, Michelle. He couldn't speak English and I could only speak bits of French but we got on well. Jackie would assist where he could in translation. Anyway, I learnt lots of ways to speak colloquial French rather than my O level grammar stuff.'

'Get on with Graham; I'm shutting up in two minutes,' said Gina.

'OK, just a minute then. Well I had just started attending The Holy Trinity Church, where Giles mentioned the bonfire night burning of Catholics, and this Sunday I was there. I was hoping to bond with the local congregation and meet make some friends. It was absolutely freezing as I took my seat next to a beautifully dressed, old but quite attractive French lady. Feeling confident I thought I'd use my new found French I'd learned of Michelle and Jackie and wish her well and mention how cold the weather was. She greeted me with the usual *'bonjour monsieur and ca va?'* and I answered *'ca va bien merci'*...and thought I'd tell her it was cold, so I said *'ca caille'*. She looked at me as if I had just farted, her face screwed up and she turned to move away, mumbling and cursing in French. I sat alone all through the service with the ladies whispering and pointing at me. End of my brief moment of religious freedom.'

Françoise looked at him, she knew what he had done, and he wasn't quite correct but she didn't want to spoil his story so she asked him to explain if he could what he had said wrong.

'Well I didn't have a clue until I came here for a beer at twelve. I told Giles and he laughed and said where I learnt *'ca caille'*. I said that I always said *'C'est froid'* which I took to be, 'it's cold' but Jackie told me the common way to say it was, *'ca caille'*. And every time I saw the lads in the bar I said *'ca caille'* and they just nodded, shrugged as they do and answered back, *'oui, ca caille'*. So, what was wrong with that? Giles laughed and told me. *'Well 'ca caille' can mean a few things but for 'the lads in your bar' it meant; 'my balls are frozen' or 'it's cold enough to freeze your balls.'*

A laughing Giles interrupted Graham. 'On that note we'll go, shall we? I don't think Graham is joining the Vicar's tea party anytime soon. Are you back in tomorrow Françoise?'

'No. I am spending the day with my aunt, and then flying back the next day. It was great to meet you all. I'll tell Jack all about the place.'

'Same here. Good to meet you. Give Jack and his family our love,' Gina said and kissed her each side of her cheeks.

'Tell Jack you've been locked in Yousef's cellar and watch him twitch,' Giles shouted after her laughing.

She took the RER back and cleaned up for dinner with her aunt. Over dinner they talked about the day and the coded message in the cellar.

'Well to me Françoise it's possible the lake of Avalon is where your King Arthur is supposed to have been taken up to heaven. What it has to do with vines I do not know. But I bet 'the cup' is referring to the Grail and we now know it was held in Tintagel, Arthur's castle.'

'It seems amazing that King James or whoever in his court would know all that those days and write it on a cellar wall and that it is still secret today and we have to decipher it now,' Françoise said, still shocked at how things were unravelling and how fast.

'I feel many over the years have known what the code means. But few know where the 'cup' is now. If indeed any one person does. Avalon puzzles me. I have never heard Jean-Luc speak of Avalon or the vine; only of the 'one who holds the secret of the vine'. Maybe it is just all about Christ's last supper and the cup he used to pass the wine around - the Holy Grail of all those King Arthur tales. Avalon is in your part of England isn't it?'

'I have no idea. Let me Google it.' A minute or so later she had found out that Avalon was indeed not far from Teignmouth and was thought to be Glastonbury, in Somerset.

'Lots of mythical and arcane history around there aunty and it's full of weirdoes and pagan worshipers every summer at the festival. The abbey is thought to be sacred for many cults and religions. So maybe there is something linked to our message on *The Bitter End* cellar wall and Tintagel. What it is though, I can't be bothered to think about anymore. I really need to sleep Aunt Edith. I am worried about you when I leave. Come and stay with us? Or go down to see Mother in Brittany please.'

'No, my darling, I will see my time out where Jean –Luc and I had so many happy memories. I am sure my love is watching over me wherever he is and his friends will not let me down. Go back to your lovely husband and find that what lost. I will be in touch if you get near. I feel you may need help when you face the two who need it so much.'

Françoise kissed her aunty goodnight and the next day she flew back to Exeter. What a story she had to tell Jack. And what a story he had to tell her.

CHAPTER THIRTEEN

Jack met Old Jim Smith in *The Ship Inn.* Jim was a regular and was comfortable with the pub. *The Ship* was an old pub that overlooked the estuary and the back beach. Immensely popular with tourists and locals alike for its ambience, location right on the beach and fishing quay and it's very good food. Today it was busy, but most were drinking outside on tables or the wall next to excellent *Crab Shack* seafood restaurant, so Jim and Jack managed to get a couple of stools in the bar corner next to the window that overlooked the estuary with stunning views up to Dartmoor.

Jim talked about Françoise and where was she. Jack explained that she had gone to see her aunt who had told her that somehow she was linked to French invasion and she really was interested now in all of this treasure hunt. Jim looked worried and anxious and said so. 'Jack, I really don't know how you both got involved in this but maybe it's too deep for all of us. Charlie told me that he gave you his part of the code. Did you find out what it means?'

Jack was unsure of where to go. Was Jim really going to help or was he one of those trying to stop them. The more he told, the more the risk of not finding it or, worse, getting hurt. He looked at Jim and decided that if Charlie had come clean after all these years then maybe Jim should be trusted now. So, her told him of the Church and what they'd found. He did not say anything about the two men.

'Wow. So, there was a grave of one of the family's ancestors with a secret message buried all the way in Dartmoor. I really was never told that. I think only Albert must have had that link and Charlie. He was probably my great, great, great grandfather who was with the other smugglers who stole the Frogs' treasure. Have you spoken to one of the Jobs yet?'

'No, who are they?'

'Like the many branches of my family, they were here in the beginning and were on the boat that smuggled the treasure. The French were so angry they burnt all their ships and homes and they were exiled to live in Torbay. When they recovered, they started the Teignmouth fishing in Newfoundland and set up their fishing business at the New Quay. Which is why the pub next door is called *The New Quay.* One of the old men is still around. He lives in Newton Abbott. I believe he could be one of us; a keeper of clues.'

'Well thank you for that Jim. Let me get you another pint. What are you having?'

'I'll take a Tribute thank you, Jack,'

Jack came back with the beer and asked Jim if he had anything else to tell him.

'Well Jack, like Charlie, my uncle handed down the same garbled type of message. I brought it along. Here, read it and tell me what the hell it means.'

Where the Angels sing and the Bishop broke the bread. The Chalice hides the truth.

Jack looked again at the message. No idea what that all means. All he could think was the clue they had surmised at Widdecombe was linked to this:

Look for the rabbits in the church who point to the nuns and he who wears the crown will show the Grace of God.

Françoise had convinced him that the nuns referred to Trinity School old convent in Teignmouth. What that had to do with a mythical crowned figure he had no idea.

'Jim, who wrote these messages? And surely they can't have been here forever. The grave was moved in Widdecombe from its original place. So, if these are ancient then it would not be relevant anymore as new developments come on stream, people die, buildings knocked down'

Jim said, 'There are four of us who hold the clues. We were sworn by Albert to keep this secret and never to reveal the clues to each other or anyone else. It is the pact we make on taking up the responsibility. Albert would tell us if any of our clues needed changing. It seems he was responsible for managing the clues and changes to their locations. He must have inherited the role of keeper of the clues.'

Jack looked puzzled and said so, 'Why bother with clues? If Albert was told the location of the treasure why didn't he just keep it secret and pass it on to next keeper of the location?'

'Because if the one keeper died suddenly then it would be lost forever or if he had the clue information safe somewhere and it was burnt or lost, then again it's gone forever. I believe our ancestors wanted all to share the responsibility but not everyone to have all the knowledge. They hoped to protect each other and to allow the man who bore the biggest responsibility to have a failsafe option in the event of his death or capture and loss of the final solution. Not perfect I agree but no one ever expected to learn what we were protecting or ever let anyone know how to find out. It seems Albert is the first to die without passing on his responsibility and the first to set in motion the quest to solve the clues and find the treasure. And for some reason, known to him, he was trying to tell Françoise what it was and where to find it when he passed away. If he hadn't, we would have been waiting for his successor to come forward. If no one did, then we have all sworn to get together to attempt to solve the clues and find the location. We were sworn however to keep it secret again and appoint a *keeper of the clues*. Albert seems to have thrown a spanner in those works.'

'It seems a bit complicated and unnecessary to me. But I guess it's worked for four centuries,' Jack said, not really understanding why they just didn't bury the thing somewhere and write the location down and give it to a lawyer in the event of death to be given to the next holder.

Jim semi-explained his question: 'It was the old way and we have kept that tradition. All we were told is that this bloody secret would change all that we believe to be right here in our small world of Devon. We were never told that anyone from the rest of the world would be so interested or do anything to find and destroy it. To the people here over the years it was really a family tradition that we all bought into and kept away from outsiders. A bit like being in the Freemasons, you know some things but not all, and only the highest degree can know it all, if indeed he knows that. We still believe someone was controlling Albert. And like the Freemasons we are sworn to keep it to ourselves. A bit of fun we thought and tradition, that's all. I guess Albert has decided it's time to give it up. Well, best of luck. We hope you share what you find with the four of us. After four centuries it would be good to know what we have kept hidden.'

Jack confessed some of the recent history. 'Jim, I'm not sure really I want to carry on with this. There are people out there who seem to want to stop Françoise and at any cost. This may be dangerous.'

'You have to Jack. If Albert has not given to knowledge of the location to a successor then it could be lost forever. The clues must be deciphered and the location known. If you don't want to discover what it contains and what it means, then one of us four will take up Albert's position and we will move the location to prevent those that you have said are chasing you get to it. I am sure Albert didn't want it given to people for harmful things and if he wants you to discover it, then maybe you should and we can all sleep in our beds at last.'

Jack took a drink and nodded. He didn't really agree but he was thinking about the man in graveyard, the one dressed in black with the local accent, who had warned them that he wanted to be given it and 'use it for his own good'. It seems he wants to reveal or use whatever it is publicly and will hurt people to make sure it is. So, Albert will get his way if they give it to him. Why not just do what Albert wanted? Or did he want this man to have it? He may well get violent if they let Jim and the keepers hide it again. He shook his head. This was altogether too puzzling and also becoming terrifying. It was time to have another beer. And he did, so he walked down the road to the oldest pub in Teignmouth and one that may well have held the booty stolen off the French ships all those years ago; *The Jolly Sailor*. And there he met Charlie and the buoys again on their twice weekly walk about town.

'Do you know that this pub has been here since eleven thirty-two? It was where the Teignmouth to Shaldon Ferry docked originally and was called *The Ferryboat*. Do you know buoy that the Teignmouth to Shaldon ferry has been running since at least twelve ninety-six and probably was here in Roman times? Nearly a whole thousand years this pub has been here,' Bert said. He carried on his normal history lesson. 'When the French invaded, they searched the pub up and down for something people say. They left he standing as even the French needed a drink and he was the only ale house. What they were looking for no one knows. The booze the buoys nicked off the ships was long gone up to Bishopsteignton they say. The pub was once on an island, Rat Island, as the River Tame then flowed into the Teign and cut the Jolly off. He be called Rat Island because of the rats that lived in the wooden houses built on the back beach and quayside those days. The back room here was once The Smugglers Bar, the French should have looked up the chimney, it's where the monks used to hide during King Henry's reformation and also the Royalists during the Civil War. If there was anything hidden, he might have been up there?'

'Maybe that's where the ghost hides?' said Roy, the other member of the Three Tenors.

'What ghost?' Jack asked.

'What he says?' asked Bert to his fellow band members. Deaf Bert was what Jack affectionately called Bert as he lived habitually in a world of misunderstandings and out of context conversation. The habitual ear syringing by his doctor had little effect on his hearing.

'Get your lugs done! You owld bugger you,' Charlie shouted across Jack and Bert. 'He's asking about the ghost hiding up the wassel.'

'Oh, the ghost,' Bert said, happy to be back on track: 'Yes Jack, that ghost still haunts the place. It seems it follows Darren the landlord's missus around and moves chairs and things. This place has many secrets. He also be doing smashing *Jail Ale* and grub - nothing better.'

106

Jack saw Charlie look at him in a strange unfamiliar way, as if he knew something but was not about to add to the conversation. And he suddenly changed the conversation completely as if to distract Jack and Bert from talking any more about *The Jolly* and its secret past. 'The Old Quay pub had a ghost. They reckon he be the ghost of Ringo.'

Jack smiled, seemed like we were back to the old days on the docks yet again and he played the usual game of 'tell me more lads'. 'I've heard of Ringo.'

'Yeah, He was Stan, Marty's father in law's monkey,' Charlie answered.

'A monkey in the pub; that must have been a laugh then,' said Jack, happily knowing fine well that he was about to hear tales of mayhem in *The Old Quay* pub.

'Yes, Ringo was...' and he was interrupted by a lost Bert.

'*The Jolly* has loads of history and the food here is bloody great. I could eat...' Bert interrupted, back still on his original conversation having not heard a word.

'You daft bugger, we are talking about Ringo the monkey now,' Charlie said exasperated.

Bert in blissful audio compromised ignorance continued unabated, 'There is a ghost in Shaldon. He be the ghost of the highway man who shot a coach driver in the seventeen hundreds on Picket Hill.' The other three just stood shaking their heads and let him finish. 'Commons Old Road is known as 'Murder Lane' and still has steps cut out there for the passengers to get out of coach to allow it ascend the hill.'

'Thanks Bert,' Jack shouted. 'Charlie is talking about Ringo the Monkey.'

'Oh arh? I goes and has a cig.' And he left to smoke outside.

'One day I'm going to buy Bert a bloody ear trumpet,' Jack said. 'I saw one on Amazon. I'll get him it for a laugh for Christmas. Anyway, what was the craic about the monkey?'

'Stan used to keep him in the rafters of the pub. *The Old Quay Pub* was our main drinking den for elevenses. Bill Arnold the landlord was always trying to catch Ringo and stop him causing mayhem. But the monkey was a clever sod. The monkey jumps down from the rafters and picks the crisps from anyone's packet. Kev tries to eat one of his and Ringo bites him and took the top of his finger off. He pinches the bag and runs all over the pub chased by a bleeding Kev.'

Jack and Roy smiled. Roy had heard all this before. He had been a friend of Charlie for nearly 70 years and they holidayed together in the Wild West of America many times with families. Roy had adopted the

American cowboy accent and when pissed, which was often, he spoke American cowboy language and would break into song in a Nashville country accent. Hence, he was named The Teignmouth Yank.

Charlie continued with his simian story. 'On elevenses Lofty was looking forward to his pint and sandwiches when he pulled out of his box a Kit Kat. He was chuffed because this was a real treat. He strips the silver paper off and was about to eat it when Ringo swings down from the rafters and pinches it out of his hand and runs back up. It sat eating it, chattering way at Lofty as he tried to bash it with Bill's sweeping brush. The money just jumps and sits and eats some more, chattering down and laughing.'

'It seems to have caused some grief to the buoys Charlie?' Jack said.

'Not as much as it did to Bill's ginger tom cat. The cat came in looking for some scraps from the buoys' pasties. Ringo sees the cat and jumps down from the rafters. Matey swaggers over, swinging his little body from side to side like *Buster Scroggs* the gun slinger, and gets behind the cat and jumps onto its bag. The cat hisses and howls and tries to arch its back and whirls around like a banshee. The monkey just holds on like an American rodeo rider and stays on its back as the cat jumps across the stools and tables scattering beer and pasties. Stan shouts to Bill, '*Catch him!*' Bill howls back, 'You *bloody catch him. I'm not getting near the crazy bastard.*'

Charlie chuckled as did Jack and they took another drink. 'Yes, that monkey caused some wassel. Matey used to jump down and pinch the change on the bar if Bill put it there for a customer. He'd run up his pole to the rafters and throw it down at them. Kev's dad won the fruit machine jackpot and Ringo pinched most of it and put it in his mouth. The pockets in his cheeks were full up and he sat staring at Kev's dad in law chattering away. No one was brave enough to prise its mouth open. He be hiding up in the rafters. Bill had to get ladders for Kev's dad to try getting the coins back while Ringo kept biting his fingers. We laughed like hell!'

'Poor Bill, he seems to have a pub with character, if not a zoo!' Jack cracked.

'Oh, there was everything in there buoy. He had his own chicken on the bar. She was called Dolly. She had only one leg and stood on the bar. When he pulled pints, she'd have a drink out of them; days long gone before environmental health and all that. She laid an egg in his till one day. When Bill opened it up the egg rolled out, he dove and tried to catch it before it hit the floor and broke his nose on a crate of beer and ended up on his arse, covered in egg. We howled at the daft bugger. Dolly just hopped up on the bar and took a sup out of Marty's beer.'

'Some bar that mate,' Jack said.

'Aye buoy, he certainly be. Kev was only a young lad when he joined the quay. He started with Bill before Bill took the pub on. They both had to count slates all day, every day. They had to earn their positions. Marty and me were top gang by then. Kev drank in there as a kid when it was run by Plymouth Breweries and one day he was sitting at elevenses and he nearly collapsed under the table and keeled over with a heart attack. Bill had pulled out a twelve-bore shotgun from under the bar and loosed off two barrels at the floor next to Kev, just missed his feet. 'What the hell was that for?' Kev shouted.

Bill shouted back, 'That bloody rat, I'll get it one day,'

Jack and Roy chuckled and Charlie was on a roll about Bill and the old *Quay Pub*.

'Bill ran he like an Indian trading post. If matey asked for a brandy or whisky, he'd look around him his eyes moving like a shit house rat, then he'd nod and wink at matey and he'd whisper: *'Above or below the counter?'* Which meant did we want the smuggled stuff under the counter? It was cheaper and stronger. His downfall was he agreed to be filmed by the TV. Us still has the VCR tape. They interviewed him in his pub, standing at the bar, no Dolly, Ringo, rats, parrots, cats, or donkeys and dogs but just barrels and bags of food and provisions which he told them were 'donated' by the good captains of the ships and that he helped out the poor with then. He foolishly says he pays cash for it. Two weeks later he was raided by the Customs and Excise 'black gang'. Sadly, the stuff he had out for TV he normally kept under the counter and sold on to the buoys in the bar. It seems the Customs buoys weren't too pleased with the cash changing hands and lack of duty paid on the goods. After that he parted company with the pub.'

Bert came back in and butted in. 'There be another ghost in the Castle pub in Holcombe...'

To be greeted by all three, 'For God's sake Bert, get them syringed.'

Charlie just continued over Bert. 'The next one to take over was Monty. He was a barrel of laughs, he'd just stand and watch the lads getting pissed and smoking and then he'd say, 'When you see the floor full up with cigarette ends buoys, there's an empty ash tray over there. He was dry as anything. Mind you his customers were something out of the Star Wars bars. When he would watch them and their antics he'd say,' *we once called it family; here we call it in breeding!'*

'I'll get this round in buoys, 'Bert said, 'and anyone wants a pie?' Bert loved his food.

'I don't bloody eat and drink,' Charlie exclaimed. 'In the old days us only ate at lunch and then only a pasty. Elevenses were for a drink. *The Quay Pub* for elevenses and then *The Teign* for lunch an hour later. Most were half pissed by elevenses as we have had a drink over the rail with Captain at about six am or eight. Our coffee was always topped up as well by bottles of brandy from the ships. No one took the Cognac good stuff mind, only the cheap Three Barrels stuff. The Cognac was for sale. You could tell who had worked on a good ship as they all had red faces, half pissed!'

'These pies are lovely...Jack are you making some for the next City game?' Bert butted in again, blissfully ignorant of the Quay story.

Charlie just ignored him, as he had done for thirty years and continued. 'Harold the store man loved his elevenses and his lunch. If you were not on peace work loading or emptying a ship, you were put into Harold's store on day rate work. He did nothing but give you the huge bags and barrels to hump around. Then he'd go to *The Quay Pub* for elevenses. He'd come back for an hour and then go for his dinner at *The Teign*. He'd come back after an hour or so and wait a while and say, 'I'm just heading off to sort the tickets out for the queer fellow' and you'd find him blooted in *The Quay Pub* when we finished work.'

'A character then?' Jack enquired, stating the obvious and expecting more. He was not disappointed.

'Most days he sits with two of his mates. No one dare sit in their seats. It's like that bloody Social Club, the Legion now; pain of death to sit in their seats. They all drinks rough cider, about a couple of pennies a pint. It was lethal stuff. They also never stopped sniffing snuff from little wooden boxes. I fixed Harold's hinges for him in my Carpenters Arm's store. In between the lethal rough cider and the snuff, they drinks from their cough medicine bottles. He be having morphine and cocaine in the formula *'for our coughs from the grain and sand boats'* they says every time they took a drink. They were stoned most of the time and their noses dripped because of the snuff, like cocaine addicts now. Droplets hung off the old buggers' noses and I watches one day when a huge droplet falls into Harold's cider. It looked like an oil slick. He looked at he for a while floating on top and then supped he.'

Roy and Jack laughed again. Bert stared singing, *'Paint it black,'* he was into his Rolling Stones mode now.

'The funny thing about all this was one day a young lad came in. Those days you'd call him a beatnik. He had longish hair and a Beatles

110

type suit on. Harold turned to his mates and said, loud enough for the young lad to hear, *'Look at him. Those beatniks are all drug addicts.'* As he took a large swill of his umpteen percent scrumpy and his mates overdosed on snuff and narcotics from their cough bottles. Yes, we had good old days in *The Quay Pub'*

'Let's move on *The Devon Arms*. As The Animals sang, 'we *gotta get outta this place,'* said Bert, drinking off his beer.

Roy staggered into his Elvis pose, hips loose and bent, hands outstretched at his sides, and puts on his American twang. 'That's right buddy, there's a whole lotta drinking we buddies gotta do and whole lotta loving.' and as he swung his hips and arms Elvis fashion he broke into – *'On a cold and grey Chicago mornin'…in the ghetto'.*

'Come on you daft twats. I'm thirsty,' Charlie exclaimed for the hundredth time in his life to the Two Tenors and they walked to *The Devon Arms*.

As they entered Roy immediately put several Elvis songs on the jukebox and did his Elvis impression in the middle of the bar, much to the amusement of the assembled masses… *'uh, uh, uh, love me tender, love me…'* Bert just sang Stones' songs to himself watching the floor show. Charlie shook his head and Jack told Charlie in a moment of privacy that he had met with Jim and knew about the ways of their secret agreement.

'I didn't want to say anything buoy as I am never sure what I can say. But if Jim also knows what I knew and is one of us and has talked, well, let's get on with it all and move on. I hope you talk to old man Job, I bet he knows more than most. They are the oldest family around, along with the Hooks. And the family was massively important to the town after the invasion. You should head over to Shaldon and talk to Gordon Hook as well, we'll come with you. Roy loves singing over there and Kev likes a stroll. Mind you Roy is still traumatised over what he saw there as a young one. It's changed a bit now with all these posh and rich Londoners coming in. Did I tell you the last time we were over?'

'No Charlie,' Jack replied, knowing fine well even he had, he'd still hear the story.

'As you know we all lives in Kingsway. The council estate always thought as the roughest ever since we were kids. And as you know we have the best views in Teignmouth though; over the Ness, the estuary and the sea and overlooking Shaldon. We face South West too so get the sun all day and evening sunsets. Shaldon is in the dark most of the morning and nearly all winter. And they pay a million pounds a house! Daft buggers: Well anyway. Kev, Roy and me are standing taking a breather after walking from *The Shipwrights Arms* to *The Ferryboat* to have one last pint and take the ferry back over to Teignmouth when this couple comes up to us and the man, says in a very posh accent, *'It's beautiful here isn't it?'* We grunted. He carried on. *'We've just arrived from the South East, haven't we darling?'* His partner said nothing but smile and he continued, *'bought a beautiful house on the hill. It's wonderful but the views are spoilt by that monstrosity over there.'* And matey points to our estate over the water on the top of Teignmouth. He then says, *'I am raising a petition to the council and I am well connected with... 'The Party' so will contact the local MP, to get it knocked down and decent quality development built there. God only knows the type of people who live there.'* I stopped Kev hitting him. Roy put his best Yank accent on and in heavy Don Corleone speak told him, *'Heh buddy, we all lives in that monstrosity. And if you don't **** off, you'll sleeping wi the fishes in the lazy river there a ways.'* I just told his nice maid, *'Best take him back to London. The natives are restless.'*

Jack chuckled at this. 'There are some posh buggers over there for sure. But it's full of pubs and some characters and I'm sure everyone has a story to tell mate.'

'I've always thought that the secret was buried over there somewhere. Maybe moved onto The Salty when it was built in the estuary or was always under the river there; buried with the treasure from The Black Pig. They say *The London Inn* goes back as far as *The Ship* and *The Jolly*. There were smugglers' tunnels from *The London Inn* to the beach and when it was coaching house it probably had smugglers and highwaymen hiding in the tunnels. I've always loved history and tales of pirates and guns and things. Did I tell you I used to have lots of antique weapons?'

'Yeah, I think you did mention it mate.'

'Us had collected lots of guns; many from British history and some from the American West. It was a sad day I lost them.'

'Why? What happened, Charlie?'

'It was the day after the Black Gang had arrived and locked up Col. My wife was frightened that if they had found the booze and the guns I'd have been locked up for years. She told me to throw them off the quay. So, the next day I took them all down to the quay and threw them in. The next day I came to work and there were the police with divers dragging the river next to the quay! I was terrified and thought about jumping on a ship out. They dragged but then all they come up was a pile of dead fish and fish heads and guts. But I expected them to arrest me any minute; someone must have seen me throw them in and reported me. But I then found out that a local bad lad had pulled a gun on a bank official in Newton Abbott and he'd confessed to the police the same day I threw my guns in that he'd thrown his in the quay too!'

'Bloody hell Charlie. That was unlucky. Did they find them?'

'No, they didn't. Yes, it was unlucky. Who the hell would expect that? Anyway, there must be my set of guns buried in the river somewhere. Maybe they'll find them when they find the treasure! And my mate hadn't thrown the gun in anyway, he was telling the coppers porkies - the bastard and I lost my collection and could have been banged up for it.'

Roy stopped singing Elvis songs and came over and had picked up on the craic about guns. 'Jack, us enjoyed America buoy, guns everywhere and the country songs were great. I could dance line dancing and we'd drink till dawn. Charlie used to tell them all about the quay and his guns. They loved the one about the Queen and the black lads.'

'Sounds good, Roy; what was that Charlie?'

Charlie chuckled a bit, took a drink and explained: 'The first darkies that ever came here on the ships were from Papua New Guinea. They were great workers and great buoys. They came from the same tribe in the wilds of New Guinea and were the first of their community to come to England. The missionaries had taught them about the Queen and all that stuff and when they sailed into the estuary and past Bittern Park, where the council offices were, they saw the grand offices. When they talked with us on the docks, they were desperate to meet the Queen as they thought something as big as the council offices must be Buckingham Palace!'

'It must have been amazing for anyone if you have lived in the jungle and sailed across the world to see a building like that?' Jack suggested.

'It was buoy. And they had never seen a gun in their lives. Us had found an old Martini Henry rifle in a boat full of scrap: the gun that the British used to stop the Zulu at Rorke's Drift. I had fixed he and put he in a vice in my store, *The Carpenters Arms*. I asked them to come and see how he worked. They had never seen a gun or heard of one in their lives. I filled he with ball bearings, gunpowder from all the fireworks Pete, Jackie's dad had got from the store below, and had a rope fixed to the trigger. I told the buoys from New Guinea let's hide downstairs. I pulled the rope and the gun exploded. The bugger blew the *Carpenter's Arms* home- made bar to bits with the ball bearings and gun powder! It took me ages to fix he. The New Guinea lads loved it all. They were the best workers we had and the Cape Verde Islanders and Filipino and Indonesians were great, lovely people and hard workers. The Poles were not so good and then we got the Russians...they changed after Perestroika. They were terrified to do much before that as the KJB on board controlled them.'

'Come on: let's head to *The New Quay* and *The Ship*. My taxi's due at four,' Bert shouted across Roy singing, wriggling his hips and arms again *'uh uh uh uh, the wonder of you,'* Jack declined the offer. Also, he would leave the Russian invasion of Teignmouth till another day.

The next day Jack had to meet Françoise when she arrived back from France and they needed to get to Trinity school to search for the *'nuns and the crown'*: whatever that meant and now sort out the other clue he'd been given. He had heard nothing from her since her visit to her aunt and was looking forward to updating her. He did not know that Jimmy the Hat in *The Devon Arms*, not talking of course, had heard everything said in *The Ship* with Jim and in *The Devon Arms*. He left after Jack left and phoned a man in London.

CHAPTER FOURTEEN

Françoise met Jack in *The Pavilions*, the recent modern theatre and performing arts addition to the town. It has a cafe and restaurant that overlooked the sea and was in magnificent form today as the sun rose over the English Channel and The Grand Pier. It was constructed between 1865 and 1867 and is still a main attraction to for visitors and locals alike. Nearly washed away in the great storms of 2014, it held firm and plays host to many who enjoy the English sea side pleasures. *The Pavilions* since opening had given opportunities to many local and international artists, performers and societies to please the visitors' and members of the fine establishment. They both met for a coffee and an update.

Françoise told Jack about her adventures in Paris and the banlieues of Le Vésinet, Croissy- sur -Seine and St Germain. He was shocked and scared. 'Françoise, this is really getting out of hand. What started as a joke really is now a serious life-threatening thing. We should go to the British police. Surely we can trust them?'

'I am not letting my aunt get hurt again. We can do this Jack. Let's just get this cracked and then give the bloody thing to whoever wants it. Men in black or secret societies who want to create a new world order based on Jesus Christ's bloodline, I don't care. I just want Aunt Edith, my family and yours safe. Best way is to finish. Let's head up to Trinity and see what the hell that first clue meant. I contacted them and asked if we could write an article about the old convent days and would they let us look at the chapel and the old grounds and particularly where there may be sign of nuns or their graves or crosses.'

They walked up to the school and entered by the main gate to the school administration building, 'The White House'. There their identification was re-checked and cleared and they were given their pre-vetted visitor passes and a very helpful and knowledgeable admissions manager and very mature and respectful head girl of the school had been allocated to help and escort them through the grounds on their research.

The young admissions manger Lewis explained a lot about the history of the school.

'The site was originally a house of Religious Formation and Studies for the Redemptorist Order of priests and brothers on a farm which in 1796 was called 'Bugridge'. The estate was bought by the congregation of Notre Dame de Namur who opened it as a boarding school in 1901. On the 21st December 1976 all parents were informed that the

Convent School in Teignmouth was to close. It was widely felt that this would be a tragedy and, as a result of the action of some of the parents and the Anglican Chaplain, an attempt was made to save the school. This was eventually achieved through the hard work of a number of interested parents and staff. It was agreed early on that the school should be a Christian foundation and the joint Roman Catholic and Anglican foundation was established with the blessing of the Roman Catholic Bishop of Plymouth and the Anglican Bishop of Exeter, who became the joint Patrons. The parents' association committee, on historical grounds, had favoured St. Joseph's as the name for the school, picking the title of the original Redemptorist monastery on the site. This was felt by the Roman Catholic authorities to be too specifically Roman Catholic for a joint foundation and the name Trinity was eventually chosen since this was the third Christian foundation that had existed on the site. Trinity School opened on schedule in September 1979. Trinity School is a charitable trust and a company limited by guarantee. The trust bought the school from the Notre Dame order. Now we are a very successful co-educational school from early years to eighteen years old with a wide catchment across South Devon of day and boarding students of all abilities with many of our International boarders coming from all over the globe. Now we pride ourselves on providing a multi- cultural safe and challenging environment and a holistic education to students of all beliefs, non-beliefs or abilities. We are proud of the citizens we put out into the world.'

Françoise whispered to Jack, 'The kid's I've met from here seem to be very well rounded and helpful like this nice girl with us. Pleased I came, learnt a bit more today.'

Jack nodded in agreement and said 'Lots of mention of nuns and Trinity but where is our crown?'

Françoise pointed in front of her at large cross planted upon a grave and exclaimed, "Wow, there's one!'

They both moved quickly to look at the grave and the headstone. The headstone was a stone cross and on the vertical apex of the cross was a single crown carved into it. Across the transverse stone was written, "Rev. R. L. Schofield' and underneath, *Convictor Natus: 1892*.

'What are you looking for?' the nice admissions young man asked.

'Well, we have an old quote we found in our research in an ancient book which seemed to say there was a link to Trinity. It said '*look for the nuns and he who wears the crown will show the Grace of God*'. Weird I know, but we are in a graveyard full of nuns and here is a crown. Who was this Reverend?'

'I have no idea. He is not in the official history. I can Google him,' the young man said, and he opened his smart phone and searched. Jack did the same.

Françoise looked around the grave and the headstone and tried to line it up with something. She looked around at the other smaller stones and began checking them. All were nuns and some monks; none had any crown or any link to the 'crown stone'.

Jack shouted over to Françoise. 'He doesn't exist, as far as the internet is concerned,'

The young man kept plugged away at his phone. 'I am trying a few sites but nothing. I does seem that Convictor Natus means 'old friend' or it means 'born' I assume he was born eighteen ninety-two...but OBIIT means *he died* so I guess he died same year! Maybe it is just *old friend who died 1892.*'

Françoise had not been listening as she had stopped at a grave which also had a cross as a headstone but no crown. 'Do you know anything about this grave?'

The young man and the head girl walked over to Françoise. Jack continued searching on his phone for some link to the 'old friend' that might mean anything.

'Oh, that is Bishop Robert Coffin, at one time the Bishop of Southwark, He was a Redemptorist father. He died in this monastery in 1885 and was buried in the cemetery within the grounds. He often came here; it was if he was searching for something either spiritually or physically. He died suddenly and again it is strange but he is the only Bishop of Southwark never to been buried back in his Diocese. We have always wondered why that was and what was so important that he was buried so far away and here.'

'He is a Catholic I guess?' Françoise asked.

'Well he was an Anglican and was educated at Oxford. He was the Anglican vicar of the church of Saint Mary Magdalene but he left that faith to join band of the Oxford converts to modern Catholicism lead by Ambrose Lisle Philips at a place called Grace Deus and after that he was ordained a priest in Rome in 1847 and a Bishop in 1882. Interestingly, he was a member of the Association for the Promotion of the Unity of Christendom which was founded by a multi denominational group of religious leaders lead by Amboise Phillips. He himself had been an Anglican vicar until a meeting with strange Abbé sent over from a group of people in Paris. He was transformed into

117

visionary and aesthetic who was convinced the Anglican Church should be reconciled with Rome. It seems our Bishop Coffin was a member of this society and Teignmouth must have been important to him in his mission for those at Grace Dieu to be buried here.'

Jack had been looking up all this on his phone whilst the young man spoke and couldn't help but wonder if this was indeed 'the crown' they had to find. The Bishops crown. And certainly the death and burial here at a place mentioned in the clue and where the treasure was lost seemed much too co-incidental to him. *Maybe it was buried under his head stone?*

'I think this is the man the book referred to Françoise,' Jack interrupted as he walked over to the grave. 'The crown is reference the Bishop. A crown is the chess symbol for a Bishop and they are effectively crowned by the Holy See.'

'Sounds like it to me, 'the admissions man concurred, 'but what do you do with that information now? Didn't you say the book had another strange quote in it?'

Françoise who had been thinking seriously about all of these co-incidences had said nothing but she knew she had solved the clue. She knew nothing could be gained by carrying on in the graveyard and she decided to cut the tour short and answered blandly and untruthfully. 'Oh, nothing really: it's obvious now, the grace of God and the crown, just points to the Bishop. The book must be trying to describe his life and his dedication to his ecumenical work to unite faiths. It was a book on religious sects anyway. But that is great. We can write our book and include the Bishop and Trinity school as really interesting part of British Church history. Thank you so much for both of your help. Can we go back now?'

As they walked back down to Teignmouth, they both were lost in thought. Jack said he fancied a beer and as they ended up at the rail station, he suggested *The Brass Monkey Pub*, as it sold excellent St Austell's Tribute beer, was an accredited Camra Real Ale pub and had Bob, the only landlord who could do two cross words, write his tote double numbers and the lucky draw and write down the questions to the weekly pub quiz while serving a beer. It too was an old pub having been owned by successive Earl's of Devon as an old coaching Inn. Bob was the longest serving landlord apart from those in *The Devon Arms* and *The Castle*.

Jack explained. 'Don't expect him to have riveting conversation while he does it mind. Bob is a man of few words. *The Brass* is great when we want to sit and talk about this because you won't get him interrupting you and rambling on to you about anything but Aston Villa football club, his time as Michelin chef and the Sun crossword clues. No politics: no Religion and no lunatics, he keeps a good pub. We can talk and sort this out there. Mind you if his lovely wife, Jan is working, we might have to talk, as being from Lancashire she can chat and so can you, so we'll get nowt done. Let's hope Bob is doing his crossword and we can talk.'

Indeed Bob was working. He greeted them warmly, poured the beers and went back to work on his quiz and what 5 down was. Jack had often enjoyed the football craic with Bob at the bar when the crossword was done but today he took Françoise to a table and they tried to make sense of the morning's work.

'What do you think of all that then,' Jack asked Françoise as he enjoyed a cool beer.

Françoise smiled. 'I think I have solved what the Widdecombe clue meant. Well, no idea what to do next but I'm sure I know what it means. It seems to me that it may still be cryptic and point to something beyond our reach but you need the clue that Jim gave you to solve it. Think about it.'

Jack did think. He wrote the clue on a beer mat: He thought deeply.

and where he who wears the crown broke the bread the points the way'

'Well, we know he who wears the crown is probably Bishop Coffin. Oh, maybe the treasure is in his coffin?'

'Could be,' Françoise said. 'But the other clue says **where the Bishop broke the bread points the way**. And the Widdecombe clue, **Look for the rabbits in the church who point to the nuns and he who wears the crown... will show the Grace of God**. I think breaking the bread and the grace of God refer to Holy Communion and we have to now look for where this Bishop took Holy Communion to find the way to the treasure.'

'But that could be any Church! He was a Bishop for God's sake,' Jack uttered a bit too loud, as he seemed to disturb Bob on 'clue 25 across' and Bob shouted over, 'Another pint Jack?'

'No thanks Bob. In a minute please.' And he turned to Françoise and whispered, 'Françoise, he could have taken communion with the Teignmouth monks, at Southwark Cathedral or any church in his Diocese. And what about this Grace Deus stuff. I checked that out, there was an abbey built where this guy Ambrose De Lyle lived. It was located on a holy site from very early pagan and founded in 1235 and dedicated to St Mary and the Holy Trinity. Which might be interesting as the Bishop was a rector of another Saint Mary Magdalene church.

Anyway Ambrose built his manor near the priory. So, the whole Grace Dieu thing in the clue or maybe it's a secret society, could be where the Bishop broke the bread for them all?'

'I have thought that myself. I think there is more in this Grace Deus thing and why was the Bishop buried here and not at his Cathedral or if he had been a member of the Grace Dieu society, then why not take him back there? It is all too much Jack really. I think the people who have kept this secret treasure hidden for four centuries are more likely to reference local clues than this wild goose chase we seem to on with Priory of Sion, Grace Dieu, Holy Chalice's, Christ Blood Lines, Mary Magdalene and now a secret Bishop... think about the words of the last clue'

Where the Angels sing and the Bishop broke the bread. The Chalice hides the truth.

Jack thought a bit, took a drink, and suddenly had a thought, and he said out loud, 'Angels sing in Heaven!'

Françoise nodded. 'And also they can sing in Church. So, Jack, what is that to do with the clue?'

'We look for a Church with Angels I guess.'

'And where the Bishop broke bread; and when do you break bread?'

'At Holy Communion,' said Jack finally understanding.

'And just down the road we have St Michael the Archangel. Anglican I know, but this Bishop seemed to want the whole of the Catholic and Anglican Church to join together again as one European rule, so he may well have broke bread there. It hardly matters, the clue points to that being correct and it's the only option we have unless we go hunting around Leicestershire and Southwark. I think everything points to Teignmouth, and Saint Michael's, hence the Bishop's burial here.'

'By George I think she's got it!' Jack shouted out, in mimicry of the musical 'My Fair Lady'. And he shouted over to Bob, who had finished The Sun crossword and was looking through his facts books to write another Quiz clue, 'Bob two more mate.'

Bob looked thoughtful and picked his book and pen up and walked over to pull the beer. 'By George'...That could be a good clue Jack – 'Who said that, and then, what musical?' Thanks mate.'

Jack came to the bar and chuckled at Bob. 'You have to be careful Bob with quotes from that movie. Deaf Bert and The Teignmouth Yank, Roy were singing 'On the Street Where You Live' the other day when Charlie and me realised that you really shouldn't be singing that these days; you'll never get away with it. It's all about a man who stalks a lady by walking up and down her street peering into her window all day and night.

'*I often stalk down the street you live*' As Charlie always says: '*you just canna say that anymore*'. And if you do it, well you'll be banged up. God knows what George Bernard Shaw would have said.'

The retired Dole Catcher Tony had overheard and laughed. He was on his weekly few beers with his mate, Robbie the ex postman, and he said, 'Hello my hansom, let me buy you and Françoise that, and come and join us.'

Jack said, 'Yes ok,' and he asked Françoise to join him at the bar. He fancied a laugh after such a serious morning and Robbie was always fun. Eccentric of course like most of the locals around these parts and he could hardly understand his broad Devon accent when he was pissed and also, he spoke like a machine gun normally, fast and in bursts.

Françoise joined them and seeing Tony in shorts with his leg looking nicely healed she asked kindly, 'I see Rollo's bite has healed nicely Tony.'

'Bloody dog, thinks I'm still working for Christ's sake. That's the last time I drink in that end of town.'

Robbie the postman got excited and stammered out: 'Dogs, they were the bane of my bloody life. Did I tell you about the T Rex?' And he didn't wait until anyone answered and stammered out his terrifying tale.

'This dog was bulldog thing. He had jaws like a T Rex. The bloke was a nightmare and he wouldn't keep he in or on a lead. So, head office wrote a letter to him to tell him I'll stop delivering unless he ties dog up or keeps he in. I takes the letter and luckily the dog isn't out. Us knocks on the door as he be recorded delivery. Matey shouts from inside an open bedroom window *Sod off* I knocks again, this time after a minute, he shouts out, *Bloody Jemima Witnesses*…and then the bastard empties a bucket of water over my head.'

Everyone laughed; Jack loved the '*Jemima witnesses*', typical Robbie misunderstanding. The poor water sodden man continued his tale:

'The post office sent him another letter. I looks over the wall and up the drive and the dog is fast asleep and I thought I sees a leash on him. So, I goes up the big hill of the drive and half way up the bloody dog wakes up. He becomes one of them T-Rex's and starts chasing me back down the hill. The milk man had arrived and all he hears is a small bark and couldn't see the bloody reptile running down from its lair. He shouts at me laughing, '*What's wrong Robbie; it's only a dog man.*' And just then the dog comes around the bend and stands up on its two legs just like a T Rex and hurtles down, his teeth chattering like a crocodile. The milk man says, *'Sod this,'* drops his six bottles of milk and both of us leap over a hedge and try to hide.'

Robbie clearly excited and still traumatised, got into a bit of a stammer, the rest were howling with laughter, but he continued the tale of woe again:

'The bloody owner strolls down in his pyjamas, puts his reptile on a lead, and says *'sorry'* and walks back up the hill, dragging the beast still snarling at us. We are still cowering behind the hedge. The dog stops, drinks a lot of the spilled milk and then seeing my post bag, lying in the milk and as it was Valentines' day with all the cards lying around the bag, the bloody dog cocks its leg and pisses all over my bag. The bloody owner just turns and smiled and said, *Happy Valentine's Day.* I looked at Alf, the milkman, and just said, *Well bugger me!'*

Everyone howled at poor Robbie's fate and the laconic way he took it. Jack thought what a lovely and kind man - a loss to post office and community when he retired.

Tony's wife came in on her way to her work. She said hello and Françoise decided to collar her as she was now Curator of the *Teignmouth and Shaldon Heritage Centre* or locally known as the Museum. She wanted to ask her if she could come and see her to search through the history of Teignmouth the museum kept as she was researching for a book on the French invasion and what happened to the town after. Lou told Françoise that they had an extensive library and documents and that many people in the town had written books which they kept and just lately someone had written a poem about it. They both agreed to meet up.

Jan arrived to bring Bob his sandwich lunch. And she stayed to join in the conversation with Françoise and Lou. The men's talk moved away from ferocious canine dinosaurs and French invasions to more mundane talk about gardening and horse racing and Aston Villa football club. The quest for the treasure would have to wait for another day.

But in the City of London two men were dining together. One of them was a Minister of the Crown, and in the British Government's Cabinet, the other was owner of a Merchant Bank. They were discussing a phone call the banker had had received from a man in St Germain-en-Laye. Both were worried and both were unsure what to do. But one thing was sure they could not let the two country bumpkins in Teignmouth destroy what they had built up over centuries. They talked about how to stop them.

CHAPTER FIFTEEN

The Minister spoke quietly across the table. 'Are you sure the items are safe? No one has tried to access it?'

The banker shook his head. 'No one; No one has opened the safe deposit box since it was bought from Saunière and deposited here the beginning of the century. However, the call from Saunière's relative in Saint Germain is disturbing. I am shocked that he knows about the two straw sucking amateurs from a country town in the West Country could find what was lost and unravel what we have kept secret in two thousand years.'

The Minister stared out of the window and looked at the view across London. His mind drifted to the last scare they had and curiously enough it had been in the same town. This could not be a co-incidence. It sounded as if the real secret was definitely located somewhere there. But apart from that, the man in St Germain was perennial problem. They had paid off his grandfather when he found the Cathar documents in the Church of Saint Mary Magdalene in Rennes le Château. The deal being that for his secrecy they would pay him and his descendants a considerable legacy each year for the return of the copy. Sadly, however Father Saunière and his advisors were not stupid and they had photographed the ancient documents which they kept in a secret place with the legal documents they had signed. They threatened if the money ever stopped, they would release these photographs. The originals were in the vault of the Merchant banker having lunch.

For one hundred and twenty years they had both kept this deal. Saunière, nor his descendants knew that these documents did not tell the whole truth, or tell what sensational purpose the Priory was going to use them for. The true secret had been lost in Teignmouth. The threat of revealing a false truth without any real proof was not great enough to destroy what they had worked for centuries but it was enough to cause too many prying eyes looking into their true purpose and the real truth. The sums of money were nothing to the Priory, and well worth keeping the Saunière's family quiet. The Priory still controlled the Templar wealth and secret treasure found under Solomon's Temple and secreted away during the Pope's crusade against the Templars and the Cathars. These funds had accumulated into fabulous wealth which could bring down governments so the few million paid to Saunière were nothing. These funds were controlled in part by the banker having lunch. The strategy they would be used for was in part managed by the other diner, the British Minister. Both were senior members of The Priory of Sion and its English brother, Grace Dieu.

He cursed the fact that this same town where the two were seeking the treasure also held another source of irritation and potential upset to their centuries' old plans. Those two sisters they kept in luxury in Cliffden at Mules Park had been a nuisance, but that was all. He cursed the fact that their ancestor had been the lawyer who had drawn up the agreement between Saunière and the Priory and he too, like Saunière, had wanted his share of the Templar treasure for him and his offspring. It was a small price to pay for their silence.

He cursed the fact that that interfering Bishop turned up at the Redemptionists' priory, the site of the new Trinity School in Teignmouth, searching for the truth. Despite his conversion to the true faith and joining Grace Deus, he was not senior or ready to know the esoteric secret he persisted in seeking out. They just could not trust another Saunière type of enlightenment and conversion and possible blackmail if he found what was hidden. They had him followed and carefully watched as he sought out the keepers of the clues in Teignmouth. Sadly, when he got close to finding the hiding place, he died suddenly. Only the Priory knew that he had been poisoned by someone in Teignmouth to prevent him finding it. No one wanted a scandal or any investigation into his sudden death or why he spent so much time away from his own Diocese and flock; so he had been quickly embalmed to destroy any evidence and buried in Trinity School graveyard. Another potential leak and drain on finances avoided.

The Minister thought deeply:

And *now Saunière's descendent was running scared because he knows if the true documents are revealed by the two bumpkins, he loses his hold over us, and that which means everything to him - the money. So, he is pursuing the two in Devon to get the documents and destroy them. He would then be the only holder of the truth and can blackmail us even more. But he doesn't know it is the real and only truth that he will find in Teignmouth, not the false knowledge his father uncovered. He can never be allowed to know what only a few in the world knew. He would certainly use that against us. But whatever, he thinks or does it must not stop the secret being found again. The time is ripe now to use it for the absolute power that Sion has sought for so long. They will monitor this man and his friends. If he gets too near, then it can only lead to his death. All will be unimportant if the Priory regains the secret and the grail and also the proof.*

He stopped his thinking and spoke. 'I think we have to up the ante with The Cornishman. He is very low in the organisation and working on a shoe string and practically on his own. As we have planned, he can never be allowed to know the whole truth, only his petty Cornish part. I never expected this to amount to anything. Certainly, I didn't expect those amateurs to have gone so far. The Cornishman is a bit of a sledgehammer to crack his own small nut. We need a rapier to skewer the whole beast. Let's send in the Knights of Malta to help him. Now is the time to find and release the documents again and show the world the proof. Britain is moving away yet again and Europe may break up. It's time for the truth to bring us back together. We have to get Sion back and the true faith restored.'

The banker nodded in agreement and added his own concerns. 'Let's hope we can do better than last time. It was silly to try to release those false documents in the fifties with that stupid French admiral having lost any real proof we had to those idiots in Devon back in seventeen hundred.'

'They can't be that idiotic my friend. They have frustrated our attempts to get it back for four centuries. They keep moving it when we ever get near and we've never broken their loyalty and their bloody clue code. Only that nosey Bishop Coffin has come near in years,' said the Minister.

The banker nodded. 'I guess you are correct. History will tell that after the Second World War and in the fifties, Britain proposed to France to merge the two countries under the one crown. What it won't tell is that we manipulated that, and have manipulated that result for centuries. We manipulated and controlled that in 1690. But we lost the truth and the power behind it in Teignmouth. Not for our own purpose and not the political groups who seek economic power, but for a united Europe under the one true crown and the one true faith ruled from Sion, not Rome or Brussels. De Gaulle stopped that he opposed any development of a supranational Europe and he was anti- Britain.'

The Minster took a drink of an excellent Château Latour. 'Yes, everyone thinks he just hated us as Brits. He hated the Yanks too. If only they knew his real reason to stop Britain and the rule of our Monarchy was that he was a devout evangelical Catholic and Rome had influence on him. Mind you he was very correct in that both of us did not want a France and Britain ruled by the current British monarchy and the Defender of the old Faith. Oh, what a twisted web we all wove. And in the end when old French bastard died and the new Pope came in, we finally got what we had tried in sixteen ninety, a united Europe. Now possibly it was secular enough and enlightened enough for us to reveal the true faith about Sion and destroy Rome's hold on it once and for all. But we didn't have that bloody proof to convince the rest of the

Alliance. Bastard Devon farmers and smugglers! We should have tortured the whole lot of them.'

'We would have! But with the grail and Sion proof lost, even though William of Orange won at the Boyne and stopped the French and Stuart Catholic rule of England, we couldn't stop the hard Protestant rule of Britain after the Act of Union and the Act of Succession. The people weren't ready in any of the Union of Britain for the true faith and the Royal Blood British King of a European Alliance we planned. And without the document we had lost the bargaining power in that sleepy bloody Devon town,' said the banker.

'So true my friend. Anyway, we have to get moving. Now after Brexit and the UK are leaving, all our plans might go astray yet again. We have to get the secret, get the people to see what we have known for ever. We can make this country great, put the true King on the throne and we can change the world. We must get that treasure those idiots are chasing down now in Devon. After lunch phone the Grand Prior, and get the Knights down to *Worzel Gummidge* land quickly. Tell them to help The Cornishman and to stop Saunière the Frenchman getting that secret - at any cost.'

CHAPTER SIXTEEN

Françoise decided to head off to St Michael's Church herself the next day as she had a shift that allowed her sometime in the afternoon. She was standing in the body of the church looking around. It was a very spectacular design and in an unenviable location right on the pretty sea front of Teignmouth. Each pew carried its own hand made kneeler. Each one designed and embroidered individually. Each design was a work of history and art in their own right. At an initial examination she could see nothing that stood immediately out that may indicate anything to do with Bishop Coffin or anything remotely linked to her Aunt's stories. This could be a dead end she thought. She strolled around the impressive building looking at every nook and cranny and all the art, plaques and statues. She could find nothing that resembled a Chalice...

The Chalice hides the truth

She had almost given up when she met an old lady who had just lit a candle and prayed. The old lady could see her looking puzzled and thoughtful and she walked over and asked if she could help her. Françoise saw a kind and helpful face that had lived a long and difficult life. She felt comforted by this person, so she confessed that she was looking for something that would mean a lot to her but all she knew it was something to do with a chalice. Maybe that could mean The Holy Grail.

'Well my dear. The chalice for Communion is kept locked away by the Warden but maybe it doesn't mean the Holy Grail. All those stories are just daft. It might mean the Communion itself. Do you know what it represents my dear?'

'Well, yes, it's The Last Supper isn't it?' she answered remembering her Catholic upbringing all those years ago in France which she still held quite close despite her lapses.

'Correct. And maybe I have an answer for your question. Follow me please.'

And they walked across the nave and up towards the altar. The lady took her to the left of the altar and there on the wall was a picture she had seen but had ignored as a possible clue.

'And what's that my dearie?' the lady asked, pointing at the small painting.

'Ah!' It suddenly dawned on Françoise: 'The Last Supper.'

'Yes, it is. Leonardo Da Vinci's painting. It is lovely isn't it? Anyway, I have to go. I hope I have helped you. Take some more time in here. Maybe say a prayer. You look troubled my dear. He will take your burden, just ask.'

Françoise shook her hand, and for some reason she felt she had to give this old lady a cuddle. Maybe she hadn't had one in years. The lady held on tight and Françoise knew she'd done something kind. She felt uplifted again.

She stood looking at the painting and the inscription on the plaque describing who had donated and why. There was nothing that hit her that might help. She racked her brain for what she knew about this famous painting. And then, with start she remembered what she had read about this in *The Holy Blood and the Holy Grail* at her aunt's house in Le Vèsinet. Many thought that the disciple who was cuddling another to left of Jesus was a woman and that it was his wife, Mary Magdalene. And the reason Da Vinci had a distinct V shape shown between the woman and Jesus is that it depicted the shape of her womb. And her womb was the Chalice that carried the Holy Blood, Christ's child; the Sang Grâal.

She also had read that Da Vinci was probably a Grand Master of the Priory of Sion and was painting a medieval clue to the royal bloodline descended from Christ. He was sworn to protect this bloodline and restate the true King to the throne of Europe.

This must be it, she decided. *It's just too much of a co-incidence. So, what is it hiding? Was it only telling her what she had read or was the painting it actually hiding something else?* She decided that there can't be much else hidden in the painting that hundreds of scholars, conspiracy theorists, theologians and history experts had not already explained. Then again in a burst of common sense she got it.

It wasn't to be analysed as a painting but it was physically hiding something.

So, she looked around the church. There was only one man sitting at the back praying. So, she worked fast. She lifted the painting and looked behind. Written on the wall, like that in Giles's cellar in Saint Germain–en–Laye, was yet another clue.

Find the Unicorn in the palace of the Prince du Sang.

She took a quick photograph and tilted the painting back, she felt rather than heard someone behind her. She turned quickly and there trying to sit down clumsily was a large man in shorts and tee shirt who had been quietly praying at the back holding his mobile phone as if videoing her. He looked to and fro nervously and was obviously uncomfortable in a church as he tried to cross himself but looked more like he was drawing a figure eight on his chest. Françoise knew that he was not what he seemed.

She put her phone into her handbag and turned to walk through the door and out into the fresh summer air. As she came out of the door, she began to pick up walking pace but turned around to see that the man in shorts was following her. She accelerated her pace. The man accelerated too until he was behind her. She was frightened now and trembling but she ducked to one side and ran around a large gravestone trying to reach the gate at the far side. The man was faster and he cut off her exit. She shouted 'What do you want?'

'I want the phone and the photos you have taken. I want you to tell me what it means.'

Françoise stood behind the grave stone. Her pursuer moved across the grave and moved to trap her. She shouted again. 'I don't know what it means, that's why I took the photo.'

'I can't let you find the treasure and give it to them or publish it. You have been told that. Your Aunty has already had one swimming lesson. Do you want her to take another bath? Give me the phone!'

Françoise moved as if she was taking the phone from her handbag and then suddenly burst away from the headstone to run around the church and seeking another exit. The man pursued her, running much faster and after only a few metres he'd grabbed her by her shoulders and was squeezing her tightly. He threw her to the ground and stood menacingly above her.

'Give me the bag,' he said much quieter now and breathing deeply.

Françoise was about to hand the bag over when from behind a large raised tomb mausoleum a body flew out in the shape of a man. He launched himself over a distance of three metres with the speed of a tiger pouncing. Within seconds he had the man in shorts in a Japanese stranglehold and squeezing the life out of him. The squat man squeezed until the man became unconscious and then allowed him to fall to the ground. He put his hand out to help Françoise up and spoke for the first time. 'Are you being aright maid?'

A surprised but grateful Françoise said,' Yes thank you,' as she was helped up from the ground.

'Us sees matey follows you in here. I don't be liking men following maids all alone like, so I waits and sees. Sure enough my training paid off. Matey was a wrong un wasn't he, maid?'

Françoise looked down her the unconscious stalker and agreed that indeed he was a 'wrong un'. She now could look more clearly at her

129

rescuer and she recognised him as Jungle Jim, a man who had recently arrived in town and mixed with the locals. It appeared he had spent time in far climes working in forestry or the World Health Organisation and was returning to Devon, his home county. He had told MI5 Mick under scopolamine masquerading as Hunt's *Bull Walloper Cider*, that he had been in the jungle quite a while, hence his nick name. Also, that he had no interest in following Exeter City football club. He was quite dapper, medium height and tanned. He had a presence about him. Françoise quite fancied him.

The 'wrong un' stirred and was regaining his faculties. 'You best leave maid. Us be taking care of this one,' her knight in shining armour said.

'Oh, be careful Jim. He's dangerous.'

'I can handle him. Sorted much more dangerous men and I have my Amazonian throwing knife fixed again. He'll not get far with that between his shoulders. I be taking matey down town to the police.'

Françoise panicked a bit. She didn't want the police called; her aunt's life was in danger. She had heard about Jim's Amazonian throwing knife which Huggy the Indian welder, had fixed for him. She certainly didn't want that embedded in her attacker's chest. That would be certainly curtains for Aunty. 'Jim, just leave him here buddy please. I don't want any bother. I think he was just a mugger, might be a druggie or something and desperate for a few bob.'

Jim looked at her, puzzled. He wasn't stupid for sure and he could tell she was lying. But he was a gentleman (well in the terms of a man with manners; not in terms of gentle and controlled violence). But she was a maid and he had done his duty. If she wanted him to show mercy well what could a gentleman do? He'd knock him out with a kung fu blow, put him over his shoulder and chuck him over the railway embankment. Best be merciful. It was a churchyard after all.

Françoise said thank you and left Saunière's goon in the tender tropical sun- burned arms of Jungle Jim.

She walked down the bank and into The Teign Brewery. She needed a drink. Rollo climbed off his bench to greet her. Paul was standing in the corner drinking his rough cider as he did every day. His carrier bag at his side, what it contained no one knew, but whatever he had in it seemed to feed him and keep him in a state of eternal youth. He never gets any older and his sharp mind and intelligence never failed to impress her. Françoise thought; *must be the rough cider and the carrier bag; the food of life.*

She took a pint in her own Tankard off Kay, Dawn's partner and owner, and sat down to think.

'Would you like a quickie?'

While Françoise was searching in St Michael's church for impossible clues, and being rescued by her knight in shining armour, Jack was standing at the bar in the Teignmouth Social Club, known by all by its past history as the British Legion. He was trying to rationalise what was happening to them both and the amazing revelations that they were being exposed to. He did believe in secret societies that held mysterious secrets, because he had discovered and revealed one of the most dangerous and sought-after secrets in the world, 'The Paradise Secret', which would change the known world forever. He had hidden down here in the lost world of Devon from those in Asia who had wished to keep it secret. Now he was worried that the men who followed them and threatened them, may also be part of some global secret society that were also going to punish him for his frightening and life changing revelation in Asia.

He was shaken out of his anxiety and silent thought by the question from Bingo Pat. He looked down at the charming and still beautiful old lady who had seemingly asked him if he would like some pleasures of the flesh. Well that was what he thought when she had first asked him years before. Many may not have thought that was what she may be inferring, but he had lived in Asian areas where asking someone if they *'wanted a quickie?'* or *'a happy ending'*, did not mean a short fairy story where the Princess finally finds her true love with Prince Charming.

Jack answered with a smile as he had always done for the last two years, gave her a cuddle and said, 'Only from you my dear.' Pat chuckled and sold him a one-pound quickie bingo ticket. Bingo Pat sold her tickets always starting off with the microphone to the assembled geriatric inmates of that home for the bewildered Jack inhabited - Teignmouth Social Club asking everyone, *if they would like a quickie.* Normally saying *she hadn't had one for years; anyone had one this week.* She also loved to call out the meat draw ticket number 69 out; again asking anyone *who would like one?*

Pat moved off to proposition Silent John, Yorkshire Bob, Bill Hook and Shaky Tom. As Jack drank his Teignworthy *Reel Ale* beer he kept thinking, *what to do now? If they were after him, should he move up sticks again? Surely there was no other place to hide, anywhere more remote than the West Country.* Mandy the lovely stewardess could see he was worried and tried to cheer him up with a bit of black

131

humour. 'Cheer up Jack. Your mate Al will be here soon. He'll make you laugh.'

Her husband and the steward Birmingham Alan leant over the bar and in his inimitable way, he rubbed it in. 'Al told me last night he had to work this morning so he'll be a barrel of laughs again today Jack.'

God no, Jack thought. He'd learned never to talk to Al after work. He often physically assaulted people who did. His misery knew no bounds. But once he'd had a beer or two, he'd cheer up to a level between cantankerous to depressive. Purple Alan, or Grumpy Al, depending on Jack's mood, and also the outside temperature which when wet and freezing, which was most of the time here in the UK, turned him purple.

Purple Alan, had become purpler every time Jack met him. It is a medical condition caused by excessive cider, malnutrition and cigarettes. Cider and tabs (cigarettes) sadly do not support good microcirculation in the extreme regions of the body, nor does living on them without the food and vitamins essential for healthy blood and circulation. So, Alan continues to go purple and grumpier. Well, he told Jack that he had always been grumpy and had hated almost everyone for as long as he can remember, so maybe his extreme misery and grumpiness aren't caused by Reynard's Syndrome. Jack believed that was because he comes from Leicester and supports Manchester City. Another syndrome he would claim to have discovered one day: Grumpy Al Syndrome.

Today he had to face him at the Teignmouth Social Club during that wild rave and sexual wonderland of a Saturday afternoon bingo, tote double and meat draw lunchtime session (and he thought he'd left Purgatory). The week before he'd told the purple one that his friend Davey the author was thinking of writing a book about life in Teignmouth and he wanted to include Al. Jack told him that he was about to become famous when Davey's book is sold in its millions. People from the known world will seek him out. Especially the Asians: and particularly the Japanese, who will all want his photograph. Grumpy Al was not impressed with his new found fame.

'If anyone comes near me with a camera it will end up up their...Well you don't have to have studied anatomy to guess where.'

Mind you Jack mused, if they survive Grumpy Al's camera insertion, he would not be sure what the Japanese, and especially the Thai's, will think when Bingo Pat sells them their bingo ticket and asks them if they *'want a quickie?'* If our Thai visitors heard such things they may revert back to their roots and the ancient inmates of the Club may well get that long lost *'happy ending'* much to the delight of Pat.

Last Sunday in that International Court of Human Rights, which is the grumpy old gits end of the bar in *The Blue Anchor* on Sunday lunchtime, Jack was explaining to Charlie, Al and Elliott, Al's angst at becoming famous and his predication to using Nikon cameras for proctoscopy on our Asian brethren. Then somewhere in the scrumpy- induced coma of Sam's cider, Jack recalled the plight of the Japanese when visiting that other place which makes Al look like Mother Theresa – Paris. The BBC reported the effect of French people on the Japanese.

A dozen or so Japanese tourists a year have to be repatriated from the French capital, after falling prey to what's become known as Paris syndrome. *That is what some polite Japanese tourists suffer when they discover that Parisians can be rude or the city does not meet their expectations. The experience can apparently be too stressful for some and they suffer a psychiatric breakdown.'*

Jack had printed out the Wikipedia description of the symptoms to look out for to give to the local bar owners to hand out to their Japanese customers and take to the local doctors if they ever come to visit and meet the famous man.

The syndrome is characterized by a number of psychiatric symptoms such as acute delusional states, hallucinations, feelings of persecution (perceptions of being a victim of prejudice, aggression, or hostility from others), derealisation, depersonalization, anxiety, and also psychosomatic manifestations such as dizziness, tachycardia, sweating, and others, such as vomiting. Similar syndromes include GRUMPY AL syndrome, commonly found in Jack's Inferno, Devon, UK.

Jack had introduced Purple Al to Davey the author, who was researching in the pubs and clubs' facts for his book, *'Tin Baths, Hot Summers and Rock and Roll'* about life when we were all happy and young. Davey quickly realised that Grumpy Al was never happy, and he doubted he'd ever been young. So maybe he wasn't such a good subject for a warm, nostalgic and happy story. But being a dedicated man and researcher, and also a bit touched, Davey pursued his study of Al.

Pascale, the lovely lady who worked with Terry the Scouse owner and head chef, came down from the upstairs restaurant, a venue noted for its amazing sea views and cracking ambience, to take an order. Jack really enjoyed the quality food they served in both club and restaurant. He kept hoping to win a voucher for one of their sizzling Sunday roast dinners in the meat draw. Mind you, he'd really rather eat Terry's Scouse dish of liver and onions. His palate, like his brain, was really pretty simple.

One day Davey was talking about days gone by and food and realised that Al never agreed to that anything nutritious could taste like manna from heaven as he was only a lover of *Heinz Tomato Soup* and *Quavers*. The only fish he would eat was from *Bird's Eye*. So, when Davey and the other graduates of the Oxford University Debating Society in Dicey Reilly's bar were discussing the old days, before we all had to end up *Contracting with the Devil* in real work, he included Grumpy Al.

The talk was about how great those days of being caned at school by sadistic teachers like Killer Phillips, also using Izal medicated toilet paper in outside toilets, Blue Peter badges and saving milk bottle tops to save starving kids in Ethiopia, tin baths, and ice on your bedroom windows, rampant poverty, rickets, polio and many other such wonderful childhood things. The subject moved onto coming home from school and having to wait for your tea when your father came in from the hell of work, or he got out of bed after his long night shift and then everyone remembered the smell of their mother's cooking. For many they remembered freshly cooked bread, and for Davey especially, stotty cakes, with a bowl of steamy homemade broth made with a ham shank and fresh vegetables. Grumpy Al was not impressed and exclaimed: 'Broth is shite.'

This prompted another intellectual debate from the assembled masses of Mensa on the merits of a diet of broth and slightly leavened bread, interrupted periodically by Gus shouting from his cage: 'Heh Gringo! How's your Wi Fi'

So, realising that Al was incorrigible Davey gave up on him as a subject for a book on nostalgic happiness. He stood with cider in hand watching Gus sitting in the corner howling and playing his air guitar and he realised that he also was playing a phantom guitar and singing out loud to himself, *'That's me in the corner...'* He knew right there and then that he was slowly losing the will to live.

And to finally cap it all, Yorkie came over to try to persuade him to raise six goslings for Christmas in his garage and on his darling wife's manicured lawn. The resulting reactive depression finally pushed him over the edge. He decided to give up on Al and all fellow inmates of Dicey's and join the West Country Author's Society instead.

Jack reflected on his friend's encounter with Grumpy Al, Gus and of course Yorkie, and thought dolefully *maybe I should have introduced him to normal people first?*

Brian the Brickie came in and said hello to the two stewards, took his cup of tea from Mandy and stood at his usual position near the bar hatch. 'Hi Jack, are you playing today?' and he put one pound on the bar.

Jack's doom-laden thoughts were interrupted by this oblate shaped older man, whom he liked tremendously. It cheered him up. 'Aye: Go on then. You'll win the bugger anyway.'

Brian smiled, as Jack was correct, he always won the nearest loser competition. This was the game introduced by Grumpy Al, who being delighted yet again at losing the meat draw and the bingo, thought why not have bets on who was the closest to a winning number. It was the only thing that made him happy - losing. And true to form the perpetual depressive came into the club and walked to bar, his *'Warmer Windows'* work clothes covered with silicone sealant and plaster. Jack decided retreat was the better part of valour and left him to Brian, who was infinitely more patient and kinder than Jack, to humour the irascible man. Jack would wait until the purple man had had two pints of larger and two cigarettes before he attempted to talk to the irascible single- polar man. He also wanted to talk to yet another Hook.

He moved across the bar, carefully, with no sudden movements, to talk with the gang of four at the other end. He said hello and was delighted when Silent John looked down with his huge furrowed brow and he nodded. Jack thought *Christ, he communicated. I must be doing ok.* Of course, Yorkshire Bob looked down at him and through his huge and gnarled features and just grunted. *Nothing new there then* Jack mused, but he didn't hit me so again I must be doing ok. Both were ex-military and pretty precise in all they did, including talking to idiots. Bill said hello and continued his pint; another not gregarious, but careful and polite man. Shaky Tom was smiling and asked Jack how he was and how was Davey's book going. Tom had bought one month before from

Amazon and enjoyed it. Tom was much more gregarious than his fellow members of the gang of four, well at least to strangers. Jack he found useful and also someone he could talk too about life over in Asia as Tom had worked and lived there himself.

Jack answered his question on Davey's book. 'I've no idea. I think Davey may be trying to write a book about the smuggling history here in Teignmouth.'

'I hope it's better than that last shite he wrote,' interrupted Yorkshire Bob. Silent John just looked at Jack and attempted to smile. But it seemed to fail before the lips could move upwards. *Uhm* Jack thought, *Davey better not try to write anything that might upset the locals. He may well end up in the Bishop's grave.*

He decided to head back and join the Depression Anonymous corner. He joined and Al looked at him and just grunted. 'Hi Al, had a good morning?' Jack said, more for devilment than curiosity. Alan the steward perked his ears up and turned and smiled at Jack, knowing precisely the answer, and he shook his head.

'Do I look as if I've had ******* good morning,' the grumpy and purple man grunted rhetorically at Jack without turning his head to face him.

'Well maybe not,' Jack said, not bothering now in slightest as he knew the ways of the man well now. He continued, not phased with the answer he may or may not get. 'Anyway, I heard Schultzie's funeral went well.'

'Aye it did,' Brian said warmly. 'Did you go Jack?'

'No mate, didn't really know the man, but heard he was well loved and a character of course. I was talking to Françoise that Frog lass the other day. She went to it; told me some great craic about the old days on the docks. She also mentioned about when the French invaded and she reckons they might have had some treasure or map or something onboard that the lads pinched when they smuggled the booze.'

'That's shite,' Grumpy Al interjected.

'Why's that Al?' Jack asked not really expecting a sensible or polite answer. Alan and Mandy behind the bar just smiled in anticipation.

'It's just yet another one of your daft mate Davey's conspiracy theories. I think you are going that same. That's your problem how many times have I told you not to talk to anyone? It's your own fault you get into stupid conversations with any bastard. I hate everyone therefore I don't talk to anyone. You are just stupid. Don't talk to anyone and you won't need to worry. That's your problem. How many times have I told you that!'

'Well that told you then Jack. Can I get you another Teignworthy?' said Alan from behind the bar, while Mandy smiled and turned away. She heard it all before. Jack nodded to Alan in agreement that more beer was indeed needed to allow him to talk to Al without strangling him. Nicki the Baptist came up to him and said hello. She was a lovely woman who attended the Baptist church and every Saturday she brought her elderly father to the Club for his beer and maybe ending with bingo and maybe a happy win the meat draw. She asked Jack if he wanted to support a Church youth group. Jack talked a while and when she left Jack introduced her conversation to the two manic depressives in his company. 'Lovely lady Nicki: She wants me to help out with something at the Church. I really am up to my eyes that weekend, sometimes I wonder why I offer these things.'

'That's your problem. You are stupid. Why would you want to help anybody? I help no one. That's your problem, you talk to people. How many more times...'

Before Grumpy could finish, Jack, uninterested anymore in being verbally abused, walked over to The Gorgon to get a meat draw ticket. This lady sold the tickets and when Al and he had first started to come to the Saturday afternoon debauched orgy that was the bingo and meat draw they were so terrified of her stern face that they were scared to buy a ticket, so they sat still and drank. Mind you they had to avoid the punches thrown by Billy Bob the Boxer; an elderly man from Exeter who loved to come on the bus to the seaside three times a week and who drank continuously. He also could not talk without throwing his hands around and around just like an off- centre windmill. Grumpy Al swore that if he didn't stop swinging at him, he'd kill him. After the second black eye Grumpy Al just knocked him out with a head butt.

The stern-faced lady was named The Gorgon, after the mythical woman who had a head of snakes which turned you to stone if you looked her in the eyes. After several months of just sitting ducking and weaving in between Billy Bob's lefts and rights, Jack decided that maybe The Gorgon was not so lethal, as he had not seen anyone turn to stone statues after buying a ticket and she always seemed to laugh and joke with her potential victims and they with her. He told Grumpy that he was going to be brave and face up to her. 'She looks a lovely and kind woman Al,' he said, ducking low to avoid a right from Billy Bob.

'That's your problem. You think everyone is nice you daft bastard. Haven't I told...,' Jack got up before Al could repeat his lesson and he walked the green mile walk to the Gorgon's lair. She smiled and engaged in a nice friendly conversation. He had been doing the same thing every since that day but now Jenny, the wonderful lass always gave him and his ticket a kiss every time for luck. A smashing person: Even Grumpy Al realised that she was a lovely engaging person but only after he spent six months in Exeter jail for the manslaughter of Billy Bob! He would have received a conditional discharge for extenuating circumstances or a crime of passion as the Judge had drank with Billy Bob before, but as he was explaining why he would let him off, Grumpy Al interrupted him with, ' that's your problem, you like people, and you think I deserve compassion. You are a **********...' The last thing Grumpy heard before he finished his expletive was, 'Six months. Send that man down!'

Jack left the club after the meat draw. Of course, they won nothing as Grumpy Al predicted. Brian won the happiest loser prize and looked pleased with himself. He had enough money to go to Redfern's the wonderful family butcher who supplied the excellent, local supplied meat for this and *The King Arms* and *The Courtenay* meat draw and to buy his own meat. Grumpy told him, 'That's your problem, you actually want to win. How many times have I told you; never win anything; it just makes you happy.' As Brian put his hands around Al's neck, Jack left.

He was walking out when Bingo Pat shouted over, 'Jack would you like to join the bowls team? I can show you how to play with your balls. We could have a quickie on the green tomorrow if you fancy?' Jack shook his head, his brain mashed; *this just wasn't easy was it...*

CHAPTER SEVENTEEN

Françoise phoned Jack up and told him of what she had found out at Saint Michael's and about her lucky escape. She told him about the clue.

Find the Unicorn in the palace of the Prince du Sang.

'What the hell does that mean?' Jack asked, becoming increasingly frustrated with one dead end after another.

'Well I've spent some time on the internet and popped in Teignmouth library and museum to see if I can find out. And I have one idea.'

'What's that then?'

'Well Prince du Sang is French for Prince of the Blood. But my research says it means Royal Blood.'

'Not bloody Holy Royal blood lines again!' Jack said, getting exasperated with this entire esoteric gobbledegook. 'So, we look for yet another offspring of Mary Magdalene. I thought that was King James Stuart according to you and your aunty? Are we trying to find his ancestor and his palace now?'

'No, I believe we are much nearer than Edinburgh or Saint Germain. We have our own family here in Devon that is born of 'Princes of the Royal Blood.'

Jack was stunned. 'Surely not; this is a joke?'

'Non, mon ami. The Courtenay family are descended from the founder of the French Monarchy in the year of our Lord four hundred and twenty AD. In the twelfth century Reginald de Courtenay moved to England after falling out with King Louis. Through royal blood lines the Courtenay family could lay claim to the French throne and be Royal.'

'So, what has that got to do with us here in little old Teignmouth and Unicorn's?'

Françoise smiled to herself. She thought she had done well to research this and was sure that what she found was too much of a co-incidence to be wrong. She answered Jack. 'The Courtenay family is one of the most ancient in England and the current head lives just up the road from here.'

'Oh, 'said Jack, 'where's that?'

'Powderham Castle: He is Charles Courtenay. The nineteenth Earl of Devon.'

'Bloody hell! A belted Earl. Are you sure it means him?'

'Well the guy has a palace. Well, not as such, but a castle. I guess that is bigger than some palaces. He has thousands of deer at Powderham but I've never seen a Unicorn mind,' Françoise said laughing.

'What about his coat of arms?' Jack said, suddenly enthused again, thinking she may well have something.

'Nope none there; I checked.'

'Well what do we do now?'

'You do nothing cheri, I am meeting the Powderham management tomorrow at ten am. I hope to meet the Earl. If not, they may well have a clue about Unicorns'

'You know what Françoise; you are becoming one hell of a detective. This could make an Agatha Christie novel for sure. Most of her books are based in her home county of Devon. There are more secrets and deaths here than in The Midsomers.'

'I guess so Jack. I hope it doesn't end with Poirot finding a murderer. That body could well be one of ours.'

'Don't be so morose Françoise. You have done great up to now. We can get through this together. The more we find the more all of this is linked to Devon and the West Country and in some way the Royal Blood line and this secret Priory society seem to crop up every stone we turn. Now we have an Earl in the loop and his castle- the ancient seat of Devon itself. Maybe the lads put the treasure and the Grail there?'

'We have only two of the clue keepers come forward so I have a feeling there's more turns in this story yet. But who knows the Earl may well be one of the keepers. Nothing surprises me anymore. Anyway, I have to go to work. I'll meet you after the meeting somewhere'

'Ok. I will be having a few beers in Dawlish in the *The Lansdowne* with Andy the landlord and Steve from *The Castle* in Holcombe tomorrow. I had a sniff that there may be some link to all this at another landed country house; Luscombe Castle there has its own family chapel. I've been to the Christmas carol service there as a guest of AIMS, the local Charity that helps parents and children with special needs here. It's a beautiful chapel and the grounds are magnificent. But I am sure I noticed a plaque on the wall with some reference to a buried Bishop, maybe Bishop Coffin. I may be mistaken but it sticks in my mind. I'd like to try to get a visit. I'm sure one of the landlords knows the owners. If not Steve, then Norma his bar lady will. She knows everybody.'

'Ok I can meet you maybe in *The Teignmouth Inn* or *The Marine Tavern* in Dawlish? I can park near there. It's a hard life for some; Au revoir Jack.' And she put the phone down.

The next day she drove to Powderham Estate which was only twenty minutes away from Teignmouth. She arrived early as she wished to walk Piaf and take in some of the shops there with a nice coffee and croissant. She pulled into the car park. The multitude of apple trees was showing resplendent with fruit. She loved this place in the spring when the whole place was lined with daffodils. Piaf got lost amongst them, her head popping up every now and then amongst the gently waving yellow landscape.

She walked along the path towards the Exe estuary. Through the fence the herd of deer could be seen in the distance grazing over near the Castle and the marshy estuary ground. In the autumn she walked past and Piaf would be curious on her lead to hear the rutting of the males and the loud booming cries of their mating calls. The sweet chestnut trees were her favourites as she gathered up her store of nuts to roast. It reminded her of her walks with her aunty in Le Forêt de St. Germain, particularly over towards Chambourcy, where les châtaignes, small sweet chestnuts, grew in abundance. Hopefully here at Powderham she wouldn't meet the sanglier, wild boar, that she and her aunt had met the first time they went gathering nuts.

On her return to the car park she walked to the farm shops that contained a host of quality goods and food with much of the produce coming from local suppliers of clothes, crafts, arts, garden goods and food. She treated herself to a couple of venison steaks for her and her husband who had returned from another trip fixing marine harbours in Cornwall. The butcher there supplied Powderham venison and really excellent local meat and game. In the same place she purchased a couple of pasties and some quiche for her husband for his working breaks over the next two days. Great food and value she always thought as she browsed around. She had tied Piaf up at the dog pole outside the Castle shop cafe and took a takeaway coffee and an almond croissant from the bakery to eat on the wooden garden tables outside with her hound. As she sat there in the rapidly warming air, she reflected on how she had come to be here waiting to go to the Castle, not as visitor as usual, but as a guest.

Could Powderham Castle and Estate contain the treasure? Is the Earl somehow linked to this whole Royal blood line story?

What if anything was the Unicorn? And more worrying, what will she do when those who want the secret come calling on her again? She sat watching the visitors arriving for their Castle tours, all looking so happy and content with the beautiful surroundings and weather and suddenly she wished she had never nursed Albert and could go back to being ordinary and safe like all these happy people.

Ten minutes later she was sitting in the office in the castle talking about her reason to be there. She had told them she was writing a book about Devon's secret history and was hoping to have some form of historical treasure hunt and charity raising event on the back of it all. She asked if Powderham would be happy to support the event. She knew they held music festivals, local festivals, and spice festivals and they agreed to talk. Twenty minutes later she was on an escorted tour of the castle and she hoped sincerely she could find out about the unicorn and anything else that might make sense.

She passed the magnificent mahogany staircase. It was decorated by many wooden and plaster carvings depicting ancient heraldry. She chuckled to herself when she recalled a story a good friend had told her of a similar but much grander staircase. Barry the Romancer was a lovely older man who had tried unsuccessfully to woo her. He was a dapper, old navy man and a bit of a lothario with the fairer sex. He was a member of The Monday Club in *The Blue Anchor*, along with Red Martin. She wasn't sure if he was linked to the security services in any way but he drank with MI5 Mick and Jimmy the Hat each Monday too.

He had worked at one time providing silver service to the rich and famous. On many occasions he was at the House of Lords and he met the heir to the Huntley and Palmer fortune on the terrace over a silver service lunch. Lord Palmer showed him a picture of his staircase which was solid silver. He invited Barry to come and see it. 'You can help my men clean it,' he said in his aristocratic voice. 'It takes a whole week and three of my men to clean it. They scrub it morning till night with bran mash. I love to watch men work with their hands; don't you?'

Barry being left of Karl Marx, like Red Martin, declined to comment.

But certainly this one looked impressive too. Françoise thought she wouldn't fancy polishing this with wood cleaner all day. They entered the music room and then the dining hall and she stood amazed at the history and architecture that surrounded her. But she was impatient to get to a conclusion so she asked her very helpful lady marketing lady if she knew if there was a unicorn in the place.

Mikaela thought carefully as they walked past the grand chimney in the dining room. 'I can't really say we have one which isn't in some heraldic crest somewhere. The kids may have had one as toy at one time. Oh, wait a minute...'

And she phoned up someone on her mobile. 'That tusk thing, the whale tusk. Is it called anything? I seem to remember we had some more information about it.'

She listened for some time and spoke again. 'It's the lady who wants us to support a charity event and book. She wants to know if we have a unicorn.'

She went quiet again as whoever was on the other end spoke. Mikaela spoke again. 'Are you sure? I can ask her, Sure. Ok I will.'

'Françoise, why do you want to find the unicorn and what do you want to know for. I have been asked to ask you this before we go any further.'

Françoise thought deeply *now we are getting somewhere. There must be ne and they think it's important. What do in say for God's sake?* She decided to be more honest, after all if they stop her dead then that's it- a dead end.

'Well it's that a lovely old man who died told me that I would find a unicorn here and that would lead to secret that might change Devon forever. I know it sounds crazy but I have followed this across many places in Devon and it seems to end here; with this unicorn and the Earl.'

'Just wait a minute please. I need to talk to someone. I'll be back. There are some lovely paintings to look at here. Maybe one will jog another memory for you.'

Françoise waited for her guide to come back. *Had she upset her and who ever she spoke to?* She pondered as she looked at the ancient paintings. A few minutes later Mikaela came back and asked her to follow her. They walked through the halls and through a locked door which her guide opened. *Where was this going?* Françoise asked herself. Then very soon they reached an oak door upon which Mikaela knocked. 'Come in,' someone answered. They came through the door and a tall, casually dressed man was sitting at an antique wooden desk, writing. He got up and greeted

143

Françoise. 'Hello I am Charlie Courtenay. Please sit down and take a cup of tea. Thank you, Michela you can leave us now.'

As she drove back towards Dawlish, she pulled into *The Ship Inn* in Cockwood right on the small tributary of the Exe estuary which held the fishing and leisure craft that were at this time stranded on the mud of the small tidal harbour. She needed to get her head around the last hour she had spent with the 19th Earl of Devon. She took a pint of the excellent Dartmoor *Jail Ale* she always drank there and sat on her own in the small bar and reflected on what she had been told. The young Earl had been charming and helpful. Too charming because she soon told him a lot of what she knew; about Albert; the keepers; the possible secret that might change Devon or the world. But she did not mention the people chasing her or what secret society and esoteric past they had. She told him that the last clue she discovered had led her to here and to a unicorn. He had been very polite and empathetic with her and he revealed his own personal secret and the meaning of the unicorn over a nice cup of Darjeeling tea.

The earl had shown her the tusk of a Narwhal. A one tusked whale that lived up in the frozen North and had for many years he explained been thought of the Unicorn legend. It had been in the family for many years. He believed it may have been given by the families on Teignmouth who fished the seas in Newfoundland and the Arctic. His father had told him that one day someone may come asking about it and if they were Teignmouth people to tell them the story. And now she had arrived. He wished her well on her quest and hoped the information on the whale that was a unicorn was helpful. They said goodbye and Françoise went to the ladies who had helped her and thanked them so much for their assistance. What this meant she couldn't fathom. *Why a narwhal's tusk? Who gave the Earl it?* She really needed some help from Jack so she drank up, said goodbye to Anna, the landlady and drove past Starcross and the ferry across to Exmouth and then Cockwood and finally through Dawlish Warren, with its holiday beaches and fun, to meet Jack in Dawlish.

After hearing the tale, Jack smiled, as he understood the meaning of the tusk pretty much immediately upon hearing it. He believed they had made a giant leap again. 'Françoise, we have been told that the families who were part of the smuggling of the secret were also fishermen and some went off to Newfoundland and the Northern seas to fish and build businesses. As far as I know from David Attenborough's shows about the frozen North, narwhal's live there. Surely the Narwhal tusk and the Earl's father passing the story down that they only tell where it came from to Teignmouth people must mean the next clue must be with one of the fishing family's descendants. My guess is either a Hook or a Job.'

'Mon Dieu, you might be correct Jack. We have to meet them.'

Jack said it was maybe time they popped over to Shaldon to meet the old grandfather of that branch of the Hook family and then maybe meet an old member of the Job family. And they agreed to arrange it.

Jack arranged to meet Gordon Hook in *The London Inn* in Shaldon as he was heading over with Charlie and the boys on the weekly pub crawl on Wednesday. He asked if she wanted to come.

'No thank you Jack, an afternoon with you lot is just too much for me. I'll try and get a contact for old man Job and fix up a meet in *The Cider Bar* in Newton Abbot. I'll take the train mind, after a pint of that Sam's cider from the barrel or a Sam's' cider and maybe an Elderflower wine or two; it's wise to be safe.'

'I would come with you but whenever I go, I never get home. Well if I do, I have no idea how I did. I am addicted to the stuff. I think they put heroin in real scrumpy. My wife's mother loves the Elderflower wine and the peach. It's great to have country wines and cider from the barrels and no beer. The only one left in Devon they say. It's iconic.'

'I love their baguettes, 'Françoise said. 'Half a loaf and huge slabs of ham or cheese and onion; mind you, a bit much for a petite French mademoiselle. I always give the rest to my husband.'

'Me too,' said Jack, licking his lips, 'I can only eat half. The cider helps wash it down. Did I tell you that when I first went there, I asked if I could put my pewter tankard up with the hundreds of other jugs and pots hanging on the ceiling and over the bar?'

'No, you didn't.'

'Well, the cracking bar lad, told me I'd be better off with a ceramic pot. Many years ago, everyone thought that the reason that heavy scrumpy drinkers were a little bit touched and ended up in the loony bin was the fact that the cider was made with dead rats and things in it and had hallucinogenic properties. It seems the real reason was they supped it out of pewter tankards and the cider was so lethal it sucked the tin and the lead out of the tankard and they supped it with every pint!'

145

Françoise laughed: 'So no pewter tankard then?'

'For sure; there are all sorts of cups, tankards, mugs, and vessels hanging on there. Mine is pure ceramic with a hard glaze. Even natch or diesel won't rot that. Well, I hope so!'

'It's not affected you yet,' Françoise chuckled. 'Well apart from the twitch and nervous tick.'

'I was told that in the old days on the docks, natch cider was the cheapest booze you could drink. No one really drank it if they had money. You knew when a man's wages had run out if they were on a pint of cider. It was only about four pence and lethal. So, drinking cider was not allowed in the lounge where women might be. Tony Sawyer, the old owner of *The Teign Brewery* used to bar people drinking cider in the lounge. He was ex Marines and ran the pub like a barracks, not like *The Quay Pub*. Ashtrays were for cigarettes and cleaned after every cigarette was stubbed out. Heaven forbid if you used the floor.'

'I guess people got legless on the old cider then?' Françoise asked, knowing the answer really.

'The lads tell me that the last bus up to Kingsway was a double decker and it was called the 'Cider Express'. The bus conductor used to carry the younger girls and the worse off male bodies to their front doors to make sure they got home all right. Bloody good customer service those days. Problem was the next day most were still legless from the apples. Mad Jock Macfay just drove straight down and smashed into Shaldon Bridge causeway. The police were told he was blinded by the sun at nine am when it was still behind him. But they knew the craic and let him off. Yes, the cider express was famous.'

Françoise chuckled again and then cut the phone conversation. 'Well, I have to go now. I'll try to sort out a meet with old man Job. Let me know how your piss up goes with the lads and if you have any success with Gordon.'

'Will do. Have a good shift and talk at the end of the week.'

Jack met Gordon early before the crazy gang walked over Shaldon Bridge from their homes over on the sunny side of the Teign to rape and pillage the nice folk of Shaldon again. They met in the excellent London Inn. Tim and Katie, the owners were proud of their beer and their food and Tim served them a beer. Jack took a pint of *Otter Ale* and Gordon a half of lager and they retired to the tables outside, opposite the immaculate bowling green and quaint cottages that surrounded it. The London Inn was filling up with the usual diners who came from far and wide for the excellent food and ambience of the old coaching and smuggling inn. After a few minutes of talking about their known acquaintances and Jack's reason for chatting, Gordon decided to tell a lot more about his chequered career in Devon and Cornwall around the world of fishing, smuggling, engineering, and business and many things which Jack suggested would make a good book for his mate Davey the demented author. But they soon got to the reason for the meeting.

'So, my handsome, Charlie was one of us then,' Gordon surprisingly confessed. 'It makes sense. Good old buoy Charlie and his family, and Albert knew a good one when he saw one. I always knew one day we had better just let this whole thing die and let everyone get on with their lives. So, what do you want to know?'

Jack was delighted and also shocked that it was so easy. He had expected a wild goose chase again but maybe this was the break they were looking for.

'I was wondering if you were a 'keeper of a clue' and if you'd be kind enough to let us have it?'

'Well me beauty, you would not have had a hope if Albert hadn't set this adventure in motion. But I guess as I said before, it be time we all moved on. I am not a clue keeper anymore. Albert, I believe passed that on to Old Man Job in Newton. I am travelling a lot now I am retired and I asked to give he up. Best go see if Old Man Job will talk to you.'

'Actually, Françoise is going to do that,' said Jack. 'But thanks for helping out. We are so pleased to get some way forward at last. I'll buy you another pint.'

'No that's all right buoy. I have to go now. Enjoy your drink with the crazies from over the water. We did some daft things in those old days on the Quay and the river. Matey, your author friend, should write that book.'

They shook hands and Jack was sad to see such a grand character stroll off into the distance. He knew that there were not many of the old buoys left who could tell such magical tales of the sea and the river. He really had to get Davey to write about these people. He'd phone him and try to persuade him to brave the crazies in Dicey's again the next day and meet up. Too much social history to lose it all he thought.

He strolled along the estuary, past The Salty, the huge sandy island, which was exposed at low tide. The yachts and small pleasure boats were stranded on the sandy gravel and mud. The estuary and river Teign shimmering in the midday sun. The oyster catchers, dunlins and sand pipers were picking among the mussel and oyster strewn sand and gravelly river bed. Tina from *The Kings Arms* was raking among them, picking a bucket of cockles to cook and give to anyone in the pub who fancied a few. *It's hard to get anything more picturesque and calming* he thought as he strolled along, looking up the river to the beautiful Dartmoor National Park.

He waved at Tina diligently raking the pools and river bed at her mammoth mollusc hunt. She waved back and wiped her brow. Jack walked along the river towards Ringmore and entered *The Clipper*. The men from Teignmouth were already in.

'Get him one in,' Charlie said, 'and the other buoys,' as usual pulling out a roll of money and paying.

'Where you been Jack?' Roy, the Teignmouth Yank asked.

'Oh, I met someone, Gordon, in *The London Inn*. Trying to get some old stories about the old days for Davey's book.'

Charlie looked knowledgably at Jack. No doubt Gordon had contacted him by now.

'Well he knows more than most. He'd have been a pirate in the old days,' Kev butted in.

'He was a bloody pirate!' said Charlie, much to the amusement of his mates.

'Aye, he knows some stories. He and the Tooleys seem to have been characters around here for years,' Jack retorted.

'Mad as March hares all of them. Fred was mayor of the town. An ex-boxer, he'd greet you with a full punch in the bread box. I cringes and tightens my stomach muscles every time he comes near on the quay,' Charlie explained.

'Remember when he sent that old tramp upstairs to the bosses' offices to play that violin he carried for KP,' Kev said.

'KP gives him a drink too after he'd played,' Charlie added.

'How did a tramp get onto the quay,' Jack asked, amazed.

Charlie explained. 'Oh, Fred invites him on the play for the buoys. Those old days everyone came on the quay. We used to get the tourists every year coming on to watch what we did. One couple brought their son in a wheelchair each year. We used to put a pallet in front of his chair to stop him rolling into the dock. One of the bosses came down one day when us had some visitors
148

from the blind hotel with their dogs. He goes mental. Fred walks over and grabs his arm,' Clam down buoy. It's ok man. Can't you see they are blind? They can't see us are on the piss and not working.'

Everyone chuckled at Fred's simple consolation and easing of his bosses HSE angst and swallowed yet another pint on long lost memories. The Teignmouth Yank started singing to an old Elvis song.

'Shut the hell up Roy. It's only twelve thirty,' shouted Kev and looking around at the ladies and gents drinking coffee and eating lovely scones and cake, 'and it's pretty posh in here too.' Despite being posh, the general public appreciated the Teignmouth Yank's valiant attempts to swing his hips and do his *uh...uh...uh* vocal in the middle of an empty bar. Kev continued, 'Fred seemed to rub the bosses up most days. He loved to take the piss. Remember when the quay burnt down. Fred ran up next to a boss with a bucket of water and throws it on and starts to run off to get another. The boss grabs his arm and tells him 'to bring petrol next time!'

They chuckled at this memory. 'Why did the man want it burnt down?' Jack asked.

'Allegedly, everyone knew the quay wasn't doing so good with money at the time, that's all us hears,' says Jimmy the old man sat in the corner with his small Jack Russell at his feet. He'd been listening and had worked on the Quay long before the men drinking with Jack. He continued. 'Mind, Fred would have done that just for a laugh, he didn't have to be told. His brother Tony was even more crackers. He caused me to be black balled in The Masons the bastard.'

Kev grabbed Jack by the wrist as he is about to take a beer and whispered. 'You should offer him a whisky, he'll not tell you the *shakey leg* tale till he gets one.'

Jack nodded, understanding the ways of the old dockers by now and he offered a nice Scotch from the top shelf. Jimmy took it gratefully, patted his rough haired terrier and finished his tale of Tony and the Masons.

'I was having a beer in the old *London Inn* before the Lodge meeting. It was a full dress, white shirt and all. Tony comes up and throws a bottle of Indian ink all over my white shirt. *'You bastard'* I shout. He laughs and tells us to wait. A few minutes later he be gone; he be disappearing ink Tony'd got from the toy shop.'

149

Everyone smiled as they recalled the incident, Jack laughed as this was the first time he'd heard. Jimmy took another sip of his whisky and continued. 'After the shock I thinks meself this is a hoot. I'll get a bottle and throw it over the Grand Master. I asks Tony where did he get it and does he have another one. He pulls one out of his pocket and gives it to me. I buys him a pint of cider. And off I go to the Lodge. We are all assembled before the dinner and I walks to the Master of the Lodge and throws the bottle over his white shirt. Everyone goes silent; the Master looks at the huge black stain rapidly expanding into his starched white cotton shirt and glares at me as if I am about to have my bowels ripped out at low tide at midnight and thrown over my shoulder. I am the only one laughing and I looks at the fierce stares and grunts from my fellow brothers I quickly tries to break the ice. *'It be all right Master. It's disappearing ink'* and I nervously laughs again. Everyone tries to laugh but all they does is watching the ink spread. *It's talking longer this time* I thinks and tries to wipe his shirt. He knocks me back and growls at me. Five minutes later in deathly silence we waits and the bastard just gets deeper and deeper stained. Then it dawns on me and he - Tony had switched the bottles; it was real ink — the bastard.'

The bar fell about laughing at the poor man's plight. The Teignmouth Yank broke into a song from Oklahoma, *'Oh the corn is as high as an elephant's eye,'*

Charlie interjected. 'There were no elephants in bloody Oklahoma you daft bastard. Shut the hell up. Come on, us be heading back to the ferry back to Teignmouth; one in *The Con Club* and the last ones in *The Ferryboat.'*

Standing in The Ferryboat, they watched as the tourists came in and out taking their drinks and food into the terrace and beer garden overlooking the beach and the Shaldon Ferry across to The Back Beach. Jack couldn't help thinking what an idyllic spot to have a pub. He loved the ferry ride across the short estuary mouth, through the moored yachts and fishing boats. When a cargo boat came in led by the harbour master and pilot boat, it dwarfed the small craft and the ferry. You could not help be amazed at the majestic and skilful bit of master mariner seamanship every time. He just stood as many did and looked in awe of the beauty and majesty of the place.

Matt the landlord, who had been the steward at Teignmouth Golf, greeted them warmly. Jack couldn't help thinking that this man and his wife Michelle had been very lucky with their choice of work. Teignmouth Golf Club must have had the most beautiful and panoramic views of any course you could mention. And now they had a pub right on one of the most scenic and pleasant beaches and waterside views in the UK.

Roy went to the juke box to put on the ubiquitous Elvis and oldie songs, this time he started off with Gene Pitney and *'24 hours from Tulsa'*. Gyrating around the bar shaking his hips and hands outstretched from his sides he growled out his song. Many perplexed tourists just smiled at 'the local character' as they ordered their meals and beer. This was Devon after all.

The talk once again came around to the old days on the Quay and Tony Tooley and his exploits. Kev told of the London Inn again as Roy broke into *'Oh Lord, please don't let me be understood'*. 'Remember Charlie when Tony switched the water with a bottle of vodka for his mate?'

'I does; I does,' Charlie answered, putting his beer down on the bar. 'His mate a recovering alcoholic only drank a small whisky with a lot of water from the jug on the bar. Tony threw half the water away and filled the jug up with one hundred percent lethal vodka from the Russian ships in the Quay. Two hours later his mate collapsed, was rushed to Torbay hospital and was in a coma for days. Tony and the buoys laughed for ages. He was mental.'

'I think that was the same night when the comedian from up North was on at the old *London Hotel* and Tony throws a gateau over Fred dressed in his mayor's suit. And then that huge German comes in off the boat in the quay. The buoys winds him up, just like they does with Schultzie about two world wars and one world cup, but this big German bugger knocks two of them clean out. The bouncer goes over and the German does no more than pick him up under his huge arm and smash the fire doors open with the bouncer's head. No one wants to be on with the huge bastard, but luckily the German gets maudlin and guilty so he pays the owner of *The London* twenty quid for the broken door and the broken head of the bouncer and goes off to *The Blue Anchor* for the tarts.'

Charlie said. 'That comedian from up country just gave up with all the mayhem, didn't he? He walked off stage and was never seen again. Just as well coz he speaks just like that buoy from up country who worked on the Quay. We called him 'Flob a Lob weed' coz he spoke like one of Bill and Ben's flowerpot men. Us couldn't understand a bloody word he says.'

'*As the snow falls...*' Roy was moving his repertoire back to Elvis and by now he had gained quite a small appreciation society of tourists, curious to know if it was the cider that made people crazy around these parts or just the sea air.

Kev, by now oblivious to The Teignmouth's Yank's songs, ignored the tourist's cheers and clapping at the pathos of Roy's adaption of the song's tragic end, '*and his mother cried,*' and he went on about Teignmouth's own Tommy Copper, Tony Tooley:

'Tony was scared of no one. I remembers when the London gangsters came down. Matey was in *The Teign Brewery* with a nice gold watch on his wrist. Tony sidles up to the man and says, '*That be a nice watch buoy, can I have a look at he?*'
The cockney says, 'of course mate, here take a look' and takes off the watch. Tony takes it and looks at it moving it around in his hands feeling the heavy weight. '*Wow buoy, this must have some gold in he me hansom*' The cockney heavy says,' '*It's worth a grand mate.*' Tony whistles, '*Is he waterproof too?*' and he promptly dropped it into the fish tank on the bar.'

Jack laughed out loud: 'The mad bugger.'

Kev took a drink and he hadn't finished the story. 'That wasn't the end Jack. You sees the tank only had one fish in he. He be a huge Piranha. Even the big cockney wouldn't put his hand in. Tony just laughed and walked off to torture someone else.'

'Us had some right dangerous Cockneys come down here in the old days; dressed in camel hair coats and flash suits. They were on the run as one told me his brother had been nailed to the kitchen floor. We all gives them buoys a wide berth. Mind you Marty and me were like gangsters up in the country. KP always helped the town and he let us build the carnival float and paid for it all and the booze. He liked to help his home village in Dartmoor and sent Marty and me to fix their houses for them. We put Tyrolean finish on house all week one time. Us was like the Cockneys up there buoy. We were moving Russian booze and cigarettes to everyone but the Hound of the Baskervilles. They all thinks we are gangsters.'

'I needs a piss; laughing too much,' Charlie says and leaves.

This prompts Kev to tell yet another story about the Quay. 'I remembers when Charlie and Appsy used to go on the piss till about two thirty every day. Fridays were worst. They comes back to the boat and I'm on the hatch this day. They walks past me and both are bursting so they piss like horses into the hold. There must have been gallons of it. Then the Captain sees the water and brings an engineer to look at it as he is scared there is a leak. They both dip their fingers in the piss. They are checking if it's the main bilge tanks, if he be salty it be's bilge. Obviously, he wasn't so they goes over where Appsy had pissed to check if it be ballast tanks and are about to dip their fingers in again when I takes pity on them and owns up that I'd let a bobcat radiator tank leak.'

'You were always too soft Kev,' Charlie said as he came back and overheard the last bit of the story.

Jack smiled again. *Another great afternoon, Davey must write a book and call it 'Tales of the Demented'.* They supped up their last pints and headed for the ferry. Roy stopped at the tourists' tables to render one verse of *'I often stalk down your street at night,'* until Charlie grabbed him by his collar and dragged him off to the ferry on the beach. He left to rapturous applause from the visitors. Some of whom were murmuring amongst themselves. *'Was that really Elvis?'*

On the other side they walked into *The King Billy* pub; yet another old Teignmouth ale house. Jack couldn't help think how linked things were in this town with the quest he and Françoise were on. *The King Billy*, William of Orange and St. James Church, *The Kings Arms*...all Kings and all intertwined by some in their royal priesthood sect and carrying a mysterious secret that still seemed beyond his grasp. Jack stood and wondered *what could they do next to break through the roadblocks that seemed in their path?* He was about to get an answer.

CHAPTER EIGHTEEN

Françoise sat with Old Man Job in *The Cider Bar* in Newton Abbott. She had taken the short train journey along the beautiful Teign Estuary. As she passed Bishopsteignton Village on her right, she remembered that there was a vineyard there. Maybe the *'keeper of the vine'* her aunt kept talking about referred to someone there? Or what she saw on the cellar wall in St Germain-en-Laye *'Avalon is the Vine and the Cornerstone'* in some way might mean Bishop. She made a note to visit the Vineyard and its nice restaurant; maybe she'd try a bottle of the Devon wine. It might persuade the owners to talk to her about the past. Or she'd try the pubs there. *The Bishop John* and *The Ring O' Bells* both sounded linked to her findings about Bishop Coffin and St James Church. Then she sat back and decided she was getting far too paranoid. What about *The Cockhaven Hotel* and of course that cracking Brewery and drinking venue, *Red Rock Breweries?* What could they have to do with the clues? She just couldn't do all of it. She'd go to Bishop another day. Let's hope Old Man Job comes up with a clue.

And sure enough he did - but only after a few of Sam's *Devon Scrumpy* special cider and a huge Cheese and Onion sandwich.

'The family started with John Bulley who set up in Newfoundland fishing in seventeen fifty and my relative John Job married his daughter. The company finally grew and grew to be big player in the fishing business. The French destroyed our ships that day and our warehouses so we had to move to Torbay for a while. Eventually we moved on to bigger things. The bloody French didn't stop us. But we stopped them. When the buoys pinched their booze, they also found a small chest in the Captain's cabin which one of them opened. In it were a parchment and a cup. They took the chest and a small group of five asked the Squire to read it for them. It has been passed down in rumour, that what he read shocked them to their core and they swore on their families lives to the Squire to hide the chest along with what it contained. The five swore that no one should know what it contained and formed that day in sixteen ninety the 'keepers of the secret'. Appointing one man to know the location of the hidden chest and four others the clues to where it was. The Squire held the location too in case *the keeper* was accidently or deliberately taken or killed.'

154

Françoise was fascinated by all this as it confirmed a lot of what they had been told. He asked about The Squire. 'So, at any one time two people know of where the chest is hidden? I guess that is protection for both?'

'Yes, you are correct. If matey comes looking for the treasure and tortures one, they will never know the name of the other, as even they don't know each other. They communicate through drop points in the town.'

'So, do you know who 'the Squire' is now? Albert was the keeper of course?'

'No, I does not. All we four keepers of the clues hears is a written note sent to each of us...telling us to co-operate at last with a French lady who comes to talk to us. The modern-day Squire is still a shadow for us.'

'But you know something for sure?' Françoise decided to be direct.

'Aye, maid, I does, you want a clue, don't you?'

'Yes please.'

'Here I have paper I've had for ten years. Given to me by Albert when they last moved the chest I was told.'

And he handed it to Françoise.

Look where you might find and Albatross and a pilot flying together. A girl's name points the way.

She shook her head. *Another puzzle to solve,* she thought.

Seeing her despair, Old Man Job, sympathised. 'Aye, maid, I has no clue either what he means. Anyways, I goes back now. Thank you kindly for the cider and the dinner. I hopes it all turns to the good and those bloody Frogs get a good hiding.' And seeing her smile he qualified it. 'Of course, not you maid. You are nearly Devonian!' He laughed, got up and left.

She took the train back to Teignmouth. On the way she phoned Jack to tell him of her findings and arranged to meet with him in Dicey Reilly's where he was drinking with Davey the author whom he had finally persuaded to return to the place he'd had his last nervous breakdown.

Two men separately switched off their phones, having listened to her conversation. The Cornishman smiled; we were getting close now. The Frenchman Saunière was not so happy. He was still annoyed that his man had been overcome by the mastery of Jungle Jim and was still in Torbay Hospital along with his other man, recovering from the attack at Widdecombe churchyard. He slammed down the phone and

155

whispered, '*Merde; these Devon lunatics are becoming a nuisance. It's time to call in his best soldiers: They won't fail.*'

Singapore Jack was trying to convince Davey the author that the people he drank with in Dicey's were normal. A difficult task he knew, but he was determined to try. Certainly, the Irish owner and landlord, Dominick, or Dom, was not. But everyone knew that.

He was like a whirling banshee most days. He never stopped either whizzing around with jobs to do or talking and joking in the way only the Irish can. Dicey's was his reincarnation of his career in the Irish Navy. It was ship shape and Dublin fashion every day. Poor Alice, the lovely student barmaid, had little knowledge of domestic chores and the use of a mop was beyond her. Jack watched as Dom was showing her how to swab the decks (something he did every hour on the hour). He started on the small area of the bar to show her how she should do it.

'Let me show you how to do this small bit for you and you can do the rest,' Dom was saying.

Thirty minutes later he was finishing off the whole pub while Amy stood watching and chatting to Ricki Pesci, the irascible Irish reincarnation of Joe Pesci in Goodfellas. Ricki Pesci, was a wonderful funny but sometimes cantankerous Irish manifestation of Tommy DeVito's maniacal angry character, Joe Pesci in '*Goodfellas*'. Ricki was a cracking, intelligent and caring fellow, but sadly never finishes a joke without breaking into laughter at the ultimate ending and he was chatting to Alice, Jack and Davey about cowboys:

'General Custer was riding into the Black Hills of Dakota looking for Crazy Horse and Sitting Bull. He asked his scout to come to see him. His scout came from Newcastle and was a Geordie and called Geordie. Custer took a big draw on his cigar and said to the scout: '*Geordie take some men and see if you can find where the Indians are camped.*'

Geordie said: '*Wye aye general,*' and rode off in the dust and the sun with three more ethnically coloured scouts than our immigrant from Tyneside. Sometime later Geordie returns in a flurry of horses stamping and snorting with dust covering both him and his men. He rode up to Custer who was sitting on his grey horse surveying the Black Hills who asked him: '*Did you see any Indians Geordie?*'

Geordie brushed the dust off his long coat and answered: '*Nah, boss, but I heard lots of drums over the far hills towards the Little Big Horn River.*'

Custer took a drag of his cigar and looked concerned. He asked another question: '*Were they war drums Geordie?*'

Geordie looked at Custer with a puzzled look in his eyes but answered truthfully: *'Nah, General, they were their drums.'*

The End.

Alice was puzzled by the ending but the men of the world told her the translation - in Geordie dialect the plural pronoun 'OUR' is translated as 'WOR' i.e. Our Drums, equals Wor Drums. To paraphrase Basil Brush the stuffed fox of TV fame…Boom! Boom!

Recently Charlie had told Jack of similar days at the movies in his youth. They also used to shout at the cowboys and Indian movies. Their favourite was whenever a Boot Hill cemetery came up and the men that the bad guys or good guys had wiped out with their six guns were about to be buried, they'd all shout, to the bemusement of anyone not from Kingsway council estate.

'Put him in the hole Ted!' Ted was the local gravedigger.

Again, he waxed about happy times then – 'Now you canna do that. If you did what we did at the movies you'd be arrested and given an ASBO and electronic tag as an anti- social maniac.'

Dom finished the decks and handed Alice the mop and bucket. She started at it as if it was a Quantum computer and gently stroked the head across the sparkling, pristine hospital operating theatre floor while Dom ran down the cellar to change the *Guinness* beer barrel. She was still leaning on the mop wondering how it worked when Dom ran back up carrying a huge axe and ran out the door and attacked a mountain of tree logs. He rushed back in with one that resembled a Californian Redwood trunk and threw it next to the unlit log fire. He ran back to Alice who had by now figured that the mop needed water in the bucket to work, grabbed the mop and bucket and ran back to the fire to mop and scrub the small amount of wood chips that had fallen on the wooden pub floor. He returned the mop back to Alice. He ran behind the bar and poured Davey the pint of cider he'd waited for while Dom cleaned the deck of the Dicey Reilly Bismarck. He ran past Alice, leaning on the mob against the stanchion and chatting lovingly with Ricki, a wonderful smile on her face as usual and he ran into the toilet with a screwdriver to fix the women's lavatory door.

'Does he ever stop?' Davey asked Jack.

'Nope: Anne Marie says only when they are both on holiday does he slow down.'

'He's making me dizzy and a bit guilty,' said Davey. 'I haven't worked that hard in twenty years.'

'It's normal. He's actually slowed down,' Jack said.

'Morning folks.' In walked Grumpy John. He is a somewhat milder version of Grumpy Al but without the misery and venom of the master. Much to the misunderstanding of those he engages in conversation and introducing mischievous cutting humour, he can sometime provoke unexpected reactions.

Ricki Pesci nodded and said,' Hello John,' And he then stood back. Jack and Davey both stood at either side of the two bewildered men, facing each other off like gunfighters in Ricki's cowboy jokes. Most conversations went wrong between the two. A typical conversation may be: John: 'you looking happy today Ricki. You must have had a better morning today than yesterday.'

Ricki slowly putting his pint down and feeling for his Colt 45: 'So you think that, do you?'

Cue another communication meltdown between Clint and Lee Van Cleef, as crazy Gus sat in the corner and whistled the theme from *The Good, The Bad and The Ugly... 'Whoo, whoo...whoo –whoo - whoo.'*

Wolverhampton Col came in pushing his charming diminutive wife, Trudy in her wheelchair. Col had left his home town of Dudley, in a region of the West Midlands what is quaintly termed the Black Country. Jack was never sure why this place is called this. He always thought they were all from Birmingham. However, this is a life-threatening belief and is heresy for anyone to say this to either Birmingham people or Black Country people. One can be excommunicated and burned at the stake or just head butted, whatever is the easiest. In fact, he never understood the West Midlands mainly because until moving to the lost world he had never met anyone from there. He had travelled the known world and worked in many industries and with many people, however like the Spitting Image song and video, *'I've never me a nice South African,'* He'd never met a Brummie: until his job prospects and mental state deteriorated enough to move to the 'Twilight Zone' of Devon.

There can't be many people left in the West Midlands as they all seem to have moved to the relative heaven of Devon where there are no 'Peaky Blinder' psychotic maniacs, concrete motorways or Black things at all, never mind Black Countries. They obviously love the peace, tranquillity and lack of gang warfare and homicidal maniacs in this beautiful corner of the world. He guessed who wouldn't.

Col had moved here with his endearing and charming wife, Trudi who struggled valiantly and courageously with motor neurone disease. He eases his worries and constant care of his wife by the odd pint of beer, football and sharp wit. Jack's knowledge of the geography of the West Midlands and indeed Britain was questioned and enhanced by

158

Col. He was grateful to him. He never realised that Birmingham people were Cockneys. Cockneys were from the sound of Bow Bells in London he thought. Nope: untrue according to Black Country Col.

He proved this to Jack as he challenged a pub full of Birmingham City and Aston Villa football supporters who were watching a local derby match.

'Heh you Cockneys why don't you piss off back to London.'

Jack thought here we go another who'd lost the plot. There are many such inmates in Dicey Reilly's. Col was told by those he knew what he meant, to go and boil his head (well not really but this is a family book.) The others just glowered at him and continued watching. Col continued with his baiting and Jack felt I had to ask him why he thought they were Cockneys. But Col shouted again at the two groups of separate supporters.

'You lot you're nearer Watford gap than God's country. The Black Country is the only West Midlands. You lot are Cockneys. Fifty miles from Watford Gap! All Cockneys the lot of you.'

Jack stood drinking his pint and shaking his head. He'd heard so much rivalry between football local teams. Dear me he drank for 10 years in the Asian Glasgow Rangers bar and for bigotry and pure stubborn refusal to give anyone from either Celtic or Rangers an inch, that city beats them all. And Davey told him back in his old home they even argue who has the best shopping centres and Newcastle flaunt their superiority over the fact that the Regional airport is actually called Newcastle airport and they have a bigger bridge. But he'd never met a nice South African and he never knew that Birmingham was in London.

Charlie, Kev and Roy were drinking at the bar and waxing literal about how teachers were a nightmare in the old days. Roy was talking of Killer Phillips, a psychopathic teacher at their junior school who used to have several canes in a bucket. As you were hauled up by the neck to face his wrath, he'd take out each cane and whip it into the in the fluid movement of caning he'd perfected. Roy said: 'He acted just like 'Zorro' in the movies, whipping his canes in the air like Zorro's rapier sword before thrashing you half to death.' When he was happy with the weight, spring and lethality of the cane, he would thrash the unfortunate pupil as hard as he could – then break into an ecstatic sweat as he finished.

They were also talking about the latest funerals and what had killed the poor deceased friends. 'One guy was diagnosed with bar disease not long after he died,' Roy said.

'What was that?' Jack asked.

'Oh, the Doc saw that he had a bad fungal infection under his forearm. He said he'd got he from leaning on the bar every day and the yeast from the beer had infected him. Think it finally killed him matey. It be a worry.' And they all stopped leaning their arms on the bar.

Burglar Bob was leaning on the bar in the horse racing corner with his fellow aficionados of the Sport of Kings. He heard of Killer Phillips had some very wise words on the subject. Burglar Bob is an itinerant odd job man. It is rare to see him at work however between the hours of 3 pm to 10 pm that is when Dom's fine hostelry is open. Like many contracting folk he starts early and finishes in time for a few beers before his dinner. It is also rare not to see him in plaster, putty, paint stained jeans hanging off his arse showing his builders bum and a cigarette hanging out of his mouth, regularly coughing up large bits of tar and plaster from his chest.

He has no transport for the tools that he carries, therefore he is apt to stand after a day's graft outside his client's house and place of work smoking and lounging with intent, looking highly suspicious to middle class elderly vigilantes and waiting for a taxi to his second home in Dicey's. So, it was when he was accosted by Davey's neighbour and his rather large son and asked what he was doing hanging around the neighbourhood looking like an itinerant Albanian refugee after working on the author's bathroom. (Strangely, for some unknown reason they had accosted Davey when he first arrived). Bob's rhetorical reply of: *What's it ******** got to do with you,'* didn't really help matters. So, Davey named him Burglar Bob.

Bob was standing drinking with his jeans around his arse again, he burped loudly and coughed his day's paint fumes up and turned his head and looking over the top of his 'one pound from the charity shop' thick black rimmed glasses and spoke these sagacious words. 'When I was at school the teacher asked me what I wanted to be when I grew up. I looked at him and told him I wanted to be a Lollipop man (a normally retired elderly person who saw children over the road on their journeys to and from school, stopping the traffic with assign shaped like a 'lollipop.'

'What on earth for boy?' the teacher enquired of the then youthful Bob.

'Coz I won't have to start work till I'm retired,' Bob answered truthfully and hopefully. 'The bastard caned me for saying that too!'

In Bob's days, children should be seen and not heard or ever hope of better things than an early retirement and the grave, in those happy days child beatings by teachers were the norm for anyone with acerbic wit and a perceptive brain.

Into the pub came Rugby Steve, his brother Lee and Wee Mark the baker. They had been to yet another funeral, at St James Church and then Teignmouth Rugby club. Mark provided the warm, delicious bread, pastries and patisserie from his quaint, family business, The Wee Shoppe Bakery in town and in Dawlish., The fruit and veg from his brother's family vegetable shop, Tibbs. Mrs Tibbs, his mother was one of the stalwart old characters of the own and she always had a friendly and gracious welcome for every customer. Jack liked to shop in both and particularly to talk to the friendly Thai wife of Wee Mark's brother. It reminded him so much of his Asian sojourn. And she could source good Thai veg. and spices.

'Another funeral buoys?' Charlie asked.

'Yes, Charlie,' Steve said.

'I missed this one. Marty and me are like professional mourners now. The vicar at Saint James church reserves a seat in the front pews now for us both. For God's sake we are getting like Mari, the funeral crasher. She went to every funeral there was. She scanned the paper every day for funerals and just turned up. She would even go to complete strangers and to go to eat the food after. Problem was she would sit there in church or as they carried the coffin out and say the most outrageous things, *'Aye, he was never her son'* or *'he was never her dad you know?'* In the old days she would have been burnt as a witch and buried at midnight.'

Scottish Bill leaned over the bar from the place he perpetually stood playing with his hand-held device and linked continually to his on line bookies. He took hold of a small plastic cage with a plastic mechanical bird in it and pushed the switch on the side. The bird started tweeting and whistling in a high-pitched way.

Bill said, 'It's the anniversary of Budgie's funeral today.'

Budgie having been one of what can only be described as 'characters' of this peculiar crowd and patron of Dom's excellent menagerie. Burglar Bob had brought the bird back from Benidorm one year to hang above the seat where Budgie perpetually sat, wearing only a short-sleeved Gilet and shorts in all weathers. He was known to talk incessantly and very loud, across any person's conversation. The bird was as loud and piercing as Budgie. Sadly, the bird had only been in situ above the iconic man for a few weeks before he passed away. Now it was a constant reminder of his ability to clear a bar in five minutes with his voice. And a memorial to his lasting place in the hearts of many. But whilst he was one of the most generous men most had met, his voice and constant chatter were an anathema to many.

'If I woke up in bed with Budgie on my arm; I'd bite my arm off to get out before he woke up and started talking!' Chel said, offering her own parody on the old male joke about waking with an ugly woman. It possibly says it all about Budgie and his chattering.

Charlie interrupted; 'Aye Budgie could talk. When he was the tower crane driver at the Quay, the electricians used to switch the power off to stop him coming down at lunch and talking to us in the cabin. We always paid his loving wife to make him a three-course lunch in case to keep him up there during the break. He was like a Muslim Imam trapped in his crane; the whole town thought they were being called to prayer when he started shouting down to get freed.'

Everyone laughed. Budgie would remain a fond memory for most.

'Budgie reminds me of another funeral,' began Kev. 'Fred was always borrowing money. He was good at it. Budgie being the kind man he was, lent him a tenner. He didn't pay he back and Budgie's wife gave him hell to get he back. One night they are both in *The Teign* pub and Budgie spots Fred. He slips away and gives him a tenner to pay him back in front of his wife to save him getting any more grief. Fred does a runner out of the back door with Budgie's other tenner!'

The racing corner cracked up again at one more tale of Budgie's woe. The caged bird chattered away in memory. Charlie added yet one more tale of the man's woe:

'At Fred's funeral I was sat with Budgie. When we walked out and saw the collection plate. There was a tenner on he. I turned to Budgie and said, *'take he buoy; he be the last chance you'll ever get to get he back!'* He just grimaced and put a fiver on the plate. Good buoy was Budgie.'

'Even Fred's daughter knew the craic,' Kev continued. 'At Fred's funeral reading his eulogy she said, *'I guess he owes you all a tenner?'* He was still borrowing when in his wheelchair. But not so daft, he had two grand stuffed in it they found when he went to hospital.'

'Fred could be a bit crazy though,' Charlie had to finish off the story. 'We used to have baby milk powder boats come in. He was seen violently stabbing the bags in the hold with his knife for some form of fun. The captain was terrified and wanted to call the police. We told him Rambo had just come out in the movies. He liked Rambo. Marty calmed him and we got the bags shifted. Yes, he didn't have any fear. He must have been selling mythical Christmas hampers all over the Teign Valley one year because a group of seriously big gypsy and farmer types arrived on the Quay from up Dartmoor way. They came to get their hampers but none of us buoys had a clue. It got really naughty. There was no sign of Fred all Christmas. He'd buggered off with his hamper money to Spain, leaving us to face the gyppos.'

Yorkie had come in and was standing nearby and had heard Charlie talking about Fred's dealing. Yorkie, coming from deepest Yorkshire was unintelligible to most in the bar. Some years ago, he left in a hurry and he was a young and handsome lad. He has worn a bit now but is always dapper and smart and always carrying a wedge of money from where, who knows or cares, but he knows a good horse and a deal when it arises. His dad was a scrap man of some wealth, and Yorkie followed him into the trade and then butchery and it seems they both were, shall we say, Jack the lads in those days. He began talking about his own Christmas deals he'd pulled, few understood what he was saying, but they all nodded and laughed when Jack laughed. Jack was the only one who understood him.

Dom understood Yorkie, but he'd ran out of the toilet, upstairs to his charming and pleasant wife, and pick up his VAT returns to run down to the other end of town to Greenwoods the Accountants and onto bookies to place a bet. Before he hurled up the stairs, he stopped and said hello to all:

'I hear you talking about funerals and graves and things. My brother before died he bought two plots, one for him and one for investment. He made sure his lawyer had a covenant but on the other grave so that it could only be sold to English speakers so that he could talk to them. True men; its fact.'

Dom then took the mop off Alice which she was now thinking must have some magical powers and continued in full Irish flow while he mopped up around Steve, who looked down through his aristocratic nose as if Dom was mental - which of course he was.
Dom continued 'the craic':

'He once bought a greenhouse. I went to see him in late summer and he was full of the hell. He was looking at his grow bags in the greenhouse; empty of tomatoes. He moans, *'Mary, Jesus and All the Saints I divn't understand this gardening Dom. Those tomatoes, I have been fecking waiting for the whoors to grow for months. And not a ting. Do you know what might be wrong with the whoors?* I asked where were the plants? He says, *'what fecking plants?'* I say, 'The ones you planted.' He says, *'I didn't plant any. The feckers are tomato grow bags, aren't they? I have watered the feckers and there are no tomatoes growing. I'm going back to the garden centre for me money back Dom.'*

'Indian Jack is a bit like that with funerals,' Jack said, moving on from tomatoes, as Dom ran upstairs. 'He is like Dom's brother; he wants to make sure he is ok after death. He's bought his plot already and his coffin and got an agreement with the funeral parlour here that when he is dead that they cut his wrists to make sure he is dead. Takes all kinds, I guess. Anyway Yorkie, what about that Christmas Turkey?'

'Aye: Ah wor listening to yon tale about the Christmas hampers. When ah wor a butcher at Christmas, we all got Christmas turkeys. One year, we are in t'pub drinking our bonuses in Christmas Eve and t'young apprentice was being a bit of t'lad. So, we thought we'd teach him lesson. I went back shop and swopped his turkey. I put a load of old guts and huge chunk of cheap dog meat in't bag. I took a severed turkey's neck and head and placed it out of t'bag and tied it tight. Ah took it back and gave it t'lad. He wor chuffed. He took a bus home. But after another couple of beers I felt sorry for t'lad's mother, so I took bus t'hor house with his turkey. I knocked on t' door and she opened it. I told her about the tale. She looked shocked, t'lass and told me what had happened t'lad.' He took a drink of his half of cider.

'What happened you daft bugger? Jack, can you translate mate?' Burglar Bob asked.

Yorkie continued. 'Well the lad wor pissed sat on t' bus with his bag of guts and turkeys head sticking out t'bag. Another pissed up bloke told him that he'd buy his Turkey off him because he had gotten pissed at the office party and forgotten to buy one for his family of six. So, t' young lad sold him the bag for a fiver. The daft bastard on t' bus took home a bag of beasts' guts and turkeys head and neck to his wife and kids for dinner. And he'd paid five poond for it!' Everyone laughed once Jack had translated. Yorkie finished the story. 'T' olwd lass was chuffed I brought the turkey as she'd belted hor lad and took fiver off him to buy Turkey but butchers wor closed. I guess I made someone a happy Christmas.'

'You are not too good with carrier bags are you Yorkie?' Jack mused with a mischievous grin.

Aye; bloody hell Jack, that darkie doctor wasn't ower pleased with t' badger wor he.'

Jack told the tale to the assembled patients of Dom's.

A few months ago, Yorkie had collapsed in the street with a suspected stroke. Many came to help and the ambulance was called. They loaded him and his carrier bag he had been carrying into the ambulance. At the hospital he was examined and a senior doctor called. He arrived and

164

tore into the poor Yorkshire man. 'Why you eat badger Mr Yorkie? It may have poisoned you?'

Now you may ask what the doctor was on about. Well it was simple. The shopping bag contained the severed head and guts of a badger. The hospital believed the intrepid Northern collector and butcher of road kill had devoured the beast and may well be suffering from TB, Bubonic plague or some other peculiar disease.

'Ah told black bugger. Ah don't eat badger. Ah wor taking t' guts and head to throw in t' sea. I sell the bugger, don't eat it.'

Yes. Yorkie's old days as a master butcher were not passed. 'Some people like badger, thou knows. Its hind quarters are called Yam, and taste just like ham. It's no point wasting road kill. I sold one t' Tim, the owner of a restaurant many years ago. I wor butchering a badger in t'house when our lass got vexed wi me. The fleas wor leaping out over t' hor and she told me to throw it in t'sea. Tim sees it as he walked on t' prom and asked what it wor? I knew he missed t'goat and organic food from his home, he wor a foreigner, to eat for himself and family. I told him it wor a badger hound!'

Everyone chuckled. 'Did he eat it then?' Steve asked, looking down at Yorkie from his great height, as usual looking disgusted at the tales of haute cuisine Yorkie style.

'Nor, he didn't. The daft bugger dropped his cigarette on it and set light to its fur. We had to throw it in t' sea again to put t' fire out. After that he always asked me if ah had more of them *furry mouses'*.

Jack whispered to Davey. 'Make sure you see the beast before Yorkie butchers it and sells you a nice rabbit or leg of lamb. God knows what you might eat.'

Yorkie was in full flow. 'Ah had a great life as a butcher. It's been useful here too with things since ah retired. I butchered a whole pig in t' Teign Brewery for the lads at Christmas. Where it came from I couldn't possibly say, but it had its own apple sauce.' And he winked at Jack. Jack chuckled and thought *a lot of small holdings of places with apple orchards around here.* Yorkie continued. 'Ah even managed to sell the scraps and t' guts. Some daft bugger took them in t' black bucket ah wrapped up in t' Christmas paper with a nice piece of leg sticking out of the paper. That wor only meat - just like t' Christmas Turkey yon your apprentice sold!'

Rugby Steve shook his head, unimpressed. Scottish Bill, looked up from placing bets and said, 'What about swapping the steak for mince you crafty bugger?'

Yorkie took another drink of cider and explained to the waiting masses. 'Ah forgot that Bill. A posh wifey used to come in t'shop and wanted fillet steak minced up for her bloody Pekinese dog. She would pay for steak and owner would take i'nt back to the mincer and mince it and give it t'hor and t'bloody hound would slaver as she put in t' shopping bag. Ah couldn't afford steak them days and bloody dog gets best cut. But one day the owner let me serve her. I did that but after a few weeks of this ah thouwt why should dog get t'best meat, so every day she came in I started mincing up the shite leftovers from the floor and I put the fillet steak in mah pocket and took it home t'wife. She thought I wor marvellous saving mah money and treating hor every Saturday night t' fillet steak and half a bitter.'

'You're a bloody rogue you olwd bugger,' said Enid the lovely older lady as she passed, hearing the tale, who came in every day with her ex-navy partner Alan. Enid had known many like Yorkie and the lads in the bar. She had had a glorious life as a landlady to the lost and bewildered and Yorkie was a favoured rogue of hers.

Yorkie didn't catch what she said and turned to watch the races. Sadly, the badger-induced stroke had affected Yorkie's sight and his hearing was not great now, so he sometimes made big mistakes. He had the day before walked in and right up to a stranger and tourist from up country standing at the bar enjoying Dom and Anne Marie's excellent *Guinness* in the company of his partner. With his dodgy eyesight he thought he was a certain lovely lad with a certain affinity for the ladies. He leant into him and looked up at him and said, 'you dorty stop out you! Bet you were drinking and shagging all t' night that lass you picked up in here.' Wrong man! - the lady left alone after slapping her partner.

'He must have hundreds of tales Jack?' Davey said.

'He has. Some will have to wait till the statute of limitations is over!' And grabbing Yorkie's arm, 'Heh, Yorkie, tell Davey of the posh owners you worked for in the butchers and the sausages. I love that one.'

Yorkie came nearer and shuffled near Davey and he said, 'A Thatcher's wouldn't go a miss young man. We pensioners struggle tha know.'

Davey smiled, got his money out and called Alice over. She was still mopping the area around her feet. Yorkie told his tale. Jack translated for Davey.

'I wor working as a young lad at really posh family's butcher's shop. This night ah'd had a night out wi mah dad and ah couldn't drink them days like him and his mates. I wor going out wi young lass who wor tax

166

inspector. Dad had a dodgy mate in his pub who was being investigated. Dad and his mate had asked me to offer hor a monkey, five hundred pound, for t' tax file. Ah took money and met hor and asked if she'd fancy a holiday with me if she'd hand me t' file. The bugger said she fancied a career instead!' And he chuckled. Then he summed up the doomed relationship. 'We were obviously not compatible Jack, so I broke up with hor.'

'A bit sad that mate,' said Jack sympathetically.

The great man took a sup of his half a cider and lamented. 'In a way Jack, but a straight tax inspector would nivva have worked out. Bit like marrying a poliss wife. Me father would have nivva have slept reet agin. But was silver t'lining you knows as we supped a lot of the five hundred quid that neet in consolation and ah got drunk. The next day I was rough with t'drink. I wor sent in t'cellar to mek sausages. T'cellar was boiling hot, low roof and t' big vat of boiling meat and fat wor reeking. I wor sweating with the drink and feeling ill. Then my stomach heaved and I spewed everything up in t' sausage mix. Ah bends down to get a ladle to ladle up the spew and it had disappeared. The boss is shouting down all the time for t' sausages, so ah had to mek them. I kept looking for spew as ah filled t' skins but kept being sick. All the time t' boss was shouting down. Anyway, I took his sausages up to sell and after working all morning later went in the back room where we all had dinner every day. They wor posh so me, t' boss, t'owner and his fat stuck up wife dressed up like dog's dinner. She bollocked me for being so hung over and kept giving me stick. She opens the dish on t' table and bugger me, t' dinner is sausage and liver casserole; the sausages ah made. She ladles some onto hor plate with some vegetables. Ah looks on while the others do t' same. The fat wife then bites on hor sausage and a white bit of spew oozes out of t'skin down side of hor mouth. She teks her silver napkin ring and wipes it off and swallows the whole lot of the rest. Ah runs out holding the spew in mah mouth and vomits on the pavement.'

Everyone smiled at the poor man's misfortune and Yorkie finished his tale of sausage woe. 'Ah couldn't eat t' liver and sausage casserole for yors'

Even Davey laughed but when Yorkie began asking him again if he wanted to put six goslings in his garage and his wife's lawn and grow them for Christmas, he decided to go talk to Enid and Alan. The final straw being when he said he'd butcher them at Christmas when they were fat geese along with a couple of badgers which he'd sell as pork in a Christmas meat package.

Charlie was chatting about early drinking and how *The Old London Hotel* was always open early for drinking if you were resident. But the Quay boys could get in at nine if they had no boat to work on and were laid off for the day. This prompted another Yorkie story. He said he nearly had the sign off the hotel when they were knocking it down. 'It wor probably worth a lot of money as it wor the Queens Head and Arms and reet gold coloured. We dressed pretending to be as painters and I wrote a sale agreement for it. We wor up ladders screwing it off when the last screw kept slipping in't its hole. We wor worried it would fall and smash. And then there wor huge banging at back of hotel and some men who had been boarding the windows up as young lads from t'town had been chucking bricks through windows. They shouted at us, *'who the hell are you!'* Ah takes me dodgy sales agreement to them and tells them to phone owners. They bugger off to phone box and we do a runner. Bastard had the sign away hisel. He was selling it in *T' Teign* next day.'

Jack thought *the ways of the transgressor are hard.*

This put Yorkie was on a roll and he took a drink of his Thatcher's and said to Jack, 'Did I tell you bowt the non-stick frying pans lad?'

Jack, who had heard the story but forgotten it in a haze of Jail Ale and Devon Red, replied in the negative. He too enjoying the errant Yorkshire man's tales.

'Well Jack, those days ah wor a young jack the lad. Me and me mate had bought a load of dodgy non-stick frying pans from someone who worked at Tower factory. They wor all skipped as t' coating was crap. Ah bought thyem for fifty pence each. We took them in t'van tut Pennistone market. Ah has a butane bottle and gas burner grill at back of t'van and ah have bought to good pans from the shop which ah put bacon, eggs in and with t' fat. Ah shouts out to the market, 'Come and get yr bacon eggs, non-stick pans   two for a fiver!' Just like Del Boy on't *'Fools and Horses'*. Ah gets loads of punters coming ower. They see the bacon and eggs sliding all ower t'pan and start getting their brass out. A new Tower non-stick frying pan was seven poond at time. Ah sold loads of them. Ah had about fifteen left to sell about two in the afternoon when ah sees this wifey walking down the street with t'pan in hor hands. Eee, she looked angry, so ah says to my mate, *'get fire out quick, we're doing a runner'.* The bloody woman arrives just as we are trying to get t'van sorted and shows me t' pan. It wor covered in black shite of the non-stick coating and the bacon and eggs of hor husband's breakfast wor burnt and stuck all ower t' thing. Ah tries to jump in't van but she grabs me. *'My husband has been at work all neet and I cooked his*

168

breakfast when he got up at two and this bloody mess happens. A want me money back! Or I'll brain you with this heap of shite.' And she lifts pan up to bash me heed. Ah gives her a couple of quid and jumps int' van and me mate accelerates away. Just our bloody luck, the only punter to cook something afor we could sell the lot. But ah made a bob or two that day Jack.'

'You always do you old villain you,'

'Afor ah go to t'bookies ah'll tell you another Turkey tale. Me fatha got me a butcher's shop and ah had a deal with lad in t' Salford to sell me two yor old Turkeys. They'd been frozen for ower two yors. Ah buys then for one pound a pound and sells them for fower. This young lass used to come in t'shop and was getting married. Ah used to try to flirt with hor. She comes in afor Christmas and asks for a capon for hor mother in law and father in law. Ah tries tap hor up, but she has just been married so she laughs and says she'll be back if capon isn't good. Ah thowt sod bloody capon ah'll sell t'hor an old frozen small turkey like all t' rest. Ah used to defrost them but they wor blue with the cowld so I'd warm them up with t' hairdryer and rub salt into them to brighten them up and sell em as fresh turkeys. After Christmas ah teks all left overs and t'olwd turkeys and am trying to fresh them up agen when in comes hor mother in law. Ah thinks here we go she's sussed me owt and ah hides in't freezer. Me boy meets hor and ah hears hor say she loved the bird, and wanted to buy more! Ah comes out of hiding and ah sells hor all t'd old frozen turkeys as fresh bloody capons. Daft bugger she gave me big kiss. But ah had a reet good Christmas that yor.'

'You owld bugger. Christmas as well. No wonder Davey doesn't want to grow your bloody geese for you in his garage.'

'Ah nivva cheated mah mates Jack. Mind ah did mek a bob or two out of some punters. Ah always knew if a punter knew abaht t' meat. And those wifey's who were clued up ah gave best cuts to. The others ah'd give the owld meat from the boiler cows ah'd buy cheap of the knacker yard. Loved it when there wor two wifeys in t'shop and one would come in and say *'That joint you sold me last week was tough as boots Adrian.'* Ah'd say, *'never Mrs Johnson'* and ah'd say t' wife who ah sold good beef to, 'What *wor yours like Mrs Wood?'* She'd reply, 'Mine *wor lovely Adrian, tender as owt and beautiful taste.'* Ah'd turn to other wife and say, 'Your cooker must be a bit dodgy Mrs Johnson.' She'd say, *'Aye it must be. I'll have it looked at.'*

'You con man you. Poor lasses,' Jack said chuckling.

'A working man has to earn a spare bob or two Jack. Best thing wor ah sent me mate around to fix hor cooker. We made a fiver between us.' And he left to clean up at the bookies.

Gus had started wailing and playing his Bob Marley air guitar in the corner, 'No woman no cry...' Dicey's was becoming Davey's nemesis, he could tell he was about to need the tablets again and he went to talk to Grumpy John. Stumpy Tony came into the bar. A large ex-biker who had lost his leg in an accident when young and still walked with a crutch. He took up a seat at the end of the bar. Yorkie's tales were not for him, nor were Gus's electric guitar solos and howling. He too like Col was a Wolves supporter and avid Black Country independence man. Today he was wearing a tee-shirt with 'Pikelets - not ****** Crumpets' printed on. This a major cause of angst in the lost midlands. To Tony and Col they are pikelets. To the rest of the world they are crumpets. In Wolverhampton, crumpets are for wimps. It is a problem worse than the Schleswig Holstein question or the Brexit backstop. Only Black Country men can solve it.

Tony has a wealth of scientific theories; one of which is the effects of Jamaican tobacco and cider on the motor neurone function of one-legged bikers and the longevity of Siamese fighting fish. It seems that if you smoke Jamaican tobacco, drink ten pints of cider and attempt to descend the flight of stairs from your friend's upstairs' bedroom, you may forget you only have one leg and try to place the missing limb on the top step. This has an effect not unlike entanglement in quantum theory where a related event anywhere in the universe will have an effect in a completely different part of the universe. In Tony's experiment, his attempt to place a missing leg on a vertical staircase had an 'entangled' effect on the Siamese fish living in the fish tank at the bottom of the stairs. Namely, his head ended up smashing through the glass and the fish disappearing down his throat into a huge black hole!

Who says God doesn't play dice...?

Charlie was talking about how woodwork at school was useful to them as none of them were going to be Classics lecturers at Oxford. Roy was asking why was it that all woodwork and metalwork teachers, like Killer Phillips were sadistic lunatics. Music and art were lost on most at school and Maths might as well have been Swahili to many. Enid threw in that her son was not good at art and his school report said, 'He is good at tidying up'. Stumpy said his maths teacher had written off his mate's ability, 'I hear he's good at football.'

They laughed. Charlie just grunted in appreciation of how the world has changed. 'The way schools are now with white boards, gender neutral, LGBT by x-squared toilets; teachers canna say that about kids these days. In our day they could beat you to death and your fatha would do same when you got out of hospital.'

Françoise came in and she and Jack retired from the circus which was the bar to the top lounge. Jack said hello to the two brothers who came in there every day in their shorts and purported to run some form of internet business. Davey had told him he doubted that they ran anything, he was becoming more convinced they were part of the spy ring that included Jimmy the Hat, Queer Richard, MI5 Mick and possibly Red Martin, who may well be a communist sleeper, turned mole for the CIA. And don't get him on about the cider man with the bag in *The Teign*. Jack passed him another *mandy* to calm him down.

Dom ran in and said hello to Françoise, ran behind the bar, took the mop off Alice who was admiring its grace and simplicity, scrubbed around her feet, gave her it back and poured Françoise a coffee.

Françoise talked for some time about what she had heard from Old Man Job. They were now at a bit of a stalemate. The clue didn't make sense to each of them.

Look where you might find and Albatross and a pilot flying together. A girls name points the way'

'Why do they make them so obtuse and cryptic?' Jack said.

'So that no one can accidently solve them I suppose,' Françoise sighed. Her phone rang. She answered and listened quietly. The Budgie memorial bird was still chattering and whistling away in the background so she had to ask the person to speak up. Jack thought, *it's as if the bugger was still alive. He's haunting us.*

Françoise ended the call and said, 'Well we might know tomorrow.'

'Why's that Françoise?'

'That was that man that sounds Cornish. I know he's Cornish now because he talks just like that Navy man downstairs who never sits down, Alan, Enid's partner. He is in *The Smuggler's Inn* with two people from France who want a meeting. They want to know where we are and what we are doing next. He says if I don't co-operate bad things will happen again. I have to meet them in *The Castle* pub in Holcombe.'

'I'll come with you.'

'No Jack, he just wants me. They say we must be close now to the treasure and these two French people have come to make sure we don't cheat them out of what is rightfully theirs. Who the hell they are I have no idea? This is getting out of hand Cherie.'

'I am beginning to think we should throw the towel in go to police and tell your aunt to go to the Gendarmerie.'

'Let's give it one last shot. I will meet them and see what they say. We still need one more clue. We only have three keepers who have revealed themselves. And now we have a Squire to think about, whoever he or she is.'

'Ok, it's time to go, I think. Crazy Gus is playing his air guitar. Stumpy is about to bash him with his crutch. Yorkie's boys have brought him a suspicious looking carrier bag with a hoof hanging out and Grumpy and Ricki Peci are squaring off in gunfighter mode like Buster Scroggs and Surly Joe. By the way I think I'll rename Purple/Grumpy Al, Surly Al. Did you ever see *'The Legend of Buster Scroggs'*? No. Well it's worth watching. Grumpy/Purple/Surly Al, Ricki Pesci and Grumpy John could make a fortune on a sequel. Oh God! Julian, loud Phil, the Welshman and the two Dawlish boys that never work more than one hour a day on roofs have come in. The noise levels will destroy your ear drums and Davey is twitching and reaching for his anti-anxiety drugs again. I fear he is going to need more *mandies* to get over this session. He is close to another breakdown. Oh no! Gus is about to sing. Best head out the back way.'

And they did.

The two brothers in shorts, seemingly deep in thought and discussion about cricket on the telly or web design or something, said goodbye as they passed. One of them took his mobile and phoned France.

CHAPTER EIGHTEEN

The Cornishman met the two who had been sent by the Priory in *The Smugglers Inn* on the border of Holcombe and Dawlish. They had come at the insistence of the Minister in London and were given specific instructions by The Abbott/Grand Master to help The Cornishman in the treasure search and his mission to stop Saunière destroying the secret. They were not what he had expected. For some reason he thought they would be huge, dangerous and violent men. He was surprised to see two women turn up at the pre- arranged lunch they were having. Both were French and both were slim and attractive. Both spoke perfect English. He sat looking over the fields and cliff tops to an azure and sparkling sea and the ambience helped calm him down from the anger he felt at being humiliated when The Prior had told him he needed help. It was such a lovely day and the stunning views and peace of the place helped keep his temper in check. The two pretty girls also helped.

'What have they found out up to now?' one of the ladies asked, lighting up a cigarette and taking a drink of her chilled white wine.

'They have solved a couple of the clues and I believe they have now found three of the keepers of the clues and are close to meeting the fourth. I have the phone tapped and they have to keep us updated on fear of their lives if we need to know more.'

'Any sign of Saunière's men?' the lady with the smartly cut sun dress asked nonchalantly.

'Not since the incident at St James Church. The one I floored with the wooden branch at Widdecombe churchyard is still recovering in hospital it seems. The one who accosted and chased Françoise, who was thrown over the railway line by the jungle juiced crazy, has disappeared. So, at the moment we have no indication if he has sent any others over yet.'

The girl in pale blue shorts spoke. 'So, what do we do next? The Abbott wants the treasure found urgently. It seems the signs are aligning in the heavens and across Europe. Now is our time. The Priory will awaken and we will establish Sion where it should have been for all time.'

The Cornishman looked at them both. He was never interested in their fantasy of establishing Sion or revealing the true faith. His mission was to get Cornwall back to where it was ordained to be by the Holy hand of God and by the feet and blood of Christ - for Cornwall to rule from Sion. These Devonians who accidently stole our destiny must soon be routed and the truth and the Royal assent be published. Only then would his family who have sought and protected this be at rest. He would die to reveal the truth. The Divine Right of Cornwall and Sion was his dream, his life and his destiny. No one, not these French girls, not these Teignmouth bumpkins nor Saunière's devilish offspring would stop him.

He was broken out of his vision by one of the lady assassins. 'Well, what do we do next, monsieur?'

'We wait and we talk to the two of them who are near the end. We remind them of the risk to them and their families and we watch. We have waited two thousand years another few days won't stop what we know is right. And now we eat.'

He waved over a waiter to order some lunch. Ben, a student on summer vacation came over and handed a few menus and explained the extensive and fabulous carvery options. The Cornishman had eaten here a few times now. He liked the place. Despite it was one of the most popular venues in South Devon for eating and drinking with fabulous views, he always liked the personal service and friendly ambience. Nick the owner and his son, and his huge friendly Rottweiler always made everyone welcome, both tourist and local. The new managers Bernie and Natalie had made him welcome and Ben was his favourite waiter as he was helpful, respectful and a laugh. He'd enjoyed a few |Sandford Orchard Devon Mists and Dartmoor Legend pints at the bar with Nottingham Forest Colin, listening to his tales of woe. A great professional and bringer of joy, as no one could have the mishaps that happened to Col, one could count one's blessings.

He also adored the steak and kidney puddings. Hand made every day; they were the best he'd ever eaten. He had to accept it that some good things came from Devon. But don't get me on about Scones and Jam and Cream; there was only one way to eat them and he would fight for that right. Also, pasties were Cornish, not bloody Devonian. Everyone knew they had been invented in Cornwall with the big crimped pastry on the top side of the pasty so that the tin miners could eat them holding the crimped pastry which they then threw away as it was contaminated with tin and heavy metals. He'd had a fierce argument with an ex docker one day last week in *The Blue Anchor* bar in Teignmouth, who told him in no uncertain terms that pasties were pasties not *Bake Off* show stoppers. *'Don't you be daft buoy? Do you think a working man in the mines is going to worry about dirty hands and is going to pick up a pasty just by the crimped edges? Have you tried to eat one like that? You spill all the filling all down your gob man. And don't get me on about the fairy story you buggers from Cornwall spread about pasties having one side savoury and the other sweet. Do you think us is daft here? A working man down a mine doesn't have a desert or pudding for Christ's sake. And his tin miner's wife is going to bake a pasty with two special separated compartments one for meat and two vegetables and the other nice crème brûlée.'*

Charlie the man was called he remembered. Bloody Devon locals, all smugglers and turnip munchers, like those Somerset buffoons. We are God's chosen race; Bretons, Ancient British even Welsh for God's sake but not bloody English. Descended from a Holy line and soon what we have sought for centuries will get us that Independence from those Anglo Saxons in London. And then that bloody man in there with his questions and attempts to get me to support Exeter City football club. Everyone knows Plymouth Albion is the only team.

His two Gallic countrymen, well women, chose the carvery options and when they returned, they couldn't believe the amount that they could eat and the choice of vegetables and meats. Both had one piece of meat and a salad. They were French.

'We will walk back to the farm house bed and breakfast in Holcombe Village after this and you should ring this French girl Françoise. We would like to meet her and reinforce to her the danger her aunt is in and that she must keep us up to date. I will guarantee her safety from Saunière's men. We can kill a lot more effectively than the crazy Amazon knife throwing Tarzan. Believe me.' And she looked at the man from St. Austell straight in his eyes. *Yes*, he thought as he saw the cold steely blue eyes and realised why these two had been sent, *I believe you.*

'Ok, I'll phone her and we can meet in *The Castle Pub* in Holcombe.

The Castle is a lovely country pub in the small village of Holcombe, nestling between Teignmouth and Dawlish above Smugglers Cove which is accessed down the historical Smugglers path to the red sandy beach which stretches all the way to Spray Point and onwards to the expansive sandy beaches of Teignmouth. Françoise had walked along the sea wall from Teignmouth. She passed the old historic pier, The Grand Pier, built in 1865 and could hear the amusement machines whirring and clanging away as the kids were enjoying themselves inside the pier on their school holidays. She walked along the prom and passed Mr Grumpy's *East Cliff cafe*. She smelt the bacon cooking and smacked her lips as she enjoyed many a pot of steaming tea and bacon butty sat overlooking the Channel, winter or summer. It was pleasant stop after a session swimming in the heated outdoor Lido pool next door. She hoped the lido would not suffer further funding cuts as it was her favourite facility in the town. Today the sea was sparkling and Mr Grumpy was slightly less grumpy than his usual 'tourist attractive' personality. He wasn't even wearing his 'bah humbug' black and white Christmas hat, so something must have cheered him up. Must be wind she thought. It took her about thirty minutes to walk to Holcombe and she counted two trains passing on her left side as they travelled along Brunel's finest railway. She never stopped wondering how this iconic engineer had designed and built this unique and historic railway line so close to the raging English Channel. And it had lasted nearly 300 years. She waved at the tourists as they looked out of the train windows over the sea wall across the beach to the shimmering sea they would soon be paddling and swimming in.

She spotted Pixie walking his huge Great Dane on Holcombe beach. She waved at the small and stocky, long haired docker. He was being pulled along the beach by his hound. The hound was taller than Pixie Dave. It amused her to see his struggle to contain the beast. She was pleased she had Piaf, no arm wrenching walks there. Pixie waved back.

Françoise walked on and reflected on the recent events that might see the end of this beautiful beach. Due to excessive wear and tear of the cliffs the railway company had submitted proposals to collapse the cliffs and move the railway line offshore, destroying the beach. Madness, and to many local and tourists alike, an act of wanton disregard for the reasons people come to visit and live in this beautiful part of the world. She and Pixie had joined the 'Save Holcombe Beach' campaign just last week. She grinned to think of any railway official trying to stop his huge hound from enjoying its drag of little Dave along the beach. And being French she may well don her Yellow Jacket and set her Gallic bulldog, Piaf on their ankles. Vive les gilets jaunes!

She reached The Salty Dog cafe at the end of the sea wall and bumped into Anne Marie, the landlady from Diceys and her friend on their weekly power walk as they took a well-earned drink there. The Salty Dog was like an oasis for anyone walking the beautiful sea walks and provides life-saving good food and drink to thirsty travellers. 'Hi Anne, how's Dom today?' she asked as she stopped next to the walking couple at the cafe.

'Bejesus Francoise, he's no different. He was fixing a new head onto the mop for Alice when I left. It seems she has mastered the art of mopping now and worn the bloody thing out. Now they both have rubbed off the paint on the bar floor with the mop, he's training her how to paint the whole floor during the forst half of the Man United match on Saturday afternoon in time for her to serve the drinks at the half time rush. Bejesus, she's just a young lass I tell him, she'll nivva do it. It took Tom two years to master that one.'

'Does he ever sleep?' Francoise asked comfortingly.

'Only on holiday. But he keeps mumbling and waking up the first couple of days, with the nightmares. It seems he is having the same one as he wakes up screaming, *'Gus, Gus, no, you'll need a bigger stool. I don't fecking know how my fecking Wi Fi is!'* Then he calms down for a few hours. It seems that Davey that author has a similar dream too. Must be the lack of Guinness on holiday.'

'Well send him my love and the kids. I'm off up that hill to *The Castle* to meet someone. See you soon.'

She climbed the road from Smugglers Cove up Smugglers Lane her mind drifted to yesterday's conversation with the man who had saved them at Widdecombe churchyard. She really did not want to get involved anymore with these shadowy people but the thought of her aunt or her friend Jack being hurt was too frightening not to accept the meeting today. She climbed up the steep path amongst the overgrown tress and clear stream rushing down the steep banks to the Cove. The rushing water, green creepers, bird calls and forest smells made her think she could have been in an Amazon rain forest. *And maybe* she thought *this was the path that the smugglers took after looting the French ships all those centuries ago. Maybe here in some long-hidden cave in the stream banks was the treasure. Well maybe soon she'd know if they could decipher that last clue.* Or maybe it was buried under the curious and very strange stone statue of a Lady's head that nestled amongst the trees high above the falling stream. It was a constant question of why someone would put a twenty-foot statute of someone's head looking only into the darkness of the tree lined gully. *Maybe to hide the treasure* she mused as she passed it on her left.

She passed Holcombe Orchard on her left and exited the steep wooded path to main Dawlish Road. She crossed over and followed the road along Hall Lane past the houses on the right until she reached the single-track old London Road that wound its way up the hedge lined narrow road to the top of Dawlish Road and onto Teignmouth. *The Minadab*, a quaint thatched, five-star roof bed and breakfast marking the end of the single road. She took the other direction up the steep hill past the thatched cottages that mark this pretty Devon village and then the small, pretty village church on her right. She had attended a couple of her patients' funerals lately there and was mightily impressed with the Church and its vicar, a lovely lady called Chris. The gardens and the remembrance wall were particularly beautiful with smashing sea views. She always reflected that it would be nice place to be put to rest. As she looked over into the garden and remembered why she was coming here today, she hoped that she wouldn't need Chris's kind and holy obituary soon.

The Castle was one minute away and she entered the small bar. Norma the constant presence behind the bar, and many days also in the small quality restaurant, greeted her warmly as she always does.

'Hello Françoise; what brings you up here today? And what would you like?'

'Hi Norma: I'm meeting a couple of people for lunch. I'll have a drop of that lovely spiced rum and ginger beer from the Two Drifters local brewery, please.'

Françoise looked around for a stool at the bar. To the right the usual lunchtime crowd of displaced, and often demented, regulars sat discussing the world's woes. Norma's pets, she called them as they needed constant care and attention when let out of their own kennels and hutches. Norma tended to her flock daily; she was indeed the Good Shepherdess. One of her favourite pets, Scottish Ken, shouted across to Norma and put his cider glass on the bar as she was serving Françoise.

'Norma! Can a man not get some service in here? Gassing with women all day; we'll have to retire you soon.'

Norma ignored the banter, as she did most days. 'What can I do with them Françoise? Their poor partners or carers need their respite and I have to send them home to them every day. It's a constant battle to stop them getting too drunk.'

Françoise smiled, Norma was a very kind, caring and moral person and she understood Norma's dilemma, sell them drink to keep her employer Steve in vast quantities of red wine, or deny them the medicine that their long-suffering partners or doctors had mostly banned them from imbibing in large quantities. Most days she controlled them with the subtlety of a true bar professional, and also a rabid dog handler.

Françoise knew most of them and she sat down next to Robbie, a quiet, charming local man, who seemed some days to be misplaced amongst the most disturbed of Norma's flock. He appeared to be quite sane.

Botanic Bob was sitting in the corner next to Graham, the Old Bill, he called over to Françoise. 'Hello Françoise, what are you doing up here this early?'

'I am meeting some people for lunch. How are you keeping now?'

'Well, I'm fine now thanks. Norma keeps me in check, don't you my dear?'

'Someone has too. All of you need help,' Norma answered whilst taking the money from two customers who had finished lunch.

Françoise chuckled again. Botanic Bob was a cracking man, so helpful and kind. But like most in here, some days he needed, and was subject to, Norma's psychotic therapy. A life of living amongst shrubs and trees and the vagaries of Brussels and the European community and Civil Service mandarins had turned him slightly strange one day and he fell into the caring kennels of Norma. He had been there ever since.

'I knew Doris Day before she was a virgin.' Scottish Ken was chatting about women again. The 'kennel club corner pets' angst knew no bounds when it came to the many ladies' clubs that lunched in *The Castle*. The sound of their merriment and chatting that emanated from the open dining room next to kennels was the cause of much discussion and distress.

'What would you call a collection of noisy women?' was a perennial question as the sound levels and laughing and chatting grew to aeroplane take off decibels. The winner was voted upon. It was; 'a cackle of women'.

The talk of women and how they tortured the poor men was normal, healthy conversation in the kennel club. And it was no different today. Ken continued his woes about the fairer sex.

'Years ago, when I was young, I once was in a bar in London and this wonderful, and amply sized barmaid kept serving me Guinness. She was Australian and could take the banter from the lads. A few were trying to hit on her. I thought why not, I'm better looking than these. And her bosom was just magnificent and I told her so. I also asked if she'd write her phone number on the Guinness top rather than the shamrock she carefully drew with the beer tap. She said of course she would and brought the pint over. She did no more than lift her left tit out of her blouse and wrote, 'bugger off' and then put it back saying, 'that's the closest you ever get to these you pommy bastard.'

'Language Ken!' Norma whispered over to her errant patient. She monitored them for expletives with like the loving care of Jamie, the Teignmouth Baptist minister. Not that religion or politics was allowed to be discussed much. Women were easier to talk about, but quietly, mainly because everyone lived in fear of Norma and her retribution - no beer.

'We're not in Church Norma,' Twelve Wheel Bill, the Man City supporting retired lorry driver explained.

'Aye, bloody hope not too,' said Ken. 'Did I tell you Françoise about one time in Glasgow when I went into one of the dark gloomy windowless bars?'

'Nope Ken. But I guess you are going to.'

'Well this razor scarred man came up to be and asked, *What religion are you?*' As you know up there if you are the wrong one you can get badly hurt. I said, *'None. I am an atheist'.* He looked at me puzzled, went away and kept looking back at me scowling. I worried that I'd upset him. He then put his drink down and came over. *'Heh Jimmy, are you a Catholic atheist or a Protestant atheist?'* I drank up and hurried out. They are mad up there.'

Welsh Jim, nodded, 'They aren't much better in the valleys boyo.'

Françoise looked around and thought maybe it was the same in here. Turkey Pete came in a rare daytime visit. 'Hi Françoise; Are you ordering a turkey from me this Christmas maid?'

'Yeah: I'll have the normal one. It's a bit early isn't it? Poor birds I hope you don't let on to them what their fate is just yet,' she joked.

'What about the Irish Turkey then?' Botanic Bob shouted over.

'What about it?' Turkey Pete asked naively.

'It was looking forward to Christmas,' Bob chuckled and ordered another beer from his trainer.

'I always feel for Turkeys,' Françoise added. 'Can you remember that Christmas advert for a big supermarket store, I think? It showed all those cartoon turkeys pecking around and happy in the sunshine. And then one snowflake falls. They all look up to the skies and one just goes *'gulp'* and its Adam's apple goes up and down with such a sad face on. It makes me cry every time I think of it.'

Rex, Norma's husband, looked on. He was a hunting man, 'pheasants and turkeys were bred for it and they like it' and not in great sympathy with Françoise's sadness.

The talk had moved on to golf. Bob was talking about his days up North where he had joined the Craft Club. This was a gentleman's club within the golf club where each of the members planted a spring flower bulb in a pot in the autumn. They then bet a bottle port on whose bulb broke through first.

Old Bill Graham was puzzled. 'Sounds riveting, a bit like the Leek Growing Show that mad bugger Sunderland Dave has introduced here; Bringing leeks from County Durham. He's another cracker pot that one. What was the fun in growing a bulb?'

180

'Well, everyone gets absolutely mortal drunk. Most are carried out by their wives. A lot are dead now,' Botanic Bob explained.

'Why the CRAFT club? There's no craft or skill in planting a bloody bulb,' lamented Twelve Wheel Bill, his Lancashire practicality showing through.

'Well it meant '**CAN'T REMEMBER A** ******** **THING**'.' Bob explained, taking a drink and chuckling.

'Language!' Norma shouted through from the kitchen.

'Bloody woman. Ears like a bloody bat,' Scottish Ken concluded, but quietly in case she actually heard. He still needed one more pint for his quota.

The Cornishman and his two French 'hit girls' came in. He tapped Françoise on the shoulder and she apologised to the circus animals at the bar and they took up their place a reserved table away from the others near the restaurant window. Steve, the enigmatic tenant of the pub took their order. Steve was like Bob from *The Brass Monkey* and he competed for the longest tenant of the same public house. Steve with Heavitree Breweries and Bob with St. Austell's and the granddaddy of them all the landlord of the Devon Arms. He was now both cook and waiter with his ex-partner Julie. He cooked and served really good fine food in a cosy atmosphere. Most lunchtimes it was full with locals, women's groups, walkers and general country folk. Today it was quiet, which was what Françoise was hoping. She did not want her problems passed around.

'These are my colleagues from France,' The Cornishman started the conversation and drinking a first mouthful of Steve's best Tarka Otter Lager.

Françoise scowled. 'I hope you are not part of those that hurt my aunt? If you are, I might just walk out.'

The lady with the steel eyes, stared menacingly at her and said,' If it had been us Cherie, she would be floating on the Seine by now. Calm down we are not here to hurt you. Just to help keep you focused on what we all want. The treasure: The secret.'

'Françoise, tell us where we are now? Maybe we can help you and Jack?'

'I'd rather you kept out of our lives.'

The steely eyed lady whispered. 'You know we can't do that. It's gone too far now. The men who attacked you will not stop. We are your only hope, so co-operate. It's the only way.'

So, over lunch she explained about the last of the clues they had found and solved. How they now were looking for an Albatross and a pilot.

'Well we will expect you to get these last hurdles jumped and you will keep us informed. Remember we are always here and we will hurt you and your friends to get our dreams accomplished. You are nothing. We have waited two thousand years for this. A simple French woman from this remote wilderness won't stop us. Think carefully and co-operate. If not? Well you know what.'

The three left the pub and Françoise felt she needed to wash the bad taste out of her mouth so she moved to go back to Crufts in the bar. However, she was stopped in her tracks by a revelation that she never expected. Norma sat down next to her. She looked at her through her kind eyes and shook her to her bones. 'I believe you are looking for the last keeper of the clues. Well, here I am. What do you want?'

CHAPTER NINETEEN

Françoise was stunned. Never in a thousand years would she have thought Norma, a humble lovely person in a beautiful Devon village would be her possible saviour. How on earth was this possible? And she asked Norma.

'My mother's family is linked to this area for centuries. Dad was Cornish, but they all say he couldn't help that. My family were part of the French ship raid. I am the last link and Albert warned me just before he died, I might need to give up the burden soon. So here I am. I heard most of what those two horrible persons were telling you.'

Dear me Françoise thought, *Norma misses nothing, she always seems to know what is going on. Maybe she is the best of all of the keepers.*

'Yes, things are dangerous Norma. I really do not want you involved or please don't tell anyone about these people. They are evil I think.'

'I understand my dearie. I guess you want what I keep?'

'It would be great if you can help.'

'Well, all I have is this.' And she took a piece of paper from her pocket.

Françoise opened it up and read it:

'On a hill far way He was lost then found. On the hill that overlooks the Hound. X marks the Grail.'

'What on earth does that mean,' Françoise exclaimed, to no one but in frustration again.

'I have no idea. I have thought and thought about it for many years ever since Albert gave me it. I know most of what goes on around here and have walked, ridden, rowed almost all of the hills, coves, rivers but still can't understand it.'

'One clue we have refers to an Albatross, a pilot and a girl's name. Maybe it's the same hills?'

'Well, the only Hound I can think of that's linked to hills, is Hound Tor. The granite outcrop on Dartmoor where the Hound of the Baskervilles was supposed to have roamed,' Norma suggested.

'Dear God. Dartmoor is a big place. I know of no Albatrosses or pilots there? Do you?'

'Haven't a clue,' Norma said and looked kindly at Françoise. 'Maybe you should just give up. Tell the police about those horrible people.'

'I can't do that. Despite the threats, I really want to get this mystery solved. I will not be beaten.'

'You just can't get the staff these days!' Scottish Ken was peering in through the dining room cider glass in hand.

'Come on I'll get you a drink. Relax a bit before you start again with this puzzle,' Norma said, stroking her friend's hand, ignoring her tormentor's pleas for more drink. And standing up she walked through to the sheep fold that contained her pet lambs.

'It's time for you all to go back to your homes. I've had enough of you.'

And they did. Quietly and humbly.

Françoise sat at the bar and couldn't get any fix on what was circling in her head. All these cryptic clues, she needed someone who could think outside the box. Nothing seemed real anymore. Or maybe nothing was real? And just as she thought she must be losing her marbles, into the bar came the one person who knew that nothing was real. She looked up as he said hello with his charming diminutive wife. He towered over ladies, a very tall, long haired man.

'How are you now after your crash?' he asked kindly.

Oh no, she cried in her mind, *Jack's friend, the crazy Professor who saved her in the hit and run. I'm not sure I can take another symposium on time or reality. But wait! Maybe this genius might be able to crack one of these clues for me.*

'I'm fine. I have to thank you both again for your help. It was so brave and kind. Here, let me buy you both a drink. Norma, can you serve them please?'

They sat down together and chatted about normal things. The pair had been walking again. It seemed they were avid walkers and loved to sample the food and beers in such lovely country pubs as *The Castle*, *The Elizabethan* at Luton and *The Royal Oak* in Ideford. Françoise couldn't understand how anyone could walk so far for beer and food, but each to their own. She decided to broach the subject of her last clues.

'I'm trying to solve a puzzle. An old relative of my husband's has a puzzle book which is linked somehow to places in the area. We are supposed to find the place and what it represents. Maybe you can help? You walk the area a lot and you both are clever. I'm not sure what is real anymore in the clue.'

'Well reality according to Bell's paradox and Barbour's interpretation of time...'

The Proff's long understanding wife, seeing Françoise's face drop, stooped him in his tracks. 'Dave, shut up. Let Françoise show us what she has.'

Françoise explained, but not all. 'This first clue I have is 'look where you might find and Albatross and a pilot flying together. A girl's name points the way.'

They thought for a while. The Proff, his long legs and arms straddling the room, wrinkled his furrowed brow. 'The only place where you might find an Albatross here is a museum or a golf course. One has them stuffed and the other is a golf score three under par. So maybe it's one of them. Maybe there is museum with an old airplane and stuffed bird in it; or a golf course on or near an airport?'

Norma came over. She had heard the Proff's answer. 'There is golf course here and there was an airport. Teignmouth golf club is actually on Haldon moor and that was where there once was an airport. You may well have given the answer Dave. Well done.'

The Proff's wife looked excited and exclaimed. 'We walk up there to Luton and *The Elizabethan* and *The Royal Oak*. What covers the moor?'

They all thought. The Proff moved his long legs, agitated and troubled with the question. 'It is relative to the time you observe the moor and any observation as quantum physics tells you will change the outcome and the reality...'

'Shut up!' all three women said, laughing.

'Heather. Heather covers the moor,' Dave's wife said.

And Françoise got it all at last. 'And Heather is a woman's name. We've cracked it folks. Thanks?'

'It must refer to Haldon Moor then, your question and quiz? What do you need to find next?' the Proff asked Françoise.

'Oh, that's about it, I think. We just have to find the place. That's one more I'll tick off. Thanks a lot.'

She was not going to give the last clue in an open space. She trusted no one now. The place could be bugged. She knew it had a ghost. Maybe the ghost that moved glasses and opened doors was there to protect the final clue.

'I think I'll walk back along the sea front. I need some fresh air and to clear my head. Thanks for everything folks and Norma, I will talk to you once I've got my head right. Take care and a bientôt mes amis'.

Descending down Smugglers Lane, Françoise looked at the huge women's head stone statue and decided for certain the treasure wasn't buried under there. If she was correct somewhere on Haldon Moor laid the next step and maybe the final conclusion to her quest. She determined not to tell her Cornish and French tormentors. She would take her chance and make her mind up what to do after she had located the hiding place.

The Great Dane trotted up the path, Pixie was being dragged behind, rolling and twisting in the dust along the ground, not unlike one of those rustlers caught by the cowboys in the movies who have been lassoed and dragged along by a horse. As he went past, he shouted,

'Save our Beach!' Françoise waved and called after the tortured man,' Vive les Chiens'.

She reached the beach and phoned Jack. They arranged to meet in *The Blue Anchor* on Sunday.

CHAPTER TWENTY

Sunday at the bar in *The Blue Anchor* was set aside for the Oxford University Debating Society, or alternatively, the Grumpy Old Gits' Symposium. Charlie was ensconced at the end of the bar next to the open door. Today being a summer's day, it was warm and with a slight breeze blowing through the door along the small wooden bar. Any other day, especially during winter it resembled *'The Polish Corridor';* except now there was no German Army to cross it and liberate Danzig. This howling gale through the open door of Luke and Adele's version of the *'Hurt Locker'* never bothered Charlie, who rain, snow or howling gale still wore a tee shirt, jeans, boots and a light cotton fleece. Having spent many years on the exposed Quay, where the wind howled up the River Teign from Dartmoor, he was immune to cold. He was also immune to Deaf Bert and The Teignmouth Yank's singing. The rest of the pub was not.

'Shut the hell up!' Grumpy Al howled at Roy as he burst into, *'I was born under a wandering star...'* 'It's only ten past twelve for God's sake. I hate it when people are happy this time of the day. That's your problem...'

Jack, who was standing with the crazed ancient rock stars, glanced smiling and knowingly at Elliott. Elliott was the hyped, and amazingly happy, too happy for Grumpy Al, barman. Elliott smiled, his teeth white between his big, suicide bomber's black beard. He had heard Grumpy's lectures on self-mutilation and isolation from normal conversation too many times. But he loved to listen to the old men wax lyrical about the good old days, the way the world has gone politically too correct, and the merits of Gene Pitney over Mick Jagger. He too was a rock star but sadly none of the men stood at the bar would be singing his new age music. Elliott had that trait and character that makes a great barman and person. Unlike Grumpy Al, who lectured him incessantly on his character faults, Elliott saw nothing but good in everything and everyone. He had to; he supported Torquay United.

Jack had heard Elliott and his partner in the group, Ted Jevans, the best singer song writer in town and the next Ed Sheeran were thinking going to write a new song about a book that Davey the author was writing. He told them they were too late and that the brilliant sea shanty band *Steve Collings and The Back Beach Boyz* were already doing that. They decided to call it *'Frog and the Teign'* and hoped to get it played at a festival at Powderham Castle and at the Teignmouth Carnival, if Sarah the lovely dedicated lady who organised it with so many other loyal volunteers, would schedule it. It would take pride of place at the immensely successful *Sea Shanty Festival* in September in Teignmouth and Mr Grumpy from the East Cliff Café was adding it to the cracking Teignmouth Folk Festival too.

'Last year it brought in more visitors than anyone. Thousands,' Jack said.

'I hates that bloody racket,' interrupted Charlie. 'Every pub us walks towards and opens the door, all us hears is, *'Haul away, haul away!'* or *'I'm on a prison ship to Australia'*. Us just shuts the bloody door and walks on. But you just canna get away from it. Every pub has the buggers in with long beards, pint pots full of ale...*'hauling away'* and chasing bloody whales. If I hears one more song about whales and Australia, I'll thump the bugger.'

'I likes Wales,' Deaf Bert butted in, only picking up the one word.

'So do I,' says the Teignmouth Yank and begins his Tom Jones stance, sticking his pelvis out and crooning, *'and there to meet me was mah momma and papa'*.

'Shut the hell up,' Grumpy Al shouted through the melody, 'there is no bloody green, green, grass of home. It's a myth. Wales is just a pile of pit heaps and empty steel works. That's all your problems, you think everything is romantic and nice, well it ******* isn't.'

'What he say?' Bert said turning his good syringed ear to Charlie.

'Nothing Bert; the usual gloom.'

'I thinks so. I'm off outside for a ciggy.'

'I loved the festival last year Jack. Remember when we watched the Back Street Boyz sing that classic *'Sid the Pacific Oyster'* in *The Devon Arms* or was it *The Ship?'* Elliot said.

'It was *The Ship*. Yup *'Sid'* was a classic. Not so sure the line about ejaculating oyster sperm into the River Teign did a lot for the recruitment of new members of the swimming club. But it was fun. That old guy who nearly died on stage singing about hauling away to Australia in *The Devon Arms* was a hoot. He must have been as old as Moby bloody Dick.'

'One day we will be famous like them,' Elliot enthused over the bar.

Elliott, in his eternal optimism and enthusiasm, was sure he and Ted would be able to take over Chris Martin of Coldplay's top spot at the Powderham festival. Also, that one day they may well be bigger than that huge mega rock band that came from Teignmouth, Muse. Grumpy Al was not impressed:

'Don't be so stupid; you daft twat. How many times have I told you to stop being such an optimist and deluded happy idiot? That's your problem. You think everyone likes you. Well they don't. I think your music is shite and so is that daft bastard's book he is writing.'

'I thinks Mick Jagger is better than Gene Pitney. *Jumping Jack Flash is a gas, gas...*' Deaf Bert was back and still on the conversation of ten minutes ago.

Roy leapt back away from the bar and stood in his Elvis pose, in an attempt to mimic Mick Jagger. He was about to sing when Luke, the laconic landlord, put some hot sausage rolls on the bar. Bert spotted them with the eye of Bald Eagle and grabbed a handful and began swallowing and munching. Roy broke into, *'You can't always get what you want...'*

Charlie said. 'Roy, for God's sake buoy: You cannay say that these days. It be too sexist man. It be not gender neutral.' Roy looked puzzled and stopped. Bert put another sausage roll in his mouth and munched and chewed, his mouth going from side to side now. He burped and continued munching. Luke looked on in wonder. Charlie saw his look and explained. 'Matey, I think Bert has three stomachs, just like a cow. He's chewing the cud.'

Luke just stood and wondered if he should call the duly authorised officer to section them all – again. And it was only twelve thirty.

Elliott took another burst of abuse off Grumpy Al for just being there and smiling. He spoke to Jack.

'Kalin says last Monday you both agreed that you both talk to Davy and he might start writing books about Grumpy Al. Like the Enid Blyton's *'Famous Five'* books. *'Grumpy Al does Brexit'*: *'Grumpy Al goes to the United Nations'*; *'Grumpy Al discusses Bipolar Disease'*. Kalin said he did time not long ago for the mercy killing of Billy Bob. Davey could write, *'Grumpy Al goes to Jail'*.'

Jack nodded in assent of how successful these books would be. 'Problem is Elliott they would be only one page. If you edit out the four-letter words and the personal abuse all you are left with is: 'Jean-Claude Junker said... Grumpy Al interjected. 'That's your problem... **** @@ **** you stupid @@@@... And Grumpy Al was arrested again.... The End.' Not great stories for kids I fear.'

'I guess so Jack. Kalin was working the bar last Monday and he said that Red Martin is back. How was he?'

'Well he's ok. Think he was in hospital as he had indigestion over too many pumpkins and vegetable curries. How he eats that shit every day I'll never know. He's planning another march on Downing Street. He's calling it - 'Up the Workers and Save the Vegans'. The Monday SPY Club was missing its quorum though when he was away and poor Barry,

189

the octogenarian Romeo, is still in hospital. And MI5 Mick was asking where MI6 Richard and Jimmy and his dodgy detective's hat were. It's a worry when the secret service doesn't know where they each are!'

Charlie heard the conversation and added his own theory. 'It's like in the westerns when John Wayne stops the wagon train and says, 'It's too quiet.' And then out of nowhere come the Indians. Same in here, when it's too quiet, something will happen matey. Mind you this bar was never quiet in the old days, everyone wanted to be here as the tarts were here and the sailors all spent their money in here. He be like a foreign exchange bank in 'ere.'

'Same now with the currency; but not the tarts: Look at all the notes all round,' Elliott said, pointing to the many foreign notes pinned up all around the bar.

'They've even got the bell. The foreign sailors, particularly the Scandinavians loved to ring the bell and buy the whole bar a pint. Especially if they had been looked after by Chicken Head.'

'Who was Chicken Head?' Jack enquired, knowing he was in for the long haul now.

'She was one of the ladies who serviced the sailors. Five quid a time; if they didn't pay, she knocked them out. She knocked anyone out if they upset her. No one would tackle her even the boxers in town were scared of her. She looked like Tommy Farr the boxer with a broken nose. As you can gather, she was no Lily Langtry. But she was rich as Midas as when she died, they found loads of bank books full of money hidden under the stair carpet.'

'Thankfully, we don't have tarts in here now,' Luke said.

'No, Adele has turned this into a cracking place. The only pub in town that David Attenborough would put an environmental protection order on,' Jack said.

For indeed Adele, much to the financial despair of her partner Luke was amazingly innovative with the decorations and various live shows she put on in the pub at regular periods throughout the year. Never mind the excellent live bands and beer festivals but also weekends of animals and plants in harmony with beach party themes with stuffed crocodiles, Halloween themes with devils and dragons, Alice in Wonderland with her own customers playing the Mad Hatter hares and the pièce de resistance the Christmas Theme, which much to Luke's bank account and Grumpy Al's despair starts straight after Halloween. Never mind the Santa Claus stuck up the chimney, there are actual reindeers in the back yard with the real Santa Claus. And artificial snow machines! This along with a back yard full of exotic plants, trees, shrubs and strange looking statues, three dogs that they own and Hovis's Bill Sykes type burglar dog, Bob, who lives perpetually by the log fire, makes the whole year seem like a series of Life on Earth - except many of the customers have not evolved yet.

'Talking of animals; did I tell you of the Teignmouth Loch Ness Monster?' Charlie asked them all. There was no need for an answer. 'A lorry driver had a dump in the Quay toilet. The turd was massive and he couldn't get rid of he but he told no one. So, every time matey went to the toilet they were faced with this monster. The management were called to sort he out. Wizzel was the plumber and he was sent with his Turd Tickler to get rid of it. But he couldn't, he just submerged under the water and around the bend only to rise again when matey went next to the toilet. Poor Wizzel, he tried time and again to tame the Turd but each time he just disappeared. All the buoys thought he lived there. Marty was sure he saw he swimming in the Teign. Just like the Loch Ness monster.'

'Poor Wizzel, he must have been demented with trying to catch it?' said Elliott, always caring.

'Wizzel was demented. He loved the Teign. Us thought he was always after catching the Teignmouth Turd as he swam every lunchtime from the Quay to the Pier. Even the bosses tells the skippers as they are loading out and sailing on the tide, *'if you see Wizzel as you pass the pier, tell him we'll meet him at The Ship pub as we are in it.'*

They chuckled at Wizzel's exercise and search for the legendary Teignmouth Turd. Bert had finished the last sausage roll and was chewing the final cud in his mouth.

'What you buoys saying?' Still masticating but muttering and strolling out to take a cigarette.

'Wizzel always had problems with water mind,' Charlie continued. 'When matey broke a broom on the deck he threw it over the side. Wizzel strips off and dives in and swims and gets it and brings it back. Matey throws it back in again. Wizzel jumps in again. Marty had to tie him to the handrail to stop him. Yes, he liked water.'

Charlie took a long drink of his Carling and continued Wizzel's water tales. 'His mother worried that he never went to the toilet when he was younger and she told him if he didn't wee, she'd have to get the doctor to examine his willy. So, he would take a full gallon watering can to bed and then run it out into the toilet. His mother in the next bedroom hears him pissing loudly for five minutes each night. She calls the doctor and poor Wizzel is whizzed off to Teignmouth hospital and gets a catheter put in!'

Jack looked at his phone and checked the time. Françoise was late. He hoped she hadn't had any trouble. But the craic was good so he chilled out and listened to the tales of past glory. Marty came in with Pixie Dave - *Oh no* Jack thought, *here we go, he'd be stuck for hours now.*

'Morning buoys,' Marty said. 'You talking about Wizzel there Charlie? Happy days. We was greedy bastards then. Did I tell you that Jack?'

'Yes, you certainly did Marty. Loads of money on peace work; the only way to work matey - time and knock and straight into the bar.'

'They hated me some days,' Marty said. 'I'd be on the deck and the gang would be shovelling away down below in the holds. I is a bit deaf sometimes so they thinks Marty canna hear them calling me the worst names you can think of. But I'd keep them shovelling.'

'Aye, you hard bugger; remember when Lofty nearly died,' Charlie butted in and didn't wait for Marty to answer. 'He shifted too many bags around him in a full hold and the other bags collapsed on him. He was buried. You shouted down the hatch *'dig around his head so he can breathe and get on with shifting the bags. We are on peace work!'*

'We got him out eventually,' Marty said, a bit aggrieved at that his attempts at filling the buoys' pockets might be misunderstood. 'I took him home after. The nurse said he was nearly dead. He collapsed in his house. One hour later we were all in *The Blue Anchor* drinking to a successful ship and he's already in there, pissed, watching Liverpool on the telly - the bastard.'

Everyone laughed at Lofty's plight and Marty's angst. Marty held the chair again. 'I tried my best for the buoys but sometimes the bosses were too smart. On one ship, the agent came to me and asked why are we working in the dark? I told him he hadn't paid for lights and I wanted paying: And for the overtime as well. He said that he'd already paid the bosses for the lights and the overtime - greedy bastards took our money!'

Yes, Jack thought someone's always got an edge somewhere but Marty was the best and he told him so. 'Aye buoy, I made some money for the buoys. I loved it when the timber boats came in. The agents and captains there were full of stuff to move. Problem was I couldn't shift all the stuff that came off them!'

'What the timber?' Jack naively asked.

'No, the buoys moved the timber and we made a good wage. I moved the booze!'

Charlie interrupted. 'Marty was the best hatch man in the business. He negotiated all our booze from the captains. If the captain wanted to sail, he'd have to get Marty's agreement. It was always from the captain *'how much, one case of brandy?'* Marty shakes his head and says, *'Impossible for the buoys to finish'*. Captain: *'Two cases?'* Marty says: *'Can't hurry the buoys; Health and safety.'* Captain says; *'Three?'* Marty says; *'That'll do me hansom.'* And we finish work and let them sail. The only good thing about the EEC was that it was EEC law that we had to take the ships rubbish so all the booze was put in rubbish bags and smuggled out. But as I says, *ya canna be doing that now at the Quay.* We all know that things are much better down there these days. Our days are long gone and it lots of ways thank Christ, especially with Health and Safety. In our days we just inhaled the grain dust, clay and slate dust, chemicals from the scrap boats now they all have air fed masks and rightly so. And I tells 'ee of all the shenanigans that went on. We are lucky to be alive and as for security? It's impossible now to do what we did. We also made good money on cockling too when you sent the tractor over to the Salty to scrape the sand for cockles. KP the boss was used to us by then one day he turned to his juniors and said, *'looks like one of ours'* and kept on working. He was looking out of his window and saw his machine not cleaning the dock but earning us buoys drinking money on the Salty. But you cannay do that these days. They have proper security now. No one can get on or off like we could. Even the tarts from *The Anchor* could move on and off the ships them a days.'

Marty remembering a classic 'That massive maid who could get down the gangway from the ship after a night onboard she was so pissed and huge. We lifted her off the deck for the captain by strop and crane and she was so drunk from the ship's booze she couldn't walk. So, we took her back to *The Anchor* on a pallet and forklift...hah... hah...'

Charlie ordered another round for them all. Bert had returned and was talking to Roy about Exeter City's result. He scanned the empty bar but nothing was left but a few sausage roll crumbs. Looking morose, he regurgitated another cud and began chewing. Roy went to find Elvis on the juke box. Luke demented again ran to switch it off from behind the bar. Hovis and the burglar dog, Bob, came in. Hovis looking more like Bob Marley every day now he had taken up a life living on an open boat on The Teign. Charlie continued the tales of yesteryear.

'We had strange boats come in and they all wanted girls from here. The Russians were the strangest because at first the KGB wouldn't let them off the boat. And their boats were so dangerous. You could poke holes in the sides. They loaded them up with old fridges, washing machines and cars to take back to Russia to sell. Some never made it as they were so overloaded.'

Marty continued with the difficulties of pre- Glasnost days: 'The Russians ships wouldn't come to Teignmouth in the old days because as the port was tidal, they could get stranded if World War broke out. It was that real the threat. I couldn't deal with captains at first because they weren't allowed to talk to us or if they managed to avoid the KGB, most didn't speak good English. Us had to deal with the KGB officer who was fluent. After Perestroika things changed as the ships started to have proper stiffeners in the cargo holds and ballast tanks. Mind you it made peace work harder. We preferred the clear straight wall holds. Death traps for the sailors but great for shovelling shit out of. We also started to get decent vodka then. Before that it was poison.'

Charlie came back from the toilet to hear the last bit and it invoked bitter memories of bad vodka. 'Remember that big ship that came and the Russian captain after Perestroika; he was called 'German'. He got the gang in at six am and put a couple of bottles of vodka on the table with hard back bread and cheese for breakfast. He kept bringing bottle after bottle. It was horrible and we paid him for apple juice to make he palatable as each bottle was worse than the last. The apple juice was hundred percent alcohol like the vodka. He be lethal that juice. Us walked back to the Carpenters Arms mortal drunk, there were three of us, each holding on to each other's belts in a line, like a drunken pantomime horse. We started singing *'hi ho, hi ho it's off to work we go'*, like the Seven Dwarfs. KP looked down at us and just shook his head. When Kev opened the door to come in to work, us were all lying throwing up in buckets!'

'Were all the crews like the Russians?' Jack asked.

'The Russians were lazy and rude mostly. They got better as the years went on. But to be honest I likes the Cape Verde, Philippine and Indonesian workers. They worked and were pleasant. The Poles were horrible and Russians not much better,' Charlie explained.

'What about the Turks?' Marty said, laughing mischievously.

'Don't get us on about the bloody Turks. You bugger, you,' Charlie exclaimed, obviously with some history of Turkish delight on the Quay. And he explained. 'This bugger is dealing with Hungarian boat or maybe Rumanian. And when he hears they have a world champion wrestling buoy on board, he tells them that I am a champion wrestler. So, every time I turns around on the boat there is this short squat foreigner squatting down with his hands out in wrestling pose. Us goes to the hold to shift some bags and sure enough facing me in the black is matey, squatting on his hunkers with arms outstretched like a Turkish wrestler moving from side to side about to pounce on me. I says, *'what* *the ****,'* and moves away. This goes on all shift with matey following me in lethal wrestling pose waiting to pounce. Us sees Marty at the end of the shift and he pisses himself and tells me the story. The wrestler is still following me the mad bastard. As I says buoy, happy days, but Marty could be a bugger.'

Françoise entered the asylum. She says to Pixie, 'I see you have recovered from the dog torture.'

'Bloody dog! Costs more than me to feed,'

'That's your problem. You like dogs. How many times have I told you dogs are for idiots?' Grumpy in good form again.

Bob the burglar's dog hearing the word dog, perked his ears up. Despite the summer heat he was lying right next to the unlit log fire in the bar. He loved that spot. Someone shouted that Elliott should put the fire on for the poor hound. 'You should ask Amy to do it,' shouted Huggy, the Indian man at the end of the bar.

'We don't have any firelighters man,' Elliot said laughing across the packed bar. Everyone chuckled who were in the know. Amy, a lovely and very personable temporary barmaid had been asked to light the fire for the first time in her life. She had duly done what Luke asked, put firelighters, newspaper, sticks and logs on, and gone back to bar to serve the waiting inmates. Sometime later when the ice was forming on the extremities of the customers of the Polish Corridor, Amy was asked why the fire wasn't on by a frozen, purple Grumpy. She was shocked as she expected the firelighters to spontaneously combust. No one had told her to use matches!

Huggy the Indian was sympathetic to Amy's angst. 'Poor Amy, if you've never put a fire on then why wouldn't firelighters spontaneously light. A friend's son did the same with a Fray Bentos steak and kidney pie tin he'd dropped off for him at University. He phoned his dad sometime later saying he had no idea how to open it as it didn't have a ring pull. He bashed it and stuck it with knives but couldn't open it. It wasn't until he U Tubed, *'How to open a Fray Bentos Steak and Kidney Pie'* and watched a video some parents had put in to help their own student son. It showed that it was quite easy if you knew how to use a tin opener!'

All the grumpy old gits agreed that the youth of today were spoilt and should have suffered the abject poverty, beatings by sadistic teachers and rampant disease of their own early years. 'Fires! We used sleep in an igloo.' 'Steak and Kidney pies! You were lucky. We ate tar of't road.' 'University! I wor fighting Japs in jungle when ah was twelve.'

Françoise said hello to the assembled debating society and both her and Jack wandered off to sit away from the insanity of the bar. She bought a jar of honey and half a dozen eggs off Gill and Derek as she passed by. Smashing stuff, she told Jack. Big Pete and Mandy were sitting next to them. Both nursing sore heads, Seems the band the night before had been special and Adele's Dartmoor beer, Devon cider and amazing assortment of spirits had taken their toll. Blind Pete and his gorgeous Alsatian guide dog were sitting next to the fire. Pete drinking his '*Jail Ale*'; Nickel, his seeing- hound loving his pork scratchings, slightly annoyed that Bob, the burglar dog, was trying to hump him; as is Bob's way. They both took up a seat next to the window.

Françoise told Jack of her findings. Jack was delighted. 'So, we now have solved most of what we were told or found. Let me sum it up so we can both be sure we haven't missed anything.'

'If you want Jack, but I think I might be near now. But go on then.'

Jack listed the progress and conclusions:

Charlie the first keeper of the clues had told them.

Look for stone in Widdecombe that marks the hook. The answer lies behind.

They had found the clues at Widdecombe Church.

Look for the rabbits in the church who point to the nuns and he who wears the crown will show the Grace of God.

Jim Smith had given them the next one.

Where he who wears the crown broke the bread points the way.

That had led them to Trinity School and Bishop Coffin. Which in turn had led them to St Michael's church and the Da Vinci painting of the last supper:

Find the Unicorn in the palace of the Prince du Sang.

And then to Powderham Castle and The Earl of Devon had given them:

The fisherman of the North will show the way.

Old Man Job had given them the next clue:

Look where you might find and Albatross and a pilot flying together. A girl's name points the way.

Finally, well they think finally, Norma gave them the last clue:

On a hill far way He was lost then found. On the hill that overlooks the Hound. X marks the Grail.

And now Françoise believed that the next step or even the treasure may well be on Haldon Moor.

'Why should it end there? We have been led a merry dance across Devon, and maybe we have it wrong? The Hound may well mean we have to search for a hill all over Dartmoor,' Jack asked, still shocked at how much people in this place had known but had not known.

'Jack, trust me, I am sure it's up on the moor near the golf course. Tomorrow we will go up there after dark and I'll show you why. What I really don't understand is why this is so important to all those chasing it. What are we missing Jack?'

Jack thought for some time and then began to look at his notes on his phone he had made about the whole revelations they both had been told and he summarised what they knew to Françoise.

The men who had attacked Françoise in her car were the members of the Frenchman Saunière's gang. The man who attacked them in Widdecombe first was also one of them. He wanted the secret destroyed or kept.

The man in black who saved them with the West Country accent was part of a secret society which Françoise's aunt had said were called the Priory. They were sworn to keep this secret. But now they had sent two more French ladies and the same man to scare them into finding the secret and handing it over to them to reveal it to cause some for some unknown worldwide catastrophic event.

Françoise's aunt had told her that her husband was also a member of the secret society that had held and kept this since the time of Christ. They had kept it in Tintagel Castle and it may well be something linked to the Holy Grail. She explained that many believed the Holy Grail was actually the proof of the offspring of Christ and Mary Magdalene and the Priory were protecting that lineage and had proof of its current descendants. The descendants were of mainly royal blood and that King James Stuart II was one.

His failure to win back his throne at the Battle of the Boyne was in some way orchestrated by Françoise's descendant, the French admiral Compte De Tourville, who was a senior Knight of St John. He was possibly in league with King William. And he lost the Holy Grail and something else at Teignmouth in 1690. Since then the Priory have been searching for it and the good people of Teignmouth keeping it hidden. Now, for some reason, it was time to reveal it to the world but only the Priory could do that for their own means. Saunière was to be stopped getting it. Françoise or Jack could not, at risk of harm to them or Françoise's aunt, tell anyone or try to hide things from Saunière or The Priory.

'It's still a mystery Françoise. What the hell happened between your Admiral relative and our King Billy? And why was the loss of the treasure or Grail so important to everyone? What with Bishops mysteriously dying and buried in Teignmouth, and not their parish when they belong to some weird religious group. And two old ladies who were kept in luxury for years by some secret fund. Why did the

Teignmouth keepers of the secret down the years keep it secret? What would change their lives if it was revealed? None of the lads I talk to here are, or seem ever to have been, very religious. And Catholic or Protestant or Jacobite or King Billy, never seems to have mattered much down here to me. They were all fishermen and smugglers for God's sake.'

'I know Jack. I have no idea still what this all about. But remember, you have forgotten I think what I found on the cellar wall in St Germain- en- Laye.

Rex quondam rexque futurus. He holds the cup. Avalon is the Vine and the Cornerstone.

'I haven't,' Jack replied, 'it's just I have no idea how that fits in.'

'Well, it must be linked to King Louis, King James and maybe anyone in The Priory or the other secret societies that abounded in France around then. I have looked up a few things. It is mentioned in Thomas Malory's ancient *'Le Morte d'Arthur'*. **Rex quondam rexque futurus** means *'The Once and Future King'* and is also a book about King Arthur written by T H White. Tintagel is supposed to be where Camelot and maybe the Grail were and Avalon was where he was buried. He is supposed to rise again and come and save Britain in a time of imminent disaster. I can't help think this is a co-incidence.'

'Why?' Jack asked.

'Because of the message; can't you see? *'Avalon is the Vine and the Cornerstone'*. Jesus was always referred to as the Vine and also The Cornerstone and will come again billions of Christian believe. This is all linked to Christ, I'm sure.'

'Talk of cornerstones comes back to Temples. Solomon's temple was built on a cornerstone. I'm sure the Templars and The Freemasons have documented rituals about the cornerstone and master mason, Hiram Assif, who laid the stone. See I haven't been sitting not listening or reading up! This could just be a conspiracy theory about secret societies and nothing else. There is no Jesus mystery here Françoise. Only the Bishop Coffin with his Grace Deus seems to have any link to organised religion.'

'Jack, this is all about secret societies man! Who do you think the bloody Priory are and 'keeper of the vine'? The whole adventure has been to keep something secret. Anyone who has read the New Testament and believes in Jesus knows that Gospel means *'the Good News'*. If it's so bloody good, then why do they all keep it secret.'

'Because maybe Françoise it isn't *'Good News'*. They are keeping secret bad news. Well bad news for many not in the know or who believe in Christ. Just saying, don't get all religious with me.'

Françoise took a drink and looked around and pondered; *who knows who in here is in some secret society or has some secret past. Or believes so strongly in something what she might reveal would hurt them so much. And I might be the one to destroy their dreams, faiths, traditions or beliefs.* She suddenly felt tired. 'Let's go home Jack. Well I am going. You can stop with your chums if you wish. I will call you tomorrow and fix up a meet on the moor tomorrow night. Bisous, mon ami. Keep safe please.'

Jimmy the Hat looked over. His hat had a small listening device placed in the band of the trilby. It's why he never took it off. *This would be good news for his controllers* he thought.

Charlie shouted, 'It's my round'.

Grumpy Al shouted across. 'No one buys me a beer. How many times have I told you? DON'T buy me beer!'

Bert said, 'what you say Charlie?'

Jack gave up hope.

CHAPTER TWENTY-ONE

In a pub outside of Exeter in the village of Ken, *The Lay Arms*, a beautiful thatched 12th century country pub, two men sat waiting for lunch. Saunière was still disturbed that both of his surveillance team had not recovered yet. He had decided to oversee the final solution to his problem himself. As he drank his glass of red wine, he reflected on what they knew and what he should do next. Whatever it was he must get the secret document and destroy it forever or his father's legacy and his dynasty would be destroyed forever. So, he had phoned the number he always kept at his side in case of events like this. The man sat opposite him was the result of that call and as he looked at the man he shivered. What had he set in motion?

Saunière had flown into Exeter Airport the day before, booked into a small bed and breakfast in Kenton, near Powderham Castle. He had enjoyed a wonderful tour of the Earl of Devon's ancestral home and stroll around the extensive groomed gardens. Now, he was sat with a strange looking Italian man whose eyes seemed to move from one side to the other side continually but never take their scary gaze from the middle of your own. The man had little time for pleasant chat. He was there for one reason and one reason only, to kill anyone who stopped Saunière securing the last copy of the Templar's secret.

Saunière believed that he had been sent to him after his call by an organisation his grandfather had called, 'Opus Deus'. But that organisation was not a secret society or bunch of assassins but a legitimate religious movement trying to revive the principles of Catholic faith. The Saunière family from the days of Father Bérenger, when he discovered the documents in the church of Mary Magdalene in Rennes le Chateau, had been controlled not by the Vatican or Opus Deus but by the Kremlin.

In 1891 when Saunière's great grandfather discovered his secret the Kremlin was controlled by Czar Alexander III and its International interests were controlled by the Okhrana, the precursor to the KJB. When Father Saunière came to Paris and met his great grandmother Emma Calvés and her esoteric and occultist friends, what he never realised that his young and all so consuming friend and controller, Émile Hoffet, was a member of the Okhrana, reporting to the head of the secret service who was based in Paris, Pytor Ivanovich Rachkovsky. Through Rachkovsky's mole in the Priory, Hoffet and Rachkovsky played Saunière and the Priory at their own game and the Kremlin were kept informed of every move and every step of the Priory's securing of the Rennes le Chateau copy of the original Cathar secret which was carried to Britain by the Templars.

It was Hoffet who gave Saunière the camera and skills to photograph the document and then blackmail the Priory to protect his future descendants. Saunière was always told and convinced that his helpers were part of the Vatican trying to protect the shattering theological facts being made public that he found out at Rennes le Chateau. They convinced him that as long as he kept the copy safe and the Priory kept funding him to do so, they would protect him. But it was not the Vatican but the Kremlin who controlled him, and now his descendants. And the man sat opposite was not Okhrana, but its post-revolutionary arm, the KGB.

The man with the moving eyes, curiously one was brown and one was blue, was a senior member the GRU and of Department V, responsible for 'wet affairs', the assassination of enemies of the state. He was trained and he was deadly - licensed to kill. He had been diverted from his task given him by the GRU to find the real perpetrators of the Salisbury poisonings of the Skripal's by supposed Novichok, to support Saunière and his attempt to recover the Teignmouth secret. He was never told the real reason for his missions, only his objectives. These were simple; ensure you recover the document. Eliminate anyone who tries to stop you.

A few miles away in Bovey Tracey, in the exclusive *Bovey Castle* on the edge of Dartmoor, two men were having lunch. One was also French, and he had flown in on the same plane as Saunière. He had been well aware of Saunière's plans as the Priory had him under constant watch and surveillance. His fellow diner was the UK government minister who he had spoken to with the merchant banker a few days ago.

'Is he really any danger to us these days?' the Minister asked, as he took a piece of his sole meunière onto his fork.

'Not really. It seems the Cornishman and the local vigilante seems to have taken out his two main assassins. We have him watched. The French ladies with The Cornishman are more than a match for him and his big bruiser he has now. He's got funds to finance mercenaries so we shouldn't be too complacent. But my spies here have him under control.' His partner tucked into a nice piece of his rack of English Lamb.

'And the French girls have the Cornishman in control?' the Minister asked, as he looked up from his plate.

'Bien Sûr. He knows their abilities and their record. He won't be a problem. He'll follow orders.'

'So, we think they are close now?' the Minister posed.

'Well it appears they both met in some God forsaken pub in Teignmouth yesterday. We never got the full conversation and she hasn't said anything on the phone. So, we're assuming they will talk at some point. But we have them continually watched. We have key people in all their known haunts. It's been hard to recruit sane people to look and act as bizarrely as the locals they seem to befriend in that weird place. But we have a small few now. The locals don't seem to have sussed them out. It's like the Star Wars bar every day down there. Give me Paris any day. I worry they may know too much mind.'

The Minister put down his knife and fork and sat back. A waiter came over and took his plate away. He picked up a glass of Chablis and took a drink. 'How much do they really know? Do you think they really know about the rise of the new Holy European Empire? The absolute rule of Europe and the true faith. I doubt it. They may think they know where the Grail is and the treaty but not its purpose. Do you think two country clowns would understand we have been struggling for years to put a common European Constitution, with common laws and regulations under the control Sion? That we have fought the Vatican to control that Constitution since the secret was lost. It has been prophesied in the Bible, in Daniel and Revelations that one day an empire will arise North of Jerusalem made up of ten nations which would be led by a disciple of Christ who will rule over Europe. No, I doubt they know that.'

The Frenchman also finished his plate and answered him. 'You may be correct but if Saunière finds the proof and destroys it or the two of them find it first reveal it prematurely or worse, hide it again, we will have Brexit and the chaos surrounding global affairs. Now is the time to show the world the true faith and the Union of States to be solidified under the Defender of the Faith. Britain cannot be allowed to be separate from that. Britain is the key and the cornerstone of it all. Without Britain it is lost.'

'So true my brother,' said the Minister, and passing his glass over his dining partner's in some secret symbolic bond of brotherhood. 'We must ensure that we take back the Grail and the truth. It is a long time since Rodger de Vere, our prior, brought the vessel to Britain that Jesus used. It took some time to return it to Sion. Now we are close to getting it back and the return of the True King to Avalon at last. Let's drink to that my brother.'

A few miles away from both *The Ley Arms* and *Bovey Castle*, The Cornishman was stood on the cliffs at Babbacombe, Torquay, overlooking a shining and aquamarine sea. He could see Teignmouth and Labrador Bay to the left of him and in the far distance Exmouth and Budley Salterton. He squinted through the summer haze dimming the far horizon and thought he could see the beginning of the Jurassic Coast and Dorset. He had to admit it was impressive but never as good as his home. Cornwall was the rightful ruler of this place and he would ensure his long search for that proof would soon be over.

He considered his next steps. He wanted the protocol document and the final proof of what was rightfully given to him and his countrymen. They could have the bloody cup or chalice or whatever that was. It was all bullshit anyway, the religious stuff. He was interested in the law, the rights of his fellow Bretons and the rule of the West Country. Holy Roman Empires, Sion, the Vine, and Mary whoever, well his overseers could take them. He had had enough of that. When they brought the French girls in, he said, *'bugger that'*, I am bigger than that. And so is my cause. I will force these two Devon idiots to give me the location and not tell the French.

As he walked along the cliff path towards Babbacombe Harbour he knew this was going to be a risky strategy, his employers and fellow Priory members were dangerous people but he was hell bent on winning now - at any cost.

In Paris the Grand Master of the Priory was taking a walk along The Seine. In the Master's head were many thoughts. Can they really finally be nearing the end of days when they can declare the true faith and recover Sion and save Britain and Europe? Do any of those chasing the Grail, except the higher degree orders, know the history and the truth? The Grandmaster was the only one who knew the whole truth. As the Grandmaster looked towards the City and the beautiful buildings and ancient churches, Saint Sulspice came into mind and how the Catholic modernist movement had come into being there, culminating in alignment with the Anglican church and the creation of Grace Deus, the conversion of so many Anglicans and Catholics, including Bishop Coffin, securing the copy of Saunière's secret Cathar copy (we should have realised he'd make another) and the attempt to align the faiths into the one true faith. A one faith and a new Holy European Empire built on the ancient esoteric knowledge and rights of the Gnostic Essenes and Cathars, Freemasonry and the Holy Knights Templar and Hospitallers.

Only the Grandmaster knew, that Sion was held sacred in their esoteric higher degree rights, only those in the higher Royal Arches knew that it referred to 'the stone that the builder rejected - *The*

Cornerstone. Sion was the cornerstone of the new temple and the new temple was built by the son of the Great Architect. And it was built in Britain, not Jerusalem or Rome.

The Grandmaster knew all this and also that only in Teignmouth would the proof of all of this be found. So, as she walked along the streets of Paris, she decided it was time she went there.

On the banks of the River Thames, in Vauxhall, London, the head of the Service, put down the phone from the Prime Minister. She thought for time and then she phoned her best agent in Teignmouth. She told the person that the time had come to mobilise and prevent the Grail falling into the hands of anyone but the British Secret Service. That person switched the phone off, took a drink of his *Jail Ale* and smiled. At last he was set free to do what he did very well. Like his opponent sat in *The Ley Arms* having lunch, he too was - licensed to kill.

Not far away from the recipient of the call in Teignmouth, Françoise and Jack were about to set out on their final deadly adventure.

CHAPTER TWENTY-TWO

'There must be somewhere up here where there is a place overlooking a hound and a cross,' said Jack, looking at his piece of paper with all the clues written on. 'This last one from Norma says, *on a hill far way He was lost then found. On the hill that overlooks the Hound. X marks the Grail.* If girl's name Heather means anything then we're in the right place as my legs are scratched to death with the bloody stuff and this gorse.'

They were standing on the top of Haldon Moor. It was dusk. They had decided to go and look when no one would be around. They had taken back packs with water and an ordinance survey map, a compass, small bird watching binoculars and were armed with only Jack's Swiss Army knife. He also carried a spade, a screwdriver and a chisel.

'Well this is where the airfield was, I am told,' said Françoise, as she stood in a field of heather. 'And if you look towards the sunset you can see Dartmoor.' She took the binoculars out of her bag and looked towards the sun setting in the West. The moon was rising early over the sea to the East of them. 'I can't see Hound Tor, but I'm sure I can see Hay Tor. Maybe that's what it means. We are actually looking towards the Hound.'

'Well there's no way you can see any cross in this lot. We need to find some stone or marker or something which has an X on it. Let's walk further down the moor,' Jack suggested.

'Ok, makes sense. Look Jack, quiet,' she whispered and pointed towards Dartmoor. Some way off among the sparse trees on the moor were three Roe deer, quietly grazing. They must have heard her whisper, because one looked up and at them and all three quickly disappeared over the edge of the heather bank. 'It's beautiful up here Jack.'

'Sure is Françoise. Let's hope it stays that way and nothing happens to us. Let's head down here. There looks like there is a clearing of grass or shrub or something. It looks a bit like a runway to me.'

They walked on through the dusk. In the silence, they could hear the crickets and the last songs of the larks and yellow hammers and finches as they headed off to roost. In the distance they could hear the crows as they headed towards the trees on Ashcombe Estate. They reached a large expanse of clear ground covered in short stubble. It did indeed look very straight and stretched in one long twenty-metre wide line Eastwards. They soon realised that another line the same width stretched Northwards and Southwards. Jack peered at the intersection of the two lines. His eyes brightened in the gloom.

'Françoise, I may be stupid but that looks very much like a cross to me.'

'It does to me,' replied an anxious but curious Françoise and looking behind her, 'and it is looking over at the Tors on Dartmoor. This may be it. X marks the spot Jack. It really does.'

They both walked the twenty metres or so to what they thought was the centre of the cross. Françoise looked all around and up at the stars shining quite brightly now. She grabbed Jack excitedly, 'Jack I believe we may well be in the right spot. Look up what do see over there along the line of the transverse cross?'

Jack looked over towards the top of Dartmoor and then upwards to the sky. 'I am not sure. What should I be seeing?'

Françoise pointed up to the sky. 'That's the North Star rising and it marks the end of the Plough, The Great Bear. What's the North Star commonly called?'

Jack thought a moment and then he smiled, his teeth brightening the growing the gloom. 'Of course, the Dog Star. The bloody Hound! '...*on the hill overlooking the Hound. X marks the spot.*'

Françoise was delighted. 'So, the treasure may well be buried here, just like we always thought, Captain Hook's treasure, but not guarded by Rollo the dog or buried on The Salty like Gordon Hooke's contraband, but under here. We can't dig everywhere Françoise. We have to concentrate on the centre. The only way to get the centre accurately is pace out from each corner diagonally and measure where they intersect. It's not great but it's only thing we can do.'

'Ok. Let's get moving; it's getting darker.'

After a short while they marked what they believed to be the centre of the cross. An owl flew across the rapidly darkening sky and the last few crows headed back to their roost. 'Right I guess the hard work starts now. Guess I do it?' Jack said, chivalrously.

Fran responded, chuckling. 'Of course! A mademoiselle like me couldn't spoil her hands or figure doing that.'

Jack dug for about ten minutes. It was very hard going as the heather roots were impacted and the grass roots very long. But then he felt the spade hit something immovable and harder. He dug a bit more and took his torch out of the bag and shone it into the hole. Sure enough there was something wooden and solid. Excitedly, he shouted out in glee, 'Look Françoise! There's a chest or something.'

Françoise bent over and peered into the hole and she felt her heart race. Finally, here it was. After all this grief and pain, it really did exist. She nearly fainted with relief. 'Jack quickly, get it out of there. We have to get this somewhere safe. Away from the Cornishman and whoever else is after it.'

'Ok. Just let me dig a bit deeper. I'll use the trowel to get around the bottom.'

After another ten minutes Jack lifted the box onto the moor. The first star could be seen in the Southern sky. They could see the box was old. It was bound by metal but only about the size of a large cubic shoe box. It was heavily built but not too heavy. It had a keyhole so someone must have a key. They looked at it for some time and then Françoise picked it up and turned it around. They could see still quite clearly as the starlight and moonlight were now reaching their peak.

'There is no way of opening it but to bash it I think Jack.'

'Let's take it back to one of ours and see if we can open it with a screwdriver or chisel or something. Best get out of here Françoise. You know they have a habit of turning up at the wrong moment. I'll carry it if you take the spade.'

The intrepid treasure hunters packed up. Jack filled the hole in and they walked with some difficulty in the darkness back over the moor towards their car they had packed on the road near the golf course. Eventually they reached the car.

Not too far away while they were digging, The Cornishman had returned to his car. He was grinning and out of breath. He had picked up the two French assassins from the farm house in Holcombe and told them that from his phone surveillance and his spy in Teignmouth Jack and Françoise were heading to the moor to finally find the secret. The girls had packed their automatic Manurhin 7.65 pistols in their small back packs and they set out in The Cornishman's car. He drove them the short distance up Exeter Road and they parked up in a car park just off the moor and the forest surrounding it. The Cornishman had told the girls to follow the forest path down towards the valley and the sound of the traffic from A38. He had followed a short way behind. Then he shouted that he had forgotten his map and torch would run back and get it. He told them to walk slowly down until they reached fallen tree and wait there. He crossed himself for the first time in years as he jogged back. '*Thank God they fell for that. If they hadn't, he feared for his life*'. He opened the car door his hand shaking, jumped in and started his car. He drove out of the car park and back onto Exeter Road. He headed back toward Haldon Moor, leaving his puzzled and very lost Gallic killers on Ideford Moor.

He had seen the two treasure hunters' car parked at the side of the golf course when he arrived from Ideford. He parked up farther along the road pulling the car out of sight in amongst the trees. He walked steadily and cautiously towards Jack's car. There was a small clump of trees nearby. He hid behind them and waited. This time he was armed. He had brought his hunting knife. He anticipated no trouble with his opponents but he was perfectly capable of handling them as he did at Widdecombe, he would take no chances now he was so close. He did not notice the man who was lying in the heather perfectly camouflaged with his green and brown army clothes, striped green and black face and woollen hat with clothed in heather. He was holding his Russian supplied silenced Stechkin machine pistol close to his body. His breathing was very slow and relaxed. He had no fear or anxiety. This was what he was trained for and very, very good at.

The two treasure hunters approached their car with the small wooden chest. Jack pressed his key fob and his boot opened. They reached the car, stepping over the small ditch from the moor. Jack put the chest into the back and they pulled their back packs off and threw them in. Françoise leaned the spade by the driver's door. Suddenly the Cornishman ran out from his hiding place and confronted them with the six-inch knife:

'Stop there, Jack. Both of you just step back please. I only want the chest.'

Jack was stunned. Françoise screamed in shock. They both stood and stared at their pursuer. The Cornishman moved closer as the two stepped back. 'You were warned that you had to tell me what you were doing. Do you think we wouldn't have had you bugged at all times and watched? Silly fools - anyway, I won't harm you if you step over there onto the golf course and let me take this beautiful thing you've found.' And he reached into the boot.

Jack and Françoise were just too shocked and depleted of all their excitement; they were just both tired of it all. They both just walked backwards and towards the golf course. Jack took Françoise's hand and they looked into each other's eyes. There was great sadness but also as they saw deep into each other's pain, they both saw something warm, compelling and affectionate and it stirred an emotion that they had not felt before – love.

The Cornishman picked the chest out of the boot and was walking back to his car when of a sudden he fell into a heap. His left leg had crumpled below him and he just tumbled into the ditch by the side of the road. Slowly from his hiding place in the gorse and heather, the Italian GRU man rose up, his silenced gun in his hand. *A nice knee shot* he thought as he rose, *I'm good aren't I*. He walked over to the

Cornishman rolling in agony in the ditch, picked up the chest and said, 'Sorry my friend but I have someone who wants this more than you. It's only a wing shot, but I'd get to a doctor soon if I were you. It looks a bit dirty in there.'

He walked back towards the stunned pair of treasure hunters. As he approached he spoke again. 'Sorry all your efforts are for no good. Take comfort that you could never have stopped me taking this. He will recover. You may not if you try anything stupid. So, do you have a way of opening this? I need a light too. Come here, no sudden moves.'

Jack and Françoise walked slowly the few yards to the open boot of the car. The Italian placed the chest in the boot. 'You,' and he pointed the gun at Jack, 'come here and get me a torch and if there is a key give me that.'

Jack stepped over the boot and took his torch from the back pack. 'There is no key. But I have a chisel and screwdriver.' Trembling he handed the camouflaged man the tools.

Françoise had moved next to him and whispered nervously in French, 'I think there is a hammer here.'

'What did she say? Speak up, you silly woman. What are you pointing at?' the Italian said forcefully and moved to the centre of the boot. He peered at what Françoise was pointing at. Françoise leaned slightly to her right and picked up the small heavy spade and with a sudden rush of strength, hate and anger she brought it down on the man's head. He collapsed in a heap at the back of the car. Jack was absolutely shocked into a complete sate of catatonia. He stared at the body and couldn't move, Françoise slapped him across his face. 'Wake up man. Get his gun quickly. Where are the keys Jack? What did you do with them?'

Jack just stared at the body, which was stirring now; he'd only been temporarily stunned he knew. *Dear God what do we do now?* He was still in a state of shock. 'Jack! Jack! Come on my friend. For God's sake get moving. Look in your pockets. Where are the keys?'

Jack came too. He fumbled in his pockets while Françoise put the chest in boot. He couldn't find the keys he pulled his pockets out and they still weren't there. 'They must be in the boot with the back pack, 'he shouted, panicking and fumbling his pockets back. They both went to look over in the boot.

'Move away from there!' a voice cried out. They turned and to face the Cornishman who was holding the gun that Jack had failed to pick up. The Italian made to stand up and the Cornishman smashed the gun against his temple and he keeled over in a heap yet again. 'Where are the keys?' the Cornishman cried out in pain holding his knee as he tried to walk nearer the two, still pointing the gun.

'They're here!' Jack shouted as he finally found them lying next to his bag.

'Ok,' grunted the Cornishman. 'Now let's get out of here before he wakes up again. I can't drive, you have to take me. And don't try to do to me what you did to him maid. I'll not fail to shoot you. Come on let's go.'

Jack took the wheel and Françoise sat next to him. The injured gunman crawled into the back with his gun and put his leg up on the back seat. He pointed the gun at Françoise and told Jack to drive. Françoise turned and spoke gently to the man. 'Why don't you let me take a look at your leg? I'm a nurse you know. We could drive to the hospice and I can get you into the infirmary and treat you.'

'I know all about you, maid. I know more than you will ever know. But that isn't such a bad idea. I'll never get back to my people like this and I can't go to hospital yet until I have the box opened and get what I've chased for years. If we go there, we open the box there. Can you guarantee no one will be there?'

'At this time of night, there won't be too much activity but emergencies happen. I can't promise that some emergency won't crop up. But it's our best chance of getting the equipment and dressings I need.'

'Ok then. Drive slowly and don't get picked up by the police. When we get there, you maid will go in and I'll have your friend covered here. Any, and I mean any funny business and he'd get hurt. Do you understand?'

Françoise nodded. She grabbed Jack's left leg and squeezed. He turned and looked at her. Their eyes met again and with the feeling that rose in his heart he knew somehow it would end well. She was not so sure.

They did not see the man dressed all in black put on his motor bike helmet and climb onto his bike. He had lain hidden just fifty yards away from the where the Italian lay. He had observed it all. He was about to take out the Italian when Françoise had knocked him out. He had watched as the Cornishman crawled unseen to confront them and knock out the Italian again. He thought carefully about his next move, should he intervene and take the Cornishman out or not? He thought a little and decided he'd let them take the chest somewhere safe and he could neutralise them all there. They had already been lucky with the late-night traffic and no one spotting the incidents here. Yes, let's follow them and finish this whole thing somewhere quiet and safe from accidental witnesses. He walked over to the Italian and tied his hands and feet with the cord he carried for garrotting his enemies. He cut a piece of the camouflages and tied it as gag. He then rolled the body over into the ditch. He took the GRU man's car keys just in case he was freed by a passerby. That should keep him quiet for the time he needed to finish his business. He switched on the tracking device he had attached to the bike. It immediately located the transmitter he'd placed under Jack's car. To be doubly safe he switched his phone to tracking mode and could follow wherever his Françoise's phone went. He made a call to one of the sleepers in Shaldon and drove off after the car. Very soon he would deliver to his country the final solution to the 1690 Teignmouth smuggling problem.

CHAPTER TWENTY-THREE

They arrived at the hospice and Françoise used her pass key to enter. She came out shortly after to advise that all was quiet and the infirmary was free but they should enter via a fire door at the back of the building close to the medical room which she had opened. The Cornishman shuffled out of the car pointing his gun at Françoise and then Jack alighted and took the chest and tools out of the boot. They entered the room via the fire door and pulled it shut. Françoise asked the injured man to hop onto the treatment table and she cut up and through his trousers to expose the wound. It was bleeding still and but the knee and bone appeared to have been missed and luckily the bullet had gone straight through the lower thigh. She injected a local anaesthetic, prepped the wound and sewed up both wounds. Finally she bandaged it. During this time, Jack had been instructed to work on opening the box.

'It's come free!' Jack shouted with some glee, despite their predicament. He really couldn't wait to see what it contained. He forced the lock open. The Cornishman hopped off the table with a grunt of pain and grimace that belied his own joy.

'Out of the way! Let me look.'

He peered into the open box and took out a faded brown stained parchment, about current A4 size, rolled into a cylinder shape and sealed with a wax seal. 'The Royal seal of England,' the delighted man exclaimed. 'This was it.' He sat back on the table and rested for a while. He looked to the sky, in some form of divine praise or inspiration. 'After all these centuries - mine at last.'

Jack took the opportunity of the Cornishman's prayers to look in the box. There was nothing else, just the rolled-up parchment in the man's hands. Disappointed he closed the box. *No Holy Grail? No proof? What a disappointment* he thought.

'So now you have your secret, what are you going to do with us?' Françoise asked, disturbing the Cornishman's worship.

He looked at her and smiled. 'Nothing much maid, you really can't harm me too much now I have what my family have sought for centuries. But don't think about doing anything daft.' And he waved the gun at them. 'Would you like to see what they have tried to keep hidden for aeons of time?'

'Sure, we haven't risked out lives just to end sat here in a medical room. What does it say?' Françoise asked. Jack just leaned against the fridges watching and hoping for some way of overcoming this madman.

He had perked up since the early incidents and got his bravery back and maybe he'd make a mistake.

The Cornishman gently broke the seal. It had been intact since July 1690 when King William III had pressed the Royal seal on the wax at Torbay, Devon in the presence of Vice - Admiral of the French fleet, Anne - Hilarion de Costentin, the Count of Trouville and grand prior of The Knights of Malta. Present also and a signatory to the protocols the scroll contained was Charles Colbert, marquis de Croissy, secretary of state for French foreign affairs. He was the most powerful man in France next to The Sun King, King Louis XIV and he signed the protocols on behalf of his King. He was also Grand Master of the Priory of Sion. King William was the head of the Holy Roman Empire Alliance and was signing on behalf of them all. He too was a Master in the Priory and leader of all Dutch and British members

The Cornishman unrolled the parchment, careful that he didn't break it. He read carefully the 18th century French. He had learned this French over many years in the eternal hope that one day he would have this in his hands. As he read his face couldn't help but show his pleasure and then, peace and delight. *A form of God's Grace seemed to overcome him* Françoise thought. *What could it say?* And she spoke breaking her thoughts. 'Can you tell us what it says please?'

The Cornishman rolled up the scroll and tied it with small piece of bandage that was left on the table. He spoke softly and deliberately, his smile gone and has manner firm and decisive again.

'I summary, it sets out an agreement, a binding Treaty, by the Holy Roman Empire, England and the French. It agrees that through the power and infiltration of The Priory of Sion in French Aristocracy, The French secret society will ensure that King Louis does not interfere in the defeat of Charles Stuart by King Billy and will hold back its fleet and allow King Billy to prevent Charles's reclaiming the English and Scottish thrones. For such an intercession The Priory and France will be given the West Country as part of their dominion and all parties will form a grand European Alliance, ruled by a united Britain under one King, King William, a protestant descendant of the Stuart line - the Holy Blood.'

Françoise and Jack just stood and stared, both were thinking simultaneously *What on earth did that mean and how could that happen?*

And, *what on earth has any of that to do with now or cause people to search for it for centuries and possibly kill for?*

Jack broke the silence. 'I really don't understand any of that. You have told us many times that this is so important to you and your family. You are Cornish and what could a grand European alliance mean to you or indeed, losing Cornwall to the bloody French!' and realising his xenophobia might upset his Gallic friend, he smiled and apologised, 'Sorry Françoise, just in a manner of speaking.'

Despite the seriousness, she smiled back. She turned to the injured Cornishman. 'It really doesn't make sense to us.'

'Maybe not to you but I am a member of the Priory as well as a loyal Cornishman. I am not high enough up the degrees to know all that they know and can manipulate. They say that what this chest contained can be used now to ensure that the people they have infiltrated into all governments and financial institutions and also monarchies to re-establish what this agreement was signed for. But for me it's simple. Cornwall has always been British, never English. We are linked right through to the Celts and before them all the way to the Egyptian people who kept to true knowledge of the Supreme Architect. Indeed many believe we are the lost tribe of Judah. We should be rulers of our own kingdom and aligned to Bretagne rather than London, or heaven forbid Rome. This paper proves that we are divinely and royally a separate nation, a ruler of a West Country that is a free state within the new Holy Roman Empire from which Cornwall will rule, not London or Paris or Rome.'

Jack and Françoise just looked on. *This can't be what this what all about surely? The guy's gone loopy.'*

'So I will use this for my own purposes. I will make up with my French colleagues and we will begin the process of winning back the power for Cornwall and for Sion. Give me your car keys and I think the leg's stable enough to drive now.'

Jack handed him the car keys, feeling pretty pleased that this was now all over. This lunatic can do what he likes with a three hundred year piece of paper, Cornwall will remain Cornwall surely, Britain will leave any Holy European Empire and it won't change the world. They can go back to normality.

The Cornishman placed the scroll in his shirt and opened the fire door. As he exited something forced him to hurtle backwards, smash into the dressing table and slip down unconscious, his nose smashed to a pulp. The two left were gobsmacked and their heart beats rose quickly. They stared at the open door in fear of their lives yet again.

A man dressed solely in black entered. He wore a back full face bike helmet. He had a Walther PPK hand gun in his hand and as he closed the door behind him he began to take his helmet off. He took the helmet off and placed it on the white clinic bench. He looked at the body and nodded his head in satisfaction. He stood facing his two frightened treasure hunters, PPK in his hand. He shook his blond hair and looked again at the trapped couple and said in perfect Queen's English:

'Hi. My name is Jim...Jungle Jim.'

CHAPTER TWENTY-FOUR

You could have knocked Françoise down with a feather. Here, in front of her was the local lunatic who had rescued her at St Michael's Church yard. Now he was standing there speaking perfect English, dressed like some paid assassin and carrying a handgun. *What the hell next?* she thought. And then she panicked again.

Jungle Jim walked over to the Cornishman and kicked him a few times. He smiled as he turned to them. 'He'll not be eating too many pasties for some time.'

'It's you? Françoise stuttered. 'The graveyard: The man on the tracks: Isn't it?'

'Yes Madam. It is moi. Here to serve all good people, particularly pretty French ladies.'

Poser Jack thought. His jealousy rising for some reason he did not understand. *If he didn't have that gun...*

Françoise felt a flutter. He was dashing for sure. But she soon fell back into worry. 'What are you doing in all this? I don't understand any of this. It is getting more frightening by the hour.'

'No need to be frightened now. The Italian is fixed and now the Cornishman. All I need now is that which is sticking out of his chest and I will leave you. A pity as I'd like to get to know you a little more. This town has been pretty slim for the International jet set I am used too but I could possibly stay a while for you. But sadly no: M would not be too happy... and Moneypenny? Well you know what she might say.'

Dear God Jack thought another loony tune. *He thinks he's James Bond.*

'Can you hand me the scroll my dearest please,' Jungle Jim asked.

'Françoise pulled the scroll from the unconscious West Country fanatic, not caring any more for his laboured breathing and blood pouring out of his smashed nose and mouth. She was getting hardened to this.

'Vauxhall will be happy now. This needs deep sixing in their vaults forever. We can't have nasty foreigners interfering with our Constitution or our Monarchy. That's just not British is it? Yes, this will be buried and a great thank you from the British Government. Now I must go.'

'Wait, please Jim,' Françoise pleaded, 'We've come so far I'd like to read what it says and at least touch what we have risked our lives for. I can't believe it's just what that idiot there said. Come on let me see,' and she gave him her best flashing eyes bit and smile. Jack got even angrier.

'Ok, here take a look. M says its dynamite what was in the box. I have no idea. I am only told what to do. Of course I enjoy myself doing it. After all, I am licensed to thrill - Hah hah hah. From what I heard behind the door from the poor man lying there its crazy stuff, but heh ho, that's spying and governments for you.'

Jack hated him more. Sleazy bastard; if only...

Françoise carefully read the document. It was as the Cornishman had said. It seems as if the French Priory in line with the Grand Alliance and the Pope had a plot to over throw King Louis after it was all signed and completed. King Louis had been duped by his Priory infiltrators that a French revolution was near unless he stopped the war and made up with Pope. However, the Priory's objective was always to cause the next French revolution and avenge the Cathar massacres, which they eventually did with Guillotines, Mary Antoinette's head, the lot, and oust the Bourbon's and put on the throne of European Alliance the rightful heir to the Royal Bloodline, the British protestant monarch, the Defender of the True Faith. It appeared that the West Country would be annexed by France under Cornish control to assuage Louis temporarily until they could remove him. But eventually the objective was to neutralise the Pope as well and Roman authority and rule the new European Order from the West Country, and from the New Jerusalem, Sion.

As she read, she was still puzzled. So much plotting; So many religious dynasties and beliefs to overcome to achieve this. France and Italy and most of the Eastern and Southern states of the Grand Alliance were Catholic. Surely they wouldn't be ruled by a Protestant Dutch/English King? They were fighting the Catholic King Louis for sure and trying to stop a Catholic Stuart gaining the throne and strangely the Pope supported them in stopping that and thus allowing King Billy, a staunch Protestant, with his Act of Union to rule over a untied Britain and Ireland. And with King Billy's Act of Succession there could never be a catholic Monarch of Britain aligned to Rome. What on earth was the Pope up to allowing all that? What a tangled web. Something was missing here surely. Also, what or who was Sion? And why is the West Country so important to that? Why would it be a New Jerusalem?

She stopped reading, as she just couldn't believe that this had all been signed and agreed by the highest powers in Europe. But what other thing would make them all fall into line? All were so biased in their religious faiths and their petty dynastic squabbles. Something was missing for sure. And where was the Holy Grail in all this? Is that all the Grail was - a protocol, a document? There is no world shattering religious proof here that her Aunt and others spoke about. It was just old powerful men agreeing a dirty rotten deal between them all to carve up Europe.

She was about to put it down, when she noticed a small codicil to the Treaty. It was just an annotation that looked as if it had been added later and signed and dated by the French Foreign Secretary and the English Secretary of State. She struggled to read it was so small but when she did she laughed out loud.

Jack looked over shocked; 'There can't be much to laugh about surely?'

'Oh Yes there is. I now know why our friend's family in Cornwall have sought for centuries to get this published and announced again.'

Jack shrugged his shoulders. 'So do I. It's because the daft sod thinks England will give up Cornwall and the West Country to the French and Cornwall will rule. Deutschland uber Alles and all that; Like Hitler, he's bloody mad man.'

'Well maybe not,' Françoise answered smiling. 'Shall I read what the codicil says?'

'Well you will, so go on.'

And she did. 'Here goes, you'll love this.'

Herewith on this day in July 1690 all peoples listen: The King of England and his Parliament agree that Cornwall shall be afforded Royal Privilege and the Royal Seal of Bakers for joining with France and helping form the new European Alliance and leading Sion in the West Country. Let all peoples of England know that from this day and forever, all scones will be eaten the Cornish way; with the jam spread on first and then the cream. It will be heresy punishable by hanging drawing and quartering to eat them the Devon way with cream first.

'No wonder the good people of Teignmouth kept this secret for years. They weren't interested in Grand Alliances, Holy Roman Empires, and mythical Sion's. They would never put their jam on first for God's sake. This must have shocked the original smugglers to the bone, their new Dutch King legalising their worst nightmare. Under English common law it's probably still legal today. That's why they kept it hidden for centuries.'

Jungle Jim brushed his long blonde hair back. He laughed and spoke in his polished English. 'I always wondered what all the fuss was about jam first or last while I hid down here. I thought you were all just crazy like all those folks in the pubs here. And to be honest it makes sense to put the jam on first. The Cornish may well be correct but surely M

218

hasn't had me living undercover to this flea-bitten town to stop this happening. I think there is more to this than how to eat your damned scones, Françoise. But for sure, it's a shock to the Devon system for sure if it ever becomes legal again. Jam first! We'd have riots on the streets. Anyway, enough chit chat. I must take your scones and Sion and all that jazz and place them in the capable hands of Her Majesty's Secret Service, whose duty I serve.'

'Bugger off then. And take your bodies with you. We don't want the Police involved,' Jack replied, his frustration and dislike for the preening spy showing a little too much.

'I'll need your car for that. I'll help you dump him back on the Exeter Road with that other unfortunate. Did you know he was Russian GRU? An Italian, but definitely Russian. We've tracked him since he arrived. This one here, he'll wake up and once you explain about me when he inevitably gets back to you, he'll go quietly away. Drop me back here and I'll take the bike and head off. I'll give the Treaty to double oh nine and he'll head back tonight with it. I plan to meet the boys from the Monday Club for one last celebratory drink tomorrow in *The Jolly Sailor*. Maybe you'll join us? Mine will be a *Jail Ale*, shaken but not stirred.'

'Oh just piss off,' Jack said. Françoise whacked the shocked double oh seven with a roll of gauze. And they all left the scene.

The treasure hunt over: The terrible secret that Teignmouth had kept secret for years would be 'deep sixed' again.

Devon was safe again - or so they thought.

CHAPTER TWENTY-FIVE

Françoise and Jack sat in the kitchen of her house. It had been a long difficult night and much had happened to them. They really tried hard to understand the terrifying events and the amazing revelations that emerged. Jungle Jim had left them on his bike to meet his accomplice 009. Jack was not sorry to see the back of him and he certainly wouldn't take up the offer of a drink with him even though he would dearly love to find out who was 009 and who were the agents planted all over Teignmouth. He was still shocked to find out that those he believed were ordinary folks out for a drink and relaxation were indeed on Her Majesty's Service or where in the pay of some deranged Cornish liberation gang or some Global esoteric secret society. He hadn't been this paranoid since working for a living with his bosses The Iron Chancellor, The Big Yin and KT the Terrible. It had to stop.

They both understood from Jungle Jim that it was pointless to approach the authorities as he was indeed 'The' authorities. And who would believe them anyway. Jack sat drinking his coffee and decided best let sleeping spies lie. However, he would give the basis of the plot to Davey the Author, this conspiracy was right up his sleeve. Even better than the one that the Titanic didn't sink or Skirpal was poisoned by Donald Trump. In a moment of sanity as he supped his Mocha he looked at Françoise and out of the window towards the river and he thought he'd tell Davey to call the book *Spies on the Teign*.

The open treasure chest was sat on the table. Françoise had stared at it long and hard over their coffee. She was still in some form of shock at what she had seen and heard but she really could not comprehend that all the fuss was over a long-lost historical treaty and a King's edict to eliminate the Devon tradition of how to eat bloody scones. *People were prepared to kill for that? No, that was not it all. It couldn't be.* She told Jack of her thoughts. He agreed with her. 'Well it's certainly not what I expected. All these clues referring to the Holy Grail, the man who died on a hill far away, Avalon, Sion and Vines. Were they all just bullshit to confuse the hell out of the seekers of the treaty? If so then it's been a bloody long and pointless wild goose chase we have been on.'

'What I really can't understand is why this man Saunière would want this so badly to send that Italian or Russian or whoever the bugger was to kill us for it. My Aunt said he had a copy of the real truth about Jesus Christ and the Magdalene and that he needed the copy lost and supposedly in this chest. Her husband and this Priory society had kept this hidden for two centuries as it could change the world for ever. I really can't see a long dead treaty and letting the Cornish eat scones with jam first is going to change our world Jack. It's just all nonsense.'

Jack looked concerned. He got up and rinsed his coffee cup and placed it on the stainless-steel draining board. He took another glance at the treasure chest. *Was this it? All the heartache for this?* He needed a drink. 'Have you got a beer in the fridge Françoise?'

'Yes, but I hide them in the vegetable tray. My husband just drinks them all if I leave them on show.'

Jack opened the tray and took out a can of Dartmoor Legend. As he gripped the ring-pull he suddenly had a wonderful thought. *What if the chest was hiding something in a tray or compartment?*

He put his beer down and walked over and picked up the chest and turned it around and upside down. 'Françoise what if there is a secret drawer or compartment in this? It would make sense if there was something else more sensational hidden away that was never discovered by the Teignmouth smugglers or known about by the British Government, Jungle Jim and his James Bond mates; known only to the Priory and to Saunière.'

'Maybe Jack, but if it is, it's defied the searches and handling of centuries by the Teignmouth keepers of the secret. How can we find it?'

'We look. They probably only saw the treaty got scared at it as it was signed by the new Monarch and they could well still have had their heads chopped off those days without any bother. And of course which Devon person would want to be forced to eat scones with Jam first. Its criminal, if not as the treaty says, heresy. They just hid what they saw. Why would they think there was anything else? They wouldn't.'

Françoise looked at Jack and her face dropped. 'Jack, if there really is something else hidden that is more important and world shattering them what Jungle Jim has taken then we are still in real danger with this chest.'

'Yes, I guess you are right. So let's get in with it and find the real secret what they keep telling us 'was lost'. At least we will have a bargaining tool to get our arses out of this safe.'

They both studied every part of the chest but could not fathom out if there was a secret drawer or compartment. Then Jack had an idea. 'Have you a tape measure?'

'Yes. My husband keeps a small one for small house jobs in the kitchen drawer.'

'Jack took the tape from the drawer. 'If I measure the dimensions and then the inside and the thickness of the wood then I should see if there is a discrepancy in the measurements.'

'That's a good idea matey. Let's do it,'

After a few measurements it became clear that the top to the bottom of the chest was not accurate. The distance to the base inside was shorter than it should be given the thickness of the wood. 'Jack, this is exciting. The base is much thicker than it should be. There could be a compartment in there. Well done ma cheri.' And she grabbed him and kissed him. But this wasn't the polite, social kissing the French do with close friends but a full blown, lasting amorous kiss. Jack responded is the same way. All his passions of the last twenty-four hours arose and fulfilled. The kiss lasted and they gripped each other closely. Too close for just friends.

They did not hear the kitchen door open. But they did hear the angry voice. 'What the hell are you doing with my wife?'

They broke apart and both took one step back from each other. Françoise looked at the direction of the voice and cried out. 'Jimmy, I didn't think you were back till...'

The man looked Jack up and down and said, 'Obviously. Who the hell is this?'

'He's Jack. The man who has been helping me with the charity treasure hunt I told you about. It's nothing Jimmy, just a kiss in celebration we've got a treasure chest to open,' Françoise replied, telling the same lie she'd told him for some time now.

Her husband appeared to calm down and told them both the sit down. Jack had looked around for anything he could use to defend himself. The man was a fit, much younger man than him or Françoise and this was dangerous stuff. Found kissing another man's wife in his own home and after midnight. He would not be amused himself.

Jimmy sat down himself opposite them, he answered Françoise. 'Looks a bit more than a happy kiss to me, but let's not let that stop what you were doing eh?'

Françoise was puzzled this wasn't what she expected. 'What do you mean? What we were doing? We just had a quick kiss as we opened this box.'

'I think not Françoise. That wasn't a quick peck. I heard most of what you both were talking about. I'd like to see what you have found in that box.'

Françoise was really puzzled now. *Why would he be bothered about this more than catching her in flagrante with Jack? He wasn't normally this quiet*

222

tempered. In fact he'd battered a few men who had looked at her badly and said something nasty. He was a strong aggressive man. This was not in character at all. She asked him to explain. 'Jimmy you were listening? Why not come in? You weren't back until Wednesday and what does this chest mean to you Jimmy. It's not like you.'

Jack just sat and waited. He was very tense. This wasn't how he would have expected a man to react finding his wife in the arms of another. He was scared and ready to protect himself and Françoise but he knew he had little chance of physically defeating the large man unless he used the small hammer he'd seen in the drawer when he found the tape measure. He slowly opened the door.

'Well to be honest Françoise. It's not me who wants what is in that box. I really don't care. What we kept secret for years to stop those damned Cornish I now hear has been taken to London by that posing bastard Jungle Jim. If its lost then that means Devon is safe from the bloody Cornish and we can sleep again in our beds.'

'What!' Françoise shouted out, clearly shocked and frightened at what she was listening to. 'Who the hell are you Jimmy? What do you know about Jungle Jim and the secret? Who the HELL are you? You are my husband for God's sake and you knew all along about what we were searching for?' She almost collapsed on the table after the outburst. This was all getting far too difficult to grasp. Jack opened the kitchen drawer slowly.

Jimmy crossed his legs and sat back. He waited until Françoise had calmed and answered her. 'Of course I knew about the hunt. I set it in motion with old Albert all those days ago.'

Françoise jaw dropped and she stared wildly at her husband. Or whoever he was. She wasn't sure anymore. He continued.

'I have known every move you both made. Well, most of them. The phone bugs helped and our spies in the town told us the rest. Even tonight we heard most of what went on. Jungle Jim isn't so clever, the posh twat. Zero Zero Nine is one of ours. Jack, you know him as Jimmy the Hat. And I wouldn't take what you are looking for out of the drawer matey. I'll break your arm.'

Jack closed the drawer. *Who the hell was this man? I wish this was all over,* was all he could think.

'But you are my husband Jimmy. How could you do this?' Françoise whispered clearly upset and tears rolling down her eyes.

'Yes. That's true my beauty. But I have a stronger love and affection and that was to the people of Teignmouth and lately, the Priory. I am The Squire - the ultimate 'keeper of the secret'.

Jack took Françoise's hand and squeezed it affectionately in sympathy for her pain. She looked into his eyes and saw what she hadn't seen for years in her husband's – love. He decided to have his say. 'So you've deceived this lovely lady and all your friends for so long Jimmy. How could you do that?'

'Oh Jack. What a twisted web we all weave. Ever since I was young I was groomed to be The Squire as I am linked all the way to Zebediah Hook, the pirate smuggler. Albert was groomed take over as Squire from Doctor Mules in the Cliffden. When he died Albert took over but as I grew up into manhood he groomed me to be the ultimate Squire which he handed over to me two years ago. The clues are kept locked in the lawyer's Scott Richardson's vaults and I the only one with access. The problem was Albert never told me the location of the chest. He was waiting for the right time. It never came before his death. I never got there in time but you did. Then two years ago I was approached by the Grand Master of the Priory. Somehow they had known for some years I was the Squire. I then joined their cause to find the secret and reveal the truth. None of us could solve all the clues. And then you took over. We let you carry one as you both did much better than us.'

'Oh Jimmy this is incredible. How could you keep that secret from me?'

'It wasn't easy Françoise. I did love you once but it was always fate that this would happen between us. You see you have always been the key to all this. You are the one destined to find the Grail and the truth; whatever the truth is. I was never told that.'

'How on earth am I the key and who chose me to find this bloody thing?'

Her husband got up from his chair and opened the kitchen door. As the person entered the room he said:

'Meet the person who chose you; your aunt – The Grand Master of the Priory of Sion.'

CHAPTER TWENTY-SIX

Françoise momentarily fainted. Jack sat staring into the void, his mouth agog. Edith walked into the room, no wheelchair in sight. She was dressed in a smart designer dress and her grey hair was tied up in a bun. She looked years younger that when Françoise had last left her after the near drowning incident on the River Seine. She came over and hugged her niece and kissed her four times on the cheeks. Françoise just mimicked the same not really knowing what she was doing. This was now a dream she was convinced. A fantasy, *Rollo the dog and Captain Hooke were nothing to this nightmare.*

'Oh my dear girl, please forgive me. This must be a shock to you. I really never hoped this meeting would be so traumatic for you. You have been so brave. And your friend,' Edith looked over at Jack, 'he is so brave too. Please forgive us Jack. This is greater than family or love. Jimmy why don't you pour us all a long shot of that Scotch you were keeping for this day?'

Jimmy left to bring his bottle of fifteen year old Glen Morangie. Françoise took her aunt's hands in hers as Edith sat next to her at the table. 'Aunty, this is all too much for me to take in. Tell me it really isn't true.'

'I'm sorry ma Cherie it is. I am the Grand Master of the Priory. I have been ever since your uncle died. I took over from him. I have been watching you carefully through all of this. Please understand, I would never have let Saunière or anyone hurt you. We were in control most of the time.'

'Most of the time!' Jack shouted. 'It took a man with some camp, posh crazy James Bond fetish to save us on the moor. Where were you?'

'Do you think the Cornishman could fool us? When he left our French girls we had followed him and the girls hopped on the motor bike we gave them and got to the moor and hid. They watched it all. They would not let the crazy Cornish or the Italian harm you.'

Jack sat back. It was too much. Every bit of heather seemed to have some form of assassin hidden behind it and every pub had the cast of Tinker Taylor Soldier Spy. He had given up thinking now.

Jimmy returned and poured out four glasses of whisky. Françoise and Jack swallowed theirs in one gulp. He poured them another. Françoise had got her voice back. 'Aunty, if you were searching for that Grand European Treaty then it's gone. Jungle Jim has taken it to be hidden away again in the vaults of Westminster. So what was all the point? You've lost.'

Edith stood up easily. No hint of any arthritic pain or disability. 'We always had the French copy of that. Only King William's signature was missing. Your great Grandfather was sent to get that. It's enough for our purposes if we have the real truth.'

'You see,' said a wakening and angrier Jack, 'that's what pisses me off with you lot. Secret societies, spies, treaties and still no truth. You wouldn't know the truth if Donald Trump spat it out at you. You are all just living in a dream world made up by old men who like to dress up as grand wizards, knights and ******* priests. I'm sick of the lot of you.'

'Calm down Jack,' whispered Edith and she reached over and grabbed his hand in some form of comfort. He pulled away. Edith continued, 'It's understandable you feel that way. The truth is known only to me and partly by two others both leaders of their countries. Of course it's difficult to take in. Maybe if we can show you it you might believe us?'

'How are you going to do that?' Jack said sarcastically.

'By opening this box - watch me.'

And Edith took a key she had in her small handbag and placed it in the lock. As she turned it a door opened at the base of the chest. She pulled the small, five centimetre, drawer down and put her small finger into the rectangular hole, now the width of box. Slowly she pulled out a slim wax coated rectangular parcel, bound in leather. It was about A4 size. 'Eureka: That what was lost!' Edith smiled broadly as she spoke.

She put the packet on the table and took a long drink of her whisky. 'Well, there you have it. What was lost in 1690 and stolen by Jimmy's family and their mates. Hidden ever since then; now we can tell the world and Sion will rise across Europe.'

Françoise sat and took another sip from her glass. She was actually underwhelmed. What she expected she wasn't sure. *Where was this Holy Grail they'd heard of? Another piece of paper in the wax coated jacket? What can that do?* Her whole mind was numb.

'You look upset my dear. What's troubling you?' Edith asked compassionately.

'What's upsetting me is simple. I still don't know why this piece of old leather is so important that my life has now been ruined. My husband is not what I thought and deceived me. You have deceived me. I have been manipulated and lead to put this kind and caring man into danger. And you still don't tell me what it was for. I really wish you'd both just go and leave me and Jack to get on with our lives. So, will you go; Now!'

'Oh Cherie, please don't get so sad. This is a wonderful day. We have all made sacrifices over centuries. Think of all those who were massacred, tortured and excommunicated to keep this secret until the time was right. Our own family; do you think my husband died naturally? Of course he didn't. Those who wish to keep the rule of Rome and Jerusalem have killed many to get to this small packet. Now we have it. I can only say sorry that you have been instrumental in finding it but you have done a great service to your family, your country and to God. You will receive your reward on this earth and the next.'

'For Christ's sake! Well, if there is a Christ after all the bullshit we've been told and learnt, tell me what it is and go. Get out of my life forever; both of you.'

Edith took the waxed leather packet and placed it in a small leather briefcase that Jimmy had supplied her. She put it next to her. Then she told her story.

'In here is the missing Gnostic Gospel, written in Aramaic so you will not understand but I know what it says. It was written by the followers of Christ - his disciples and the Essenes. It was not buried at Qumram with the other Dead Sea Scrolls but under Solomon's Temple and was discovered by the Knights Templar in their diggings in the eleventh century. Its knowledge and truth had been followed by the Cathars since the first century and then given to them after the persecution of the Templars by the Pope and Rome. They have never given up searching for it. Finally it was taken to Britain and kept at Tintagel until your great, great grandfather lost it at Teignmouth. He was bringing it back to us to use to prove and enforce the creation of the Grand European alliance between King William, The Holy Roman Empire and France. It would cement the Alliance until we could remove the Pope and Louis and form the new order and to do that we needed the Gospel and the proof. When he lost it we lost the opportunity and the war just carried on to its final defeat of Louis and the Treaty of Utrecht in 1713. From then on we have manipulated and changed European order with the one goal. To use what is in that packet to change Europe and then the world, to a united group of States that are built on a modern, liberal religious order of both Catholic and Protestant far removed from the rule of Rome, the Church of England or any established faith. A faith based on Sion and ruled from Sion by a monarch that rules over that place and the faith.'

Jack looked at Françoise and shook his head. *Crazies again* he mimicked. He spoke out. 'So you still haven't told us what's in it have you except your weird theories and conspiracies it's just a story isn't it?'

Edith smiled. 'So many people think that or write false and hurtful untruths. We too have released documents to hide the truth and keep everyone on the wrong track. The Pierre Plantard *'Dossiers Secret'* my husband helped release at the Bibliotheque national de France. But now is the time to release the truth. This packet contains the Gospel that proves that the son of God did die on the cross and was resurrected to finally come again and judge the living and the dead. It also proves that all the esoteric beliefs and that followers of the secret that Mary Magdalene carried a son to Europe and therefore Christ's bloodline lives on, are also true.'

Jack interrupted her, 'So it is true that Jesus had a son?'

'No, of course not, that was just misinformation. Mary Magdalene had a son but the father was definitely not Jesus. He was Jesus' uncle, Joseph of Aramathea. Mary was his aunt. Why do you think Jesus was so close to her? Why she was always around and the first to find him after his resurrection. And why Joseph bought and paid for his tomb. Only Jewish family would have done that in those days.'

'Wow. It makes a bit of sense,' Françoise said, perking up now that the historical treaty stuff was out of the way. 'Never did get that Jesus was married. Mind you I was brought up a Catholic. I thought you were Aunt? What's all this true faith, modernist liberal stuff?'

'Yes I was brought up that way because your great Uncle knew nothing of the destiny I had after marrying your Uncle, the Grand Master. It changed my life. We are bound to the Great Architect, to the all-seeing God. And we are bound to his son, the Master Builder. We know that all peoples should live in awe of him and his work and live together; free in the knowledge that truth, brotherhood and charity are the virtues that make good citizens. You see Jesus built this faith not in Jerusalem but here in England. This is what the gospel also tells us.'

Jack poured himself another whisky. He needed it. *Was this woman for real? Or just another loony tune like the Cornishman.* 'Oh really,' he said sarcastically, in response the whisky making him braver and remembering what his old friend, Steed, in Singapore would have replied to any inane or stupid statement.

'Yes Jack really. It is all set out in the Gospel. You see it has been known by many throughout the ages that Joseph of Arimathea was a wealthy merchant and that he traded with Britain, the Tin Islands, for the metal. He visited Cornwall for sure. And he also visited Devon looking for tin. Then on one trip he brought Jesus with him, his nephew.

'Oh come on,' Françoise said 'Jesus never left Palestine. Well except to escape to Egypt after his birth. He couldn't have been here.'

'Why not? His Uncle came here, it's well documented, and why wouldn't he bring his nephew. And we know nothing about his early life. The four gospels and New Testament only talk about him from his baptism by John the Baptist until his death on the cross on that hill far way. All we are told is that he was a Carpenter. And that wasn't particularly true.'

'What are you saying aunty, Jesus wasn't a carpenter?' Françoise said, astonished again.

'Well you have to understand what we have known for thousands of years. There are many references in the known scripture that Jesus was a master builder not a carpenter. *'The stone which the builders rejected'* in Mark's Gospel *'the stone which the builders refused is become the head stone of the corner'* the Psalms. You see we know that the stone, the cornerstone is the Rock of Sion. Not the actual rock outside Jerusalem but that Sion is the cornerstone of the Church that Jesus built. Both the actual stone and the spiritual one. Did he not say himself, *'Destroy this temple and in three days I will raise it up'* Yes, we know he is the master-builder.'

'That doesn't explain anything. You are just building in your own links to ancient free masonry and Knights of the Temple,' said Jack, sarcastically again.

'Well, you may not know too much about your bible my boy and you certainly don't know anything of our Ancient Rites, but let me explain in simple terms. According to John, when Jesus' Aunt, Mary Magdalene met him in the garden beside the empty tomb after his resurrection she said to him: *'Rabboni*; which is to say, *'Master.'* Now you may say this may well be a sign of his spiritual leadership to her. But we know that Rabboni was not Aramaic for master but derives from two Hebrew words. It is a crucial password in our highest Royal arch degree and it means 'Master Builder'.'

Jack just shrugged his shoulders. *So what,* he thought, she could tell him anything.

'You don't look convinced Jack, or you Françoise. Sometimes you have to accept the sacred knowledge we have is founded on real events and records. From the dawn of Egyptian civilisation we have kept this knowledge and we keep finding many things to confirm it. The Bible does not, lie about this. A lot was missed out of course as the Roman Empire and the Bishop of Rome chose what truth to put in to confirm Rome's primacy over the new Christian Church. But this Gospel tells a lot more than those which were put in the Bible and confirms that indeed that Jesus was the cornerstone and the architect of the real Church - of Sion itself. Why wouldn't he be? He is the son of the Great Architect himself.'

'Time for break, I need a wee,' said Françoise, and she got up to go to the toilet. Jimmy followed her. 'So, I'm a prisoner in my own house then?'

'Sorry my dearie, but can't let you get in touch with anyone about this. Not until its safe in the Priory's hands.' Françoise dropped her head and thought she might cry again. This was so much to take in.

When she returned Edith explained more. 'So you must see that there is no reason why Jesus could not have been trained in the Master builder craft and travelled with his rich uncle to Britain. Indeed you all know he did. You sing about it at every rugby match. Even when you beat us at the French stadium last January, Scare bleu, a bad day that.'

'*Swing low sweet chariot?*' Jack retorted. 'That's a negro spiritual song. Guess it's about the Jordan River but that's a bit loose connection.'

'A bit closer to home than Jordan Jack,' Edith said.

Françoise had been studying and thinking and she threw in a possibility. '*Jerusalem?* But that's a long way too.'

Edith started to sing: '*And did those feet in ancient times walk upon England's mountain green? And was the holy Lamb of God on England's pleasant pastures seen?*''

'Oh of course but that just a song surely? Patriotism and Religion mixed up in Victorian John Bull stuff?' Jack sneered.

'It was written by William Blake, a Grand Master of the Priory my friend. And it tells of when Jesus came here with his Uncle and he started to build the new temple, the new faith and the new Sion. *I will not cease from mental fight, nor shall my sword sleep in my hand, till we have built Jerusalem... In England's green and pleasant land.*'

Edith took a sip of whisky and finished. 'And that my friends is what we have never stopped doing, we have not slept, we have taken up arms and we are about to build Jerusalem here again.'

She stood up and placed her whisky glass on the table. 'But now I am tired. I am still an old lady even though the wheelchair was a front to confuse Saunière and those from Rome. I need my sleep. I will retire to the spare room. I guess you won't want to sleep with Jimmy?'

Françoise just shook her head. Her aunt continued and looked at Jack,' well; maybe the two of you will kip in the big bedroom. Jimmy will sleep on the sofa with the door open in case you get itchy feet. We will have the phones please. Also don't think about anything else as the two lovely French girls are in the car outside and watching every move.

This time they will stop you. I am sorry but this is my life's dream and I can't let it drift away. We will talk in the morning. Tomorrow I will tell you what the world has been waiting to hear.'

CHAPTER TWENTY-SEVEN

They lay close to each other and held on tight. Both knew that their lives had changed that night. Françoise life had been upturned and her husband and Aunt were lost to her now. Jack was sure he was in the beginnings of love with her, emotions he had not felt since the loss of his wife in a car accident five years ago. Both were too emotional to do anything about their feelings but hold tight comforting each other on top of the bed fully clothed, their minds troubled by the events that unfolded in the kitchen. They fell asleep about three am and slept until Edith knocked and opened the door and asked them to come down for a coffee. She had to get moving and back to Paris.

They all met for the last time around the kitchen table. Jimmy had taken Piaf for her walk along the Back Beach and she was quietly sat in her basket next to the back door. Edith kicked off their final and mind-boggling lesson.

'I am scheduled on the nine fifty five train to Paddington station. I have to meet some very important people in London with this packet. We now begin the process we started in sixteen ninety. We will stop all this Brexit nonsense; we have enough of us in power here and in Brussels to do that. After all they have been sabotaging it since the British voted to leave.'

'Bloody Remainers! I'd shoot the lot of them,' Jimmy interjected.

Edith smiled knowingly. 'Now then Jimmy, remember what the person we are about to talk about said, *Father, forgive then for they know not what they do*'. And for sure, few people know what we do or who is doing it. Our chosen people are not 'Remainers'; they are the most unlikely Brexiteers - those of us from the most powerful of families and the establishment. They are now, and will be, the elite of Europe; the chosen ones. The New Testament says of a line of spiritual leaders who will be: 'You are *a chosen generation. A royal priesthood, a holy nation, a peculiar people.*' And we will drive the creation of that holy nation.'

Jack kicked Françoise under the table. She looked up from her coffee. His look said it all. *'Here we go again'*, she's crazy.

Edith saw his sneer and Françoise's blank look. 'I guess you both think we are all crazy sons of bitches as it would say in the American movies. Well let me show you some of our members.' And she took out of her briefcase a sheet of paper with an organisation drawn with Edith at the top. They both took deep breaths as they saw names whose faces they had seen on Newsnight, CNN, the BBC TV evening news and all the mainline European press over the last couple of years of the Brexit shenanigans from all sides of the fence.

'Dear me auntie, is this really happening? I don't know what is real anymore.'

'It is real Françoise and it is happening. Do you really think Brexit could have been as messed up as it is unless there was some secret, underlying mission to do that by people of real power in politics and finance. This Gospel will make sure of that. With this the peoples of Europe will see that it has always been divinely ordained that we shall all live as a holy nation ruled by that royal priesthood. That priesthood will have at its head the Monarch of England, the Defender of the True Faith, and the spiritual home of all these peoples shall be here, in the West Country at Glastonbury. Glastonbury is Sion. It is where the Cornerstone of our faith first walked and the stone was laid. Where the first Church was started by Jesus Christ and built by his Uncle and his nephew, Mary Magdalene's son.'

Françoise got up and poured herself another coffee from the cafetiere. She sat down and faced her aunt. 'How do you know that?'

'It is all written here in the scroll. Joseph wrote it and returned it to Jerusalem and hid it with the Essenes leaders in the temple until the world was fully aware of the Supreme Architect's son's work and had adopted that. Mary left to France with her daughter, Joseph's child, soon after Jesus's resurrection. She landed in France and spent some time there, around the area of Rennes le Chateau. She was always heading towards Britain and eventually once he had sorted out affairs after Jesus' ascension, she was followed by her husband to Avalon, or in today's language, Glastonbury. For fifteen years they evangelised in the West Country. You see Mary was the first to meet the risen Christ. It should make sense if she was his Aunty. And it was unknown of in the first century for a woman to be given the most important role in anything, never mind the most miraculous and world changing story of all time. The published gospels are true in this. Why? Because any sensible fraud and forgery of the gospels would have written in that a man would have been the first to hear the 'good news'. Where they got it wrong was that the 'good news', a risen Jesus' message of love was not first spread by the apostles but by Mary. She brought the Grail containing the physical 'blood of Christ', his DNA to England. She also preached his 'good news' the Gospel. And Joseph, her husband, is credited by many building the first church in the world, at Avalon. You see Joseph was the first to clean and care for Jesus' body. He took care of Jesus's crucified body and for any who read the known gospels that the *'Body of Christ'* is a synonym for *'The Church'*. During this time they had a son carrying Jesus and King David's bloodline to carry on the Holy Priesthood, the Royal Blood. This son was born in Avalon and his eventual descendant was King Arthur and would be buried here too. Avalon was always Sion; the rock, the cornerstone that that Royal Priesthood was founded upon and it was always in England.'

'Sounds a bit logical even though fantastical, but why England?' Jack asked, needing some clarity to all this.

'Simple really: listen to the hymn *Jerusalem* again. Jesus did come to Britain with his Uncle. He did walk here and he did start to build the new Temple and the New Jerusalem here. He laid the actual cornerstone of the temple for his Uncle. He then went back to Palestine to finally start his eventually fatal but victorious mission. He came to Cornwall first, hence our Cornish friends believing they have the right to rule the new Sion. And this is what we told them and wrote in the agreement in 1690. But that was never our plan. Our plan was to build upon Avalon and also here, beside the River Teign in Devon - the new Jordan.'

Françoise put here cup down hard. 'Now you are living in a dream world. I think it's time you left us alone.' And she started to get up.

Edith grasped her hand am dulled her down with surprisingly a much stronger hand than Françoise would have thought. 'Please, sit down my dear. It's all here in this scroll; this is the word of Jesus's blood relatives, Joseph and the Magdalene, not me. Just listen a while longer and you will agree with us that it's time to realise that dream you think I have.'

Françoise sat down. She looked at her aunt and still couldn't believe the transformation from quaint, old matriarch to scheming, physically fit leader of a secret society that contained some the most famous faces on television. But she had to finish this and she spoke again. 'Why Devon then? And why here, Teignmouth, or the river Teign?'

'Maybe it's time to show you something before I answer that. Let me show the proof we have sought and what will ensure we change Europe then the world.' And Edith began to split open the wax jacket and prise the leather binding that covered the Gospel. As she peeled the layers, Françoise couldn't help feel the shiver down her back and the hairs rise on her hands. *Could this really be the truth about Jesus? Did he really come here?*

It took one large pull to open the final seal exposing a rolled up ancient parchment, sealed with a wax seal still. Edith broke the seal and rolled the parchment straight. The writing was faded and was in Greek or Aramaic, Françoise did not know, but it wasn't Latin or French for sure. Lying in the middle of the seal were four items; one a small piece of wood; two locks of black hair and the other another piece of what looked like fair or red hair.

'Well, after all these centuries, they are still there,' Edith broke the silence.

'I guess these are some form of icon or medieval trick are there?' Jack asked cynically. Françoise sat and stared at them. She was getting a strong feeling that her aunt may well be telling some amazing truth.

'No Jack, they are not medieval. Three are from the first century AD and they contain the DNA that will show the Holy bloodline and the proof of Jesus' death on the cross.'

Edith then carefully pointed at the wood. 'See here, this is part of the True Cross. Mary and Joseph took it after the crucifixion along with the body. The stain you see is Christ's blood. Before you say they could be medieval hoaxes, carbon dating will prove the date of these.'

The room went quiet, all but the deep breathing of everyone. They all began to believe they were experiencing something magical, something personal and something divine.

Edith waited a while, watching the faces of her audience. Then she pointed at the first piece of hair. 'That is a lock of Mary Magdalene's son's hair; the DNA on the wood and in the hair will show he was a filial match to Jesus. The second lock is that of Joseph which will show the son was not that of Jesus but both Joseph and the Magdalene and finally rid the world of that lie that he was married or never died on the cross. The third red lock is that of King Arthur, kept by Merlin and his successors. Merlin was one of us, skilled in alchemy, our esoteric knowledge and the truth. It was placed there by Hugh de Payen the first leader of the Knights Templar when he opened the scroll in the eleventh century after rediscovering it in the ruins of Solomon's Temple. That will show the blood line of Jesus passed through the rightful heirs of the British Throne. A Once and Future King both spiritually and dynastically. And when he returns, he will rebuild Solomon's Temple, on Sion, England's green and pleasant land.'

'If that is true then nothing much has changed has it really?' Jack stated, getting frustrated with it all. 'Jesus died on the cross. His aunt and uncle had a kid. That won't change the world. It might stop the rubbish about him not dying on the cross, having kids and marrying Mary but really it could be anyone in the first century's blood couldn't it? Nothing world changing here.'

'Jack you are doubtful but you may think you are correct in your delusion but the Gospel tells it all, including the blood line and how the proof was added to the scroll. It can be dated by paper and ink to the time of Jesus. It also tells us that Jesus began his ministry here, in England. It proves that the rightful Church should be here, based on that ministry here and not ruled by a Roman dynastic bishop. Rome and the Catholic Church chose the New Testament. Certain Gnostic Gospel's were missed out so that Rome would be the founder and foundation of the Church and rule from there. This Gospel has remained hidden, its contents and knowledge known only to a few chosen descendants of the Essenes, the Cathars and always us. You see Jesus, performed his first miracle here, in Britain, in England and in Devon.'

'What!' Françoise came back to life. 'Surely not; that would break the whole story of the Bible gospels. He performed his first miracle at Cana, in Palestine, turning water into wine, and when he was about thirty. From what you say he was only in his late teens or early twenties when he came here with his Uncle Joseph. What does the scroll say then? I really can't believe that.'

'Yes, it is mind-blowing and will drive the established Church apart if it published. And that is precisely why Rome and the other established Churches have tried to find this and hide this for centuries. The Church of England has sought this ever since King Henry the Eighth conned everyone into believing he was anti Rome. That was lie. He was Catholic and remained one. He destroyed the monasteries seeking all hidden truth; particularly any evidence the Arthur was the true King of England and of the Blood Royal. The Established Anglican Church has done exactly the same for centuries. It still follows the liturgy and the sacraments created by the Roman Church in the first centuries after Christ. Only those who understand the true faith based on ancient arcane knowledge and the all-seeing Great Architect could change this order. Those who joined the sectarian liberal movements, the new ecumenical modernist faiths, those who believe in a united people living under one supreme leader and one God will change the world. We will release this information and break finally the chains of established religion and petty nationalism.'

Françoise interrupted Edith's monologue again. 'Yes, yes. I think I get that now. You are trying to create a new European based on a Holy Sion Order, not Roman, ruled from Britain, by our Queen...'

'Not your Queen, she cannot be the defender of the true faith,' interjected Edith.

'Why the hell not?' Jack exclaimed.

'Because she does not have Royal Blood,' answered Edith.

'Yes, she does she is a House of Windsor,' said an increasingly frustrated Jack.

'That was just made up my boy to make them look more English. They are really Saxe – Coburg. They were German and descended by marriage through George the first and the House of Hanover. This broke the Holy Blood Stuart dynasty hold on the Throne; for whilst King Billy was a public Protestant, he was also a Stuart and therefore descended from King Arthur and the rightful true faith successor. He was the Priory's head here and committed to religious modernism but he had to break Rome's rule over his countries and people so he created the Act of Succession. He also was committed to unifying the warring countries of Britain as a first move to control Europe and therefore he created the Act of Union. Our next step would have been the Unification of Europe but we had lost the Gospel a few years previously at Teignmouth. So, we have lived with the 'Windsors' until now. But soon a descendent of Arthur will be on the throne.'

'Charles you mean,' Françoise said, pleased she knew enough of British history to contribute.

'No not Charlie, but his son - William. He has Royal Blood through his mother Diana. You see the Spencer's and therefore the Churchill's are all descended through the blood of Arthur and therefore Christ. Where do you think Harry's ginger hair comes from? It's from this lock here, this ginger lock taken from the head of King Arthur. This has been known by the Priory for centuries. His antecedent Winston Churchill was a Spencer and one of us and he too strove to unite the peoples of France and Britain. What he never knew was that his bloodline would one day be King. William will rule Sion. Just like King Billy should have all those years ago.'

'For Christ's sake! You are mad,' Jack had had enough. 'I'm going out for a walk. Come on Piaf I'll take you.'

'Sorry Jack. You can go nowhere until we have left,' Jimmy stood up and pushed him back. 'The girls outside will take you to dark places matey if you don't behave.'

Jack sat back down and crossed his arms. He had heard enough. *This was insane. If it was true then so be it. Let them get on with it. If it was a crazed woman's imaginings then again, so be it. They'll lock her up anyway when the duly authorised officer comes to take her away.* Françoise was not so convinced. She really could not believe so many people for so long would keep this stuff secret if there was no truth in it. And people were prepared to hurt or kill for it. There must be something real here. 'So where does Christ and his mission in Devon come in?'

'Well, settle down and I'll tell you something you will never forget. Joseph brought Jesus with him on his trip to Cornwall to buy tin and they spent time there. Joseph heard that on Dartmoor there were isolated tin miners and he decided to sail up the coast to try and do business with them. He sailed into the Teign Estuary in the year twenty-two BC. They sailed up to Newton Abbott and onwards by road to meet the tin miners on Dartmoor. They traded with the miners and returned back to their ship by horse and cart and loaded the tin on the ship and rowed back up the River Teign. They settled in an inn on the Back Beach, it may well have been at the Teignmouth to Shaldon's Ferry Inn, the precursor to *The Jolly Sailor*. There they were invited to the local tin and clay merchant's daughter's wedding which was being held on a small hamlet along the river.'

'How do you know all this? Are you dreaming?' Jack asked facetiously.

'No my friend I'm not dreaming but reading. It is all written down in here. And we have other written evidence taken from Joseph's account when he returned to Jerusalem. That was buried with this gospel but was kept by the Cathars and the Templars sent that to Malta. Our Knights of Saint John, The Hospitalers, have kept this since then. Believe me this is true.'

'If you say it is,' Jack mumbled, staring to wonder if he was the one dreaming.

'Anyway, I must move on the train time is approaching,' Edith replied, uninterested in her 'Doubting Thomas'. 'At the wedding Joseph noticed that everyone was drinking fruit juice and water and mead. He asked why no wine as in the Jewish custom. He was told there were no grapes here only apples and they drank the juice from them. *'If you want to have a real drink, have a jug of mead'* he was asked. He tried it and was nearly sick with the sweetness and roughness. Jesus also spat it out. But as he took another cup of apple juice he walked towards the large vat of juice that all the guests were drinking apart from the couple of drunken fathers who were stuck into the mead. Jesus must have decided it was time to help these unfortunate sober guests because he took his cup and poured the juice out of the vat. He told his Uncle to *'look again into the vat, and sample the new wine.'* Joseph and the two fathers of the bride and groom walked over with their mugs and poured it out and tasted it. One father fell to floor in front of Jesus, *'It is a miracle, Lord you are the bringer of the vine and the life'.* Joseph drank another large draft and he knew that history had been torn in two. Jesus had turned the apples into cider. All the guests were in awe of his act. He sat down on a small mount and he spoke kindly to them about how they needed to give up their pagan ways, love each other and worship the one true God, as God had shown them he could turn apples in wine, He would turn their sadness into gladness. Joseph wrote down on an old tin sale tally note exactly what Jesus preached that miraculous day on the hill on The Teign and then copied that to the Gospel.'

'Oh for God's sake man! I can't take anymore. Tell me you are not Monty Python in disguise,' Jack exclaimed.

'It's all here and has been for two centuries. It matters not that you believe it but millions will once it is carbon dated and the other scroll dated and revealed too. The first miracle Jesus performed was here, in Teignmouth, and Devon is where the miracle of cider was first brought to the world. It's a pity the smugglers never knew about the hidden Gospel in the chest. They could have made millions from pilgrims to the site of the first miracle and cornered the market in cider. As it is, the father of the bride decided to give up his trade as a thatcher, and he took his idea back up to his family in Somerset and started his own business. The husband of the bride, Sam, started his own orchard near Torrington, a few miles from here, and opened the first ever Cider Bar, in Newton Abbott.'

Françoise had about decided that this was so fantastical that it must be true and was curious to find out more. 'Aunty, so if Jesus began his ministry here in Teignmouth. I guess Christianity must have started here then? So Teignmouth is your Sion?'

'Yes, in one way you are correct. But the bride's father who was a thatcher took the first Christian message to his home in Somerset and asked Jesus and Joseph to help him start his own Church to preach the Good News, the Gospel. He chose a place where his new business would also thrive. He chose a place called *Ynys Afallach* in Ancient British, *Insula Avallonis* in Latin or to us now, The Isle of Avalon – Glastonbury.'

'Oh I think I understand now. So that is why Glastonbury is so important in all our myths and legends?'

'Indeed my dear, Glastonbury was chosen as it is also called after the Celtic word, *abal*, for apple. *Ynys Afallach* means Island of Apples. The surrounds of the Tor and the lake were covered in apple orchards, the raw material for his new cider business. The new Church was founded by Jesus, by now a Master Builder in the making, laying the first stone at what is now Glastonbury Abbey - the Cornerstone. His Uncle came back after Jesus' death and resurrection and completed the work. He built and completed the body of Christ, the Church.'

Edith stood up and put her coffee cup on the draining board. She made to get moving to catch her train but she had some final closing words:

'You see all the Bible references Old and New to the *'stone that was rejected'* and *'the cornerstone'* of the church being built on Sion, always referred to Christ and the first and last temple to be built to the Great Architect. That church was the New Jerusalem, it was the cornerstone, Sion, it was first built in England's green and pleasant land and it was the birthplace of Christ's first ministry and the death of its true King, Arthur. It is spiritually and, soon constitutionally, where the King will rise again – here in the West Country we are in the cradle of Christianity, and the new world order will rule and arise from here.'

Edith looked tired and at the same time content that now everything was revealed.

'Now I must go and make that happen. Goodbye my darling Françoise. You have played your part and one day you will forgive me. I advise you keep this all a secret between us all until we have moved on with London, Paris and Brussels. The two French ladies will stay close until that happens.'

Françoise had a few more questions which bugged her. 'Aunty, before you go. Can you tell me why our great, great grandfather, the Count, came here to Teignmouth when he could have just sailed off to Paris with the treasure chest? It seems strange to do that.'

Edith stopped leaving the room and faced her niece. She knew that Françoise now believed her. Jack she cared nothing for, he was stupid and stuck in the old ways. He'd soon be back drinking with his buoys from the Docks again and enjoying the tales, this revelation long forgotten after a few Scrumpies. She hoped he would care for Françoise; it seemed that relationship may well move to a higher plain. It was time to close it all out. So she told Françoise about the Holy Grail.

'The Count came to Teignmouth because he wanted to see where Christ first walked and preached. He had with him the Holy Grail, The Chalice, which he had taken with the Gospel and DNA proof from its keeper in Tintagel Castle. The Grail was the cup that Jesus drank the first cider from here on the Teign. He carried with him everywhere and was the cup he took his last drink from at The Last Supper. Joseph brought it with him to be lain at Glastonbury. It stayed near the Chalice Well and was thought have mystical power. During the Dark Ages it was taken by us back to the Temple Mount to be saved from the Danes, Vikings and barbarian hordes. The search for the Holy Grail by King

Arthur was in fact an allegory for the adventures his Knights had taking it back to Jerusalem to be saved. The Templars found it with the Gospel and brought them both back to Britain - to Tingagel, and there they lay until your grandfather brought it to Teignmouth. He lost it when the smugglers stole the booze and the chest within which it lay.'

'So where is it now?'

'We have no idea. The good people of Teignmouth have kept it hidden ever since. I hoped it was in the chest but that was not to be. They have it somewhere. But even Jimmy who was The Squire has no idea. There must be yet another secret society of Teignmouth people who keep that secret. My God, there are enough suspicious people in all the pubs here any one of them could be the Grail Squire. We would love to have it because it contains the saliva and fingerprints of Christ on it. Which, when they match the blood on the true cross, will prove even more conclusively what we are about to declare.'

She picked up her bag and turned and said, 'Au revoir Françoise, soon we will meet again but it will be in a new much better place.' And she left.

Françoise sat looking at Jack in shock. Even Jack seemed to accept there was far too much told and shown to them to be a fantasy. This was certainly going to change their lives. After a few minutes of silence Françoise spoke. 'Jack let's have a walk. It seems a millennium since we walked that first day on the Back Beach. I need to clear my head and think.'

'Sounds a great idea. Let's take Piaf and get out of here. I feel quite sick.'

They walked along the beach. The weather was changing and the dark clouds were rolling over Dartmoor up the Estuary. The French girls were following about 30 metres behind. But by now, being followed, bugged, tracked and assaulted was the norm. They ignored them. Françoise looked up the Estuary and at the clouds over Dartmoor wondering *if that moor contained any more secrets it hadn't revealed?* She then looked across at Shaldon and the huge Ness rock, thinking about the Smugglers Tunnel that ran through the massive rock down to beach; *she wondered if the smugglers of 1690 had hidden The Grail in there?* She waved at the two brothers who drank in Dicey's every day. They were in shorts taking their morning stroll before work. *Were they Grail keepers?* Tina, the landlady from *The Kings Arms* jogged past and waved. *The Kings Arms* was on French Street and a brass plaque to the invasion was right next to the pub. *Was the Grail hidden under that manhole type cover or maybe in a deep cellar in Gareth's pub under one of the Kings Arms carved inside the pub?* As

241

they came back to the old *Ship* pub, *maybe the Grail was buried in its cellar like the one in St Germain or maybe in the priest hole in The Jolly Sailor. After all Jesus may stayed there with his uncle and had his first cider there?* She shook her head; she knew she couldn't stop this. This was all consuming; she knew she had to get this itch scratched and final closure. She could never rest now.

She sat down on the wall next to *The Ship* and *The Crab Shack* sea food restaurant overlooking the beach, admiring the bobbing yachts and fishing boats on the beautiful River Teign Estuary. She saw Joe Simmons loading the shell fish from the fishing boat at the Fish Quay, the seagulls screeching above the boat. She listened to the melody of the wind chimes and metal sheets of the yachts jingling in the strong Westerly breeze. They all seemed to be whispering solely to her. She now knew this was her fate. She could see clearly for the first time in years. She spoke out loud, not facing Jack and staring at the beauty of it all.

'Jack, can't you see clearly now? His feet did walk in this beautiful land and he left His footprints on the Teign all those years ago. Now all the good local people we have met in this adventure have left their own stories, their own footsteps in this wonderful place for their children to follow. This could be the greatest story ever told Jack. I pity all those crazed lunatics we have met. They only have their own petty historical religious and political goals to comfort them. These are so incredible they would be laughable if we hadn't seen the history and met these people in person. But they are bound to fail. The building of empires based on power, religious doctrine and nations are not what that good man came here all those years ago to tell us. He spoke of nothing but love, for everyone. He came to us to build a Kingdom, but not of countries and borders but of love. Surely the good people of this world aren't that crazy? Are they?'

And she pointed up the river past the boats towards Dartmoor and said, 'But you know what Jack, when all their plotting has ended we will still have His message and all this beauty. They will end up with nothing but hate and bitterness.'

She picked up a piece of driftwood and threw it down towards the Estuary and her little dog scuttled after it. She turned to Jack and looked into his eyes which showed a hint of doubt but also surprise at the once hidden passion emerging from his new friend. Françoise turned back towards the river knowing at last that her life had been carefully and lovingly built for this moment. She knew now that she would finish the work started not by a Holy Roman European Emperor or a British

King but by a simple traveller and builder of lives who laid the Cornerstone which from which all this started. She stood up and took Jack's hands in hers. She pulled him away from staring lovingly into her eyes and they both turned to look up the River Teign estuary. She whispered, as if she knew the crazed French psychopaths, Jungle Jim, the KGB and strange men from Cornwall were still listening.

'This place is so beautiful Jack. Can't you feel the awesome presence of an almighty God at work here? And if His son came here to help and save us with a love so amazing that he bled and died on that hill far away for me and you, then I am damned sure we can help him now. I know I am only a crazy French girl but I am going to find his precious cup. I will use it to stop those raving loonies. I think we should start a Treasure Hunt here in South Devon for the Holy Grail. Will you be the first to join me?'

Come to sunny Devon, and eat your scones the correct way and meet us all. You can help Françoise find the Grail and you can join in with the Footsteps on the Teign Charity Treasure Hunt any day.

www.aimsfamilies.org/2019/05/footsteps/